Percy Sadler, C. F. Guillette

Petit Cours de Versions

Percy Sadler, C. F. Guillette

Petit Cours de Versions

Reprint of the original, first published in 1864.

1st Edition 2022 | ISBN: 978-3-75259-267-2

Verlag (Publisher): Salzwasser Verlag GmbH, Zeilweg 44, 60439 Frankfurt, Deutschland
Vertretungsberechtigt (Authorized to represent): E. Roepke, Zeilweg 44, 60439 Frankfurt, Deutschland
Druck (Print): Books on Demand GmbH, In de Tarpen 42, 22848 Norderstedt, Deutschland

PETIT COURS DE VERSIONS;

OR,

EXERCISES FOR TRANSLATING

ENGLISH INTO FRENCH.

BY
P. SADLER.

Revised and Annotated by
C. F. GILLETTE

FIRST AMERICAN EDITION.

PHILADELPHIA

1864.

INTRODUCTION.

STUDENTS who need practice in translating *English into French*, beyond the routine of grammatical exercises, as an introductory course to French composition, can find no book better adapted to their requirements than Sadler's "Petit Cours de Versions."

The varied topics of its entertaining anecdotes afford exercises admirably calculated to promote proficiency in the French language, at the same time that they impress moral truth and noble sentiments. Hence the popularity of this little work notwithstanding a serious impediment thrown in the way of the learner, in the *Paris edition* (the only one hitherto published), which, being intended for French scholars studying English, contains directions in regard to the *English idioms*, instead of the *French;* an anomaly in the hands of Americans, and also a puzzle, as they must throughout take the reverse of the explanations given.

It is in order to remove this difficulty that the present edition is issued, with the following changes:

THE PARIS EDITION	THIS EDITION
Contains explanatory notes of the *English* idioms, and references to the *English* grammar.	Contains explanatory notes of the *French* idioms, and references to the *French* grammar.
Opens with a list of idiomatic phrases without *direct* connexion with the text, so that they can be applied only by analogy, which requires from the pupil more mental labour	Opens with a list of all French idioms contained in the book, for which there was no space in the notes. Reference is made to the page where they are to be

than can be reasonably expected. They are, moreover, presented without order, and the difficulty in finding the one looked for, renders them almost useless.

Has a dictionary lacking many words.

found, and they are presented so as to be used without any difficulty whatever.

Has a *complete* dictionary, with the following important additions:

To the *verbs* and *adjectives* have been joined the *prepositions* to be used before *infinitives* and *complements*. (See Appendix, page 263.) This cannot fail to be considered an improvement by all who have experienced the difficulties arising from the lack of such directions.

It will be noticed that the *French language* has been retained in the notes, it being admitted by all experienced Teachers, that pupils, when sufficiently advanced, derive more benefit from studying in French texts.

The grammatical explanations introduced in the notes bear exclusively on idiomatical peculiarities, which learners are generally inclined to lose sight of. They will save much trouble to both students and teachers, without lessening in any way the rôle of the latter, as the leading rules have been left untouched, this book being not intended to be a grammatical instructor.

As may be inferred from the above, it has been the aim of the author of these alterations to appropriate this edition to the use of Americans, just as the Paris one is to that of the French. He ventures to hope that the work thus submitted will prove both useful and agreeable to students, and therefore meet the approval of all interested in giving French instruction.

C. F. GILLETTE.

KEY

TO THE

IDIOMATIC WORDS AND LOCUTIONS

CONTAINED IN THIS WORK,

AND WHICH ARE NOT TO BE FOUND IN THE NOTES.

PAGE
11. To ask a question, *Faire une question.*
12. To make some amends, *Dédommager un peu.*
14. To lose every tooth in one's head, *Perdre toutes ses dents.*
16. At the expense of, *Aux dépens de.* (The word *expense* is to be translated *dépens* s. m. pl. and not *dépense* s. f. in the sense of *at the sacrifice of, at the loss of.* Ex: To grow rich at the expense of others, *S'enrichir aux dépens d'autrui.* He saved her life at the expense of his own, *Il lui sauva la vie aux dépens de la sienne.*)
18. The next time, *La prochaine fois.* (When Time refers to a number or repetition of times, it is translated *fois;* and when to a while, *temps.* Ex: I see him sometimes, *Je le vois quelque fois.* We stopped there for some time, *Nous y restâmes quelque temps.*
23. To be at war, *être en guerre.*
38. To give a sprat to catch a herring, *Donner un œuf pour avoir un bœuf.*
35. How old are you? *Quel âge avez-vous?*
37. What do you mean? *Que voulez-vous dire?*
— In such a manner, *D'une telle manière.*
40. The height of presumption, *Le comble de la présomption*

IDIOMS.

PAGE
42. To bear witness, *Témoigner,* or *Porter témoignage.*
42. To happen to overhear, *Entendre par hazard,* or *entr'ouir par hazard.*
43. It is said (when commencing a sentence) *on dit;* (when not at the commencement) *dit on.* Ex: It is said he was killed, *on dit qu'il fut tué.* He was killed, it is said, *Il fut tué, dit-on.*
46. To have some sport, *S'amuser un peu,* or *se divertir un peu.*
47. On his return, *à son retour* (on his arrival, *à son arrivée;* on his departure, *à son départ;* on his entrance, *à son entrée).*
55. An old man with a white beard, *Un vieillard à barbe blanche.*
57. To laugh heartily, *rire de bon cœur;* more heartily, *de meilleur cœur.*
58. Some years ago, *il y a quelques années,* (ago, *il y a,* must be placed in French before the word or number expressing the time elapsed.)
63. To be for a long time, *être long-temps.*
64. At that time, *dans ce temps-là.*
— To take refuge, *Se réfugier.*
66. Such a paltry sum, *Une somme si chétive,* or *une si faible somme.*
67. To be petrified with horror, *Etre pétrifié d'horreur.*
70. Another account to settle, *Un autre compte à régler.*
75. You are at liberty, *Vous êtes en liberté.*
79. As much at sea as on shore, *Aussi bien sur mer que sur terre.*
85. Refused to let them in, *Refusa de les laisser entrer.*
89. To hurry off, *S'en aller en hâtant le pas,* or *s'en aller précipitamment.*
91. Having furnished himself with, *S'étant muni de.*
96. They were traced to, *On en suivit les traces jusqu'à.*
97. With whom he had slept, *Avec qui il avait couché.*

IDIOMS.

PAGE
- 98. To fall in with, *Rencontrer.*
- 102. Had scarcely recovered from, *Etait à peine revenu de.*
- 106. To run up a wall, *Faire élever un mur,* or *une muraille.*
- 107. Wished them good sport, *Leur souhaita bonne chasse.*
- 110. Understand what you have to do before you set about it, *Comprenez ce que vous avez à faire avant de le commencer.*
- 111. My duty is to see them executed, *Mon devoir est de les exécuter.*
- — It is not for me to, *Ce n'est pas à moi de.*
- 114. Go and find it, *Cherche, cherche là.*
- 115. Running about by himself, *Courir tout seul à l'entour,* or *courir çà et là.*
- 116. To stick up bills, *Poser des affiches.*
- — For fear of, *De crainte de.*
- 117. On the occasion, *A cette occasion.*
- — She had recognised him by, *Elle l'avait reconnu à.*
- — On being asked, *Quand on lui demanda.*
- 119. Would change his faithful subjects to, *Changerait ses fidèles sujets en.*
- — And make his throne, *Et ferait de son trône.*
- 120. To discharge (a servant), *Congédier.*
- 123. To remain idle (money), *Rester sans emploi, improductif,* (a person) *oisif.*
- 124. And boasted how he had, *Et se vanta de la façon dont il avait.*
- 126. At the same time, *En même temps.*
- 128. About five o'clock, *Vers cinq heures,* or *à cinq heures environ.*
- — Here, take care of my horse, *Tenez! ayez soin de mon cheval.*
- 131. To have another laugh at him, *Pour se moquer encore de lui.*
- 132. Our wit, *Notre bel esprit.*
- 134. We are not such fools, *Nous ne sommes pas si fous.*

PAGE
136. All was not fair, *Tout n'était pas en règle*, or *qu'il y avait quelque chose sous jeu.*
144. Drunken lethargy, *Ivresse (s. f.) léthargique.*
145. To be fast asleep, *Dormir profondément.*
148. A holy day, *Un congé.*
— To go roving about the country, *Aller courir les champs*, or *rôder dans la campagne.*
151. They contrived to take out the cat, *Ils imaginèrent d'enlever le chat.*
152. Secretary to, *Secrétaire de.*
153. A relief from solitude, *Un soulagement à la solitude.*
157. The person to whom she applied bid her, *La personne à qui elle s'adressa lui dit.*
162. And cause my sword to fall harmless on his neck, *Et de faire que mon sabre tombe sur son cou sans lui faire de mal.*
166. The first wife to Henry VIII., *La première femme de Henri VIII.*
167. I was offered a golden angel for him by a servant of .... *Un domestique de .... m'en a offert un ange d'or.*
169. The depth of winter, *Le cœur de l'hiver.*
170. The family all came out to meet him, *Toute la famille sortit à sa rencontre.*
171. Before my face, *En ma présence.*
— You have had the animal about that time, *Il y a à peu près ce temps-là que vous avez l'animal.*
— To see justice done, *De veiller à ce que justice soit rendue.*
172. Took no other notice than, *N'y répondit qu'en.*
173. Most gladly, *Avec le plus grand plaisir*, or *on ne peut plus volontiers*, or *de tout mon cœur.*
— For you both, *Pour vous deux.*
174. To restore to happiness, *Rendre au bonheur.*

CONTENTS.

	PAGE
INTRODUCTION,	iii
Idioms,	v
Integrity of a Soldier,	9
Walter Scott at School,	11
Cruelty of King John,	13
Humanity of Louis XIV.,	14
Courageous Devotion of an Officer,	15
A Mystery cleared up,	16
Diamond cut Diamond,	18
The Cunning Cutler,	20
Abstraction, or Absence of Mind,	21
Honourable Conduct of King John of France,	23
Desperate Patriotism,	25
The School-boy and the Bunch of Grapes,	26
Feminine Resolution, and Attachment to the Unfortunate Mary Stuart,	28
Interested Attentions,	30
Scarce Articles,	32
The Value of Time,	33
Cross Questions,	35
Infamous Turpitude,	37
Magnanimity of Louis XIV.,	38

CONTENTS.

	PAGE
Excessive Politeness,	39
Dignity Maintained,	40
How to make a Friend of an Enemy,	41
Justice is Sure, though sometimes Slow,	ib.
The Scholar's Answer,	42
Learning and Riches,	43
Early Rising,	ib.
The Horse and the Beet-root,	44
The Dog and the Eels,	45
The Dog and the Patties,	47
The Lucky Fall,	ib.
The Dog's Will,	49
The Danger of Confiding in Strangers,	50
The Double Lesson,	52
A Curious Exculpation,	53
Modesty of a Youth,	ib.
Virtue in Humble Life,	54
The Queen of Spain has no Legs,	56
The Dilemma, or the Lawyer outwitted,	57
A very Black Affair,	58
The Doctor who received the Life of his Patient in Payment for his Visits,	59
Embarrassing News,	60
Ventriloquy,	62
On the Folly of Believing in Ghosts,	64
The Page and the Cherries,	68
The Dervise and the Atheist,	70
Canine Sagacity,	72
Gratitude,	73
Filial Affection of a Page,	76

CONTENTS.

	PAGE
Marine Logic,	78
A Singular Justification,	79
The Immortal Elixir,	80
Heroic Conduct of a Sailor,	81
Abuse of Hospitality,	83
The Wise Fool, and the Professor of Signs,	86
A Trial of Courage,	90
A very Singular Excuse,	92
Delicacy of Alphonso, King of Aragon,	93
We must not always judge by Appearances,	95
Anecdote of a Hoax played on the Londoners,	98
Benevolence,	101
A Lesson of Perseverance from a Spider,	103
The Mysterious Englishmen,	105
Understand what you have to do before you set about it,	110
A Happy Expression. Unexpected Politeness,	112
The Four-legged Thief-Taker,	113
The Chimney-Sweepers' Feast, or the Lost Child found,	115
Noble Blood. A Lesson for Pride,	119
Real or Intrinsic Value,	122
The Biter Bitten,	123
How to Catch a Pickpocket,	125
Before you promise, calculate your ability to perform,	127
Deaf as a Post,	128
A Warm Joke,	132
A Salutary Pill,	136
The Danger of being Ungrateful,	137

CONTENTS.

	PAGE
A Curious Decision; or Smelling and Hearing,	138
One Crime generally begets another,	140
The Bagpiper Revived,	143
A Singular Precaution,	144
Avarice Punished,	146
The Students Outwitted,	148
The Double Metamorphosis,	150
Instinct and Cruelty,	151
Quackery,	154
Youthful Benevolence,	156
The Miraculous Transformation,	160
The Turbulent Youth Corrected,	163
La vieille Ganache,	164
Impartial Judgment,	166
DICTIONNAIRE,	177
APPENDIX TO THE DICTIONARY,	262

SADLER'S EXERCISES.

Integrity of a Soldier.

A king of Northumberland, named Anlaff, having been deprived of his kingdom by Athelstan, king of the West Saxons, assembled a numerous force and marched to[1] attack the invader. The two armies met and prepared for battle, and Anlaff, wishing to learn the strength and the arrangements of his adversary, disguised himself as a[2] harper and went into Athelstan's camp. Having played on[3] his harp from tent to tent, he was at length conducted to the royal pavilion. The king was so well pleased with[4] his music that, on his departure, he gave him a handsome recompense. Anlaff, disdaining to keep the money that his enemy

---

[1] *To*, signifiant *in order to*, se traduit *pour*.

[2] En français, *se déguiser en* (*to disguise oneself in*).

[3] En parlant des instruments de musique, on dit en Français *to play of* (*Jouer de*).

[4] So well pleased with, *si content de*.

had given him, buried it in the ground before he left the camp.

This excited suspicion in a soldier who observed him, and on[1] approaching he recognised him notwithstanding his disguise. As soon as he was gone the soldier presented himself before Athelstan, and said, "Sire, the harper who has given[2] you so much pleasure, and whom you have rewarded so handsomely, is no other than Anlaff, your mortal enemy."—"Traitor," replied the king, "why did not you tell me that while he was in my power?"—"Because," answered the soldier, "I am not a traitor; I have served in his army, and have sworn never to betray him; if I had done it, I should be as capable of betraying you; but I advise you to alter your arrangements before you give battle."—Athelstan followed the soldier's advice, and changed his quarters to another part of the camp, by which means his life was saved, for the same night a party of Anlaff's troops entered[3] the camp and murdered all who were in the pavilion that Athelstan had left. This attack brought on a general battle, which ended in the total defeat of Anlaff and his followers.

P. S. (*Historical.*)

---

[1] *On* devant un participe present se traduit *en* (in).
[2] To give pleasure, *faire plaisir, causer plaisir.*
[3] To enter, *entrer dans.*

Walter Scott at School.

It appears that when this celebrated author was at school, though very laborious, his intelligence was not brilliant, and his great success in after-life[1] was owing to[2] his indefatigable perseverance.

The following anecdote is found in his Autobiography[3] lately published.

"There was," says Walter Scott, " a boy in my class who stood always at the top,[4] and I could not, with all my efforts, supplant him. Day came after day,[5] and still he kept his place : till at length I observed that, when a question was asked him, he always fumbled with his fingers at a particular button on the lower part[6] of his waistcoat while seeking an answer. I thought therefore[7] if I could remove the button slily, the surprise at not finding it might derange his ideas at the next interrogation of the class, and give me a chance of taking him down[8]. The button was therefore removed without

---

[1] In after-life, *plus tard dans la vie.*
[2] Owing to, *l'effet de, dû à.*
[3] Autobiography, *histoire de sa vie, écrite de sa propre main.*
[4] The top, *le haut, la tête, la première place.*
[5] Day came after day, *les jours se succédaient.*
[6] The lower part, *la partie inférieure, le bas.*
[7] Toutes les fois que *that* est sous-entendu en Anglais il faut l'exprimer en Français.
[8] Of taking him down, *de le faire descendre, de le supplanter.*

his perceiving it[1]. Great was my anxiety to know the success of my measure, and it succeeded but too well.

"The hour of interrogation arrived, and the boy was questioned: he sought, as usual, with his fingers, for the friendly button, but could not find it. Disconcerted, he looked down[2]; the talisman[3] was gone, his ideas became confused, he could not reply. I seized the opportunity, answered the question, and took his place, which he never recovered, nor do I believe[4] he ever suspected the author of the trick.

"I have often met with[5] him since we entered the world, and never without[6] feeling my conscience reproach me. Frequently have I resolved to make him some amends[7] by[8] rendering him a service; but an opportunity did not present itself, and I fear I did not seek one with as much ardour as I sought to supplant him at school."

(On trouve cette anecdote, avec beaucoup d'autres également intéressantes, dans la vie de Walter Scott écrite par son beau-fils Mr. Lockhart.)

---

[1] Without his perceiving it, *sans qu'il s'en aperçût.*
[2] To look down, *baisser les yeux, regarder en bas.*
[3] Talisman, *talisman, charme.*
[4] Nor do I believe, *je ne crois pas non plus.*
[5] To meet with, *rencontrer.*
[6] On emploie en Français l'infinitif présent au lieu du participe présent après toute autre préposition que *en* et *après.*
[7] To make amends, *faire dédommagement, dédommager.*
[8] By devant un participe présent se traduit *en* (in).

Cruelty of King John.

The Jews, since their dispersion, have been frequently treated with cruelty by Christian kings. John of England, being much in want[1] of money, and knowing that many of the Jews in his kingdom were very rich, taxed them very heavily, and threw them into prison, to remain there till[2] they would pay. Several of them gave all they possessed; but the king was not satisfied, believing they had yet money concealed: he therefore ordered them to be tortured until they would acknowledge it.

Some were deprived of an eye, and one in particular[3], from whom a sum of ten thousand marks was demanded, was treated with yet greater cruelty. The king ordered that one of his teeth should be pulled out every day till he paid the money. The Jew, not being disposed to reduce himself to poverty, resisted during a whole week, and thus lost seven of his teeth; but, unable to bear the

---

[1] To be in want, *avoir besoin*.

[2] *Till* or *until* devant un verbe à un mode personnel, c'est-à-dire un verbe ayant un sujet, se traduit *jusqu'à ce que*, et alors le verbe doit être au subjonctif.—Dans tout autre cas traduisez *jusqu'à*.

[3] In particular, *particulièrement, surtout*.

pain any longer,¹ he consented on the eighth day; and thus preserved the rest of his teeth at the expense² of his fortune; otherwise he would have soon lost every tooth in his head.³ Happily for that people, they live now in a less barbarous age. No one⁴ need fear punishment unless he deserve it.

P. S. (*Historical.*)

Humanity of Louis XIV.

During the reign of Louis the Fourteenth⁵ an Italian chemist named Poli came to Paris, and having obtained an audience of the king, informed him that he had discovered a composition ten times more destructive than gunpowder. Louis was fond of⁶ chemistry, and ordered the Italian to prepare the composition, and to make the necessary experiments on a certain day in his presence. It was done, and every thing succeeded according to the wishes of Poli, who then observed⁷ to the king that

---

¹ Longer, *plus longtemps*.

² At the expense, *aux dépens* (idiôme).

³ *In his head*, ne se traduit pas.

⁴ No one, *personne nul*.

⁵ En parlant des monarques, il faut employer les nombres cardinaux.

⁶ Was fond of, *était amateur de, aimait*.

⁷ To observe, *faire observer*.

it¹ would give him a great superiority over his enemies.—"It is true," said Louis, "and your invention is very ingenious; but mankind already possess sufficient means of destroying each other; you shall be handsomely rewarded for your trouble and ingenuity, but I charge² you, for the honour of human nature, never to divulge your secret."

Courageous Devotion of an Officer.

In the battle of Terbillen, between the Swedes and Frederick William, Elector of Brandenburg, who was afterwards king of Prussia, an officer of the staff³ observing that the prince rode a white horse, and that it rendered him conspicuous to the enemy, requested him to change horses with him. Frederick refused at first, saying he feared no danger; but the officer insisting that he ought to preserve his life, as the fate of the battle, and perhaps that of the whole army, depended⁴ on his presence, he at length consented, and the officer had scarcely mounted the white charger when a

---

¹ *It*, sujet d'un verbe, se traduit, lorsqu'il peut être remplacé en Anglais par *this* ou *that* sans changer la signification, *ce* devant le verbe *être* (to be), et *ceci* ou *cela* devant tout autre verbe.

² "I charge you," *je vous recommande*, ou *je vous enjoins*.

³ Staff, *état major*.

⁴ To depend on, *dépendre de*.

cannon-ball killed him on the spot. Thus the life of the prince was saved by the loyal attachment of his officer, who preserved it at the expense of his own.

A Mystery cleared up[1].

A few years ago[2] some persons were travelling in a stage-coach towards London, and at the approach of night they began to express their fears of being attacked by highwaymen. One gentleman said he had ten guineas about him[3] and did not know where to hide them for safety. A lady who sat next to him in the coach advised him to conceal them in his boots, which he immediately did. Soon after a highwayman came up[4] and demanded their purses: the lady told him that she had no money, but that if[5] he would search that gentleman's boots he would find ten guineas. The astonished traveller was obliged to submit, and lost his money; but as soon as[6] the robber

---

[1] "Cleared up," *éclairci*.

[2] *Ago* se traduit *il y a* et se place, en français, devant le mot ou le nombre qui exprime le temps écoulé.

[3] About him, *sur lui*.   [4] To come up, *survenir*.

[5] Après *if* on emploie en français l'imparfait au lieu du conditionnel, et le présent au lieu du futur.

[6] As soon as, *aussitôt que, dès que.*

was gone, he loaded the lady with abuse[1], declaring she was a confederate of the thief. She acknowledged that appearances were against her, but added that if the travellers would all do her the honour to dine with her on[2] the following day, she would explain, to their satisfaction, her conduct, which appeared so mysterious.

They consented, and after[3] partaking[4] of a magnificent dinner, the lady conducted them to the drawing-room, where, showing a pocket-book[5] she said, "There is an apology for my conduct of last night; it contains bank-notes for several hundred pounds." Then addressing herself to the

---

[1] "He loaded the lady with abuse," *il accabla la dame de reproches*.

[2] *On* ne se traduit pas en français en designant un jour ou une date.

[3] La préposition *après* (after) gouverne le verbe *à l'Infinitif passé*; *en* (in, by, on) gouverne le verbe au *Participe présent*; toute autre préposition le gouverne à l'infinitif présent. Ex: after partaking, *après avoir partagé*; in, by, or on partaking, *en partageant*; without partaking, *sans partager*; of partaking, *de partager*, &c.

[4] To partake of, *prendre part à; partager*.

[5] Pocket-book, *portefeuille*.

[6] "Several hundred pounds," *plusieurs centaines de livres sterling*. Les substantifs numeraux se forment en ajoutant la terminaison *aine* au nombre cardinal, dans ce cas l'*e* muet qui termine certains nombres cardinaux se supprime.—Exceptions: a thousand, *un millier*; a million, *un million*. Les substantifs numeraux prennent la preposition *de* devant leur complément.

gentleman, " Sir," said she, " if I had not directed the highwayman's attention to your ten guineas, I should have lost my bank-notes. I therefore beg that, to make you amends[1] for your loss and vexation, you will accept one of a hundred pounds. No excuses[2], sir, for I consider myself fortunate in saving the others at that price."

The travellers were highly pleased with the lady's generosity, and complimented her on her presence of mind.

Diamond cut Diamond[3].

A gentleman of Oliver Cromwell's domestic establishment had conceived a great affection for the Protector's youngest daughter; the young lady did not discourage him, and at length he proposed a secret marriage, as there was no hope of obtaining her father's consent. A person, having discovered the secret, communicated it to Cromwell, who gave him orders to watch, and to let him know[4] the next time the gentleman and his daughter should be together. This happened on

---

[1] Voyez page 12, note 7.

[2] No excuses, *ne faites pas d'excuses, ne vous en excusez pas, ne refusez pas.*

[3] " Diamond cut Diamond," *fin contre fin* (idiôme).

[4] To let know, *faire savoir, communiquer.*

the following day, and Cromwell, being informed of it, suddenly entered his daughter's room, where he found the gentleman on his knees[1] before her.

The Protector in a fury demanded an explanation of his conduct, and the other with great presence of mind replied, "May it please[2] your highness, I have a great affection for your daughter's chamber-maid; but she refuses to give me her hand; so, thinking this young lady had great influence over her, I was soliciting that she would intercede for me."

"Oh!" replied Oliver, "if that's the case, I will see what I can do for you."—And calling the young woman, he said to her, "Why do you refuse the honour of marrying[3] Mr. White? he is my friend, and I insist that you give your consent."—The young woman, who had no objection, blushed deeply, and Cromwell said, "Ah! I see how it is —a little coquetry; go call me the chaplain."—The chaplain came, and Oliver ordered him immediate-

---

[1] On his knees, *à genoux.*
[2] May it please, *n'en déplaise à.*
[3] "Of marrying," *d'épouser.*

To marry se traduit *épouser* ou *se marier* en parlant des parties qui contractent le mariage. Il se traduit *marier*, seulement en parlant du ministre ou du magistrat qui unit les époux, ou des parents qui donnent leur fils ou leur fille en mariage. Le verbe *se marier* régit la préposition *à* ou *avec* quand il a un complément de personnes.

ly to marry¹ Mr. White and the chamber-maid. Mr. W. was obliged to submit or to expose himself to the vengeance of Cromwell, who, however, to render the bride more attractive, gave her a portion of five hundred pounds.

P. S. (*Historical.*)

The Cunning Cutler.

There is at London, in a place called Charing-cross, a very fine statue in bronze of Charles I. (Premier)² on horseback³. After the revolution and the decapitation of that monarch, the statue was taken down⁴ and sold to a cutler, who undertook to demolish it. He immediately manufactured great numbers of knives and forks with bronze handles, and exposed them in his shop as the produce of the statue which was supposed to have been melted. They were so rapidly bought, both by the friends and enemies of the late monarch,

---

¹ To marry, *marier*, voyez page 19 (³).

² En parlant des monarques on n'emploie les nombres ordinaux, que pour *the first*, premier. Dans tout autre cas ce sont les nombres cardinaux qu'il faut employer.

³ On horseback, *à cheval*. To get on horseback, *monter à cheval*.

⁴ Taken down, *abattue*.

that the cutler soon made a fortune, and retired[1] from business.

Soon after the Restoration, it was proposed to erect a new statue to the memory of the unfortunate king: the cutler, hearing[2] of this, informed the government that he could spare them[3] the trouble and expense of casting a statue, as the old one was yet in his possession, and that he would sell it to them at a moderate price. The bargain was concluded, and the statue, which he had secretly preserved, was re-elevated on the pedestal at Charing-cross, where it now stands.

P. S. (*Historique*.)

Abstraction, or Absence of Mind.

Among the many curious examples of absence of mind, that is to say, of the mind being so intensely occupied by one subject, as to be insensible to surrounding objects, we have the following laughable one[4] of the celebrated English philosopher, Newton.

---

[1] To retire from business, *se retirer des affaires*.

[2] To hear of, *entendre parler de*.

[3] Les noms collectifs employés au singulier gouvernent en français le verbe au singulier, ainsi au lieu de "informed the government that he could spare *them*," il faut traduire *it*.

[4] Le mot *one*, ne doit pas être traduit après un adjectif.

Being one morning deeply engaged in the study of some difficult problem, he would not leave it to go and breakfast with the family. His housekeeper, however, fearing that long fasting[1] might make[2] him ill, sent one of the servants into his closet, with an egg, and a saucepan of water. The servant[3] was told to boil[4] the egg, and stay while her master ate it; but Newton, wishing to be alone, sent her away,[5] saying he would cook it himself. The servant, after[6] placing it by the side of his watch on the table, and telling him to let it boil three minutes, went out; but fearing he might forget, she returned soon after, and found him standing by the fire-side, with the egg in his hand, his watch boiling in the saucepan, and he quite unconscious of the mistake he had committed.

---

[1] Long fasting, *jeûner longtemps ; long jeûne.*

[2] "Might make him ill," traduisez: *might render him ill.* Le verbe *to make* se traduit *rendre* dans le sens de *to render.*

[3] "The servant was told," *on dit à la domestique,* ou *à la servante.* Quand le verbe *dire* est employé passivement en anglais dans un sens indéfini, c'est à dire, sans mentionner par qui la chose dont on parle a été dite, il faut faire usage de la forme active en français avec le pronom *on* (one, people, they, we, somebody) pour sujet. Ex: it is said, *on dit;* I was told, *on m'a dit.*

[4] To boil, *faire bouillir;* to cook, *faire cuire;* to roast, *faire rôtir;* to warm, *faire chauffer.*

[5] To send, *envoyer;* to send away, *renvoyer.*

[6] "After placing," voyez page 17 (³).

Honourable Conduct of King John of France.

The name of John does not appear to have been in favour, either in the royal families of England or of France, as we find but one monarch of that name in each of those countries, unless we reckon the John who reigned but four days in France, from the 15th to the 19th[1] of November 1316.

The characters of the other two Johns were very opposite to each other. John of England was cruel, vindictive, rapacious, and cowardly; and during a reign of nearly seventeen years was perpetually at war with his subjects. John of France, on the contrary, whose reign was nearly as long (from 1350 to 1364), occupied himself so much about the welfare of his people, that he acquired the surname of the Good.

John after fighting[2] heroically at the battle of Poitiers, had the misfortune to be made prisoner by the English. He was taken[3] to London, where he remained until[4] a treaty was signed by which he

---

[1] En mentionnant les dates en Français, on emploie les nombres cardinaux, excepté pour le premier jour du mois. Ex. the 19th of September, *le dix-neuf Septembre;* the first of September, *le premier Septembre.*

[2] Voyez page 17 (³).

[3] *To take,* dans le sens de *to lead,* se traduit *conduire* ou *mener.*

[4] " Until," voyez page 13 (³).

agreed to pay three millions of gold crowns, for the ransom of himself and the other prisoners, and to leave Gascony, Calais, Guines, and several other places in possession of the English.

The king was then set at liberty, and returned to France, leaving the dukes of Anjou and Berry, his sons; the duke of Orleans, his brother; and the duke of Bourbon, his cousin, as hostages for the payment of the ransom. Some difficulties having arisen[1] as to the execution of the treaty, the princes obtained permission to go over[2] to Calais on parole[3], saying they should be better able to explain and terminate the differences there than in England. The duke of Anjou, however, violated his parole, and fled[4] to Paris.

John, highly displeased at such want of faith[5], immediately returned to London, and delivered himself prisoner to Edward king of England saying, "*If honour is banished from every other place, it ought to remain sacred in the breast of kings.*"

Edward assigned the palace of the Savoy to the king for his residence; but John was soon after attacked by an illness which in a few weeks

---

[1] Having arisen, *s'étant élévées, s'étant présentées.*
[2] To go over, *passer, traverser.* To go again, *retourner.*
[3] On parole, *sur parole.*
[4] To flee, *s'enfuir.*
[5] "At such want of faith," *d'un tel manque de foi.*

terminated his existence. His body was sent to France with a splendid retinue, and buried at the Abbey of St. Denis, which is the general burial-place of the French monarchs, as Westminster Abbey and Windsor Castle are for the sovereigns of England.

Desperate Patriotism.

During the wars of Napoleon in Spain, a regiment of the guard of Jerome, ex-king of Westphalia, arrived under the walls of the monastery of Figueiras. The general sent a message to the prior to demand refreshment[1] for his officers and men. The prior replied, that the men would find good quarters in the town, but that he and his monks would entertain the general and his staff[2].

About an hour afterward a plentiful dinner was served; but the general, knowing by experience how necessary it was for the French to be on their guard when eating and drinking with Spaniards, invited the prior and two of the monks to dine with him.

The invitation was accepted in such a manner[3]

---

[1] Refreshment, *des vivres.*

[2] Staff, *etat-major*

[3] "In such a manner as," *de manière à.*

as to lull every suspicion ; the monks sat down[1] to table and ate and drank plentifully with their guests, who, after the repast, thanked them heartily for their hospitality, upon which[2] the prior rose and said: "Gentlemen, if you have any worldly affairs to settle, there is no time to lose ; this is the last meal[3] you and I shall take on earth ; in an hour we shall know the secrets of the world to come[4]."

The prior and his two monks had put a deadly poison into the wine in which they had pledged[5] the French officers, and notwithstanding the antidotes immediately given by the doctors, in less than an hour every man, hosts and guests,[6] had ceased to live.

WATTS. (*Historique.*)

The School-boy and the Bunch of Grapes.

A school-boy who had just[7] returned from church, where he had heard the minister publish the bans of marriage, had occasion to pass through the

---

[1] To sit down, *s'assèoir, se mettre.*

[2] "Upon which," *sur quoi,* dans le sens de *whereupon.*

[3] Toutes les fois que *that* est sous-entendu en anglais, il faut l'exprimer en français.

[4] The world to come, *le monde à venir, l'autre monde.*

[5] To pledge, *boire à la santé de.*

[6] Hosts and guests, *hôtes et convives.*

[7] To have just, *venir de.*

refectory, and, seeing some fine grapes on the sideboard, could not resist the temptation. Thinking[1] himself unobserved, he took a bunch, and approaching it to his mouth, repeated—

"*I publish the bans of marriage between this bunch of grapes and my mouth; if any one can show cause why*[2] *they should*[3] *not be united, let him speak now or ever after hold his peace*[4]." The grapes and mouth were immediately united; but, unfortunately for the boy, the master perceived and overheard him; however, he said nothing till[5] the following day[6], when, calling the boy to him before all the scholars, he took a rod in his hand and prepared[7] to flog him, saying, "I publish the bans of marriage between this rod and this boy's back; if any one can show cause why they should not be united, let him speak now or ever after hold

---

[1] To think one's self, *se croire.*

[2] To show cause why, *faire connaître une cause pour la quelle* (idiôme).

[3] Quand *should* signifie *ought to* il faut le traduire par le verbe *devoir* (to owe).

[4] To hold one's peace, *se taire.* Les lignes en italique contiennent la formule de la publication des bans de mariage en Angleterre.

[5] *Till* ou *until*, non suivi d'un verbe, se traduit *jusqu'à*, voyez page 13 (⁵).

[6] "The following day," *le jour suivant*, l'adjectif verbal doit suivre le nom.

[7] To prepare, *se préparer.*

his peace." The urchin¹ perceived what was the matter², and instantly cried out³ with great presence of mind, "I forbid the bans."—"What impediment can you show⁴?" said the master.—"Why the parties are not agreed⁵."—"Oh!" replied the master, pleased at the ready wit⁶ of the boy, "if that is the case⁷, we must defer the marriage."

Feminine Resolution,⁸ and Attachment to the Unfortunate Mary Stuart.

A man and his wife named Lambrun had been many years in the service⁹ of Mary Stuart, and were sincerely attached to her. The tragical death of that unfortunate princess had such an effect on the husband that he did not long survive her, and the widow, Margaret Lambrun, resolved to revenge, upon queen Elizabeth, the death of two persons so

---

¹ *Urchin*, petit polisson, drôle, galopin, espiègle.

What was the matter, *de quoi il s'agissait, quelle était l'affaire.*
To enter on the matter, *entrer en matière.*

² To cry out, *s'écrier.*

⁴ To show, *faire connaître*, voyez page 27 (³).

⁵ "Are not agreed," *ne sont pas d'accord* (idiôme).

⁶ "Ready wit," *répartie*, s. f.

⁷ If that is the case, *s'il en est ainsi.*

⁸ Feminine resolution, *résolution d'une femme.*

⁹ To be in the service, *être au service.*

dear to her¹. She therefore² disguised herself in man's clothes³, bought a brace of pistols, and went to London. Soon after, when the queen appeared in public, Margaret endeavoured to make her way⁴ through the crowd in order to⁵ shoot her; but one of the pistols fell, and she was immediately apprehended.

The queen, being informed of the circumstance, ordered the man to be brought before her, and said to him, " Well, sir, who are you, and why do you seek to kill me ?"—" Madam," replied Margaret, " I am a woman ; I was a long time⁶ in the service of Mary Stuart, whom you put to death unjustly ; her execution caused the death of my dear husband, who was sincerely attached to her ; and my affection for both of them has excited me to revenge."—" And how do you think I ought to deal⁷ with you ?" said Elizabeth.—" Do you speak as a queen or as a judge ?" said Margaret.—" As a queen."—" Then,"

---

¹ " So dear to her," traduisez : *who were so dear to her.*

² " *Therefore,*" employé dans le sens de *this is why*, se traduit généralement *c'est pourquoi*, et cet adverbe doit commencer la phrase. Ex. She therefore disguised herself, traduisez : *therefore she disguised herself.*

³ Man's clothes, *vêtements d'homme, en homme.*

⁴ " To make her way," *se frayer un chemin* (idiôme).

⁵ *In order to*, afin de, pour, dans l'intention de.

⁶ " A long time," *longtemps.*

⁷ To deal with, *en agir, se conduire, en user avec.*

replied she, "you ought to pardon me."—" And what security can you give me that you will not attempt my life again?"—" Madam, a pardon granted under such conditions ceases to be a favour."—" Well then," said the queen, "I pardon you, and trust¹ to your gratitude for my safety."

P. S. (*Historical*.)

Interested Attentions.

A gentleman at London having been confined to his bed during a long time by a dangerous illness, was informed by his servants that a person, whom they did not know, came almost every day, and inquired after² his health with an appearance of great interest. The gentleman told his footman to thank him for his polite attention the next time he should call³ and to ask him for his card. He did so⁴; but judge the surprise of the master on reading⁵ when the card was presented to him:

---

[1] To trust, *se fier*.
[2] To inquire after, *s'informer de*.
[3] He should call, *qu'il viendrait*.
[4] He did so, *il le fit*.
" On reading," voyez page 10 (¹) and page 17 (²).

> W. Black, Undertaker,¹
> Funerals Furnished.²

The footman asked permission of his master to play the undertaker a trick,³ and it was agreed to say, the next time he should call, that the poor gentleman was no more⁴ and he⁵ could take measure⁶ of him for a coffin. The following⁷ day the death-hunter⁸ came, and received better news than he had yet heard; he followed the footman into a dark room, where one of the servants was stretched out⁹, covered with a sheet.

The undertaker had scarcely begun to take measure of him, when, to his great terror, he leaped up¹⁰, caught him in his arms, and the servants, after

---

¹ Undèrtaker, *entrepreneur de pompes funèbres.*

² "Funerals furnished," *on fournit tout ce qu'il faut pour les convois.*

³ To play a trick, *faire une farce, jouer un tour.*

⁴ "Was no more," *n'existait plus, était mort.*

⁵ Voyez page 11 (⁷).

⁶ "He could take measure of him," *il pouvait lui prendre mesure,* ou *prendre sa mesure.*

⁷ Voyez page 27 (⁶).

⁸ The death-hunter, *l'entrepreneur, le croque-mort.*

⁹ Stretched out, *étendu de son long.*

¹⁰ Leaped up, *se leva par un saut, se redressa.*

amusing[1] themselves at his expense,[2] told him that the funeral was put off[3], that the gentleman did not feel disposed to be interred; but that if he should change his mind[4] they had his address, and would inform him of it.

Source Articles.

George I.[5] king of England, being once on a journey[6] to Hanover, stopped at a little village in Holland, and being hungry[7] asked for two or three eggs, which he ate while the postilions were changing the horses. When they were going away[8], the servant told his majesty that the inn-keeper had charged[9] two hundred florins[10]; on which[11] the king sent for[12] him and said, "How is it[13], sir, that

---

[1] Voyez page 17 (³).

[2] At his expense, *à ses dépens* (idiôme).

[3] To put off, *retarder, remettre*. To put forth, *mettre en avant, avancer*.

[4] Change one's mind, *changer d'avis*.

[5] Voyez page 20 (²).

[6] To be on a journey, *être en voyage*.

[7] To be hungry, *avoir faim* (idiôme).

[8] To go away, *partir*.

[9] To charge, *demander, compter, se faire payer*.

[10] Florin, *pièce qui vaut environ quarante cents*.

[11] On which, *sur quoi* dans le sens de *whereon*.

[12] To send for, *envoyer chercher, faire venir*.

[13] How is it, *comment se fait-il* (idiôme).

you charge me two hundred florins for three eggs? are they so scarce here?"—"No," replied the host, " eggs are abundant enough, but kings are excessively rare here, and we must made the most of[1] them when fortune does us the honour of throwing[2] them in our way[3]. The king smiled, and bade the postilions drive on, telling the landlord, " *qu'il donnait ses œufs pour avoir des bœufs*[4]."

The Value of Time.

King Alfred, who ascended the throne of England in 871, and who, like Charlemagne, by his magnanimity and wise government, acquired the title of *the Great*, was a prudent economiser of time, well knowing that a moment lost can never be recovered. Alfred wished to divide the day into equal portions, in order to appropriate a certain space of time to the accomplishment of the different objects he had in view.

---

[1] To make the most of, *profiter de.*

[2] Of throwing them, voyez pages 12 (⁶) et 17 (³).

[3] In our way, *sur notre chemin* (idiôme).

[4] Proverbe qui signifie *donner peu pour avoir beaucoup* (voyez idiômes) ; *to give a sprat to catch a herring.*

This was not an easy matter[1], as clocks were at that time nearly unknown in Europe, and quite so[2] in England. It is true that in fine weather[3] the flight of time could be marked, in some degree, by the course of the sun; but in the night, and when the sun was hidden by clouds, there were no means of judging.

The king, after much reflection, and many experiments, ordered a certain quantity of wax to be made into six candles[4] of equal length and thickness, which, being lighted one after the other, as he had found by experience, would last from mid-day to mid-day. On each of these candles he marked twelve divisions or inches, so that he knew nearly how the day was going, as the consumption of each candle marked the expiration of a sixth part, or about four hours, and each division or inch denoted the lapse of twenty minutes.

By these means Alfred obtained what he desired, an exact admeasurement of time; and the improvements which took place[5] during his reign show that

---

[1] Not an easy matter, *pas un chose facile.*

[2] And quite so, traduisez: *and were quite so.*

[3] "In fine weather," *quand il faisait beau temps.*

[4] "Ordered a certain quantity of wax to be made into six candles," *ordonna qu'on fît, avec une certaine quantité de cire, six chandelles, &c.*

[5] To take place, *avoir lieu.*

both¹ the king and his people had learned to appreciate its value.

P. S. (*Historique.*)

Look on² your watch, and there you may survey,
How gliding life³ steals silently away,
And, mindful of its short determined space,
Improve the flying moments as they pass.

Cross Questions⁴.

Frederick the Great paid⁵ so much attention to his regiments of guards, that he knew personally every one of the soldiers. Whenever he saw a fresh one⁶, he used to put⁷ the three following questions to him. 1st⁸, How old are you? 2nd, How long have you been in my service? 3rd, Are you satisfied with your pay and treatment?" It happened that a young Frenchman, who did not understand three words of German, enlisted into the

---

[1] *Both*, suivi d'un complément, ne se traduit pas en français.
[2] To look on, *regarder à.*
[3] Gliding life, *la vie passagère, éphémère.*
[4] Cross questions, *quiproquo.* m.
[5] To pay attention, *faire attention.*
[6] A fresh one, *un nouveau.*
[7] To put a question, traduisez : *to make a question.*
[8] 1st *premièrement,* 2nd *deuxièmement,* 3rd *troisièmement.*

Prussian service, and Frederick, on seeing[1] him, put the usual questions. The soldier had learned the answers, but in the same order as the king generally interrogated.

Unfortunately, on this occasion Frederick began by the second question, "How long have you been in my service?"—"Twenty-one years," replied the Frenchman.—"What!" said the King, "how old are you then[2]?"—"One year," was the reply.—Upon my word," said Frederick, "you or I must be mad[3],"—"Both," replied the soldier, according to[4] what he had been taught.—"Well," said the astonished monarch, "this is the first time I was ever called a

---

[1] Voir page 10 ([1]).

[2] Les français emploient le verbe *avoir* (to have) au lieu de *être* (to be) en parlant de l'âge, et de l'effet produit sur les personnes et les animaux par la chaleur, le faim, la soif, la peur, et la honte. Ils disent aussi *avoir tort* ou *raison* pour *t be right* or *wrong*.

Ex.: I	am	cold,	J'	ai	*froid.*
Thou	art	warm,	*Tu*	*as*	*chaud.*
He	is	hungry,	*Il*	*a*	*faim.*
She	is	thirsty,	*Elle*	*a*	*soif.*
We	are	ashamed,	*Nous*	*avons*	*honte.*
You	are	ten years old,	*Vous*	*avez*	*dix ans.*
They	are	wrong,	*Ils*	*ont*	*tort.*
They	are	right,	*Elles*	*ont*	*raison.*

[3] "You or I must be mad," *vous ou moi nous sommes fous.*

[4] According to, *selon, suivant, d'après;* according to what he had been taught, *d'après ce qu'on lui avait enseigné.*

mad-man by one of my guards: what do you mean by it¹, sir?"—The poor fellow, seeing the king enraged, told him, in French, that he did not understand a word of German.—"Oh! is it so?" said Frederick; "well, learn it as soon as possible, and I have no doubt but you will make a very good soldier."

Infamous Turpitude.

"Have you confessed all?" said a venerable abbé to a sinner at confession.—"No," replied the latter, "I have another sin on my conscience; I have stolen a watch, will you accept it?"—"I²!" said the offended priest, "how dare you insult me and my holy profession in such a manner? Return the watch instantly to the owner."—"I have already offered to restore it, and he has refused, therefore I beseech you to take it."—"Cease to insult me," said the abbé, "you should³ have offered it again."—"I have done so⁴," replied the thief,

---

¹ "By it," *par là*.

² Le pronom personnel absolu ou nominatif d'un verbe sous-entendu se traduit; I, *moi*, thou, *toi*, he, *lui*; they, *eux*.

³ Lorsque *should* peut se remplacer en Anglais par *ought to* il faut le traduire par le temps correspondant du verbe *devoir* (to owe).

⁴ "I have done so," *c'est ce que j'ai fait*.

"and he declares he will not receive it."—"In that case," said the holy and unsuspecting father¹, "I can absolve you; but I strictly enjoin you not to commit any more thefts."—Soon after the departure of the penitent, the curate discovered that his own watch had been stolen from a hook where he was accustomed to hang it; and he then perceived that the impious thief had offered it to him, but he had refused to accept it.

Magnanimity of Louis XIV².

While the English were erecting the Eddystone light-house, which stands on a rock in the Channel³, a French privateer took the workmen and carried them to France, where they were put into prison. Some time after, Louis XIV. heard of⁴ the transaction, and immediately ordered the Englishmen to be set at liberty⁵ and the captors to be put in their places, saying, "If I am at war⁶ with England I am

---

[1] "The holy and unsuspecting father," *le pieux abbé qui ne soupçonnait rien*. (*Saint père*, traduction littérale de *holy father*, ne se dit ordinairement que du *Pape*.)

[2] Voyez page 14 (⁵) et 20 (²).

[3] The Channel, *la Manche*.

[4] To hear of, *entendre parler de*.

[5] To be set at liberty, *être mis en liberté*.

[6] "At war," *en guerre*.

not at war with mankind; the light-house which the English are erecting will be a benefit to[1] all nations whose ships navigate the Channel, and I would rather[2] protect the workmen than annoy them."

He ordered presents to be given to them, and recommended them to continue their operations without fear. The light-house was completed, and has saved hundreds[3] of vessels from wreck.

Excessive Politeness.

Queen Elizabeth was once making a journey in England; and on her approaching[4] the city of Coventry, the mayor, with a numerous cavalcade, went out to meet[5] her. On their return[6] they had to pass through a wide brook, and the mayor's horse, being thirsty[7], attempted several times to

---

[1] "A benefit to," traduisez *a benefit for*.

[2] "I would rather," *j'aimerais mieux, je voudrais plutôt*.

[3] Les substantifs numéraux se forment en ajoutant la terminaison *aine* au nombre cardinal. Dans ce cas on supprime l'*e* muet qui termine certains nombres cardinaux.

[4] "On her approaching," traduisez: *when she approached of*.

[5] To go out to meet, *aller au-devant de*.

[6] Devant les mots *retour* (return), *depart* (departure) et *arrivée* (arrival) les français remplacent la préposition *on* par à (at).

Voir page 36 (²).

drink, but his cavalier prevented him. The queen observing it, said to him, "Pray, Mr. Mayor, permit your horse to drink."—The mayor, bowing very humbly, replied, "Madam, it would be the height of presumption for my unworthy horse to drink till your majesty's royal steed has satisfied his thirst."

Dignity Maintained.

An ambassador from the emperor Charles the Fifth to Soliman, emperor of the Turks, being invited to an audience of that monarch, perceived on his arrival that seats had been placed for all but him, and that he was left standing by the Turks, for the purpose of[1] showing[2] their indifference towards his nation. He immediately, and with great sang-froid, took off his cloak, folded it up and sat down upon it. When the audience was finished, the ambassador rose and took his leave[3] without paying[4] the least attention to his cloak. An officer called to him, saying, "Sir, you have forgotten your cloak."—"Oh no, I have not," replied he; "the ambassadors of the king my master

---

[1] "For the purpose of," *dans l'intention de.*

[2] Voir page 17 (^{3}).

[3] To take one's leave, *prendre congé.*

[4] "To pay attention," *faire attention.*

are not in the habit of carrying their seats about[1] with them."

How to Make a Friend of an Enemy.

The emperor Charles IV. having learned that one of his officers had been bribed by his enemies to assassinate him, sent for him and said, "I have been informed that your daughter is about[2] to be married[3] and that you have not the means of giving her so handsome a portion as she deserves; if you will accept a thousand ducats for that purpose, they are at your service."

The astonished officer thanked the emperor with many expressions of gratitude, and immediately became one of his most loyal friends; he sent back the bribe he had received, saying he[4] was shocked at having entertained an idea of assassinating any one, and above all his sovereign.

Justice is Sure, though sometimes Slow.

The Grecian poet Ibicus, who lived about[5] five hundred and forty years before Christ, was attacked,

---

[1] To carry about, *porter*.
[2] To be about, *être sur le point de*.
[3] Voir page 19 (³).
[4] Lorsque *that* est sous-entendu, il faut l'exprimer en français.
[5] "About" devant un nombre se traduit *environ*.

robbed, and murdered by banditti. While the robbers were killing him he perceived a flight of cranes in the air, and cried out—"O cranes, you will one day bear witness against my murderers!" Some time after the assassins being in the market-place some cranes flew over, and one of the bandits seeing them said smilingly to his companions, "Look! there go¹ the witnesses of Ibicus."—A person who happened² to overhear him, suspected that he and his companions knew something of the murder, and informed the officers of justice. They were consequently taken, and, being put to the torture, confessed their guilt, and received their merited punishment.

The Scholar's Answer.

A professor of rhetoric was one day reading to his pupils a funeral sermon³ on Marshal Turenne, by Fléchier. One of the scholars, being struck with the beauties of the composition and the force of the expressions, said ironically to one of his

---

¹ There go, *voila.*

² *To happen,* devant un infinitif, se traduit *par hasard,* et doit suivre en français le verbe qu'il précède en anglais; celui-ci doit dans ce cas être mis au temps correspondant de *to happen.*

³ "A funeral sermon," *oraison funèbre.* s. f.

comrades, "When will you be able to do as much?"
—"When you are¹ Turenne," replied the other.

Learning and Riches.

A rich man, it is said², once asked a learned man what was the reason that scientific men were so often to be seen³ at the doors of the rich, though rich men were very rarely seen at the doors of the learned.—"It is," replied the scholar, "because the man of science knows the value of riches, and the rich man does not always know the value of science."

Early Rising.

A boy who was very idle, and would never rise early in the morning to study, was frequently scolded by his father for his laziness, and, like many boys who think⁴ themselves very clever, would argue instead of obeying.⁵

---

¹ Après un adverbe de temps, comme *when*, *as soon as*, &c., les français mettent le verbe au futur en parlant d'un temps à venir

² "It is said," *dit-on*, voyez page 22(³).

³ To be seen, *vus, aperçus.*

⁴ To think one's self, *se croire.*

⁵ Voir page 17 (³).

One day his father went to his bed-room, and calling him, said, "Look here, you lazy fellow!¹ See what your brother Thomas has found by rising² early this morning;"—showing a purse of money that Thomas had picked up near the street-door.— "I see it," replied Lazybones, "but I think he³ who lost it must have risen earlier than Thomas."— "You think yourself very witty," said the father, "but it is much more probable that the purse was lost last night by some one of those persons who don't go home to bed⁴ till⁵ industrious people are thinking of getting up."

The Horse and the Beet-root.

When Louis XI. was Dauphin, he used frequently, in his walks, to visit the family of a peasant, and partake of their frugal meals. Some time after the accession of this prince to the throne of France, the peasant presented him an extraordinary beet-root, the production of his garden. Louis, to⁶ reward the poor man for his attention, and to show

---

¹ "Look here, you lazy fellow!" *Regardez paresseux.*
² Voir pages 12 (⁸) et 17 (³).
³ *That* sous-entendu en anglais doit s'exprimer en français.
⁴ To go home to bed, *rentrer se coucher.*
⁵ "Till," voyez page 13 (³).
⁶ *To*, signifiant *in order to*, doit se traduire *pour.*

that he had not forgotten the rustic cottage, gave him a thousand crowns.

The village squire, on hearing¹ of the peasant's good luck, thought if he gave a good horse to the king, his fortune would be made. He therefore procured² a very handsome one³, went to the palace, and begged the king to do him the honour of accepting it. Louis thanked him for his polite attention, and ordered one of his pages to fetch the beet-root. When it was brought, he presented it to the squire, saying, "Sir, as you seem to be an admirer of the works of nature, I beg you to accept one of its extraordinary productions. I paid a thousand crowns for this root, which cannot be matched⁴, and I am happy to have so good⁵ an opportunity of rewarding your disinterested loyalty."

The Dog and the Eels.

A person had a poodle dog so intelligent that he was frequently sent on errands⁶; they used to write

---

¹ To hear of, *entendre parler de*, ou *apprendre*.
² To procure, *se procurer*.
³ "*One*" ne doit pas se traduire après un adjectif.
⁴ "Which cannot be matched," *qui est sans pareille*.
⁵ "So good an" traduisez *a so good*.
⁶ To be sent on errands, *être envoyé en commission*.

on a piece of paper what was wanted, and giving him a basket in his mouth, he would go and punctually execute his commission. One day, the servants wished to have some sport with him, and writing an order for three pounds of live eels, sent poor Fidèle to fetch them, one of the servants following at some distance. The eels were put into the basket, and the poor dog trotted off with them; but he had not gone far, when he saw some of them slipping over the edge; he set the basket down[1], and tapping them with his paw, made them go in: he then took up his load, and set off towards home. In a few moments[2] several of the eels were on the pavement, and poor Fidèle, beginning to be enraged, took them up in his mouth, shook them well, and put them again into the basket, which[3] was scarcely done, when others had crawled out. At length, quite out of patience[4], he put down the basket, and taking the eels one by one between his teeth, bit them till[5] they were incapable of crawling out; after which he took[6] them home, but from that day would never more go to market.

---

[1] To set down, *poser* ou *mettre à terre*.
[2] "In a few moments," traduisez *a few moments after*.
[3] "Which," traduisez *that which*.
[4] "Out of patience," *à bout de patience* (idiôme).
[5] Voir page 13 (²).
[6] To take, employé pour *to carry*, se traduit *porter*.

The Dog and the Patties.

Another dog, named Black-Muzzle[1], had been taught to go on errands[2], and was sent one day to the pastry-cook's, to fetch some patties in an open basket. On his return[3] he was followed by a dog that put his nose into the basket, and took out a patty. Black-Muzzle, to revenge the insult, put down the basket, and attacked the dainty robber. The noise of the combat soon attracted other dogs, and they also fell on the contents of the basket. Black-Muzzle, seeing there was no means of saving the patties, left off fighting, and in order not to lose his share of the patties, began to devour, as quickly as possible, what yet remained of them.

The Lucky Fall.

An architect who was superintending the construction of a public building, slipped from the scaffold, and fell from top to bottom[4] into the street; he, however, escaped with a few slight bruises by falling[5] on a person who was passing at

---

[1] Black-Muzzle, *noir museau.*
[2] *Aller en commission.*
[3] Voyez page 39 (⁶).
[4] "From top to bottom," *du haut en bas* (idiôme).
[5] Voir page 12 (³).

the moment, but whose arm was broken by the shock, and was forced[1] to be amputated. The unfortunate man brought an action[2] against the architect to obtain compensation for the loss of his arm. It was proved on the trial[3] that the accident had deprived him of the means of getting his bread; but the judges could not decide upon[4] punishing the architect for the effects of an unfortunate accident.

The counsellor for the defendant said that he could see but one method of rendering strict justice, which was that the plaintiff should go up[5] the scaffold to the same place whence the defendant had fallen, and that the latter should be obliged to stand in the place where the former was passing, who should then fall from the scaffold upon him. This arrangement was not approved of[6] by the plaintiff, but the architect, to make him some amends[7], gave him the place of porter at his house.[8]

---

[1] "Was forced to be," *dût être.*

[2] To bring an action, *faire* ou *intenter un procès.*

[3] "On the trial," *dans les débats.*

[4] To decide upon, *se décider à.*

[5] To go up, *monter sur.*

[6] "To be approved of," *être approuvé.*

[7] "To make some amends," *dédommager un peu.*

[8] "Porter at his house," *portier de* ou *dans sa maison.*

The Dog's Will.

A gentleman in the country possessed a valuable dog, which had twice saved him from drowning[1], and several times protected him against thieves; he was consequently much attached to him. At length the poor animal became old and died, and the master, in memory of his fidelity, buried him at the end of his garden, which was near the church-yard; he also had a monument placed[2] over him, with an epitaph in the following words: "Here lies[3] one whose virtues[4] rendered him more worthy of consecrated ground than many who are there interred."

Some busy persons[5] immediately informed the magistrate, denouncing the gentleman as an atheist. The magistrate sent for him, reproached him with[6] his impiety, and threatened to accuse him before the ecclesiastical court. The gentleman began to be alarmed, but recollecting himself[7], he said to

---

[1] To save one from drowning, *empêcher quelqu'un de se noyer* ou *d'être noyé*, ou encore, *retirer de l'eau*.

[2] Had placed, *fit placer, fit élever*.

[3] "Here lies," *ci-gît, ici repose*.

[4] "One whose virtues," *celui* ou *quelqu'un dont les vertus*.

[5] "Busy persons," *personnes empressées*.

[6] To reproach with, *reprocher*.

[7] To recollect one's self, *se remettre, se recueillir*.

the magistrate, "Sir, your observations are very just, and if my dog had not possessed almost human intelligence¹, I should merit the punishment with which² you threaten me. It would be tiresome to relate to you the history of the faithful creature, but the last act of his life will convince you of his extraordinary intelligence: would you believe it, sir, that he made a will, and among other things, has left you a hundred pounds, which I now bring you?"—"Indeed!" replied the magistrate, "he was a most astonishing dog, and you have done extremely well in paying honour³ to his remains; it would be well if every body had lived so as to⁴ merit the inscriptions that are seen on their tombs."

The Danger of Confiding in⁵ Strangers.

A farmer once sent his daughter with a considerable sum of money to⁶ pay the rent of his farm to the landlord, who lived at about a league's distance. On the way she was overtaken by a countryman in

---

Traduisez: *an intelligence almost human.*
² Traduisez: *of which.*
³ To pay honour, *faire honneur, rendre honneur.*
⁴ "So as to," *de manière à.*
⁵ To confide in, *se fier à.*
⁶ Voir page 9 (¹).

a smock frock; he asked her where she was going, and, with all the artlessness of youth and innocence, she told him her errand. He said he was going to the same place, and that he would show her a nearer way than by the high-road. She went with him, and after walking[1] some time they arrived at a by-place[2] where there was a deep well. The countryman then told her to give him the money immediately, or[3] he would throw her into the well.

The poor girl, frightened out of her wits,[4] begged him not to ill-treat her, and was preparing[5] to give him the money, when the robber, thinking he heard a noise, turned round[6] to see what it was, and the poor girl, with great presence of mind, immediately ran upon him with all her strength, and pushed him into the well. Alarmed at what she had done, she ran directly to the nearest village to seek assistance to draw the countryman out of the well; but when they arrived, he was dead, and they discovered that he was a criminal who had escaped from transportation. Take care, my dear children, how you confide in strangers.

---

[1] Voir page 17 (²).
[2] A by-place, *un lieu écarté, peu fréquenté*.
[3] Voir page 11 (⁷).
[4] Frightened out of her wits, *épouvantée, ou hors d'elle*.
[5] To prepare, *se preparer*.
[6] To turn round, *se tourner*.

The Double Lesson.

Dean Swift, a celebrated English writer, and author of *Gulliver's Travels*, was not very generous; he seldom gave anything to the servants of those who sent him presents; but he once received a good lesson from a lad who very often carried him hares, partridges, and other game. One day a boy arrived with a pretty[1] heavy basket containing fish, fruit, and game: he knocked at the door, and the dean, by chance, opened it himself,—"Here," said the boy, gruffly, "my master has sent you a basket full of things."

Swift, feeling displeased[2] at the boy's rude manner, said to him, "Come here, my lad, and I will teach you how to deliver a message a little more politely; come, imagine yourself[3] Dean Swift, and I will be the boy."—Then taking off his hat very politely, and addressing himself[4] to the lad, he said, "Sir, my master sends you a little present, and begs you will do him the honour to accept it."—"Oh, very well, my boy," replied the

---

[1] Le mot, *pretty*, devant un adjectif ou un adverbe, se traduit *assez*.

[2] To feel displeased at, *se sentir mécontent de*.

[3] Traduisez: *imagine that you are*.

[4] To address one's self, *s'adresser*.

lad, "tell your master¹ I am much obliged to him, and there is half a crown² for yourself."

A Curious Exculpation.

During the wars in Italy, a gentleman who was returning home late at night³ was robbed of his cloak by some soldiers. He complained to the celebrated chief of the brigands, Facino Cane, telling him that some of his men had taken his cloak, and saying he hoped the general would not let them go unpunished. Facino, looking at the gentleman, asked him how he was dressed when he lost his cloak.—"Just as I am at present," replied he.— "Then," said the chief, "you have not been robbed by my men, for I am sure there is not one among them who would have left you so good a coat⁴ upon your back as that⁵ you wear now."

Modesty of a Youth.

A young man who had paid⁶ great attention to his studies, and consequently had made rapid pro-

---

¹ Voir page 11 (⁷).
² "Half a crown," *un petit écu*.
³ "At night," *la nuit, dans la nuit, pendant la nuit*.
⁴ "So good a coat," traduisez: *a so good coat*.
⁵ Traduisez: *that which*.
⁶ To pay attention, *faire attention*.

gress, was once taken¹ by his father to dine with a company of literary men. After dinner, the conversation turned naturally upon literature and the classics². The young man listened to it with great attention, but did not say anything. On their return³ home, his father asked him why he had remained silent, when he had so good an⁴ opportunity of showing his knowledge.—"I was afraid, my dear father," said he, "that if I began to talk of what I do know, I should be interrogated upon what I do not know."—"You are right, my dear boy," replied the father, "there is often more danger in speaking than in holding one's tongue⁵."

Virtue in Humble Life.

During a campaign in Germany, in 1760, an officer who was out with a foraging party⁶, and could not find any corn, saw a cottage at some distance; he approached, and having knocked at the door, an

---

¹ *To take*, employé dans le sens de *to lead*, se traduit *conduire, mener.*

² The classics, *les belles-lettres, les auteurs classiques.*

³ Voir page 39 (⁵).

⁴ So good an, traduisez : *a so good.*

⁵ To hold one's tongue, *se taire, retenir sa langue.*

⁶ A foraging party, *un parti de fourrageurs.*

old man with a white beard came out and asked what he wanted.—" Can you," said the officer, " show us where we can find some forage for our cavalry?"—" Yes," replied the cottager, " if you will wait a few minutes I will conduct you."—They set off, and in about a quarter of an hour[1] arrived at a field of corn, which the officer perceiving said[2], " This is exactly the thing for us[3]."

" Come a little further," said the old man, " and I will show you some better."—He then led them to a field of oats, where they immediately filled their sacks ; but the officer said to the old man : " Why did you bring us so far ? the other field of corn is better than this."—" It is true," replied the honest cottager, " but that does not belong to me, and this does[4]."—" You are a truly honest man," said the officer, "and I will take care that you shall be paid for the oats we have taken."

---

[1] "In about a quarter of an hour," *environ un quart d'heure après*.

[2] "Which the officer perceiving said," traduisez: *in perceiving it the officer said*.

[3] "This is exactly the thing for us," *c'est exactement ce qu'il nous faut* (idiôme).

[4] "This does," traduisez: *this belongs to me*. (Les français n'emploient pas le verbe *to do* comme auxiliaire, en conséquence il faut répeter le verbe qu'il représente avec son complément s'il y en a un, toutes les fois que *to do* est employé comme auxiliaire en anglais. Souvent en réponse à une question, on peut remplacer *to do* par *oui* ou *non*.)

The Queen of Spain has no Legs.

When the German princess Mary of Nieuburg, who became wife of Philip IV. of Spain, was on her way to[1] Madrid, she passed through a little town, in Spain, famous for its manufactory of gloves and stockings. The citizens and magistrates thought they could not better express their joy at the reception of their new queen, than by presenting her a sample of those commodities for which their town was remarkable. The mayordomo[2], who conducted the princess, received the gloves very graciously; but when the stockings were presented, he flung them away with indignation, and severely reprimanded the magistrates of the deputation for their indecency.

" Know," said he, " that a queen of Spain has no legs."

The young Queen, unacquainted with[3] the etiquette, customs, and prejudices of the Spanish court, imagined that they were really going to cut off her legs. She burst into tears,[4] begging they would conduct her back into Germany, for that

---

[1] On her way to, *se rendait à.*
[2] Mayordomo, *majordome.* m.
[3] "Unacquainted with," *qui ignorait.*
[4] To burst into tears. *fondre en larmes.*

she never could endure such an¹ operation, and it was with great difficulty they appeased her. The king, it is said², never laughed more heartily than at the recital of this adventure.

(*Hume's Essays.*)

The Dilemma, or the Lawyer Outwitted.

A celebrated counsellor received a young man as a pupil to study pleading³. The conditions of his apprenticeship were, that when he should be capable of taking his place at the bar⁴, he should pay the counsellor five hundred pounds, on condition⁵, however, that he gained the first cause he should plead. When the master knew his pupil to be perfectly capable, he insisted on his taking a cause⁶, and pleading; but he refused; and the counsellor entered an action⁷ to oblige him.

The day of trial arrived, and the parties appeared

---

¹ "Such an," traduisez: *a such*. (En français l'article *a* ou *an* précède toujours l'adjectif *such*.)

² It is said, *dit-on*, voir page 22 (³).

³ Pleading, *l'art de plaider; la profession d'avocat.*

⁴ At the bar, *au barreau, à la cour, au palais.*

⁵ On condition, *à condition.*

⁶ "On his taking a cause," *pour qu'il prît une cause.*

⁷ To enter an action, *intenter un procès.*

in court¹, when the young man, approaching the plaintiff, said to him, "What do you expect to gain by this action?"—"Why,² the sum you agreed to pay me," replied he.—"But," said the other, "I intend to plead my own cause; it is my first; therefore, if I don't gain it, I shall owe you nothing, according to our agreement; and if I do³, you will have lost yours, and I shall have nothing to pay you."—The counsellor confessed that he had been out-witted by his pupil, abandoned the lawsuit, and they became afterwards great friends.

A very Black Affair.

Some years ago at Fort-l'Évêque, in America, a young spendthrift, named Châteaublond, having got into debt⁴ to a very great amount⁵, his creditors, knowing his family to be rich⁶, threw him into prison, hoping they would pay his debts. The prisoner lived very gaily in his confinement, frequently inviting his acquaintances to dine with

---

¹ "To appear in court," *comparaître devant la cour* (idiôme).

² "Why," (exclamation) *mais ! vraiment !*

³ Voyez page 55 (⁴).

⁴ To get into debt, *faire des dettes, contracter des dettes.*

⁵ "To a very great amount," *pour de très-grandes sommes.*

⁶ "His family to be rich," traduisez: *that his family was rich.*

him. One day a gentleman came with a black servant carrying some wine in a basket: and after dining¹ and spending the evening², he retired, accompanied by the negro carrying the empty bottles.

A few hours after, when the jailers went to lock up their prisoners for the night, they discovered a stranger in the place of M. Chateaublond, who, it appears, had blacked his face and hands, and gone away with his visitor, carrying the basket of empty bottles; the jailers, seeing a black man go out, thought naturally it was the negro they had let in with the gentleman. The man was tried³ for having procured the escape of a prisoner, but was acquitted, on⁴ proving that he was the servant of M. Chateaublond, and that his master had ordered him to stay in his room while he went somewhere.

The Doctor who received the Life of his Patient in Payment for his Visits.

An authoress⁵ at London, named Constantia Phillips, was reduced to the greatest misery; till⁶

---

¹ Voir page 17 (²).
² To spend the evening, *passer la soirée*.
³ To be tried (at law), *être jugé*.
⁴ Voir page 10 (¹).
⁵ Authoress, *femme auteur*.
⁶ "Till," voir page 13 (⁷).

at length some of her friends made a subscription, and set her up in a little book-shop at Westminster, where she was just able to live from hand to mouth[1]. In order to obtain a little money, she worked night and day in writing her memoirs, which, it appears, were interesting. So much exertion and such bad living threw her into a dangerous illness, from which, however, after much suffering, she was delivered by an able doctor of the neighbourhood.

Some time after her recovery, the doctor presented his bill, but the unfortunate Mrs. Phillips told him that she was really so poor that she could not pay him. After calling[2] several times, he became impatient, and reproached her with ingratitude[3], telling her that she owed him her life.—" I acknowledge it," said she, " and to prove that I am not ungrateful, I will pay you with my life ;" presenting him, at the same time, two volumes entitled " The Life of Constantia Phillips."

Embarrassing News.

In the year 1650, there was a terrible plague at Tunis, which is on the coast of Africa. There

---

[1] "To live from hand to mouth," *vivre au jour le jour* (idiôme).
[2] "After calling," *après avoir passé chez elle*.
[3] "And reproached her with ingratitude," *et lui reprocha son ingratitude*.

were at that time in the town two French missionaries, named Levachir and Guerin. The former was attacked by the malady, and in a few hours was abandoned as dead. Mr. Guerin immediately wrote to the superior of the mission in France, informing him of the loss of his friend. The letter was given to the captain of a vessel, which was about[1] to sail for Toulon, and preparations were made to bury Mr. Levachir; but as they were removing him, he showed some signs of life, and was, with the assistance of a doctor, perfectly restored.

[2]A very few hours afterwards, his friend, Mr. Guerin, was attacked and died the same night. Mr. Levachir, knowing nothing of the letter sent by his deceased friend, wrote directly to the head of the mission, to announce the death of Mr. Guerin. The vessel not having yet sailed, the letter was given to the same captain, so that the superior received, by the same post, a letter from each of the missionaries announcing the death of the other. The mystery was not cleared up for[3] some months.

---

[1] To be about, *être sur le point de, être prêt à* ou *près de.*

[2] Traduisez: *a few hours afterwards.*

[3] "Cleared up," *éclairci.*

Ventriloquy.

Ventriloquy is the art of speaking inwardly without any apparent motion of the lips or other organs of speech, and of disguising the voice so as to[1] make it appear that of another person, and to issue from another place. Some years ago[2] there was in England a man named Hoskins, who possessed this art in a very eminent degree[3], and by the aid of it[4] frequently amused himself at the expense of[5] others. He was once travelling on foot[6] in the country, and overtook on the road a carter driving a team with a load of hay. After walking some time and conversing with the countryman, Hoskins imitated the crying of a child. As there was not any child to be seen[7], the carter appeared surprised, and asked Hoskins if he had not heard it; he replied, "Yes," and almost at the same instant the cry was repeated. It appeared this time to come from under the hay in the cart, and the ventriloquist insisted that the carter had concealed a child there.

---

[1] "So as to," *de manière à, de façon à.*

[2] Voir page 16 (²).

[3] Traduisez: *at* a very eminent degree.

[4] "By the aid of it," *par ce moyen.*

[5] "At the expense of," *aux dépens de.*

[6] To travel on foot, *voyager à pied.*

[7] "To be seen," *visible, en vue.*

ENGLISH INTO FRENCH.

The poor fellow, astonished and alarmed, stopped his horses and unloaded the cart truss by truss; no child however was found, and he reloaded it; which he had scarcely done when the cry was again distinctly heard. The countryman, frightened out of his wits, immediately took to his heels[1], and running to the nearest village, told the villagers that he had met the devil on the road, and begged them to go and assist him to recover his cart and horses which he had left in his clutches. The peasants immediately set off armed with pitchforks and flails, and soon arrived in sight of the supposed devil, who having a wooden leg could not run away. After some difficulty, he persuaded them to let him approach and convince them that he was really a human being.

They were for a long time incredulous, and the experiments[2] he made of his art increased their belief in his diabolical character. At length, fortunately for Hoskins, the village curate arrived, and explained the matter to the satisfaction of the peasants, who then agreed to accompany the ventriloquist to the next public house, where he treated them with beer and a lunch. Soon after

---

[1] "Took to his heels," *se sauva, prit ses jambes à son cou* (idiôme).

[2] *Which* ou *that*, sous-entendu en anglais, doit s'exprimer en français.

this, Hoskins was engaged at several of the London theatres, where he exhibited his art to the astonishment of the multitude, as ventriloquy was at that time almost unknown, even in the metropolis.

On the Folly of Believing in Ghosts.

The ridiculous stories of apparitions which we hear and read, are generally either fictions to impose on weak minds, wicked tricks to frighten or to rob the timid, or reveries of disordered imaginations. The following story, which may be found in the *Children's Magazine*, will serve as a proof, and we hope, as a caution to children, that they ought not to listen to such follies.

A gentleman was travelling on horseback, some years ago, not far from Toulouse, and being surprised towards night by a terrible storm of thunder, lightning, hail, rain and wind, he took refuge at a small inn, near the village of St. Gabelle. The house was almost full of Spanish travellers and others, who like our gentleman had sought shelter from the tempest[1]. The company drew around the fire[2], and, after conversing some time on the horrors

---

[1] From the tempest, traduisez : *against the tempest.*
[2] To draw around the fire, *s'approcher du feu.*

of travelling in a mountainous country on such a night¹, they began to talk of supernatural appearances, of witchcraft, etc. One of the Spaniards appeared very ardent in the conversation, and firmly supported his belief in spectres, relating several stories in confirmation of it.

Among the company was a young man who laughed heartily at the serious manner in which the Spaniard treated the subject; which the latter observing² said to him, "I advise you, sir, not to laugh at what you don't understand."—"Why!" replied the other, " would you attempt to make me believe in apparitions?"—"Yes, sir, if you possessed sufficient courage to contemplate them."—The young man rose with indignation and said, "If I did not consider you out of your mind³, I would make you repent that expression."—The Spaniard, immediately throwing his purse on the table, cried out, "There are thirty pieces of gold; I will forfeit them if, in the course of an hour, I don't show you the apparition of any one of your deceased acquaintances that you will name; provided you will forfeit an equal sum if I do⁴."—"Thirty pieces!" replied the other; "I am only a student; it is more

---

¹ "On such a night," traduisez: *by* or *during a such night.*

² "Which the latter observing," traduisez: *the latter observing it.*

³ " Out of your mind," *comme un fou.*

⁴ Voyez page 55 (⁴).

than I ever possessed; I have however four, which I will risk to prove the impossibility of what you say."—"A mere excuse¹," said the Spaniard, "to conceal your fear; it is not worth while² to exercise my art for such a paltry sum."

Our traveller felt greatly interested in the discussion, and, wishing to see how the Spaniard would proceed, he threw four pieces to the young man; several other strangers followed his example, and the student was soon in possession of the desired sum.—"Now, sir," said he, "I defy you."—"Very well," said the Spaniard, "you will have the goodness to permit me to shut you in the next room, with a table, pen, ink, and paper."—The student entered, and demanded to see Francis Vialat, who was drowned³ three years before. The company, to⁴ prevent any trickery, examined every part of the chamber, after which they placed themselves, with the Spaniard, outside the door. He pronounced some mysterious words, and then said to the student, "What do you see?"—"I see," replied he, "a white vapour rising, but it has no form."—"Are you afraid?"—"No," said the

---

¹ "A mere excuse," *pur prétexte.*
² "It is not worth while," *cela ne vaut pas la peine* (idiôme).
³ "Who was drowned," traduisez: *who had been drowned.*
⁴ Voyez page 9 (¹).

student, but in a faint voice¹. The company looked at each other² with astonishment.

The Spaniard, after pronouncing some more mysterious words, repeated in a hollow voice: "What do you see, you who would discover the secrets of the tomb?"—"I see," answered he, in a trembling voice, "the vapour taking a human form! its face is covered with a veil! it raises the veil! I see its face! It is Vialat! He approaches the table! He is writing his name!"—"Are you afraid?" said the Spaniard.—No answer was returned³, and the company at the door were petrified with horror, when suddenly the young man screamed out, "He approaches me! He pursues me!... He endeavours to seize me in his arms!... Help! help! help⁴!"

The company burst open⁵ the door, found the student in convulsions on the floor, and a paper on the table, signed with red ink⁶: VIALAT. —As soon as the young man recovered his senses, he demanded the infamous sorcerer who had invoked the devil to torment him: he had however

---

[1] "In a faint voice," *d'une voix faible.*
[2] To look at each other, *se regarder, s'entre-regarder.*
[3] "No answer was returned," *point de réponse.*
[4] Help! help! help! *au secours! au secours! au secours!*
[5] To burst open, *enfoncer, briser.*
[6] "Signed with red ink," *signé en encre rouge.*

in the confusion escaped to avoid the rage of the student, who immediately rushed out of the inn swearing vengeance against him, and leaving the company to console each other¹ for having been duped by two of those confederated rogues who live upon the weakness and credulity of others.

The Page and the Cherries.

A basket of fine cherries having been sent to Frederick, king of Prussia, at a time when² that fruit was extremely scarce, he sent them, by one of his pages, to the queen. The page, tempted by the beauty of the cherries, could not resist tasting³, and finding them delicious, devoured the whole, without reflecting on the consequences.

A few days afterwards, Frederick asked the queen how she had liked⁴ the cherries?—Cherries! said her majesty, what cherries?—Why, did not Clist, the page, bring you a basket the other day? —No, replied the queen; I have not seen any.— Oh! oh! said his majesty, I will give the lickerish

---

¹ To console each other, *s'entre-consoler.*

² "At a time when," *dans un moment où.*

³ "Could not resist tasting," traduisez: *could not resist the temptation of tasting them.*

⁴ "How she had liked," traduisez: *how she had found.*

rogue¹ something a little more savoury; he then went to his closet, and wrote the following note to the officer of the royal guard :—" Give the bearer twenty-five lashes, and take his receipt for it²." He then called Clist, and told him to take the note to the guard-house, and wait for an answer.

The page, however, fearing all was not right (a guilty conscience needs no accuser³), determined to send the note by another hand⁴, and just as he was going out at the palace door⁵, he met a Jew banker who was well known at⁶ court, and asked him to carry the note.—The Jew, glad of an opportunity of obliging any one at the palace, immediately set off. On his arrival at the guard-house, the officer read the note, and telling the messenger to wait, he called out the guard⁷. The Jew, thinking it was to do honour to him, as a messenger from court, begged the officer not to give himself any unnecessary trouble.—I do not, replied he; these ceremonies are quite necessary,

---

¹ " The lickerish rogue," *le gourmand*.

² " Take his receipt for it," *prenez sa quittance* ou *son reçu*.

³ ' A guilty conscience needs no accuser," *la conscience du coupable s'accuse elle-même* (idiôme).

⁴ " By another hand," *par une autre personne*.

⁵ " *At* the palace door," traduisez: *from* the palace door.

⁶ " At court," traduisez: *at the court*.

⁷ To call out the guard, *faire sortir la garde*.

as you will find'.—He then ordered the guard to seize the Jew, and give him twenty-five lashes, which was immediately done, after which, with his honour and his back severely wounded, he was going away; but the officer told him he could not let him depart till² he had given a written acknowledgment³ for what he had received. The Jew was obliged to comply, for fear of having another account to settle.

The affair soon reached the ears of the king, who, though he could not help laughing⁴ heartily at the adventure, was obliged to confer some favours on the hero of it⁵, as the Jews frequently advanced him considerable sums of money, in cases of necessity. (*Historique.*)

The Dervise and the Atheist.

Atheists are those ridiculous and impious persons who, contrary to the evidence of their senses, pretend not to believe in the existence of God.

---

¹ "As you will find," traduisez : *as you are going to see.*

² Voir page 13 (²).

³ "A written acknowledgment," *une reconnaissance par écrit.*

⁴ "Could not help laughing," *ne put s'empêcher de rire.*

⁵ "To confer some favours on the hero of it," *accorder* ou *conférer quelques faveurs au héros.*

One of them was disputing with a dervise, and said to him, "You tell me that God is omnipresent, yet I cannot see him anywhere; show him to me, and I will believe it.—Again I say that a man ought not to be punished for his crimes by your laws, since you say that everything is done by the will of God.—You say also that Satan is punished by[1] being condemned to hell-fire[2]; now, as he is said to be of that element, what injury can fire do to itself?"

The dervise, after a moment's reflection, took up a large lump of earth, struck the atheist a violent blow with it[3], and then left him. The latter went directly to the cadi, complained of the injury, and demanded justice; the dervise was summoned to answer why, instead of replying to the man, he had struck him.—"What I did," replied the dervise, "was in answer to his ridiculous questions; of what does he complain? He says he has a pain, let him show it if he wishes us to believe him: he accuses me of a crime, yet he said that man ought not to be punished by our laws, since everything, according to our doctrine, was under the direction of God: he complains that I have injured him by

---

[1] Voir page 12 (⁸).

[2] "To hell fire," *au feu de l'enfer*.

[3] "Struck the atheist a violent blow with it," *en frappa l'athée d'un coup violent*.

striking him with a piece of earth; now he does not deny that man is of the earth, and he maintains that an element can do no harm to itself, of what then does he complain?" The atheist was confounded, and retired¹ amidst the railleries of the auditors.

To² be convinced of the hypocrisy of those infidels, we should see one of them on a bed of death; it would be a lesson for the others.

Canine Sagacity.

Among the many³ surprising stories that are told of the intelligence of that faithful animal, the dog, the following one is given as a fact.—A large dog was playing in the road near a country village, and a carriage went over one of his paws; he howled most piteously⁴, and some farriers who were at work in a shop close by⁵ came out to see what was the matter. One of them, perceiving that the poor thing was much hurt, took him up, dressed his paw and wrapped it up, after which he let him go. The

---

¹ "To retire," *se retirer*.
² Voir page 9 (¹).
³ "Among the many," traduisez: *among the numerous*.
⁴ "Most piteously," *de la manière la plus touchante*.
⁵ "Close by," *tout près de l'endroit, à deux pas de l'endroit*.

dog went home, where he remained during some days; but at length, his paw becoming painful, he returned to the farrier's, and, holding it up, moaned, to show that it pained him. The farrier dressed it again, and the dog, after licking his hand to show his gratitude, returned home, and the paw in a few days was well.

Some months after, the same dog was playing with another, not far from the spot, and a similar accident happened to the latter; upon which he took him by the ear, and with much difficulty led him to the farrier's shop, where he had been so well doctored. The workmen were much amused at[1] the sagacity of the animal, and paid as much attention[2] to the new patient as they had to the former one.

Gratitude.

The lieutenant of the police of the caliph Manoun related to one of his friends the following story of an event which happened to himself.

"I was one evening," said he, "with the caliph, when a note was brought which seemed to irritate him very much: after[3] reading it, he said to me,

---

[1] To be much amused at, *s'amuser beaucoup de.*
[2] To pay attention, *faire attention, accorder attention.*
   Voir page 17 (³).

"Go into the next room; you will find a prisoner; keep him in safe custody to-night[1], interrogate him, and bring him before me to-morrow morning, or answer it with your head[2]."—I took[3] the man to my own apartment and asked him his country.—'I am,' replied he, 'of Damascus.'—'Indeed,' said I, 'that town is dear to me, for I owe my life to one of its inhabitants.'—'Your story,' replied he, 'must be interesting, will you tell it me?'—'I will,' said I; 'It is as follows[4].'

"'Being once at Damascus, I had the misfortune to displease the caliph, and was pursued by the officers of justice. I escaped out of a back window[5], and sought refuge in another part of the town, where a citizen received me with kindness, and, at the risk of his life, concealed me in his house till[6] the pursuit was over, when he furnished me with money and a horse, to enable me to join a caravan that was going to Bagdad, my native city. I shall never forget his kindness, and I hope, before my

---

[1] "Keep him in safe custody to-night," *tenez le en prison cette nuit*, ou *tenez le sous clef*.

[2] "Or answer it with your head," *ou vous en répondrez sur votre tête*.

[3] *To take*, dans le sens de *to lead*, se traduit *mener, conduire*.

[4] "It is as follows," *la voici*.

[5] "Out of a back window," *par une fenêtre de derrière*.

[6] Voir page 13 ([2])

death, to find an opportunity of proving my gratitude.'

"'That opportunity is at this moment offered to you,' said my prisoner. 'I am the person who had the pleasure of rendering you that service.'—He then related to me some circumstances that convinced me he had been my protector. I asked him by what calamity he had excited the caliph's displeasure. 'I have had,' replied he, 'the misfortune to offend an officer who has great influence at court¹, and he, to revenge himself, has charged me with² an intention against the life of the caliph, for which, though innocent, I shall no doubt pay with my head³.'

"'No, generous friend,' said I, 'you shall not be sacrificed; you are at liberty; take this purse, return to your family, and I will answer to the caliph.'—'Do you then,' said he, 'think me⁴ capable of sacrificing your life that I have once preserved? No, the only favour that I will accept, is that you will endeavour to convince the caliph of my innocence: if you fail, I will go and offer him my head, for I will not escape and leave you in danger.'

---

¹ "At court," *à la cour*

² To charge one with an intention against the life of, &c., *accuser quelqu'un d'avoir l'intention d'attenter à la vie de*, &c.

³ "Pay *with* my head," traduisez: *pay of my head*.

⁴ "Do you then think me?" *me croyez-vous donc?*

"I went directly to the caliph, who, as soon as he saw me, demanded my prisoner and sent for the executioner.—'My lord,' said I, 'an extraordinary circumstance has happened concerning him.'"—'I swear,' cried he, 'if you have let him escape, your head shall pay for it'.—With great difficulty I persuaded him to listen to me, and I then related how my prisoner had saved my life at Damascus; that I had offered him his liberty as a proof of my gratitude, and that he would not accept it for fear of exposing me to his (the caliph's) displeasure. 'My lord,' added I, 'it is improbable that a man of such generous sentiments should be capable of the crime imputed to him; deign then to demand the proofs of it before you condemn him.'

"The caliph expressed his admiration of the conduct of my friend; a strict inquiry was made, and he was found innocent; the accuser was beheaded, and my friend appointed to his place; which he filled with honour till[3] the day of his death."

Filial Affection of a Page.

The emperor Charles V. had a page named Athanasius d'Ayala, whose father had had the

---

[1] "Concerning him," *à son sujet, à son égard* (idiôme).

[2] "Your head shall pay for it," *vous le paierez de votre tête*.

[3] "Till," voir page 13 (²).

imprudence to engage¹ in a conspiracy against his monarch; he was proscribed, his property confiscated, and he himself was obliged to flee. Athanasius was yet very young, not being² more than fourteen, and consequently did not receive any salary at³ court; his tender heart was deeply afflicted at the situation of his father, who was reduced to poverty, and he had no means of sending him assistance. At length, unable to support the idea of the sufferings of his parent, the young Athanasius sold the horse that was allowed him for his exercises⁴, and sent the money to his father.

The horse was soon missed⁵ and the page interrogated; but he obstinately refused to give any account of him. The emperor, being informed of the circumstance, ordered Athanasius to be brought before him, and insisted on knowing what he had done with the horse. The youth immediately fell on his knees⁶, and bursting into tears confessed the whole, saying, "I hope⁷ your majesty

---

¹ To engage, *s'engager.*

² Voir page 36 (²).

³ "At court," traduisez: *at the court.*

⁴ "Exercises," *récréations.* f.

⁵ "The horse was soon missed," *on s'aperçut bientôt que le cheval manquait.*

⁶ On his knees, *à genoux.*

⁷ *That*, sous-entendu, doit s'exprimer en français.

will pardon me; for, if my father has forgotten his duty to¹ his king, he is nevertheless my father, and nothing could excuse me if I were to forget my duty towards him."

Marine Logic.

A sailor who had already made several voyages to sea², had engaged³ on board an Indiaman⁴ bound⁵ to China. This was a longer voyage than any he had yet made, and one of his friends endeavoured to dissuade him, magnifying the danger, and advising him to settle on shore.

Nonsense, replied the Jack-tar, don't talk to me of danger; there is no more on sea than on shore. —Let me ask you, said his friend, what was your father?—He was a seaman.—And where did he die?—He was lost in a shipwreck.—And your grandfather?—He fell overboard and was drowned. —And where did your great-grandfather die?—He perished in a vessel that struck against a rock.— Then don't you think you are very foolhardy to go to sea, and risk your life where so many of your

---

[1] "His duty to," traduisez: *his duty towards*.

[2] "To sea," *sur mer*, ou *à la mer*.

[3] To engage on board, *s'engager à bord de*.

[4] "Indiaman," *vaisseau de la compagnie des Indes*.

[5] "Bound to," *à destination de, en charge pour*.

family have perished?—And let me ask you, said the sailor, where did your father die?—Why, in his bed certainly.—And your grandfather?—In his bed also.—Then don't you think you are very foolhardy to go to bed, where so many of your ancestors have perished? Let me tell you that God protects his creatures as much at sea as on shore.

A Singular Justification.

A reaper being at work in a field in Devonshire¹, near the banks of a river, saw a man throw himself into the water; he ran directly to his assistance, plunged in², and brought him to the shore. Having left him and returned to his work, he very soon saw him again leap in³. A second time the reaper jumped into the river, and, with difficulty, rescued him; he then recommended him to go home, and not attempt such a foolish action as to drown himself. The reaper then resumed his labour, but, in a short time⁴, saw the same man hang himself to the branch of a tree.

Finding him so determined to kill himself, he

---

¹ Devonshire, le comté de Devon.
² To plunge in, *plonger*.
³ "Leap in," *sauter à l'eau* ou *dans l'eau*.
⁴ "In a short time," traduisez: *a few moments after*.

resolved to take no more trouble about him¹, but to let him hang.

Some time after, the relations² of the man came in search of him, and finding him hanging dead on the tree, they reproached³ the reaper, saying, that he must have seen him⁴ do it, and ought to have cut him down⁵.—Not I, indeed, replied he; I had already drawn him twice out of the river, and having left him dripping wet⁶, I supposed he had hung himself up there to dry.

The Immortal Elixir.

A certain emperor of China was a great lover of the sciences, and a great encourager of learned men; but not being able to distinguish true merit from impudent charlatanism, he was frequently imposed on⁷.

One day an impostor obtained admittance⁸ to the

---

¹ "About him," *à son égard, à son suget.*

² "Relations," *parents.* m. pl. Le mot *parent* en français signifie *Kinsman.*

³ To reproach, *faire des reproches à.*

⁴ "He must have seen him," *il devait l'avoir vu.*

⁵ "Cut him down," *coupé la corde.*

⁶ "Dripping wet," *dégouttant d'eau, tout trempé.*

⁷ "To be imposed on," ou "upon," *être trompé, dupé.*

⁸ To obtain admittance, *obtenir d'entrer.*

palace, and, watching an opportunity, he presented a phial to the emperor, saying, May it please[1] your majesty, this phial contains an elixir that will render you immortal; drink it, and fear not death.

As the emperor was about to[2] take the phial, one of the ministers, who had more judgment than his majesty, snatched it from his hand, and immediately drank off a part of its contents. The monarch, enraged at[3] his presumption, immediately ordered him to be put to death; but the minister calmly replied: "If the elixir gives immortality, you will in vain try to put me to death; and if it does not[4], I have unmasked an impostor; let him be compelled to drink the rest of it, and then take a dose of poison; if he is a true man[5], he has nothing to fear; if he is not, he deserves to die, for having attempted to deceive your majesty."—The advice was adopted, and the impostor, refusing to drink the poison, was condemned to perpetual imprisonment.

Heroic Conduct of a Sailor.

The crew of an English merchantman which was at Barbadoes, were one day bathing in the sea,

---

[1] "May it please," *n'en déplaise à.*

[2] To be about to, *être sur le point de, aller.*

[3] "Enraged at," *irrité de.*

[4] Traduisez: *if it does not give it.* Voir page 55 (⁴).

[5] "True man," *homme loyal, de bonne foi.*

when they were alarmed at the appearance of an enormous shark. The men swam towards their boat as fast as possible; but the monster overtook one of them, and seizing him in his jaws, bit him in halves, and swallowed the lower part[2]. The upper part was taken[3] on board, and the mangled appearance of it[4] so affected one of the sailors, who was much attached to the unfortunate man, that he vowed to revenge his death on the shark, which was yet seen lurking about[5] in search of more prey[6]. The sailor armed himself with the cook's knife, and, being an excellent swimmer, leaped into the sea, swearing to kill the monster, or to perish in the attempt.

The shark no sooner perceived him, than he approached and opened his voracious jaws to swallow him; the sailor at the same moment dived, and rising under his belly, caught firmly hold[7] of one of the fins, and immediately plunged his knife seve-

---

[1] To bite in halves, *couper en deux*.

[2] "The lower part," *la partie inférieure;* "the upper part," *la partie supérieure.*

[3] *To take,* dans le sens de *to carry,* se traduit *porter.*

[4] "And the mangled appearance of it," traduisez: *and its mangled appearance.*

[5] To lurk about, *roder.*

[6] "In search of more prey," *à la recherche d'une autre proie.*

[7] To catch hold, *se saisir.*

ral times into his body. The enraged shark darted instantly to the bottom of the sea, but the sailor remained on the surface to take breath, and to wait for his adversary to rise again. Soon after he reappeared, streaming with blood and writhing with torture; the sailor again attacked him, and, by a few more stabs, reduced him to such a state, that, in the pangs of death, he made towards[1] the shore, followed by his conqueror.

Unable to make any further efforts, the sailor pushed him to land, where the tide soon left him dry[2]. The seaman, with the assistance of his shipmates, ripped up[3] the belly of the monster, and found in it the lower extremity of his friend, which he placed with the other part, and both were buried on the island; he took to[4] England several of the shark's teeth as a token of his victory; some of them he gave to the parents of his deceased shipmate, whose sister he soon after married[5].

Abuse of Hospitality.

In the month of June, 1818, a pedlar and his wife presented themselves one Saturday evening at

---

[1] To make towards, *se diriger vers.*
[2] To leave dry, *laisser à sec.* [3] To rip up, *fendre.*
[4] To take to, *emporter en.*
[5] To marry, *épouser.* Voir page 19 (⁵).

the door of a farm-house, and asked an asylum for the night, which was readily granted them. On the following morning, being Sunday, the farmer and his servants went to church, accompanied by the pedlar, whose wife excused herself from going[1], by saying she was not well. Shortly after they were gone, the pedlar's wife went to the room of the farmer's wife, who was ill in bed[2], and demanded the keys of the secretary. Unable to resist, she gave them; but as soon as she heard her in the next room, she crept out[3] of bed and locked her in;[4] then calling her little boy, she told him to run as fast as he could to church, and tell his father to come and bring assistance.

Unfortunately the child met the pedlar, who was returning from church before the service was finished, no doubt[5] to assist in robbing[6] his generous host. He asked the boy where he was going. The boy replied—To fetch my father.—Oh! said the pedlar, come with me, I will go and protect your mother.—They returned and knocked at the door; but the farmer's wife, hearing the pedlar's voice,

---

[1] Traduisez: *from not going with them.*
[2] To be ill in bed, *être malade au lit.*
[3] To creep out, *sortir doucement.*
[4] To lock in, *enfermer à clef.*
[5] "No doubt," *sans doute.*
[6] "To assist in robbing," *pour aider à voler.*

refused to let them in: he then told her, that if she did not open the door, he would immediately kill the child. She supplicated him to have mercy on[1] the little innocent, but did not open the door, hoping, every minute, that her husband, or the servants, would arrive to her assistance.

The sanguinary monster, knowing he had no time to lose, immediately killed the poor little boy; and having found means to climb up to the roof, entered[2] the chimney to make his way into the house. The affrighted woman heard him, and, with great presence of mind, immediately set fire[3] to the rubbish in the fire-place[4], adding also a great quantity of straw. The chimney was instantly on fire[5], and the robber fell senseless, and nearly suffocated, into the flames at the bottom. The poor woman, exhausted with fatigue and terror, then fainted and fell on the floor; but, fortunately, the husband and servants returned before the robber had recovered his senses. They forced open[6] the door, and soon discovered the fatal truth. The culprits were seized and taken to jail, and at the following assizes condemned to

---

[1] "To have mercy on," *avoir pitié de.*
[2] Traduisez: *entered into.*
[3] To set fire, *mettre le feu.*
[4] Fire-place, *foyer.* m. *cheminée.* m.
[5] Traduisez: *in fire.*
[6] To force open, *enfoncer, briser.*

death; but the poor farmer's wife did not long survive the loss¹ of her dear little boy.

The Wise Fool, and the Professor of Signs.

The following anecdote is related as true, at the University of Oxford, in England. A celebrated foreign linguist was at London, and wishing to converse in the learned languages with some of the most renowned of the English professors, he obtained a recommendation to² one of the first masters at Oxford. The professor, knowing the day and manner of his arrival, and wishing to surprise him, placed several of the students, dressed as peasants, at short distances from each other on the road leading to the town, with instructions to answer him in Latin, Greek, Hebrew, German, French, or Italian, if he should interrogate them, or to ask him some question in those languages if he did not.

He was recognised on his approach³ by one of the scholars, who asked him in French what o'clock it was. He answered him, and appeared much astonished at hearing a peasant speak a foreign language; thinking however it might be some per-

---

¹ To survive the loss, *survivre à la perte.*
² "A recommendation to," traduisez: *a recommendation for.*
³ Traduisez: *at his approach.*

son who had seen better days¹, and was reduced by misfortune, he rode on²; but his curiosity being excited, he asked the next countryman he saw, how far it was to Oxford: judge his surprise on receiving an answer in good Latin. As he approached the town, his astonishment was excited to the highest degree by answers or questions in various languages ancient and modern.

On arriving at the house of the professor, he told him he had already sufficient proofs of the superior knowledge of the members of the University, whose influence spread to the very peasants³ on the road.—But, added he, have you any one who perfectly understands the language of signs, so as to⁴ make himself immediately understood?—The professor, after a moment's reflection, replied: I will introduce you to one, if you will take dinner with me.—The invitation was accepted; and the professor, begging a few minutes,⁵ went to consult with⁶ one of

---

¹ "Who had seen better days," *qui avait été plus heureuse* (idiôme), ou *qui avait vu de meilleurs jours.*

² To ride on, *continuer son chemin.*

³ "To the very peasants," *aux paysans mêmes.* Quand le mot *very* se rapporte à un nom, il se rend en français par l'adjectif *même* (same).

⁴ "So as to," *de manière à.*

⁵ To beg a few minutes, *s'excuser pour quelques minutes.*

⁶ To consult with, *consulter.*

his colleagues upon what should be done—Let us, said he, dress up as a¹ student one-eyed George the fool, and we shall have some good sport with the doctor.—A good idea, said the other.—This George, you must know,² was an idiot, who had but one eye, and used to do little jobs for the collegians.

After dinner, the professor sent for George, and told him that a gentleman who had heard³ much of him, wished to see him, and that he must meet him at ten o'clock on the next morning at a certain place; but that the person was extremely deaf, therefore he must only talk by signs.—Very well, sir, said George, I will be there.—The professor then returned, and informed his guest that he had found the person, and that he would wait for him at ten o'clock on the following morning.—That is unfortunate, said the gentleman, for I have ordered the post-chaise to call for me at that hour, but the postilion will wait.

A little before ten, the linguist found George according to appointment⁴; they both remained silent for some minutes, and then the gentleman held up one finger; George looked steadfastly at

---

¹ To dress up as a, *habiller en, déguiser en.*

² "You must know," *il faut que vous le sachiez.*

³ To hear of, *entendre parler de.*

⁴ "According to appointment," *au rendez-vous.*

him, and held up two; the gentleman smiled, and then held up three; upon which George, with great vivacity, firmly raised his clinched fist[1]. The stranger then looked at his watch, and seeing it was late, hurried off to his chaise, which was waiting at the professor's door, telling him that his friend had surpassed his expectation.—I waited, said he, for him to begin, but seeing he did not, I held up one finger to signify there is but one God; he immediately understood me, and held up two of his, showing that there are two, Father and Son; I answered by raising three, Father, Son, and Holy Spirit; upon which he clinched his fist, as if he dared any one to insinuate, that though they were three, they were not united in one.—Finding it was late I came away[2], and I beg you will express to your friend my great admiration of his talent.

The linguist then set off, but he was scarcely gone, when George arrived in a fury, crying out: Where is the insolent fellow you sent to mock me? —What is the matter, George? said the professor. —Matter! replied George, you shall hear; he comes into the room, sits down, and after looking me full in the face, holds up one finger, meaning that I had but one eye. I did not much like it, but, however,

---

[1] His clinched fist, *son poing fermé*.
[2] To come away, *s'en aller*.

I held up two, meaning that he had two eyes; upon which he showed me three of his, as much as to say[1]—Between us two there are but three eyes. I immediately doubled my fist, and if he had not escaped as he did, I would have given him a good drubbing[2].—This story frequently causes much amusement, but its origin may be found in ancient history.

A Trial of Courage.

In 1777, during the American war, an officer in Virginia having unintentionally offended another, received a challenge to fight a duel. He returned for answer[3], that he would not fight[4] him, and for three reasons: first, not having committed any fault, he would not expose his life to gratify the caprice of an impetuous man; secondly, that he had a wife and children who were dear to him, and he would not do them such an injustice as to run the chance of plunging them into misery; and, thirdly, that as his life was devoted to the service of his king and country, it would be a violation

---

[1] " As much as to say," *comme pour dire.*

[2] " A good drubbing," *un bon châtiment, les étrivières.*

[3] " He returned for answer," *il lui répondit.*

[4] To fight, *se battre avec.*

both¹ of moral and civil duty to risk it in a private quarrel.

In consequence of his refusal, his antagonist posted him² as a coward, and he had the mortification of seeing himself shunned by the officers in general. Knowing he had not merited such disgrace, he resolved to put an end to it, and having furnished himself with a large hand-grenade³, he went to the mess-room where the officers were assembled.

On his entrance⁴, they looked at him with disdain, and several of them said: We don't associate with⁵ cowards.—Gentlemen, replied he, I am no more a coward than any one of you, though I am not such a fool⁶ as to forget my duty to my country and to my family⁷; as to real danger, we shall soon see who fears it the least. On saying this, he lighted the fusee of the grenade, and threw it among them; then, crossing his arms, he prepared to await the explosion. The affrighted officers immediately arose and ran towards the door in the

---

¹ "Both," suivi d'un complément, ne se traduit pas.
² To post one, *afficher quelqu'un, signaler quelqu'un*.
³ "Hand-grenade," *grenade*. f.
⁴ Traduisez : *at his entrance*.
⁵ To associate with, *s'associer à, fréquenter*.
⁶ "Such a fool as," *si fou que de*.
⁷ Traduisez : *my duty towards my country and my family*.

greatest terror and confusion, tumbling over each other[1] in their hurry to get out. The moment[2] the room was cleared, our officer threw himself flat[3] on the floor, and the grenade exploded, shattering the walls and the ceiling, but without doing him any harm. After the explosion, the fugitives ventured into the room, expecting to see the officer torn to pieces[4]; but, judge[5] their surprise and shame, on being welcomed with[6] a hearty laugh[7]. From that moment they ceased to shun him, and to brand him with the epithet of coward.

A very Singular Excuse.

An Irishman, accused of having stolen a gun, was taken, and brought to justice[8]. On the day of trial he was reflecting on what defence he should make[9] before the judges, when he saw a fellow-

---

[1] "Over each other," *l'un sur l'autre.*

[2] "The moment," traduisez: *as soon as.*

[3] "Flat," *à plat.*

[4] "Torn to pieces," *déchiré en pièces, en morceaux.*

[5] Traduisez: *judge of.*

[6] "To be welcomed with," *être accueilli, être reçu par.*

[7] "Hearty laugh," *éclat de rire.* m.

[8] To be brought to justice, *être conduit devant la justice.*

[9] "On what defence he should make," traduisez: *how he should defend himself.*

prisoner return from the court, having been tried for stealing a goose.—Well, said the Irishman, how have you come off¹?—Oh! replied the other, I am acquitted.—What defence did you make²?—Why, I told the judge that I had brought up the goose from the time it was a gosling, and that I had witnesses to prove it.—Very good indeed, said Paddy, who was at that moment called into court³ to take his trial⁴; stay a short time for me⁵, I shall soon be acquitted.

He was then conducted to the bar, the accusation was read, and the judge asked him what he had to say in his defence⁶. My lord, replied the Hibernian, I have brought up that gun ever since it was a pistol, and I can bring witnesses to prove it.—The judge, however, and the jury were not sufficiently credulous, and poor Paddy was condemned to be transported.

Delicacy of Alphonso, King of Aragon.

Alphonso, king of Aragon, went one day, it is said, to a jeweller's to purchase some diamonds for

---

¹ To come off, *se tirer d'affaire*
² Traduisez: *how have you defended yourself?* or *what have you said for your defence?*
³ To be called into court, *être appelé devant la cour* (idiôme).
⁴ "To take his trial," *pour être jugé*.
⁵ "Stay a short time for me," *attendez-moi un peu* (idiôme).
⁶ Traduisez: *for his defence.*

presents¹ to a foreign prince. He was accompanied by several courtiers, and the jeweller spread his finest diamonds and other precious stones before them without hesitation. The prince, after making his purchases, retired; but he had scarcely left the house when the jeweller came after him,² and requested he would do him the honour to return for a moment, as he had something important to say to him. The prince and his courtiers re-entered, and the jeweller then said that a diamond of great value had been taken by some one of his attendants.

Alphonso looked sternly at those who accompanied him, saying, "Whichsoever of you³ has stolen the diamond, he deserves the most severe punishment; but the publication of his name might perhaps tarnish the reputation of an honourable family; I will spare them that disgrace." He then desired the jeweller⁴ to bring a large pot full of bran. When it was brought, he ordered every one of the attendants to plunge his right hand closed into the pot, and to draw it out⁵ quite open. It

---

¹ Traduisez: *To make presents to a foreign prince.*

² Traduisez: *ran after him.*

³ "Whichsoever of you," *quel que soit celui de vous qui*, ou *quiconque*.

⁴ "He desired the jeweller," *il demanda au joaillier.*

⁵ To draw out, *retirer.*

was done; and, the bran being sifted, the diamond was found. The prince then addressed them, saying, Gentlemen, I will not suspect any one among you; I will forget the affair: the culpable person cannot escape the torment of his guilty conscience.

We must not always judge by Appearances.

A sailor, belonging to a merchant vessel, set off from London to join his ship, which was in the Downs. He arrived towards night at the little town of Northfleet, which is about twenty miles from the capital, on the south bank of the Thames. Being much fatigued, he entered a public house, and requested a lodging, but was told that all the beds were engaged. Another sailor, named Gwinnett, who was in the room, said, Shipmate, I will give you half my bed. The offer was gladly accepted, and after drinking a glass of grog,[1] the two sailors went to bed.

Early on the following morning, Gwinnett missed his bed-fellow[2], but thinking he had risen to con-

---

[1] Grog (du rhum ou de l'eau de vie mêlé avec de l'eau).

[2] Traduisez: *perceived that his bed-fellow was not there*, or, *was gone;* or, *perceived of his bed-fellow's absence* (*to perceive*, dans le sens de *to discover*, se traduit *s'apercevoir*).

tinue his journey, he took no notice of it, paid his reckoning, and went away. Soon after he was gone, the maid went into the bed-room to call the sailor, but he was not there. The landlord sought him all over the house, but he was nowhere[1] to be found, and some spots of blood being discovered, they were traced to the privy, which was close to the river side, where a knife was also found with Gwinnett's name upon it.

It was immediately suspected that he had murdered his bed-fellow, and thrown his body into the Thames. He was pursued and taken, and a strict search was made after the body[2], but without success. Appearances were so strong against Gwinnett, that he was tried and condemned to be hanged and gibbeted on a common not far from the spot of the supposed murder. On the day of his execution, there happened one of the most dreadful storms of thunder, lightning, and rain, that had ever been remembered[3], and the officers of justice took down the body before it had hung the usual time[4], put it into the chains, and after

---

[1] Traduisez: *but he could be found nowhere.*

[2] Traduisez: *a strict search of the body was made.*

[3] "That had ever been remembered," *dont on eut mémoire* (idiôme).

[4] "Before it had hung the usual time," *avant que le temps ordinaire fut écoulé.*

having suspended it on the gibbet, where it was to remain, they hastened home to escape from the storm.

Some hours after a boy who was driving home some cows near the spot, thought he heard a groan; he ran home in terror[1], and told[2] his master, who went with some of his men, and discovered that the body was not dead; they took it down, conveyed it home, and Gwinnett was soon restored to life. He solemnly vowed to the farmer that he was innocent of the crime, and begged he would assist him to escape. The farmer lent him a disguise, and he hastened to a sea-port, where he embarked on board a ship that was just sailing for the Levant.

While he was in the Mediterranean, the ship was boarded by the crew of a man of war, and Gwinnett, with some others of the merchantman, was pressed into the king's service. He had not been long on board the ship of war, when he observed a sailor who very much resembled the one with whom he had slept at Northfleet, and, on questioning him, discovered that he was the very man for whose murder he had been hanged. He asked him the cause of his sudden disappearance, and the sailor told him that, being attacked in the

---

[1] In terror, *épouvanté*.   [2] Traduisez: *told it.*

night by a hemorrhage, to which he was subject, he had risen to go to the privy, and not being able to open the door, he had taken his knife which he found on the table; that on his return across the road, a press-gang was passing: they took him, and he was immediately sent on board a ship going up the Straits of Gibraltar.

Gwinnett then related his unfortunate adventure, and it was agreed that, when the ship returned[1] to England, they should present themselves to the officers of justice, and prove the innocence of poor Gwinnett; but, for fear any accident should happen to either of them, they declared the whole affair to their captain. A few days after, the ship fell in with an enemy, and an unlucky shot deprived Gwinnett of his friend; however, when he returned to England, his innocence was acknowledged.

P. S. (*Historique*.)

Anecdote of a Hoax played on[2] the Londoners.

In the year 1749, the Duke of Montagu, who was very facetious, was one day in a company where

---

[1] Traduisez: *when the ship should have return* (quand le vaisseau serait de retour, &c.).

[2] Traduisez: *played to.* (To play a hoax or a trick *on* one; *jouer un tour, une farce, une plaisanterie, une mystification à quelqu'un*.)

the conversation turned on the curiosity and credulity of the inhabitants of the metropolis of England. The duke insisted that if any one should declare he would creep into a wine-bottle, there were fools enough to fill a theatre, and who would pay their money in expectation of seeing it. Some of the company denied that the English were such fools, and the duke offered a wager that he would prove it, and that he would fill a theatre by announcing such an exhibition. The bet was accepted, and the duke immediately published the following advertisement in all the newspapers:

"Hay-Market Theatre. On Monday next, the 16th[1], a person will perform the following incredible things. First, he will take a common walking-cane from any one of the spectators, and produce from it the sound of every musical instrument that is known. Secondly, he will present to the audience a common wine-bottle, which they may examine to see that there is no deception; he will then place it on a table in front of[2] the stage where, in sight of the whole house[3], he will creep into it, and, during his stay[4], he will sing several popular songs. While

---

[1] En indiquant des dates il faut se servir des nombres cardinaux, excepté pour le premier jour du mois.

[2] "In front of," *sur le devant de*.

[3] "The whole house," *toute la salle* (idiôme).

[4] " During his stay," traduisez: *during he will be there*.

he is in the bottle, any person may handle it to convince themselves that there is no deception.

"*N.B.* The persons in the boxes¹ may come in masks, and the performer will (if they desire it) inform them who they are.

"Prices—Stage, 7s. 6d.—Boxes, 5s.—Pit, 3s.—Gallery, 2s. To begin² at half-past six o'clock."

The evening arrived, and before seven o'clock the theatre was completely full. In the boxes were seen dukes and duchesses, lords and ladies; and in the other parts of the house, persons of all descriptions. After waiting a considerable time and seeing no performer the audience became clamorous, and a person came on the stage to tell them that, if the man did not come, the money should be returned. They waited some time longer; and then the genteel part³ of the audience retired, but the others remained; and, finding they were hoaxed⁴ began to demolish the interior of the theatre. The benches, scenes⁵ and other ornaments were torn in pieces, carried into the street and burnt. A regiment of soldiers arrived, but not in time to save anything. The Duke of Montagu, who had hired the theatre

---

¹ "The persons in the boxes," *les spectateurs des loges.*
² "To begin," *on commencera* (idiôme).
³ "The genteel part," *la partie respectable.*
⁴ To be hoaxed, *être joué, être berné.*
⁵ "The scenes," *les décorations du théâtre.*

for the occasion, was obliged to pay for the damage done, but he won his wager, which was considerable.

Benevolence.

The following anecdote of the same nobleman is equally remarkable, and far more laudable. During a walk in Saint-James's Park the duke observed a middle-aged man¹ continually walking to and fro² or sitting in a melancholy attitude on one of the benches. Wishing to know something more of him, the duke approached him several times, and endeavoured to draw him into conversation³, but without success, his only answers being, "Yes, sir: No, sir: I don't know: I believe so," etc.

Determined to obtain some information concerning him, the duke ordered one of his servants to follow him home, and to make all the inquiries he could⁴. The servant, on his return⁵, informed his master that he had learned that the gentleman was

---

¹ "Middle-aged man," *un homme d'un certain âge*.

² "Walking to and fro," *allant et venant*.

³ To draw one into conversation, *lier conversation avec quelqu'un* (idiôme).

⁴ To make inquiries, *prendre des informations, recueillir des informations*.

⁵ Voir page 39 (⁵).

a military officer with a numerous family; and having nothing but half pay[1] to support them, he had sent them to a distant part of England, where they could live more cheaply than in London; that he transmitted them the greater part of his pay, and lived as he could himself at London, in order to be near the War-office, where he was soliciting promotion.

The duke, after having obtained further information concerning the residence of the family, determined to do something for the officer, and to procure him an agreeable surprise. In a few days, the preparations being complete, he sent one of his servants into the park, to tell him that his master had something of importance to communicate[2], and requested that he would call on him. The astonished officer followed the servant, and was introduced to the duke, who then told him that a lady of his acquaintance, who knew his circumstances and was greatly interested in his welfare, wished very much to see him; that the lady was to dine that day at his house, and that he would introduce him to her. The officer had scarcely recovered from his surprise when dinner was announced; the duke conducted him to the dining-room, where, to

---

[1] Half pay, *demi-solde.* f. Traduisez: *his half-pay.*
[2] Traduisez: *to communicate to him.*

his great astonishment, he found his wife and family, who were equally amazed and delighted at meeting him so unexpectedly.

It appears that the duke had sent a messenger to bring the family to London, without permitting any communication with the husband; and that they had but just arrived.—After the mutual embraces and felicitations, the duke interrupted them, and presenting a paper to the officer, said to him, " Sir, I have discovered that you are a worthy man, and that your present means are not sufficient to support your amiable family; promotion in the army is slow in time of peace; I have a snug little country house and farm at your service; accept it, go and take possession, and may you live happily;" presenting him at the same time a paper in which he acknowledged that he gave the house and grounds to Mr. — and his heirs for ever.

A Lesson of Perseverance from a Spider.

The celebrated Robert Bruce, king of Scotland, after being several times defeated by the English, and almost despairing to be able to restore the independence of his country, was once out in disguise, reconnoitring[1] the positions of the enemy. Being

---

[1] " Was once out in disguise, reconnoitring," *était une fois sorti déguisé pour reconnaître.*

much fatigued, he one night took up his lodging¹ in a barn, and, on awaking in the morning, he remarked a large spider endeavouring to climb up a post that was very smooth.

The insect, not finding a firm hold for its little feet, slipped and fell several times to the ground², yet immediately recommenced its efforts. The perseverance of the insect attracted the attention of the king, and he beheld with regret every unsuccessful attempt. The spider, however, recommenced after every fall, and, at length, after twelve failures, Bruce saw with pleasure, the thirteenth trial crowned with success³. He immediately exclaimed: "What a lesson for mankind! I will profit by it, for it is the best I ever received. I have been already twelve times defeated by the superior force of my enemies; I will follow the example of the spider; another effort may be successful."—He then collected all his forces, addressed them in a most animating speech, and led them with ardour against the English, who were commanded by King Edward II. A battle took place at Bannockburn, in which Edward was completely

---

[1] To take up one's lodging, *se loger, prendre son logement.*

[2] To slip to the ground, *glisser à terre;* to fall to the ground, *tomber à terre.*

[3] Traduisez: *crowned of success.*

defeated, and obliged to fly in confusion, leaving behind him his provisions, military engines[1], and treasures.

P. S. (*Historique*.)

"Despair of nothing that you would obtain,
Unwearied diligence your point will gain."

The Mysterious Englishmen.

In the year 1767, two Englishmen landed at Calais; they did not go to Dessin's hotel, which was at that time much frequented by their countrymen, but took up their lodging[2] at an obscure inn kept by a man named Dulong. The landlord expected every day that they would set off for Paris, but they made no preparations for departure, and did not even inquire what was worth seeing[3] at Calais. The only amusement they took was to go out sometimes a shooting[4].

The landlord began, after a few weeks, to wonder at their stay, and used to gossip, of an evening[5], with his neighbour the grocer upon the subject.

---

[1] Military engines, *matériel de guerre*. m.
[2] "Took up their lodging," *descendirent*.
[3] To be worth seeing, *valoir la peine d'être vu*.
[4] To go out a shooting, *aller à la chasse, la chasse au tir*.
[5] "Of an evening," traduisez: *the evening*.

Sometimes they decided that they were spies, at other times they were suspected to be runaways. However they lived well, and paid so liberally, that it was at last concluded they were fools; which was confirmed, in the opinion of M. Dulong, by a proposition they soon after made to him.

They called him into their room and said, "Landlord, we are very well satisfied with your table and your wine, and if the lodging suited us, we should probably remain with you some time longer; but unfortunately all your rooms look into the street[1], and the smacking of postilions' whips, and the noise of the carriages disturb us very much."

Monsieur Dulong began to feel alarmed, and said if it were possible to make any arrangements to render them more comfortable[2] he would gladly do it.—"Well then," said one of them, "we have a proposal to make which will be advantageous to you; it will cost some money, it is true, but we will pay half the expense, and our stay will give you an opportunity of reimbursing yourself."—"Well," said the landlord, "what is it?" "Why," said the Englishman, "your garden is very quiet, and if you will run up a wall in the corner, you can easily make us two rooms, which is all we shall want; the

---

[1] Look into the street, *donnent sur la rue* (idiôme).
[2] Traduisez: *to give them more comfort*.

expense will not be great, as the old wall that is there will form two of the sides, and your house will be worth so much the more¹.

Dulong was glad to find so easy a method² of preserving such³ profitable guests: the rooms were constructed, the Englishmen took possession, and appeared very comfortable; living in their usual manner⁴ to the great satisfaction and profit of the landlord; though he was at a loss⁵ to imagine why they should shut themselves up in such an obscure corner. Thus passed about two months, when one day they told him that they were going on⁶ a shooting excursion, and that, as they should be absent perhaps three days, they would take abundance of ammunition. The next morning they set off with their guns on their shoulders, and their shot-bags heavily loaded; the landlord wishing them good sport. They told him that they had left some papers in the apartment, and therefore they took the key with them.

The three days passed, and so did the fourth⁷, fifth,

---

¹ "So much the more," *d'autant plus*.

² "So easy a method," traduisez: *a method so easy*.

³ "Such," devant un adjectif, se traduit *si*.

⁴ "In their usual manner," *comme à l'ordinaire, à leur manière ordinaire*.

⁵ To be at a loss, *être embarrassé, ne pas savoir* (idiôme).

⁶ "On," traduisez *to*.

⁷ "And so did the fourth, &c.," *et ainsi du quatrième, du cinquième, du sixième, &c.*

sixth, and seventh, without the return of the strangers¹. M. Dulong became at first uneasy, then suspicious, and, at last, on the eighth day, he sent for the police officers, and the door was broken open in presence of the necessary witnesses. On the table was found the following note :

"Dear Landlord,—You know, without doubt, that your town of Calais was in the possession of the English during two hundred years; that it was at length retaken by the Duke of Guise, who treated the English inhabitants as our Edward III. had treated the French; that is, seized their goods and drove them out. A short time ago² we discovered, among some old family papers, some documents of one of our ancestors, who possessed a house at Calais where yours now stands. From³ these documents we learned that on the retaking⁴ of Calais, he was obliged to flee; but in hopes of being able to return, he buried a very considerable sum of money close to a wall in his garden: the paper contained also such an accurate description of the spot that we doubted not of being able to discover it. We immediately came to Calais, and

---

¹ " Without the return of the strangers," *sans que les étrangers revinssent* ou *reparussent*.

² Voir page 16 (³).

³ Traduisez: *by* these documents.

⁴ Traduisez: *at* the retaking.

finding your house on the spot indicated, we took lodgings in it.

"We were soon convinced that the treasure was buried in the corner of your garden, but how dig for it[1] without being seen? We found a method; it was the construction of the apartment. As soon as it was completed, we dug up the earth and found our object in the chest which we have left you. We wish you success in your house, but advise you to give better wine, and to be more reasonable in your charges[2]."

Poor Dulong was dumb with astonishment[3]; he looked at his neighbour the grocer, and then at the empty chest, they both shrugged up their shoulders, and acknowledged that the Englishmen were not quite such fools as they had taken them for[4].

Judge not the action of any one, without knowing the motives.

---

[1] "For it," traduisez: *to get it.*

[2] "To be more reasonable in your charges," *d'être plus raisonnable dans vos prix, de ne pas tant écorcher vos clients* (idiôme).

[3] Traduisez: *of astonishment.*

[4] "As they had taken them for," *qu'on l'avait cru* (idiôme).

Understand what you have to do before you set about it.

Baron Sutherland, when[1] at St. Petersburg, possessed a very handsome pug dog, and the Empress Catharine having seen and admired it, he could not do less than make her a present of it. She graciously thanked the baron, accepted the dog, gave him the name of Sutherland, and made him her favourite lap-dog. He was fed with so many luxuries, and took so little exercise, that the poor thing soon died. The empress was so fond of the little animal, that she determined to have him stuffed and put into a glass case[2]. On the morning after his death, she said in French to one of her officers, "Go directly, take Sutherland, and see him stuffed[3]. The officer thought she said *empaler;* and not thinking of the dog, he went immediately to the baron's house, supposing he had committed some heinous crime, and said, Sir, you must follow me immediately.

Sutherland, not a little surprised at such a summons, and particularly at the manner in which it

---

[1] Traduisez: *when he was.*

[2] "Into a glass case," *sous verre.* (Glass case, *montre vitrée.*)

[3] See him stuffed, *faites-le empailler.* (To see a thing made, *faire faire un chose*).

was announced¹, demanded some explanation; but the officer replied, "Sir, it is not for me² to criticise the orders of her majesty; my duty is to see them executed."—"The orders of her majesty!" exclaimed the baron; "what orders can she have given with respect to³ me?"—"I am sorry," replied the officer, "to inform you that she has just given me peremptory orders to see you immediately *empaled*, and I dare not delay."—"Good God!" cried Sutherland, "me empaled! what have I done to offend her majesty?"—"That is not my business, sir."—"At least," said Sutherland, "before my punishment, conduct me to the palace, that I may hear my condemnation from her own mouth, and learn the cause of it; for I assure you, sir, as a man of honour, that I have neither done, said, nor even thought anything against the empress, or any one else; therefore be assured there is some mistake."

The officer, finding the baron so confident of his innocence, ventured to conduct him to the palace. As soon as he saw the empress, he exclaimed, How madam, have I been so unfortunate as to offend you, and subject myself to such a cruel order?—

---

¹ "In which it was announced," traduisez: *of which it was made*.

² "It is not for me," *ce n'est pas à moi*.

³ "With respect to me," *à mon égard, par rapport à moi* (with respect to, *à l'égard de, concernant, par rapport à*).

Catharine looked at him and at the officer, and then said—What is the meaning of this, sir? for I protest I don't understand one word of it.—Did not your majesty, replied he, give me orders to go and see Sutherland empaled?—Catharine immediately burst out a laughing¹, and, as soon as she could speak, said, Don't be alarmed, baron, you have nothing to fear.—Then turning to the officer, You stupid man, said she, it was the dead pug Sutherland that I told you to see stuffed², and not empaled. The baron is, I am sure, one of the last men who would imagine any thing against me.

Understand well what you have to do before you set about it, and you will avoid many blunders.

A Happy Expression. Unexpected Politeness.

In 1793, when Bonaparte was besieging Toulon, which was then in possession of the English, and from which³ he drove them, he was one day directing the construction of a battery, and the enemy perceiving it, commenced a warm fire upon it. Bonaparte, wanting to send off a despatch, asked

---

¹ To burst out a laughing, *éclater de rire* (idiôme).
² To stuff, *empailler;* to empale, *empaler.*
³ Traduisez: *from where.*

for a sergeant who could write¹. A sergeant immediately came out of the ranks and wrote a letter under his dictation. It was scarcely finished when a cannon-ball fell between Bonaparte and him, and covered them with dust: the latter, looking towards the English lines, said, "Gentlemen, I thank you, I did not think you were so polite. I wanted a little sand for my letter."

The expression, and the calmness of the sergeant, struck Napoleon; he did not forget it; the sergeant was soon promoted, and finally became a general—it was the brave Junot, whose name is so often found in the annals of French glory, and who, by his courage and perseverance, became Duke of Abrantes, a name rendered doubly illustrious by the literary productions of his widow, the Duchess of Abrantes.

The Four-legged Thief-Taker.

A Polish count named Oginski had a very fine poodle-dog, and liked him so much that he never went out without him. One evening the count went to amuse himself for an hour or two at a

---

[1]. "Who could write," *qui sût écrire*. Les français emploient généralement *savoir* au lieu de *pouvoir* dans le sens de *to know how*.

public ball at the Winter Vauxhall. He was accompanied, as usual, by his favourite dog; but the sentinel at the door would not admit him, and the master left him in the guard-house in care of a soldier. The count had not been long in the saloon before he perceived that his watch had been stolen; he complained to the police officers who were present, and they assured him they would use all their endeavours to find it.—" I have a very sure method of finding it," said Oginski, " if you will admit my dog and lock the doors; I promise you he will not harm anybody."—The officers consented, and the dog was admitted.

After a few mutual caresses the count walked around the room with him; then stopping in the middle, and tapping with his hand upon his fob, he said, "Strimki, go and find it," pointing at the same time[1] around the saloon. Strimki began immediately to examine every one, smelling their clothes, and at last he stopped short before a very well-dressed man, and began barking. The count immediately made himself known to the company, saying, " Ladies and gentlemen, I have been robbed of my watch, and that man has it. I insist on his being searched, and if it be found that I have accused him unjustly, I will answer for the conse-

---

[1] "At the same time," *en même temps*, ou *au même moment*.

quences¹!"—The company seconded the count, the search took place, and the watch was found, to the great admiration of all but one, who was immediately kicked out of the room.

The Chimney-sweepers' Feast, or the Lost Child found.²

There was formerly at London, on the first of May of every year, a superb feast given to the chimney-sweepers of the metropolis, at Montagu-House, Cavendish-square, the town residence³ of the Montagu family. The custom is said to have taken its origin from the following circumstance:

Lady Montagu, being at her country-seat, as usual⁴ in the summer, used to send her little boy Edward a walking⁵ every day with a footman, who had strict orders never to lose sight of him. One day, however, the servant, meeting an old acquaintance, went into an alehouse to drink, and left the little boy running about by himself⁶. After staying some time drinking, the footman came out to look

---

¹ Traduisez: *I will answer of the consequences.*
² Traduisez: *found again.*
³ "Town residence," *maison de ville.* f. *hôtel.* m.
⁴ "As usual," *comme à l'ordinaire.*
⁵ "A walking," *à la promenade.*
⁶ "By himself," *tout seul.*

for the child to take him home to dinner, but he could not find him. He wandered about till night, inquiring at every cottage and every house, but in vain, no Edward could be found. The poor mother, as may well be imagined, was in the greatest anxiety about the absence of her dear boy; but it would be impossible to describe her grief and despair when the footman returned, and told her he did not know what had become of him. People[1] were sent to seek him in all directions; advertisements were put in all the newspapers; bills were stuck up in London, and in most of the great towns of England, offering a considerable reward to any person who would bring him or give any news of him. All endeavours were, however, unsuccessful, and it was concluded that the poor child had fallen into some pond, or that he had been stolen by gipsies, who would not bring him back for fear of being punished.

Lady Montagu passed two long years in this miserable uncertainty: she did not return to London as usual in the winter, but passed her time in grief and solitude in the country. At length one of her sisters married[2], and, after many refusals,

---

[1] Lorsque *people* peut être remplacé en anglais par le mot *persons* sans changer le sens, traduisez *gens* ou *personnes*.

[2] Voir page 19 (²).

Lady Montagu consented to give a ball and supper on the occasion at her town house. She arrived at London to superintend the preparations, and while the supper was cooking, the whole house was alarmed by a cry of fire[1]!

It appears that one of the cooks had overturned a saucepan, and set fire[2] to the chimney. The chimney-sweepers were sent for, and a little boy was sent up[3]; but the smoke nearly suffocated him, and he fell into the fire-place. Lady Montagu came herself with some vinegar and a smelling-bottle; she began to bathe his temples and his neck, when suddenly she screamed out, Oh! Edward! and fell senseless on the floor. She soon recovered, and taking the little sweep in her arms, pressed him to[4] her bosom, crying, It is my dear Edward! It is my lost boy!

It appears she had recognised him by a mark on his neck. The master-chimney-sweeper, on being asked where he had obtained the child, said he had bought him about a year before of a gipsy woman, who said he was her son. All that the boy could remember was, that some people had given him fruit, and told him they would take him home to

---

[1] "A cry of fire!" *le cri : Au feu!*
[2] To set fire, *mettre le feu.*
[3] To send up, *envoyer en-haut.*   [4] Traduisez : *on her bosom.*

his mamma; but that they took him a long way¹ upon a donkey, and after keeping him a long, long while², they told him he must go and live with the chimney-sweep, who was his father: that they had beaten him so much whenever he spoke of his mamma and of his fine house, that he was almost afraid to think of it. But he said his master, the chimney-sweeper, had treated him very well.

Lady Montagu rewarded the man handsomely, and from that time she gave a feast to all the chimney-sweepers of the metropolis on the 1st of May, the birth-day of little Edward, who always presided at the table, which was covered with the good old English fare³, roast-beef, plum-pudding, and strong beer. This circumstance happened many, many years ago⁴, and Lady Montagu and Edward are both dead; but the 1st of May is still celebrated as the chimney-sweepers' holiday, and you may see them on that day in all parts of London, dressed in ribbons⁵, and all sorts of finery, dancing to music⁶ at almost every door, and beating time⁷ with the implements of their trade.

---

¹ "A long way," *une grande distance, pendant longtemps.*

² "A long, long while," *pendant bien, bien longtemps.*

³ "The good old English fare," *la bonne vieille chère d'Angleterre.*   ⁴ "Ago." Voir page 16 (²).

⁵ "Dressed in ribbons," *parés de rubans.*

⁶ "Dancing to music," *dansant au son de la musique.*

⁷ Beating time, *battant la mesure.*

Noble Blood. A Lesson for Pride.

A very good-king, who loved his subjects, and whose constant care was, by making them happy, to show that he considered them as his family, had a son whose disposition was so contrary to that of his father, that he despised all those who were beneath him; considering himself a superior creature, and that those whom fortune had placed under him, were unworthy of his notice, or fit only to be the slaves of his will. Unfortunately his education had been confided to men who had not had sufficient courage to correct his impetuous and haughty temper, and the good king his father saw him arrive at the age of manhood[1], possessing a character and opinions which, if ever he came to reign, would change his faithful subjects to enemies, and make his throne a seat of thorns instead of roses.

At length the prince married[2] a foreign princess and became a father; and the king, by the advice of one of his faithful courtiers, thought this a favourable opportunity to give him a lesson on the nobility of birth. For this purpose[3], on the morning

---

[1] "Age of manhood," *âge viril.* m. *âge d'homme.* m.

[2] "Married," voir page 19 (³).

[3] "For this purpose," *dans ce but, à cet effet, dans ce dessein.*

after his child was born, another infant of the same age, dressed exactly in the same manner[1], was placed in the cradle by the side of it[2].

The prince, on rising, went to see his little son; but what was his surprise on finding two children resembling each other so much, that he could not distinguish his own! He called the servants, and finding them equally embarrassed, he gave way to his rage[3], swearing that they should be all discharged, and severely punished. The king, his father, arrived at the same instant, and hearing the complaints of the prince, he said, smilingly to him, How is it possible[4] you should mistake and not recognise your own child? is there any other of such noble blood? can any other child resemble him so as to[5] deceive you? where then is your natural superiority?—Then taking the infant prince in his arms, he said, This, my son, is your child, but I should not have been able to distinguish him from the other little innocent if precautions had not been taken, by tying a ribbon round his leg: in what then, I ask you again, consists our

---

[1] "In the same manner," *de la même manière.*

[2] "By the side of it," *à côté de lui, à son coté.*

[3] To give way to one's rage, *donner cours à sa colère.*

[4] "How is it possible?" *comment se peut-il, comment est il possible?*

[5] "So as to," *de manière à.*

superiority? It arises only from good conduct and good fortune.

The prince blushed, owned he was wrong, and promised to entertain more philanthropic sentiments; but the king fearing he might relapse, took an opportunity[1] of giving him another lesson. A short time after[2], the prince being indisposed, the doctor advised him to be bled[3], and having to bleed one of the pages on the same day, the king ordered the blood to be preserved in separate bowls. A few hours after, when his son was with him, the king sent for the doctor, and having ordered the two bowls to be brought, desired him to examine the blood, and tell him which was the purest. The doctor, pointing to one of the bowls, said, That is far more pure than the other.—That blood, said the king to his son, was taken from the veins of your page, and is, it appears, more pure than yours, because, no doubt[4], he lives more simply and more conformably to the laws of nature: you see then that by birth all men are equal; they acquire superiority in proportion as they cultivate their minds and render themselves useful to mankind.

---

[1] To take an opportunity, *saisir l'occasion* (idiôme).

[2] "A short time after," *peu de temps après*.

[3] "To be bled," *de se faire saigner*

[4] "No doubt," *sans doute*.

Real or Intrinsic Value.

"The real value of a thing
Is just as much as it will bring."

BUTLER.

A lady who had more money than good sense was very fond, when she was in the country, of showing her jewels and other finery, in order to astonish the peasants, and give them an idea of her riches and superiority. One day a miller, who brought flour to the house, expressed his admiration of an elegant watch that she wore, and this flattered her pride so much that she showed him a superb diamond-necklace and bracelets.

The miller, after looking at them for some time with admiration, said, They are very beautiful, and, I dare say[1], very dear.—Indeed, they are very dear; how much do you suppose they cost?—Upon my word, I cannot guess, replied he.—Why, they cost more than[2] 20,000 (twenty thousand) francs.—And what is the use of these stones, madam?—Oh, they are only to wear.—And do they not bring you anything, madam?—Oh no.—Then, replied the miller, I prefer the two great stones of my mill: they cost me 1,000 francs, and they bring me 400 francs

---

[1] "I dare say," *j'ose dire, je ne doute pas* (idiôme).
[2] *Than*, devant un nombre, se traduit *de* (of).

a year, and, besides that, I am not afraid that anybody will steal them.—The lady was shocked at the vulgarity of his ideas, and the miller was astonished that any one could let so much money remain idle[1] in such useless bawbles.

The Biter Bitten.

A French emigrant, who, in 1789, had fled from the horrors of the revolution, and sought refuge in Westphalia, finding the winter approach, and knowing that in that country it is more severe than at Paris, thought he should do well to lay in a good provision of wood,[2] and, seeing a cart-load passing, he called the carter to ask the price. The man, seeing he was a foreigner, determined to cheat him, and, after he had praised the quality of the wood, told him he would let him have it for three louis, which, continued he, "is much cheaper than you could buy it anywhere else[3]." The Frenchman, thinking he had a good bargain[4], paid him the money, and the rogue of a carter[5], overjoyed at his

---

[1] To remain idle, *rester oisif, sans emploi, improductif*.

[2] To lay in a good provision of wood, *faire sa provision de bois, faire une bonne provision de bois*.

[3] "Anywhere else," *autre part, ailleurs*.

[4] Traduisez: *thinking that he had made a good bargain*.

[5] "The rogue of a carter," *le fripon de charretier*.

good luck, went to an alehouse close by¹, and boasted how he had cheated the Frenchman.

The landlord of the alehouse was an honest man, and told him he had done very wrong in deceiving a foreigner; but he replied, "What is that to you²? the wood was my own³, and I had the right to set my price on it⁴."—The landlord said no more, but when the carter asked him how much he had to pay, he replied, "Three louis."—"What! three louis for a little bread and cheese and a bottle of beer?"—"Yes, that is the price; the bread and cheese belonged to me, and I have the right to set my price on it: if you are not satisfied, I will go with you before a magistrate."

They went, and the carter having told his tale, the magistrate asked the landlord what he had to say. He immediately related the whole affair, and judgment was quickly given⁵ in his favour; the carter was obliged to pay him three louis, out of which⁶ he returned him the real value of the wood, and then carried the rest to the Frenchman; telling

---

¹ "Close by," *tout près de là, à deux pas de là.*

² "What is that to you," *Qu'est ce que cela vous fait* (idiôme).

³ "My own," *à moi, m'appartient.*

⁴ "To set my price on it," *d'en fixer le prix, de faire mon prix.*

⁵ To give a judgment, *rendre un jugement, prononcer un jugement* (idiôme).

⁶ "Out of which," *sur les quels.*

him not to have a bad opinion of all Germans because a scoundrel had cheated him.

How to Catch a Pickpocket.

A merchant at London, who used to walk very much in the City, the streets of which are always crowded and infested by pickpockets, was continually losing either his pocket-book, his snuff-box, or his purse, without ever being able to discover the thief. At last he thought of a very ingenious method which promised success. He went to a fishing-tackle shop and bought some strong fish-hooks, which he got sewed[1] fast in his pocket with the points turned downwards, so that anybody might put their hand into the pocket, but could not draw it out without being caught.

Thus prepared, he went out as usual to go on 'change[2], desiring one of his clerks[3] to follow him at a short distance to be ready in case he should catch a fish. On passing up Lombard-street, he felt a slight tug[4] at his coat, and immediately set

---

[1] To get sewed, *faire coudre.*

[2] "To go on 'change," *pour aller à la bourse.*

[3] "Desiring one of his clerks," traduisez: *telling one of his clerks.*

[4] "A slight tug," *un léger tiraillement, mouvement.*

off to run, but was prevented by something holding him back¹. He turned and saw the pickpocket, and said—Why do you hold my coat, sir? let me go, I am in a great hurry²; at the same time attempting to snatch the flap from him³, which drove the fish-hooks further into his hand, and he cried out—Oh, oh! sir, I cannot, you are tearing my hand to pieces⁴; pray⁵ let me go.—Ah! ah! said the merchant, I have then caught the fish that has so frequently bitten; you are the pike, or rather the shark.

By this time⁶ the clerk had come up, and a crowd being assembled around them, had a hearty laugh at⁷ the fisherman and fish, whose fin was so firmly hooked that he was obliged to go with the merchant to a surgeon, and have the flesh cut to disengage the hooks. The gentleman was satisfied with the trick, and did not send the pickpocket to prison⁸; but ever after that he could walk safely through the City, with his pocket-book, purse, or snuff-box.

---

¹ "Holding him back," *qui le retenait.*
² To be in a great hurry, *être très pressé.*
³ "From him," traduisez: *from his hands.*
⁴ Traduisez: *in pieces.*   ⁵ "Pray," *je vous en prie.*
⁶ "By this time," *pendant ce temps, sur ces entrefaites.*
⁷ To have a hearty laugh at, *rire de bon cœur de.*
⁸ "To prison," *en prison.*

Before you promise, calculate your ability to perform.

The delightful game of chess was invented, it is said, by a Bramin[1] named Sissa, in order to amuse a very tyrannical prince, and, by giving him something to occupy his mind, to prevent him from exercising so much cruelty upon his subjects. Showing him also that the king, though the most important piece in the game, cannot attack or even defend himself, without the assistance of his pawns, that is to say, his people.

The monarch was enchanted with the game, and asked the Bramin what he should give him as a recompense for having taught him to play it. The latter profited by[2] the opportunity to give him another lesson :—My prince, said he, if you count, you will find that there are 64 squares on the chessboard; all the reward I ask is that you will give a grain of wheat for the first square, two for the second, and continue doubling the number up to[3] the last.—Oh! said the prince, if your demand is so moderate, it will be easily satisfied; make the calculation, and bring it me to-morrow morning.—The Bramin did so, and the prince was greatly

---

[1] "Bramin," *bramine* (philosophe ou prêtre indien).
[2] To profit by, *profiter de.*
[3] "Up to," *jusqu'à.*

astonished at¹ finding that he had promised more than he was able to perform, and that all the granaries in his kingdom did not contain a sufficient quantity of wheat to pay the debt he had so incautiously contracted.

This, at first sight, appears incredible; we therefore recommend our pupils to make the calculation, in order to convince themselves.

Deaf as a Post.²

About five o'clock,³ one winter's evening, a gentleman on horseback stopped at an inn which was full of travellers. He rode into⁴ the yard, and, calling the ostler very loud, said, "Here, take care of my horse and put him in the stable."—"We have no room⁵," said the ostler, the stable is full."—"Yes, yes," replied the gentleman, seeming not to hear, "I will think of you to-morrow morning."—"But I tell you, there is no room."—"Ay, ay, give him a

---

¹ "Astonished at," *étonné de.*

² "Deaf as a post," *sourd comme une borne, comme un pot* (idiome).

³ Traduisez: *at about five o'clock.*

⁴ To ride into, *entrer* (à cheval ou en voiture). To ride out, *sortir* (à cheval ou en voiture).

⁵ "We have no room," *nous n'avons pas de place.*

peck of oats, and as much hay as he will eat," said the traveller;—and, leaving his horse, he made the best of his way¹ into the house.—"He must be a fool," said the ostler.—"I think he is deaf," replied the stable-boy; "but, at all events², we must take care of his horse, we shall be answerable for it³."

Our traveller now entered the house, and the landlady told him as the ostler had done, that it was impossible to lodge him. He cried out loud enough to stun her, "No compliments, no ceremony, I beg, ma'am, your accommodation will be very good. I am easily satisfied, and it is quite useless for you to speak, for I am so deaf that I cannot hear a cannon."—He then took a chair and seated himself by the fire, as if he had been at home. Finding no means of getting rid of him, the landlord and his wife determined to let him pass the night on the chair, as the beds were all engaged.

Shortly after he saw the dinner served in the next room, and immediately taking his chair, he placed himself at the table; it was in vain they bawled to him as loud as possible, that it was a

---

¹ To make the best of one's way, *se rendre aussitôt*.

² At all events, *dans tous les cas, pourtant, néanmoins*.

³ "We shall be answerable for it," *nous en répondons*, ou *nous en sommes responsables*.

private company, and they would not receive a stranger: he appeared to think that they wished to give him the top of the table, and thanking them for their politeness, he said he was very comfortable where he was seated.

Finding they could not make him understand, they let him remain; and after eating a hearty dinner[1], he threw a two-franc piece on the table to pay for his repast; but the landlady pushed it towards him with disdain, saying—What! do you suppose that two francs will pay for such a dinner[2] as you have eaten?—Oh! I beg pardon, ma'am, replied he, I insist on paying for my own dinner; I thank these gentlemen for their politeness, but I will not suffer them to pay for me.—Then looking at his watch, he went out of the room, wishing them all good night, and soon found his way[3] to a bed-room. The company, after having laughed heartily[4] at his apparent stupidity, sent a servant to see where he was gone. She soon returned, saying, he had taken possession of one of their bed-rooms.

They then agreed to go, all together, and turn

---

[1] "A hearty dinner," *un très-bon diner.*

[2] "For such a dinner as you have eaten," traduisez: *for a dinner as that which you have eaten.*

[3] To find one's way to, *se diriger vers, se rendre dans.*

[4] To laugh heartily at, *rire de bon cœur de.*

him out¹ by force; but when they approached the door, they heard him barricading it with the furniture, and talking loudly to himself. They listened and heard him say—What an unfortunate situation is mine! any one might break open my door, and I should not hear it; those gentlemen may be all honest men, and they may not; therefore, as I have some money, I will not run any risk. No, I will not go to bed, nor put out the light; I will sit up all night with my pistols cocked, and if any one should enter, I will shoot him directly. Hearing this, they made no attempt² to dislodge him; and he went to bed and passed the night very quietly, leaving the gentleman who had engaged the bed to find a lodging where he could.

The next morning,³ he came down, went to the stable for his horse, led him to the door, by which time⁴ the company were assembled to have another laugh at⁵ him. As soon as he was mounted, he threw to the servant thirty sous for his horse and his lodging, and also some sous to the ostler; then changing his manner, he said, Gentlemen, I thank you for the politeness you have shown me; I have

---

¹ To turn out, *faire sortir, chasser.*
² To make attempt to, *essayer de.*
³ "The next morning," *le lendemain matin.*
⁴ By which time, *pendant ce temps, déjà.*
⁵ "To have a laugh at," *se moquer de, rire de* (idiôme).

to beg pardon of one of you for having taken his bed; but one of my friends was refused a lodging here last night, and he has betted twenty louis that I could not procure one; so I have played the deaf man[1] to some effect.[2] I leave you to judge if I have done it well.—He then spurred his horse[3], and left them in amazement.

A Warm Joke.

A man who had more wit than money, and who, as they say in England, lived by his wits, that is to say, at the expense of[4] the credulous, was once on a stage-coach, and by the criminal imprudence of the coachman, driving furiously to arrive before an opposition coach, the carriage was overturned. Among the passengers who were severely wounded, our wit had one of his legs broken so badly that it was necessary to amputate it. The accident did not however greatly afflict him, as it furnished him with another resource for levying contributions on[5] the public.

---

[1] "To play the deaf man," *faire le sourd, jouer le sourd.*
[2] "To some effect," *avec quelque succès* (idiôme).
[3] "He spurred his horse," *il piqua des deux* (idiôme).
[4] "At the expense of," *aux dépens de* (idiôme).
[5] To levy contributions on, *mettre à contribution.*

First of all[1] he brought an action[2] against the proprietors of the coach, and obtained 200*l*. damages for the loss of his limb; with a part of this money he procured[3] a cork-leg[4], so well shaped that it was almost impossible to discover it was artificial; but, our spark[5] not being very economical, the rest of the money was soon spent, and he recommenced his old way of living.

Having once provided himself with[6] some powder of rotten wood, he went one Saturday night to a country public-house, and after joining company and drinking with the peasants and others, he began to talk of the wonders that are to be seen at London[7]. Among other astonishing things, one of the countrymen declared that he had seen a man wash his hands in melted lead. They laughed at him, and told him they were not such fools[8] as to believe impossibilities: but our hero replied, Gentlemen, it is so far from being impossible, that I assure you I

---

[1] "First of all," *avant tout, d'abord.*
[2] To bring an action, *intenter un procès, faire un procès.*
[3] To procure, *se procurer.*
[4] Cork-leg, *jambe de bois.* f.
[5] Our spark, *notre gaillard, notre espiègle.*
[6] To provide oneself with, *se pourvoir de.*
[7] "Of the wonders that are to be seen at London," *des merveilles de Londres,* ou, *que l'on voit à Londres.*
[8] "Such fools," *si fous* (*such* devant un adjectif se traduit *si*).

have seen it myself, and fortunately I have about me[1] the means of convincing you.

He then took from his pocket a tin box[2], and opening it, said—Here is a powder that I have composed, with which any part of the body being rubbed, it may be plunged into boiling liquid or melted metal; will any of you try it?—Oh! oh! cried they all, we are not such fools as you take us for[3]; try it yourself, if you please, master Cockney[4]. —Very well, gentlemen, since you are so incredulous, I will try it myself. It would be perhaps difficult to procure melted lead, so I will make the experiment with boiling water.—A pail of boiling water was brought, and taking the powder he began rubbing his leg, saying—You see, gentlemen, it is not even necessary to take off the stocking.— Then plunging his leg into the pail, he stood for some minutes, smoking his pipe with the greatest tranquillity, the peasants looking at him with eyes and mouths wide open[5].

They were all extremely desirous to obtain some of the powder, but he told them he did not sell it. —However, added he, to oblige and convince you,

---

[1] ' I have about me," *j'ai sur moi.*

[2] " A tin box," *une boîte en fer-blanc.*

[3] " As you take us for," *que vous le croyez.*

[4] " Master Cockney," *maître badaud.*

[5] " Wide open," *tout ouvert, béant.*

I will let you have it.—The powder was eagerly bought, and the countrymen hastened home¹ to astonish their wives, families, and neighbours. The next day², being Sunday, they met and invited their friends to see the experiments.

A large tub was brought and filled with boiling water, when one,³ who on account of⁴ his boldness was called the cock of the village, thinking to astonish his companions, rubbed both his legs, and jumped nimbly into the tub; but, with a loud scream, he leaped much more quickly out, and danced about the room with more animation than he had ever danced before. The company, notwithstanding the poor fellow's pain, was convulsed with laughter;⁵ and as no other could be found to repeat the experiment, they retired, leaving the scalded countryman to the care of his poor wife; and to this day⁶ they say in that part of the country, when any one runs or dances nimbly, "He runs like a scalded cock."

---

[1] "To hasten home," *se hâter* ou *s'empresser de rentrer chez soi*.

[2] "The next day," *le lendemain*, ou *le jour suivant*.

[3] "One," traduisez: *one of them*.

[4] "On account of," *à cause de*.

[5] To be convulsed with laughter, *rire convulsivement*.

[6] "To this day," *depuis ce jour*.

A Salutary Pill.

During an unfortunate campaign in which the French army suffered great losses, two peasants of a certain village were called on[1] to draw for the conscription;[2] one only was wanted to complete the number, and of the two who were[3] to draw, one was the son of a rich farmer, and the other the child of a poor widow.

The farmer made great interest with[4] the superintendent of the ballot, and promised him a handsome present, if he could find means to prevent his son from going to the army. In order to accomplish it, he put into the urn two black balls, instead of one black and one white. When the young men came, he said—There are a black ball and a white one in the urn; he[5] who draws the black one must serve.

The widow's son, having some suspicion that all was not fair, approached the urn, and drew one of the balls, which he immediately swallowed without

---

[1] "Were called on," *furent mandés, furent appelés.*

[2] "To draw for the conscription," *tirer à la conscription.*

[3] Le verbe *être* devant un infinitif est généralement remplacé en français par le temps correspondant du verbe *devoir.*

[4] "Made great interest with," *tâcha d'influencer, d'intéresser.*

[5] *He* devant un pronom relatif se traduit celui; she, *celle;* they, *ceux* ou *celles.*

looking at it.—Why, said the superintendent, have you done that? how are we to know[1] whether you have drawn a black or a white ball?—It is very easy to discover, replied he: let him draw the other: if I have the black, he must necessarily draw the white one.—The superintendent could not refuse; and the farmer's son, putting his hand into the urn, drew the remaining ball, which, to the great satisfaction of most of the spectators, was a black one; the widow's son was thus saved, and the other obliged to serve, or to find a substitute.

The Danger of being Ungrateful.

An Indian prince, who was very fond[2] of going on the water, had one day the misfortune to fall into a river; he was drowning[3], when a slave plunged in[4], caught him by the hair of his head[5], dragged him to the shore, and saved his life. When he had recovered his senses, he called for the man who had drawn him out of the water, and finding him to be a slave, he said—How dare you profane the sacred

---

[1] "How are we to know?" *comment pouvons nous savoir?*
[2] To be very fond, *aimer beaucoup.*
[3] To be drowning, *se noyer.*
[4] To plunge in, *plonger.*
[5] "By the hair of his head," *par les cheveux.*

head[1] of your sovereign lord by placing your unworthy hand upon it?—Sire, said he, it was to save your life.—Slave! replied the prince, you have polluted it;—and he immediately ordered him to be put to death.

Some time after, the prince, in stepping from one boat to another, fell again into the water, and finding no one attempted to save him, he called out for assistance[2]; but the only answer he received, was: Remember how you rewarded the slave who saved your life before.—Being unable to swim, the ungrateful prince sank to rise no more, and thus was rewarded for his base ingratitude.

A Curious Decision; or Smelling and Hearing.

A poor chimney-sweeper, who had not money enough to buy himself a dinner, stopped one day before an eating-house, and remained regaling his nose with the smell of the victuals. The master of the shop told him several times to go away, but the sweep could not leave the savoury smell, though unable[3] to purchase the taste. At last the cook came out of the shop, and taking hold of him, de-

---

[1] The sacred head, *la tête sacrée*.
[2] To call out for assistance, *appeler au secours*.
[3] Traduisez: *though he was unable*.

clared that, as he had been feeding upon¹ the smell of his victuals, he should not go away without paying half the price of a dinner. The poor little fellow said that he neither could nor would pay, and that he would ask the first person who should pass, whether it was not an unreasonable and unjust demand.

A police officer, happening² to pass at the moment, the case was referred to him. He said to the sweep, "My boy, as you have been regaling one of your senses with the odour of this man's meat, it is but just you should make him some recompense³; therefore you shall, in your turn, regale one of his senses, which appears more insatiable than your appetite. How much money have you?"—"I have but two pence in all the world, sir, and I must buy me some bread."—"Never mind⁴," said the officer, "take your two pence between your hands; now rattle them loudly."—The boy did so, and the officer, turning to⁵ the cook, said, "Now, sir, I think he has paid you: the smell of your victuals regaled his nostrils; the sound of his money has tickled your ears."—The decision gave more satis-

---

¹ To be feeding upon, *se nourrir de*.
² To happen to pass, *passer par hazard*. Voir page 42 (²).
³ To make some recompense, *indemniser un peu*.
⁴ "Never mind," *n'importe*. ⁵ To turn to, *se tourner vers*.

faction to the by-standers than to the cook, but it was the only payment he could obtain.

One Crime generally begets Another.

A bleacher in Ireland had been frequently robbed of great quantities of linen, and though he had made the greatest exertions, had never been able to discover the robber. At length he offered 100*l*. reward[1] for the detection of the thief or thieves. A few nights after, the bleacher was called by one of his servants, who told him there was a robber in the bleaching-ground[2] with a light.

The master immediately armed himself with a pistol, and the servant with a gun, and went towards the ground where the linen was spread. They saw distinctly a person with a lantern stooping down[3], or kneeling on the grass, as if in the act of cutting or rolling up the cloth[4]. They approached on tiptoe, and as soon as they were near enough, the servant took a deliberate aim[5], fired, and the person

---

[1] Traduisez: *Hundred pounds of reward.*

[2] Bleaching-ground, *blanchisserie.* f.

[3] Stooping down, *baissé, courbé.* (Kneeling, *à genoux.*)

[4] "As if in the act of cutting or rolling up," traduisez: *who appeared to cut or roll up the cloth.*

[5] To take aim, *viser, coucher en joue.*

fell dead. They ran up¹, and discovered that it was the son of a very honest and industrious man, who lived at a short distance. The cloth was cut in many places, and rolled up ready to be taken away; and a knife was found on the spot with the young man's name on it.

With such evidence nobody, not even the afflicted father, could doubt the guilt of the young man.

The servant received the 100*l.*, and was promoted to the place of foreman of the establishment. A short time after², some reports were circulated³ which excited great suspicion against him. It was discovered by some of the servants, that the unfortunate young man had supped with him on the night of the event, and that he had quitted him only a few minutes before the alarm. The master, therefore, had him apprehended⁴, and so many circumstances appeared against him, that he was committed to prison⁵ to take his trial⁶ at the next assizes.

---

¹ To run up, *accourir.*

² A short time after, *peu de temps après, quelque temps après.*

³ "Some reports were circulated," *on fit circuler des bruits, des rapports.*

⁴ To have apprehended, *faire arrêter, faire saisir.*

⁵ To be committed to prison, *être envoyé en prison.*

⁶ "To take his trial," *pour être jugé.*

Being left alone in a solitary dungeon, the conscience of the wretch tormented him so much, that at last he confessed that he himself was the thief, and that the young man was perfectly innocent. Fearing, he said, to be detected, and desirous to gain the reward, he had fixed upon[1] the youth as his victim.

He had first borrowed his pocket-knife, and then, on the evening of the fatal day, went to the bleaching-ground, cut the linen in several pieces, left the knife upon it, and having rolled up several parcels as if ready to take away, he went and asked the lad to come and sup with him; telling him, as the nights were very dark, he had better[2] bring his lantern to light him home[3]. While they were at supper, he spoke about the knife, saying he had mislaid it somewhere, and, suddenly appearing to recollect, he added—I remember dropping it[4] in the bleaching-ground, at such a spot; you can return home that way[5], and, as you have your lantern, you can look for it.—The poor young man was no sooner gone, than the diabolical wretch went to

---

[1] Fixed upon, *choisi*.

[2] Had better, *ferait mieux de*.

[3] "To light him home," traduisez: *to light him as far as his house*.

[4] Traduisez: *I remember to have dropped it*.

[5] That way, *par là*.

alarm his master, and, as we have seen, the innocent and unsuspecting youth was murdered by the real thief. The villain was hanged at Dundalk amidst the execrations of a multitude of people.

P. S. (*Historique*.)

The Bagpiper Revived.

The following event happened in London during the great plague, which in 1665 carried off nearly 100,000 of the inhabitants.

A bagpiper used to get his living by sitting and playing his bagpipes every day on the steps of St. Andrew's[1] church in Holborn. In order to escape the contagion, he drank a great quantity of gin; and, one day, having taken more than usual, he became so drunk that he fell asleep on the steps. It was the custom, during the prevalence of[2] that terrible disease, to send carts about every night to collect the dead, and carry them to a common grave, or deep pit, of which several had been made in the environs of London.

The men passing with the cart up Holborn-hill, and seeing the piper extended on the steps, naturally thought he was dead, and tossed him into the

---

[1] St. Andrew, *Saint-André*.

[2] "During the prevalence of," *au plus fort de* (idiôme).

cart among the others, without observing that he had his bagpipes under his arm, and without paying any attention to his dog, which followed the cart, barking and howling most piteously.

The rumbling of the cart over the stones[1], and the cries of the poor dog, soon awoke the piper from his drunken lethargy, and, not being able to discover where he was, he began squeezing his bag and playing a Scotch air, to the great astonishment and terror of the carters, who immediately fetched lights, and found the Scot sitting erect[2] amid the dead bodies, playing his pipes. He was soon released and restored to his faithful dog. The piper became, from this event, so celebrated, that one of the first sculptors of that epoch made a statue of him and his dog, which is still to be seen[3] at London.

A Singular Precaution.

Two young men set out together on a long journey[4]; one of them was a great spendthrift, but the

---

[1] "Over the stones," *sur le pavé* (mot à mot: *over the pavement*).

[2] "Sitting erect," *assis tout droit.*

[3] "Which is to be seen," *que l'on peut voir.*

[4] "To set out on a long journey," *partir pour un long voyage.*

other being very economical, it was agreed, for their mutual benefit, that the latter should have charge of the purse. The spendthrift soon found himself embarrassed, wishing to buy all the curiosities he saw, and not having money to do it. They slept both in the same room; and one night, after they had been some time in bed, the prodigal called to his friend, saying, William, William!—but William did not answer, till hearing him call very loud, and fearing he might disturb the people of the house, he said, Well, what do you want?—Are you asleep? said the other.—Why? said William.—Because if you are not, I want to borrow a pound of you.—Oh, I am fast asleep, replied he, and have been some time.

Finding William inexorable, the other used frequently to get out of bed[1] in the night, and seek about the room for his purse, but could never find it. At last they arrived at the end of their journey, which, owing to William's economy, had cost but very little: his companion was much pleased, well-knowing, that, if he had kept the purse, it would have been much more expensive. He then said to William, Tell me, now there is no more danger, where you hid the money every night, for I frankly confess that I have often endeavoured to find it.—I

---

[1] To get out of bed, *sortir du lit, se lever.*

expected that, said William, and therefore I always waited till you were in bed; and, after putting out the light, I hid the purse in your own pocket, knowing it was not probable you would seek it there; and taking care to rise in the morning before you were up.[1]

The young man acknowledged that he was pleased with the trick his companion had put upon him[2]; but told him it would, in future, be necessary to find another hiding-place.

Avarice Punished.

An avaricious merchant in Turkey, having lost a purse containing 200 pieces of gold, had it cried by the public crier, offering half its contents to whoever had found and would restore it. A sailor, who had picked it up, went to the crier and told him it was in his possession, and that he was ready to restore it on the[3] proposed conditions; the owner, having thus learned where his purse was, thought he would endeavour to recover it without losing anything. He therefore told the sailor that if he desired to receive the reward, he must restore

---

[1] To be up, *être debout*.
[2] "Had put upon him," traduisez: *had played to him*.
[3] "On the," traduisez: *at the*.

also a valuable emerald which was in the purse. The sailor declared that he had found nothing in the purse except the money, and refused to give it up without the recompense. The merchant went and complained to the cadi, who summoned the sailor to appear, and asked him why he detained the purse he had found?—"Because," replied he, "the merchant has promised a reward of 100 pieces, which he now refuses to give, under pretence that there was a valuable emerald in it, and I swear by Mahomet that in the purse I found there was nothing but gold."

The merchant was then desired to[1] describe the emerald, and how it came into his possession; which he did, but in a manner that convinced the cadi of his dishonesty, and he immediately gave the following judgment[2].—"You have lost a purse containing 200 pieces of gold, and a valuable emerald; the sailor has found one containing only 200 pieces; therefore it cannot be yours; you must then have yours cried again, with a description of the precious stone."—"You," said the cadi to the sailor, "will keep the purse during forty days without touching its contents, and if[3], at the expiration of that time, no

---

[1] "Was then desired to," *fut alors prié de, invité à* (idiôme).
[2] "To give a judgment," *rendre* ou *prononcer un jugement*.
[3] Voir page 16 (⁵).

person shall have established a claim to it, you may justly consider it yours."

The Students Outwitted.

Two students of the university of Oxford having a holiday for two or three days, went roving about the country, and having quickly spent their money, they did not know how to procure a dinner and lodging. However they went boldly to a little inn, ordered a good dinner and beds, leaving the payment to chance.

The next morning[1], after breakfast, the landlord sent up the bill, and they set their wits to work[2] to find some method of satisfying or deceiving him. At last one of them said, I have it[3], ring the bell[4].—The bell is rung, and up comes the landlord[5]; the student addressed him, saying, "We have not any money about us at present, but don't be alarmed, you shall not lose anything. We are scholars, and by our profound studies we have discovered that, every hundred years, things return

---

[1] "The next morning," *le lendemain matin.*

[2] To set one's wit to work, *mettre son esprit en besogne* (idiôme).

[3] "I have it," *j'y suis, je l'ai trouvé* (idiôme).

[4] "Ring the bell," *sonnez.*

[5] Traduisez: *and the landlord comes up.*

to the same state¹; therefore this day a hundred years hence² you will be landlord here, and we will come and pay you."

"Gentlemen," replied the landlord, "I have no doubt of the truth of what you say, and you will, perhaps, scarcely believe me, when I tell you that I also have deeply studied the occult sciences, and have fortunately discovered that, as you say, things return every hundred years to the same state; and last night, when hard at my study³, I made an important discovery; it is that just a hundred years ago, you came here, dined and lodged, and went away without paying. Now, I am very willing to give you credit⁴ for your bill to-day; but I will not let you leave my house till you have paid the bill of the last century, which is exactly the same amount."

The students, finding themselves beaten with their own weapons, were obliged to send a messenger to their college and borrow money to pay their reckoning.

---

[1] Traduisez: *in the same state.*

[2] "This day a hundred years hence," *dans cent ans de ce jour*, ou *dans cent ans d'aujourd'hui* (idiôme).

[3] "Hard at my study," *fortement occupé de mes études* (idiôme).

[4] "Very willing to give you credit," *tout prêt à vous faire credit* (idiôme).

The Double Metamorphosis.

An Irishman was once employed, by a gentleman at Hampstead, to carry a live hare, as a present, to one of his friends at London. It was put into a bag, and he set off. Hampstead being about five miles from London, the Irishman stopped half way[1] at a public house, to rest himself, and to drink a pint of beer. Some wags, who were drinking in the tap-room, finding what he had in the bag, determined to play him a trick; and one of them, while the others kept him in conversation, took out the hare and put in a cat.

Having finished his beer, the Irishman started with his load. On arriving at London, he said to the gentleman—Sir, my master has sent you a live hare.—Very well, said he, let us see it.—He then opened the sack, and to his great astonishment found a cat.—By the powers![2] said Paddy, it was a hare at Hampstead, for I saw it put into the bag.—Go back, go back, said the gentleman, they are making a fool of you[3].—Paddy took up the bag and trotted off again towards Hampstead, stopping, on his return, at the same public house, and telling his

---

[1] "Half way," *à mi-chemin.*

[2] "By the powers!" *par Dieu!* (idiôme).

[3] "They are making a fool of you," *on se moque de vous* (idiôme).

adventure, to the amusement of those who had played him the trick. To render the farce complete they contrived to take out the cat and replace the hare; and the unsuspecting Irishman set off again for Hampstead.

On arriving, he said to his master, Sir, do you know that you have sent a cat instead of a hare?—Go along, you stupid fellow, replied the gentleman. —Well, then, believe your own eyes.—On saying which he opened the bag, and out leaped the hare. The Irishman could scarcely believe his eyes, and appeared for some moments petrified with fear: at length he ejaculated—By Jasus, it is a hare at Hampstead, and a cat at London!—Come, come, said the master, put it into the bag and return.—By Jasus, master, I shall go no more, for if the vile air of London can change a hare into a cat, it may, perhaps, change me into an ass; and will I, think you, risk[2] going on all fours[3] during the rest of my days?

Instinct and Cruelty.

Many animals, and even insects, are known to be powerfully affected by sound, and so very susceptible

---

[1] "On saying which," *en disant cela* (idiôme).
[2] "Will I, think you, risk," *croyez-vous que j'irais m'exposer à la chance de* (idiôme). [3] "On all fours," *à quatre pattes* (idiôme)

to the influence of music that the most timid have frequently approached, and even become familiar with man, who, as instinct tells them, is their mortal enemy. The following anecdote will offer a striking example of different sentiments in different animals.

A gentleman named Pellisson was secretary to Fouquet, minister of finances under Louis XIV.; but the affairs of the treasury were so badly conducted that the minister was condemned to perpetual imprisonment, and his secretary, Pellisson, was sentenced to five years' confinement in the Bastille.

During his imprisonment, Pellisson, who knew the value of time, and could not remain idle, occupied himself in reading, in writing, and frequently, as a kind of relaxation from study, he would play on[1] the flute. On these occasions he often remarked that a large spider, which had made its web in a corner of his room, came out of its hole and appeared to listen to the music. Pellisson, to encourage it, would continue to play, and at last the insect became so familiar that it would approach the prisoner and feed in his hand.

This was a great pleasure for Pellisson; he became fond of the insect he had thus tamed, looked upon[2]

---

[1] Voir page 9 (³).   [2] To look upon, *regarder, considérer.*

ENGLISH INTO FRENCH. 153

it as a companion, and found, even in such society, a relief from solitude.

The circumstance having come to the knowledge of the jailers, they communicated it to the governor of the Bastille, who, being a man incapable of sympathy, fulfilled but too well the duties of his office, and by his rigorous treatment of the captives rendered imprisonment in that citadel one of the most dreadful punishments that could be inflicted.

Determined to deprive the prisoner of the consolation he had acquired, the governor went to his cell and said—Well, Mr. Pellisson, I hear you[1] have found a companion.—It is true, replied he, and though we cannot converse, we understand each other very well.—But I can hardly believe what I have been told[2], said the governor, and I should like to be convinced of the truth.—Pellisson, not suspecting any bad intention, immediately called the insect, which came and fed in his hand, and suffered itself to be[3] caressed, but the governor, watching an opportunity, brushed it off[4], and immediately crushing it under his foot, left the room without saying a word. Pellisson was released from prison a short time after by the king,

---

[1] Traduisez: *I hear say that you, &c.*

[2] "What I have been told," voir page 22 (*).

[3] To suffer one's self to be, *se laisser*.

[4] To brush off, *jeter par terre, faire tomber*.

who restored him to favour and loaded him with honours; but he was frequently heard to say he would never forgive the governor that act of wanton cruelty.

Quackery.

The following example of quackery, though of ancient date, is almost equal to any that the present time can offer.

A certain quack whose object, like that of all quacks, was to fill his pockets by imposing on the ignorant and credulous, once advertised that he had discovered a new method of imparting knowledge, the effects of which were so sure and so rapid, that in a single month he could teach a person of the most moderate capacity the Greek and Latin languages. To excite yet greater astonishment, and give a higher opinion of his own talent, he declared that, by his process, even beasts could be taught to understand and to speak, and that he would undertake to render an ass capable of passing an examination for a doctor's degree, in a certain space of time.

The king having heard of the impudent effrontery of this pretended scholar, determined, by giving him some employment himself, to prevent him from making a prey of his people. He therefore sent for him; and said—I have been informed, sir, that you have discovered a method of teaching animals to speak, and that you can qualify an ass for a doctor's degree; now I have an ass that appears to be very intelligent, and I should like to elevate him above the degraded and unhappy state of his long-eared brethren[1]; tell me on[2] what conditions you will undertake to make him a doctor.

After a few moments of reflection the quack replied, that he would only demand to be clothed and fed, and to have an allowance of a piece of gold every day, for extraordinary expenses; and that if in ten years the ass should not answer the king's expectations, he would consent to suffer death as a vile impostor. "Very well," said the king, "I will reflect on the subject, and let you know when you may begin the education."

The quack, overjoyed at the bargain he had made, communicated it to one of his acquaintance, who asked him if he did not fear to be hanged at the expiration of the time. "Not at all," replied he, "for if neither the king nor I should die before the expiration of the ten years, I will take care that the ass shall[3]."

---

[1] "His long-eared brethren," *ses frères aux longues oreilles.*

[2] *On*, traduisez: *at.*

[3] "*That the ass shall die.*" Toutes les fois que le verbe est supprimé en Anglais après un auxiliaire il doit être exprimé en

The king, being informed of this, sent for the man, and said to him, "Well, sir, my ass is ready to become your pupil, but two conditions must be added; the first is, that in case of my death you shall complete your engagement with my successor; and the second, that, as the ass is young, and in sound health[1], if anything should happen to him under your tuition, you shall be imprisoned till you restore the money you may have received, and you shall also be exposed every day during an hour in the public market, with a pair of ass's ears on your head."

As the quack refused to accept these terms, he was placed on the donkey, with his face to the tail, and thus conducted through the city, preceded by a man bearing a placard in large letters: "BEHOLD THE ASS AND HIS PRECEPTOR, AND TAKE WARNING[2]."

Youthful Benevolence.

A poor lace-maker with a large family, who during a long winter had been frequently in the bit-

---

français; cependant il arrive souvent qu'en réponse à une question le verbe sous-entendu en anglais et l'auxiliaire exprimé sont remplacés en français par *oui* ou *non*. Exemple : "Shall you go there?"—*Irez-vous là ?*—"I shall."—*Oui, Monsieur.*

[1] "In sound health," *en bonne santé.*

[2] "Take warning," *prenez garde à vous, tenez-vous pour avertis.*

terest state of misery, was so feeble that he was compelled to keep his bed[1]. Vainly endeavouring to rise, in order to seek employment, he fell fainting by the side of[2] his wife, who was herself dangerously ill. A girl of twelve or thirteen years watched her mother, and endeavoured, affectionately, to prevent her two younger brothers from disturbing their parents: on this child the whole care of the family had fallen.

To supply their wants, she ran to a neighbouring *Bureau de Charité*, where she had been informed that relief might be obtained; but the person to whom she applied bid her "call again in a few days." Thus repulsed, the child took the resolution of begging. This, alas! was a fruitless hope...

In vain she stretched out her little hands to solicit charity, no one answered her humble and modest claim; some even threatened her with the police. Chilled by cold and by unkindness, she sadly took her way home[3].

On her appearance[4], her little brothers immediately cried, "Bread! sister! give us bread!" On hearing the screams of the children, she exclaimed, "I will fetch a loaf from the baker's," and, in a

---

[1] "To keep his bed," *garder le lit.*
[2] "By the side of," *à côté de.*
[3] To take one's way home, *retourner* ou *rentrer chez soi.*
[4] "On her appearance," *en l'apercevant, à son arrivée.*

distracted manner, flew to a neighbouring shop, seized a loaf, and hastened away[1]! Surrounded instantly by a crowd, she was deprived of her prize, and given to the police agents to answer for her crime. Looking on[2] the crowd with a countenance of surprise and despair, she perceived a child, about her own age, whose sweet and encouraging smile cast a faint ray of hope on her forlorn mind. She approached this unknown, whose features were beaming with benevolence, and in whispers mingled with sobs she communicated her parents' address.

Whilst the poor family were[3] in the agonies of want and despair, a light step was heard approaching their chamber. A cry of joy was uttered by the unfortunates— ... a girl appeared at the door —it was not their child!—It was a little angel, with rosy cheeks and golden hair, and bearing a small basket of provisions.

Your daughter is not likely to return[4] home to day, she said, perhaps not to-morrow. Fear not— she is well—be cheerful and eat what she has been the means of sending to you[5]. She then placed ten

---

[1] To hasten away, *se hâter de s'éloigner* ou *de se sauver*.

[2] To look on, *regarder, contempler*.

[3] Voir page 21 (³) *sur les noms collectifs*.

[4] "Is not likely to return," *ne rentrera probablement pas*.

[5] "What she has been the means of sending to you," *ce qu'elle a trouvé le moyen de vous envoyer*.

francs in the hands of the mother of the family, and suddenly disappeared.

But how had these ten francs been obtained? By what means had this child been able so unexpectedly to serve this unhappy family? We shall see.

Her golden tresses, falling in ringlets over her shoulders, had excited the admiration of the neighbours. One of these, a hair-dresser, had frequently said, when she was passing his house[1], I would willingly give a louis for that beautiful head of hair[2]. When this occasion of doing good presented itself, this kind-hearted little creature, without the means of obtaining money, remembered the man's words, sought his house, and said: You have offered to buy my hair for a louis; now I will sell it to you, cut it all off quickly. Make haste, for I am in a great hurry[3]. The man, struck with the singularity of the circumstance, asked the particulars, and being of a kind humane disposition, he feigned to accept the proposed conditions, gave her fifteen francs, and added, that as she was then in a hurry, she might come again to have her hair cut off.

After having succoured the family, the girl went

---

[1] Traduisez: *was passing before his house.*

[2] "Head of hair," *chevelure.* s. f.

[3] To be in a great hurry, *être très pressé.*

joyously home, and related the whole of the adventure¹ to her anxious but happy mother, who recompensed her by kisses of affection and tears of joy.

The end of this youthful drama may be now guessed. The poor family recovered their daughter, and, with her, health, comfort, and joy returned to their humble dwelling.

The Miraculous Transformation.

Frederick the Great, King of Prussia, paid great attention to the discipline of his army, and punished with severity the smallest faults. If, during a review, a dragoon was unfortunate enough to fall from his horse, it was sufficient to subject him to a severe flogging; a hat or a cap falling off was nearly as dangerous.

In order to convince himself of the general conduct of the soldiers, Frederick would often disguise himself as² a private, and mix in their society. On one of these occasions he happened to meet with³ a soldier, of the royal guard, who was tipsy;⁴ he immediately entered into familiar conversation with

---

[1] "The whole of the adventure," traduisez: *all the adventure.*
[2] "To disguise one's self as," *se déguiser en.*
[3] "To happen to meet with," *rencontrer par hazard.*
[4] To be tipsy, *être un peu ivre, être gris, être entre deux vins.*

him, saying, How is it, comrade, that out of[1] your trifling pay you can find the means to get tipsy?[2] I receive the same as you do, and can never put anything by[3] to enjoy myself. I wish you would tell me how you manage.[4] The soldier, after eyeing him for a moment, said, You look like a jolly fellow;[5] come, give us your hand, and I will tell you how I manœuvre: to-day, for instance, meeting an old comrade, I wished to treat him; it was no use[6] putting my hand in my pocket; and it would have been equally vain asking credit at the wine-shop; so I had recourse to an expedient, I pawned some of my accoutrements, and among them the blade of my sabre.

But, said Frederick, how will you obtain money to redeem it?—Oh! replied the soldier, we shall not be called out to exercise[7] before next week, and by a little abstinence during the interval I shall be able to recover my things.—I thank you for the hint, said Frederick, and I will not fail to profit by it[8]; so, good night, comrade.

---

[1] "Out of," *avec, sur*.   [2] To get tipsy, *s'enivrer, se griser*.

[3] To put by, *mettre de côté*.

[4] "How you manage," *comment vous faites, comment vous vous y prenez*

[5] "A jolly fellow," *un bon camarade, un bon vivant*.

[6] "It was no use," *ce n'était pas la peine de*.

[7] To be called out to exercise, *être appelé sous les armes*.

[8] "To profit by it," *d'en profiter*.

The next morning the troops of the guard were unexpectedly called out to be reviewed[1], and the King, in passing attentively along the ranks, discovered his comrade of the day before. The inspection finished, Frederick placed himself in front of the line, and immediately ordered the soldier, and the one next him, to leave the ranks and approach him. They did so, and the King with an angry voice, said to his last night's companion: "Draw your sabre, and cut off the head of that scoundrel." The soldier begged his majesty to have mercy on[2] his comrade, saying he was a brave man, and incapable of doing anything to merit such a punishment. Frederick however remained inflexible, and the soldier, fearing to draw chastisement on himself,[3] said to the King: Since your majesty is inexorable, I must obey; but I earnestly supplicate Providence to interpose in behalf of my unfortunate comrade, and cause my sword to fall harmless on his neck.

Then drawing the sabre, he suddenly exclaimed, "O miracle! behold! Providence has changed the blade of my sword into wood!"

It is scarcely necessary to add that, being called to muster, and unable to redeem his blade, the

---

[1] To be called out to be reviewed, *être passé en revue.*

[2] "To have mercy on," *avoir pitié de.*

[3] To draw on one's self, *s'attirer.*

soldier had fixed a blade of wood to the hilt.—Frederick was so pleased with his presence of mind, that he not only forgave him, but also made him a present, recommending him, at the same time, not to expose himself again to the same danger, as another miracle would not perhaps save him.

The Turbulent Youth Corrected.

Henry V. of England was very wild and ungovernable in his youth; but he once received a severe and salutary lesson from a judge named Gascoigne. —While Henry was Prince of Wales[1], one of his favourite servants, having committed a crime, was apprehended by the police, sent to prison, and brought before the court, to be tried for the offence. The evidence was clear against him, and he was convicted, notwithstanding the interest that had been employed in his favour.

The prince, on hearing the judgment, rushed into the court, and commanded the judge to set the man at liberty[2], but Gascoigne told him mildly that it was impossible, and advised him, instead of encouraging a violation of the laws, and resistance to their execution, to give his father's subjects an

---

[1] "Prince of Wales," *Prince de Galles.*
[2] "To set at liberty," *mettre en liberté.*

example of obedience. Henry, whose irritable temper could not bear this reproach, rushed towards the judge, drawing his sword, as if he intended to do him a personal violence; but Gascoigne, rising with dignity, said to him: "Sir, remember that in this place I represent the king, whom[1] it is your duty to obey, both[2] as your sovereign and as your father; and now, for your contempt of the royal authority I commit you to prison[3], there to remain until the pleasure of his majesty be known.

The prince, convinced of his error, and daunted by the imposing firmness of the judge, suffered himself[4] to be conducted to jail. When his father, Henry IV., heard of the transaction, he exclaimed: Happy the monarch who possesses a judge so resolute in the discharge of his duty, and a son willing to submit to the authority of the law!

P. S. (*Historique*.)

La vieille Ganache[5].

Shortly after the marriage of Napoleon with Maria-Louisa, daughter of the emperor of Austria,

---

[1] Traduisez: *to whom.*   [2] Voir page 35 (¹).
[3] To commit to prison, *envoyer en prison.*
[4] To suffer one's self, *se laisser.*
[5] *Vieille ganache* se dit en anglais *a stupid old fellow, a thickhead.*

some political measures were adopted by the Austrian court which were contrary to the views of Bonaparte. On receiving the news he said—The emperor of Austria is *une vieille ganache*. Maria-Louisa was present, but never having heard the expression before, she did not understand it.

Soon after, when she was alone with her husband, she asked him the meaning of the word *ganache*; but unwilling to tell her the true signification, he said: Oh, it means a man of great experience and good understanding.

On[1] the following day, the Chancellor Cambaceres waited on the empress with an address of congratulation on her marriage, and wishing to pay him a compliment[2] in her reply, she thanked him heartily, saying she considered him the greatest *ganache* in the empire.

The courtiers were astonished and confounded; but of course[3] they withdrew without making any observation. The circumstance came shortly to the ears of Napoleon, who laughed heartily at it[4], and during some weeks it was a topic of pleasantry in all Paris; the empress herself being the only per-

---

[1] Voir page 17 (²).

[2] To pay a compliment, *faire un complément.*

[3] "Of course," *naturellement, sans aucun doute, cela va sans dire, il va sans dire que.*

[4] To laugh heartily at, *rire de bon cœur de.*

son who remained ignorant of the blunder she had committed.

Impartial Judgment.

In the pleasant fields of Battersea, on the banks of the Thames, near London, there[1] dwelt about three hundred years ago, a blind widow named Annice Collie, and her orphan grand-child Dorothy. They had seen better days, for the father of little Dorothy had been gardener to[2] the good queen Catharine, the first wife to Henry VIII. But when Henry divorced the kind Catharine, to marry Ann Boleyn, the servants of the former were all discharged. This was a heavy blow[3] to the family[4]; but more severe misfortunes awaited them. The brother of Dorothy, a very industrious youth, was killed by the falling of an old wall, and his death so afflicted[5] the father and mother that they did not long survive him.

The poor little Dorothy, yet a child, was thus left alone, with her blind and infirm grandmother,

---

[1] Ne traduisez pas *there*.
[2] Gardener to, traduisez: *gardener of*.
[3] "A heavy blow," *un grand malheur, un coup fâcheux*.
[4] "To the family," traduisez: *for the family*.
[5] "So afflicted," traduisez: *afflicted so much*.

and without any means of support[1]. Not knowing what to do, she procured some flowers, and a little fruit, and went daily through the streets of London to obtain a few pence; but she did not go alone, as she was accompanied by a beautiful dog named Constant, which had been given to her, when quite[2] a puppy, by the good queen Catharine, and which she loved dearly. During some time this affectionate little girl gained enough to buy victuals and drink[3] for her grandmother and herself, but at length the winter came on[4]; the old lady fell sick, and they were reduced to the greatest distress.

Dorothy could have borne her own miseries; but when she saw the sufferings of old Annice she could no longer support it, and looking at her with tears in her eyes, she exclaimed, "Dearest grandmother, it shall be done! I will sell my dear Constant; I was offered a golden angel for him some time ago by a servant of the Duchess of Suffolk."—"And can you," said Annice, "part with your favourite, the gift of the good queen Catharine?"—"Oh it will[5] almost break my heart," replied Dorothy; "but can I see you want bread?"

---

[1] Means of support, *ressources*. f.

[2] "When quite," traduisez: *when he was quite*.

[3] "Victuals and drink," *à boire et à manger* (idiôme).

[4] To come on, *arriver*.   [5] Voir page 15 (¹).

This good little creature then set off, accompanied by Constant, to go to the Duchess of Suffolk's; but she soon after returned, crying and sobbing as if her heart would break¹; for she had met a thief by the way,² who had seized her dear little dog, saying it belonged to him, and threatening to put her in prison if she dared to follow him. This was a severe trial for poor Dorothy; she saw no resource but that of asking alms of the charitable,³ and though humiliating to the lowest degree, she determined to submit to everything, in order to procure some relief for her poor blind and aged grandmother. She therefore went from door to door,⁴ telling her artless tale, and supplicating assistance.⁵ Some indeed, whose hearts were not insensible to the woes of others, gave her relief; but the greater number, thinking only of gratifying their own desires, turned a deaf ear to her prayer, or reproached her for⁶ not working to gain a livelihood.⁷ In this afflicting situation, she sadly missed⁸ the

---

¹ To break (en parlant du *cœur*) *se fendre, fendre* (idiôme).
² "By the way," *en chemin*.
³ Ne traduisez pas: " of the charitable."
⁴ "From door to door," *de porte en porte*.
⁵ To supplicate assistance, *implorer du secours*.
⁶ To reproach for, *reprocher de*.
⁷ "To gain a livelihood," *gagner sa vie*.
⁸ To miss sadly, *sentir tristement la perte de*.

company of poor Constant, whose caresses and fidelity would have offered her some consolation for the cold indifference of the world.

It was now the depth of winter, and one day, when the poor little creature had been begging[1] from morning till evening, without receiving a single penny; overcome with grief, faint with hunger, and benumbed with cold, her courage failed her, and she sank fainting[2] on the ground, whence she would probably never have risen again, but for[3] a providential circumstance.

She was suddenly awaked by a dog leaping upon her; it was her dear Constant, who was licking her benumbed face and hands, and caressing her in the most[4] affectionate manner. The surprise and joy recalled her to life, and taking the faithful animal in her arms, she said: I shall be able to reach home now I have found you, my beloved dog.

Your dog, hussey! exclaimed a footman; I'll let you know[5] that he belongs to Lady More, wife of the Lord Chancellor, snatching him at the same time from her arms.—Indeed, indeed, sir, it is my dog, it was given to me, when quite a puppy,

---

[1] To be begging, *mendier*.
[2] To sink fainting, *tomber en défaillance*.
[3] "But for," *si ce n'eut été par, à moins de*.
[4] "In the most," traduisez: *of the most*.
[5] To let know, *faire savoir*.

by the good queen Catharine, who was very kind to¹ me.—Ho! ho! said the man, in a loud laugh²: you look like a queen's favourite certainly; I see a lie will not choke you.—On saying this, he walked away with the dog, but the poor girl, cold, hungry, and fatigued as she was, followed him, though her limbs could hardly support her.

On arriving at the house, she begged the servant to let her see his mistress, that she might convince her that the dog was hers; but the man told her to be gone³, and shutting the door in her face, left her in despair. Dorothy, weeping, then seated herself on a stone, determined to wait till she could see some of the family, and at length she heard the sound of a carriage. The gates were opened and the servants came running, and crying out, Room! room⁴! for the Lord Chancellor's coach! The family all came out to meet him, but they took no notice of⁵ poor Dorothy; however Sir Thomas, on perceiving her, rebuked them, saying, "Why don't you relieve that poor little creature? don't you see that she is starving with cold and hunger⁶?"

---

¹ To be kind to, traduisez: *to be kind for*.

² "In a loud laugh," traduisez: *in laughing aloud*.

³ "To be gone," *de s'en aller, de s'éloigner*.

⁴ "Room! room!" *place! place! faites place, rangez-vous*.

⁵ To take notice of, *faire attention à*.

⁶ To be starving with cold and hunger, *mourir de froid et de faim*.

Encouraged by these kind words, Dorothy approached and said, "Indeed, my lord, I am very cold and hungry; but I did not come here to beg alms; I came to claim my little dog, which one of your servants has taken from me."

"How! you saucy vagrant," said the proud Lady More, who had come out to receive her husband, "do you dare claim my dog before my face?" Dorothy had not courage enough to answer Lady More; but she said to Sir Thomas, "Indeed, my lord, it is my dog, and he was stolen from me about three months ago."—"Do you hear that, my lady?" said Sir Thomas; "you know that you have had the animal about that time."—"Yes," replied her ladyship[1], "but you know he was given to me by Mr. Rich, one of the king's counsellors, who bought him of a man at his own door." —"And who knows," said Sir Thomas, "where that man had obtained him?" —"But," said Lady More, "she has no witness to prove the dog ever belonged to her, and so she cannot establish her right."

"Well," said Sir Thomas, "as I am Lord Chancellor, and first judge of the realm, it is my duty to see justice done: I will endeavour to decide the cause, and I think we can call a witness whose testimony will be decisive."—On saying this, he

---

[1] "Her ladyship," *sa seigneurie*.

told a servant to bring the dog. The dog being brought, Sir Thomas took him on his lap, saying, "Now, my lady, you say this dog is yours, and you call him Sultan; this little girl says he is hers, and that his name is Constant; therefore I command you to place yourselves, one at each end of the room, and call him."—They did so, and Lady More began by saying, "Sultan! Sultan! come to your mistress, my pretty Sultan!"—The dog, however, took no other notice than slightly wagging his tail.—Dorothy then said, "Constant! Constant!" and he immediately bounded from Sir Thomas'[1], leaped on his little mistress, and expressed the most passionate fondness.

"The case is very clear," said the Chancellor, "the dog has acknowledged his mistress; he is worthy of his name, and I adjudge him to her." Upon hearing this, Lady More said, "Hark ye[2], my girl! if you will sell me your dog, I will give you a good price for him."—"Oh no!" said Dorothy, "I cannot part with my dear Constant."—"But," said the lady, "I will give you a golden angel for him."—"Ah! my lady, do not tempt me with your gold," replied Dorothy, "or the distress of my poor blind grandmother will force me to accept your

---

[1] Traduisez: *from Sir Thomas's lap.*
[2] "Hark ye," *écoutez, faites attention, dites donc.*

offer."—"Oh!" replied her ladyship, "if you have a grandmother, I will also give you a warm blanket, and some clothes for her:—speak, shall I have him?"—Dorothy, bursting into tears, sobbed out[1], "Ye-es, my lady."

"Dear child!" said Sir Thomas, "thou hast made a noble and virtuous sacrifice to thy duty, and I will find thee a better employment than begging to support thy parent. What say you? will you come and live with my daughter as her maid?"—"O! most gladly, most joyfully, my lord, if I can do it without being separated from my grandmother?"—"God forbid[2] I should separate you," said Sir Thomas, wiping away[3] a tear from his cheek; "my house is large enough for you both, and the old lady shall pass the rest of her days in comfort[4]."

Sir Thomas kept his word, the little family was restored to happiness, and the dutiful and affectionate Dorothy had the pleasing reflection[5] that by her virtuous conduct she had saved her beloved parent from a miserable end, and procured her the ease and comfort necessary to old age.

P. S. (Historique.)

---

[1] To sob out, *sangloter*.
[2] "God forbid," *à Dieu ne plaise*.
[3] To wipe away, *essuyer*.
[4] "In comfort," *confortablement*.
[5] "Had the pleasing reflection," *put faire la reflexion agréable*.

" 'Tis a little thing
To give a cup of water, yet its draught[1]
Of cool refreshment, drain'd by fever'd lips,
May give a shock of pleasure[2] to the frame
More exquisite than when nectarean juice[3]
Renews the life of joy in festal hours.
It is a little thing to speak a phrase
Of common comfort, which by daily use
Has almost lost its sense; yet on the ear
Of him who thought to die unmourn'd[4] 'twill fall
Like choicest music.[5]

TALFOURD.

---

[1] Draught, *coup, trait.*
[2] "A shock of pleasure," *une sensation de plaisir.*
[3] "Nectarean juice," *nectar, jus de nectar.*
[4] Unmourned, *oublié, négligé, sans être regretté.*
[5] "Like choicest music," *comme une musique délicieuse.*

ABRÉVIATIONS DU DICTIONNAIRE.

a.	adjectif.
ad.	adverbe.
art.	article.
c.	conjonction.
f.	féminin.
m.	masculin.
int.	interjection.
part.	participe.
pl.	pluriel.
pr.	préposition.
pro.	pronom.
s.	substantif.
v.	verbe.
va.	verbe actif.
vn.	verbe neutre.
vr.	verbe refléchi.
ma.	terme de marine.

Les verbes qui exigent une préposition devant un infinitif sont suivis de cette préposition, *en caractères romains*. (à, de.)

La préposition *en italique* (*à, de,* &c.) à la suite d'un verbe est celle que ce verbe gouverne devant son régime indirect.

À la suite des adjectifs sont marquées, *en caractères romains*, les prépositions qui doivent s'employer devant les verbes, et *en italique*, celles qui doivent l'être devant tout autre complément.

N.B. On ne trouvera à la suite des *Adjectifs* que les terminaisons feminines *irrégulières* ou *exceptionnelles*. L'élève formera les autres selon l'usage, en ajoutant un *e muet* au masculin, à moins que l'adjectif ne se termine en *e muet*, au quel cas il ne faut faire aucun changement pour le feminin.

DICTIONNAIRE

DES MOTS ANGLAIS

QUI SE TROUVENT DANS LES EXERCISES.

A.

A, An, *art.* un, une.
Abandon, *va.* abandonner, *à*, renoncer, à.
Abbot, *s.* abbé, chef d'une abbaye, *m.*
Ability, *s.* habileté, *f.* pouvoir, talent, *m.*
Able, *a.* capable, de, habile à.
About, *pr.* environ; autour; çà et là; partout; à l'entour de; aux environs; touchant; concernant; sur; vers; dans; par, de.
— *ad.* en rond, de tour, de grosseur; circulairement; çà et là.
— TO, sur le point de.
Above all, *ad.* surtout, principalement.
Absent, *a.* absent, distrait.
Absolve, *va.* absoudre, de, *de*; donner l'absolution.
Abstraction, *s.* absence (d'esprit), distraction, *f.*
Abundance, *s.* abondance, *f.*
Abundant, *a.* abondant.
Abundantly, *ad.* abondamment.

Abuse, *s.* abus, *m.* offense, *f.* injures, sottises, *f. pl.*
— *va.* abuser *de*; maltraiter *de.*
Abuser, *s.* abuseur; séducteur, *m.*
Abusive, *a* injurieux, se. abusif, ve.
Abusively, *ad.* injurieusement, abusivement, outrageusement.
Accept, *va.* accepter, de, agréer.
Access, *s.* accès, *m.* entrée, *f.*
Accession, *s.* accession, *f.* avénement, surcroît, *m.*
Accident, *s.* accident, incident, *m.*
Accidentally, *ad.* accidentellement, fortuitement, par accident.
Accommodation, *s.* accommodation, *f.* convenance, *f.*
Accommodations, *s. pl.* commodités, *f pl.* arrangements logements et emménagements, *m. pl.*
Accompany, *va.* accompagner à, de, joindre, à.
Accomplice, *s.* complice.

ACCOMPLISH, va. accomplir, achever, de.
ACCOMPLISHED, part. a. accompli, instruit.
ACCOMPLISHMENT, s. accomplissement, m. faculté, f. talent, m.
ACCORDING TO, pr. selon, suivant.
ACCORDING AS, c. comme, selon que.
ACCORDINGLY, ad. conformément; convenablement, en conséquence.
ACCOST, va. accoster, aborder.
ACCOUNT, s. calcul, compte, m. nouvelle, f avis, m. relation; considération; raison, f.
ACCOUNT, va. compter, rendre compte de, estimer, faire cas de.
ACCURATE, a. exact, à, à, soigneux de, fidèle.
ACCURATELY, ad. exactement.
ACCUSATION, s. accusation, f.
ACCUSE, va. accuser, de, de; blâmer, de, de.
ACCUSER, s. accusateur, m. — trice, f.
ACCUSTOM, va. accoutumer, à, à; habituer à, à.
— ONE'S SELF, vr. s'accoutumer, à, à.
ACCUSTOMED, a. accoutumé, à, à; habituel, le.
ACKNOWLEDGE, va. reconnaitre, avouer, faire honneur à.
ACKNOWLEDGEMENT, s. reconnaissance, f. acquit, m. quittance, f.
ACQUAINTANCE, s. connaissance, f. ami, m.
ACQUIRE, va. acquérir, obtenir, gagner.
ACQUIT, va. absoudre, de, de; s'acquitter de.

ACROSS, ad. de travers; croisé.
— pr. à travers, au travers de.
ACT, vn. agir envers, jouer; se conduire envers.
— s. action, f. acte, fait, trait, coup, m.
ADD, va. ajouter à; augmenter de; joindre à.
— UP, va. additionner.
ADDITION, s. addition, f. surcroît, m.
ADDITIONAL, a. additionnel, le. de surplus.
ADDRESS, va. adresser à, présenter à, s'adresser à, haranguer.
— s. adresse, dextérité, f.
ADJUDGE, va. adjuger à.
ADMEASUREMENT, s. mesure, action du mesurer, f.
ADMIRATION, s. admiration, surprise, f.
ADMIRE, va. admirer, de; estimer.
ADMIT, va. admettre, à, à; permettre, à, de.
ADMITTABLE, a. admissible.
ADMITTANCE, s. admission, f. accès, m.
ADOPT, va. adopter, s'approprier.
ADVANCE, va. avancer à, produire.
ADVANCE, vn. s'avancer vers; faire des progrès.
— s. avance, f. progrès, m.
ADVANTAGE, s. profit, avantage, m.
ADVANTAGEOUS, a. avantageux, se. utile à.
ADVENTURE, s. aventure, f. risque, m.
— va. aventurer; risquer, de.

ADVERSARY, s. adversaire, ennemi, m.
ADVERTISE, va. annoncer à, afficher à.
ADVERTISEMENT, s. avis, m. annonce, f. affiche, f.
ADVICE, s. avis, m. connaissance, f.
ADVISE, va. mander, de, à; conseiller, de, à.
— vn. consulter; délibérer.
AFFAIR, s. affaire, f.
AFFECTION, s. affection, amitié, f.
AFFECTIONATE, a. affectueux pour, envers, affectionné, zélé.
AFFECTIONATELY, ad. tendrement.
AFFLICT, va. affliger, de, de; accabler de.
AFFRIGHT, va. effrayer, de, épouvanter, de.
— s. effroi, m.
AFFRIGHTFUL, a. effroyable, terrible.
AFFRONT, va. affronter; insulter de.
— s. affront, m. insulte, f.
AFRAID, a. effrayé, craintif.
AFTER, ad. pr. c. après; selon; après que; ensuite.
AFTER ALL, ad. après tout; enfin.
AFTERWARD, ad. ensuite, puis, après cela.
AGAIN, ad. encore, de plus, une autre fois, de nouveau.
AGAINST, pr. contre, vis-à-vis, envers, sur, vers, à.
AGE, s. âge, siècle, m. vieillesse, f.
— To be of age, être majeur.
— To be under age, être mineur.
AGED, a. âgé, avancé en âge.
AGO, ad. il y a

AGONIES, s. douleurs, agonie, f.
AGREE, v. accorder, de, à, convenir, de, de.
AGREE UPON, TO or IN, convenir de, de, s'accorder, à, sur, être d'accord, de, avec, sur.
AGREEABLE, a. agréable à, sortable, aimable, conforme.
AGREEABLY, ad. agréablement.
AGREED, a. convenu, d'accord.
AGREEMENT, s. rapport, accord, accommodement, marché, traité, m.
AID, AIDANCE, s. aide, f. secours, m.
AIM, va. viser, à, à.
— s. visée, f. but, blanc, coup, m. mire d'un fusil, f.
AIR, s. air, zéphir, maintien, m. façon, chanson, f.
ALARM, s. alarme, épouvante, f.
— va. alarmer, épouvanter, de.
ALAS, int. hélas!
ALDERMAN, s. échevin, préfet, m.
ALEHOUSE, s. cabaret à bière, m.
ALEHOUSE KEEPER, s. cabaretier, m.
ALL, a. s. tout, tout.
— ad. tout, entièrement.
ALL OVER, ad. partout, d'un bout à l'autre de.
ALL FOURS, ad. à quatre pattes.
ALLOW, va. permettre, de, à, donner, à, à, allouer, approuver, avouer, déduire.
ALLOWANCE, s. indulgence, allocation, f. appointement, m.
ALMOST, ad. presque, environ, bientôt.
ALMS, s. aumône, f.
ALONE, a. seul, en repos.
ALONG, ad. le long, de.
ALOUD, ad. haut, fortement.

ALREADY, *ad.* déjà.
ALSO, *ad.* aussi, de plus, encore.
ALTER, *va.* changer.
ALWAYS, *ad.* toujours, perpétuellement.
AMAZE, *va.* éblouir, surprendre, de, *de.*
AMAZE, étonnement, *m.* surprise, *f.*
AMAZEMENT, *s.* surprise, *f.* étonnement, *m.*
AMAZING, *a.* surprenant, de, *de,* étrange, de, *de.*
AMAZINGLY, *ad.* étrangement.
AMBASSADOR, *s.* ambassadeur, *m.*
AMENDS, *s.* compensation, satisfaction, *f.* dedommagement, *m.*
AMID, AMIDST, *pr.* au milieu de, parmi.
AMMUNITION, *s.* munitions de guerre, *f. pl.*
AMONG, AMONGST, *pr.* entre, parmi, au milieu *de,* au travers, avec.
AMOUNT, *vn.* monter à, revenir à.
— *s.* le montant, total, *m.* somme, *f.*
AMPUTATE, *va.* trancher à, couper à, amputer, à.
AMPUTATION, *s.* amputation, *f.*
AMMUNITION, *s.* munitions, *f. pl.*
AMUSE, *va.* amuser, divertir, tromper.
AMUSE ONE'S SELF, s'amuser 'de, à, à.
AN, *art.* un, une.
ANCESTORS, *s. pl.* ancêtres, aïeux, *m. pl.*
ANCIENT, *a.* ancien, ne. antique.

AND, *c.* et.
ANECDOTE, *s.* anecdote, *f.*
ANGEL, *s.* pièce d'ancienne monnaie anglaise, *f.* 12 fr.
— *s.* ange, chérubin, *m.*
ANGRY, *a.* fâché, de, *de,* en colère.
ANIMAL, *s.* animal. *m.*
— *a.* animal, d'animal.
ANIMATE, *va.* animer.
ANIMATED, *a.* animé, excité.
ANIMATION, *s.* animation, *f.*
ANNOUNCE, *va.* annoncer à, publier.
ANNOY, *va.* nuire à, incommoder, ennuyer.
— *s.* préjudice, tort, *m.* peine,*f.*
ANOTHER, *a.* autre, un autre.
ANSWER, *va.* répondre à.
— AGAIN, répliquer à, riposter à, récrire à.
— FOR, rendre compte *de,* répondre *pour,* cautionner.
— *s.* réponse, *f.*
ANTAGONIST, *s.* antagoniste, adversaire, *m.*
ANTIDOTE, *s.* antidote, préservatif, contre-poison, *m.*
ANXIETY, *s.* anxiété, inquiétude, *f.*
ANXIOUS, *a.* inquiet, de, *de,* ardent à, à, impatient, de, curieux, de.
ANY, *pro. a.* quelque, quelqu'un, tout, aucun, qui *ou* quoi que ce soit.
— BODY, *pro.* quelqu'un.
— FARTHER, *ad.* plus loin.
— HOW, *ad.* de quelque manière que ce soit.
— LONGER, *ad.* plus, plus longtemps.
— MORE, *ad.* plus, davantage.
— THING, *pro. a.* quelque chose, tout.

ANY WHERE, *ad.* quelque part, nulle part.
APARTMENT, *s.* appartement, *m.*
APOLOGY, *s.* apologie, excuse, justification, *f.*
APPARENT, *a.* évident, manifeste.
— *Heir apparent*, héritier direct.
APPARENTLY, *ad.* selon les apparences, évidemment, clairement.
APPARITION, *s.* apparition, *f.* spectre, *m.* revenant, *m.* fantôme, *m.*
APPEAR, *vn.* se montrer, paraître, apparaître, comparaître *devant*, sembler, *à.*
APPEARANCE, *s.* apparence, figure, présence, comparation, *f.* aspect, *m.*
APPEASE, *va.* apaiser, calmer.
APPETITE, *s.* appétit, *m.*
APPLY, *v.* appliquer *à*, s'appliquer, à, *à,* s'adresser, *à,* porter, à, *à.*
APPOINT, *va.* nommer, établir, prescrire, de, régler, marquer, *à,* fixer.
APPOINTMENT, *s.* rendez-vous, ordre, *m.* appointements, *m. pl.*
APPREHEND, *va.* se saisir, *de,* appréhender, de, comprendre, craindre, de, arrêter.
APPRENTICE, *s.* apprenti.
— *va.* mettre en apprentissage.
APPRENTICEHOOD,—SHIP, *s.* apprentissage, *m.*
APPROACH, *s* approche, *f.* accès, premiers pas, *m. pl.*
— *v.* approcher *de,* s'approcher, *de.*

APPROPRIATE, *v.* approprier, s'approprier.
APT, *a.* porté, à, *à,* sujet, à, *à,* disposé à, *à.*
ARCHITECT, *s.* architecte, *m.*
ARDENT, *a.* ardent, à, vif, à.
ARDENTLY, *ad.* ardemment.
ARDOR, *s.* ardeur, *f.*
ARGUE, *v.* raisonner *de,* débattre, disputer, prouver, conclure.
ARGUMENT, *s.* argument, *m.*
ARISE, *vn.* se lever.
— *to proceed*), procéder, à, provenir *de,* naître.
ARM, *s.* arme, *f.* bras, soutien, *m.*
— *va.* s'armer, *de,* prendre les armes.
ARMY, *s.* armée, *f.*
AROUND, *pr.* autour, de, tout autour, de.
— *ad.* en cercle, de tous côtés.
ARRANGEMENT, *s.* arrangement, *m.*
ARRIVAL, *s.* arrivée, venue, *f.*
ARRIVE, *vn.* arriver *à, de,* à, parvenir, à, *à,* venir.
ART, *s.* art, artifice, *m.* science, *f.*
ARTICLE, *s.* article, *m.*
ARTIFICIAL, *a.* artificiel.
ARTLESS, *a.* simple, naïf.
ARTLESSLY, *ad.* simplement, sans art.
ARTLESSNESS, *s.* simplicité, *f.*
AS, *c.* comme, aussi que, selon, suivant, si, en, parce que, autant.
AS TO, *pr.* quant à.
AS FAR AS, *pr.* jusque.
ASCEND, *vn.* monter *à,* parvenir à, *à.*
ASK, *va.* demander, à, de, *à,* réclamer *de.*

ASLEEP, *a.* endormi, assoupi.
ASS, *s.* âne, *m.* ânesse, *f.*
ASSASSINATE, *va.* assassiner.
ASSASSINATION, *s.* assassinat, *m.*
ASSEMBLE, *va.* assembler, convoquer.
ASSISTANCE, *s.* aide, assistance, *f.* secours, *m.*
ASSIZES, *s.* assises, *f. pl.*
ASSOCIATE, *s.* associé, confédéré.
— *va.* associer à, mettre en société.
ASSOCIATION, *s.* association, société, *f.*
ASSURE, *va.* assurer à, promettre à, de.
ASTONISH, *va.* étonner, de, surprendre, de, *de.*
ASTONISHMENT, *s.* étonnement, *m.*
ASYLUM, *s.* asile, refuge, *m.*
AT, *pr.* à, au, à la, chez, par, auprès.
— LENGTH, enfin.
— A LOSS, embarrassé,
— AN END, achevé, fini
— A WORD, en un mot.
— FIRST, d'abord, tout à coup.
— HAND, près, à la portée.
— LAST, à la fin, enfin.
— LEISURE, à loisir.
— ODDS, en différend, en dispute.
— PEACE, en paix.
— SEA, sur mer.

ATHEIST, *s.* athée, *m.*
ATTACH, *va.* attacher à, lier, à, arrêter, appartenir à, gagner.
ATTACHMENT, *s.* attachement, *m.* affection, *f.*
ATTACK, *s.* attaque, *f.* assaut, *m.*
— *vn.* attaquer, assaillir.
ATTEMPT, *s.* essai, *m.* entreprise, *f.* attentat, *m.*
ATTEMPT, *va.* entreprendre, de, essayer, de, attenter à.
ATTENDANTS, *s.* suite, *f.*
ATTENTION, *s.* attention, *f.* soin, *m.*
ATTRACT, *vn.* attirer à, tirer à soi.
ATTRACTION, *s.* attraction, *f.* attrait, *m.* amorce, *f.*
ATTRACTIVE, *a.* attrayant, attractif, ve.
AUDIENCE, *s.* audience, *f.* auditoire, *m.*
AUDITOR, *s.* auditeur, celui qui écoute, *m.*
AUDITORY, *s.* auditoire, *m.*
AUSTRIA, *s.* l'Autriche, *f.*
AUSTRIAN, *a.* d'Autriche, autrichien.
AUTHOR, *s.* auteur, inventeur, *m.*
AVAIL, *s.* profit, *m.* utilité, *f.*
AVOID, *va.* éviter, fuir, vider.
AWAIT, *vn.* attendre.
AWAKE, *v.* éveiller, ressusciter, s'éveiller.
AWAY, *ad.* absent, dehors, allez vous-en, hors d'ici.

B.

BACK, *ad.* en arrière, de retour, derrière.
— *va.* monter, soutenir, appuyer.

BACK, *va.* empenneler, coiffer.
— *s.* dos, derrière, revers, dossier, *m.* reins, *m. pl.*
— TO BACK, dos à dos.

BAD, *a.* méchant, mauvais, malade.
BADLY, *ad.* mal, d'une mauvaise manière.
BAG, *s.* sac, *m.* bourse, poche, *f.*
— *va.* mettre dans un sac.
BAGPIPE, *s.* cornemuse, musette, *f.*
BAGPIPER, *s.* joueur de cornemuse, *m.*
BAKER, *s.* boulanger, *m.*
BALL, *s.* boulet, *m.* bille, balle, boule, *f.*
— OF THE HAND, paume de la main, *f.*
— OF THE EYE, prunelle de l'œil, *f.*
BALL, *s.* bal, *m.* danse, *f.*
BALLOT, *s.* ballotte, *f.* tirage, *m.*
BAN, *s.* annonce, *f.* ban, *m.*
BANDIT, BANDITTO, *s.* proscrit, (qui est devenu voleur de grands chemins.)
BANDITTI, *s. pl.* bandits, brigands, *m. pl.*
BANISH, *va.* bannir *de*, exiler, chasser *de*.
BANK, *s.* la banque, digue, hauteur, rive, *f.* établi, rivage, bord, banc, *m.*
— OF THE SEA, écueil, *m.*
— *va.* élever une digue.
BANK-NOTE, BANK-BILL, *s.* billet de banque, *m.*
BANKER, *s.* banquier, *m.*
BAR, *s.* barreau, obstacle, *m.*
— *va.* barrer, empêcher, de.
BARBAROUS, *a.* barbare, de, *envers*, rude, de, *envers*.
BARGAIN, *s.* marché, accord, *m.*
— *va.* marchander.
BARK (*of a tree*) *s.* écorce, *f.*
— *s. ma.* barque, *f.* navire, *m.*
— (*as a dog*), *vn.* aboyer.

BARKING, *s.* aboiement, *m.* l'action d'écorcer les arbres.
BARN, *s.* grange, *f.* grenier, *m.*
BARRICADE, *s.* barricade, *f.*
— *va.* barricader, enfermer, boucher; *ma.* bastinguer.
BASKET, *s.* corbeille, *f.* panier, *m.*
— *Back-basket*, *s.* hotte, *f.*
BATH, *s.* bain, *m.*
BATHE, *v.* se baigner, étuver, bassiner.
BATHING-TUB, *s.* baignoire, *f.*
BATTERY, *s.* batterie, *f.* combat, *m.*
BATTLE, *s.* bataille, *f.* combat, *m.*
— *vn.* se battre *avec*, *contre*, combattre, contester *à*.
BAWBLE, *s.* babiole, bagatelle, *f.*
BAWL, *v.* criailler, crier.
BE, *vn.* être, à, exister.
BE WORTH, *va.* valoir.
BE COMFORTABLE, *vn.* être à son aise.
— IN WANT, *v.* avoir besoin de.
BEAM, *s.* rayon, *m.*
— *v.* rayonner, luire.
BEAR, *v.* porter à, *a*, soutenir, supporter, souffrir, de, endurer, essuyer *à*, de; *ma.* rester à, *à*.
— A PART, avoir part.
— WITNESS, être témoin, *de*.
BEARD, *s.* barbe, *f.* fibres, *f. pl.*
BEARER, *s.* porteur, euse.
BEAST, *s.* bête, *f.* animal, *m.*
BEAT, *v.* battre, frapper *avec*, piler; *ma.* louvoyer.
— TIME, battre la mesure.
BEAUTIFUL, *a.* beau, bel, le, bien fait.
BEAUTIFULLY, *ad.* d'une belle manière, agréablement.
BEAUTY, *s.* beauté, *f.* charme, *m.*

BECALM, va. apaiser, calmer.
BECAUSE, c. parce que, à cause de.
BECOME, v. devenir, seoir à, de, convenir, de, à.
BED, s. lit, carreau, m. couche, f.
BED FELLOW, s. camarade de lit.
BEEF, s. bœuf, m.
BEER, s. bière, f.
BEET, BEETROOT, s. betterave, f.
BEFORE, pr. avant, devant, par-devant, plus que, plutôt que.
BEFORE, ad. auparavant, avant, ci-dessus.
BEG, v. demander, à, à, quêter, prier, de, mendier, supplier, de.
BEGET, va. engendrer, produire, causer.
BEGIN, va. commencer à.
BEHALF, s. faveur, intérêt, m.
BEHEAD, va. décapiter, décoller.
BEHIND, pr. ad. derrière, par derrière.
BEHINDHAND, ad. en arrière, derrière.
BEHOLD, va. regarder, contempler, considérer. pr : voilà.
BELIEF, s. croyance, foi, persuasion, f.
BELIEVE, v. croire, penser.
BELIEVER, s. croyant, fidèle.
BELIEVINGLY, ad. avec foi, sincèrement.
BELIKE, ad. apparemment.
BELL, s. cloche, f. calice d'une fleur, m.
— *Little bell*, sonnette, clochette, f.
BELLY, s. ventre, m.
— va. faire ventre, pousser dehors.

BELONG, vn. appartenir à, concerner.
BELOVED, a. bien-aimé de.
BENCH, s. banc, établi, m.
— va. garnir de bancs.
BENEATH, pr. sous, dessous, au-dessous.
BENEATH, ad. en bas, là-bas, ici-bas, au-dessous.
BENEFIT, s. bienfait, service, bénéfice, profit, m. faveur, grâce, f.
— va. favoriser, faire du bien à, profiter à, gagner.
BENEVOLENCE, s. bienveillance, f.
BENEVOLENT, a. bienveillant pour, envers.
BENUMBED, a. engourdi.
BESEECH, va. prier, de, supplier, de, conjurer, de.
BESIDES, ad. encore, d'ailleurs.
— pr. outre, excepté, hors de, si ce n'est.
— c. d'ailleurs, de plus.
— THAT, outre que.
BESIEGE, va. assiéger.
BEST, a. meilleur, ce qu'il y a de mieux.
— ad. le mieux.
BET, s. pari, m. gageure, f.
— va. parler, gager.
BETIMES, ad. de bonne heure.
BETRAY, v. trahir, livrer, découvrir.
BETTER, s. avantage, m. supériorité, f.
— a. meilleur.
— ad. mieux.
— va. améliorer, s'avancer.
BETWEEN, BETWIXT, pr. entre, dans l'intervalle.
— WHILES, de temps en temps.
— WIND AND WATER, à fleur d'eau.

BETWEEN DECKS, s. ad. ma. entrepont.
BID, v. dire à, de, ordonner à, de, commander à, de, offrir à, de, inviter, à, de, recommander, de.
BILL, s. mémoire, m. affiche, f.
projet de loi, compte, m. carte, note, f.
BIRTHDAY, s. jour de naissance, m. fête, f.
BITE, s. morsure, fourberie, f. filou, m.
BITE, va. mordre, ronger, duper, pincer, railler.
— OFF, emporter le morceau (en mordant).
BITER, s. qui mord, trompeur, m.
BITTER, a. amer, dur, cruel.
BLACK, a. noir, sombre.
— va. noircir, rendre noir.
BLACK-BALL, s. jeton noir.
BLADE, s. lame, f.
BLANKET, s. couverture, f.
BLEACHER, s. blanchisseur, m.
BLEED, v. saigner.
BLESS, va. bénir, rendre heureux.
BLIND, a. aveugle.
BLOOD, s. sang, m. race, extraction, f.
— va. saigner, ensanglanter.
BLOW, s. coup, revers, m. en fleur.
BLOW, v. s'épanouir, souffler, venter, enfler, de, sonner.
BLUNDER, s. étourderie, faute, bévue, f.
— v. se tromper lourdement.
BLUNDERER, s. étourdi, e, sot, te.
BLUSH, s. rougeur, f.
— vn. rougir, de, de.

BOARD, s. ais, bord, navire, conseil, m. table, planche, pension, f.
— va. planchéier, aborder à, accoster.
— vn. être ou vivre en pension.
BOAST, s. vanterie, vanité, parade, f.
— v. se vanter, de, de, vanter à, se glorifier, de, de.
BOAT, s. bateau, m. chaloupe, f.
BODY, s. corps, m. matière, substance, f.
BOIL, v. bouillir, cuire, faire bouillir.
— AWAY, se réduire (en bouillant).
— FAST, bouillir à gros bouillons.
BOILING, s. l'action de faire bouillir.
BOLD, a. hardi, courageux.
BOLDFACED, a. effronté, impudent.
BOLDLY, ad hardiment, librement.
BONE, s. os, m. arête, f.
— va. désosser, disséquer.
BOOK, s. livre, m.
— va. enregistrer, écrire à.
BOOKSELLER, BOOK-SHOP, s. libraire, m. librairie, f.
BOOT, s. botte, f.
— va. servir, a, à, récompenser, de, de, botter.
BORN, a. né, pour, destiné, à, à, sorti, de.
BORROW, s. emprunt, m.
— va. emprunter de.
BOSOM, s. sein, m. amitié, f.
BOTH, a. l'un et l'autre, tous les deux.

BOTH, c. tant.
— SIDES, les deux côtés, de part et d'autre, tantôt d'un parti et tantôt d'un autre.
BOTTLE, s. bouteille, f.
— va. mettre en bouteilles.
BOTTOM, s. fond, but, motif, m.
BOUND, s. borne, limite, f. terme, bond, saut, rebondissement, m.
— v. limiter, à, aboutir, à, à, bondir.
— a. destiné, à, à, obligé.
BOW, v. courber, plier, fléchir.
— DOWN, se prosterner à.
— ONE'S HEAD, baisser la tête.
— TO ONE, faire la révérence, saluer.
— s. révérence, f. arc, archet, demi circle, m.
BOWL, s. (FOR DRINKING), grande tasse, jatte, f. coupe, f. cuvette, f.
BOX, s. loge, f. soufflet, m. boite, caisse, f.
BOY, s. enfant, garçon, m
BOYISH, a. puéril, enfantin.
BRACE, s. couple, paire, f. deux.
BRACELET, s. bracelet, brassard, m.
BRAN, s. son, m.
BRANCH, va. diviser en branches.
— vn. pousser des branches.
— s. branche, f.
BRAND, s. flétrissure, f. tison, m.
— va. flétrir, diffamer, noircir, marquer d'un fer chaud.
BRAVE, a. brave, vaillant, excellent.
— s. bravache, défi, m.
— va. braver, défier, morguer.
— IT, va. faire le brave.

BREAK, v. rompre à, avec, casser à, briser à, crever à, éclater, interrompre, faire banqueroute, percer, fendre, violer, ruiner.
BREAK OPEN, enfoncer, forcer, ouvrir.
BREAKFAST, s. déjeuner, m.
— vn. déjeuner.
BREAST, s. poitrine, f. sein, cœur, m.
BREATH, s. haleine, f. souffle, m.
BREATHE, v. respirer, souffler, exercer.
BRETHREN, s. fraternité, f. frères, m.
BRIBE, s. présent (donné pour corrompre).
— va. corrompre, suborner.
BRIDE, s. épousée, nouvelle mariée, f.
BRIDGE, s pont, chevalet, m.
— OF BOATS, s. ponton, m.
— va. construire un pont.
BRING, va. apporter à, amener à, à, mettre à, servir, à, à, réduire, à, à, exciter, à, à.
— ABOUT, faire venir adroitement, venir à bout de, de, faire réussir.
— ON, amener, causer.
— ABOUT AGAIN, rétablir.
— AN ACTION, intenter action ou procès.
— BACK, ramener.
— UP, élever.
BRONZE, s. bronze, m.
BROOK, s. ruisseau, m.
BROTHER, s. (pl. BROTHERS, BRETHREN), frère. m.
— IN-LAW, beau-frère, m.
— *Elder brother*, frère aîné.
— *Younger brother*, cadet.

BROTHERHOOD, *s.* fraternité, *f.*
BROTHERLY, *a.* fraternel, le.
— *ad.* fraternellement.
BRUISE, *va.* meurtrir *de*, froisser, égruger, concasser, broyer, piler.
BRUISE, *s.* meurtrissure, contusion, *f.*
BRUSH, *s.* brosse, *f.*
— *v.* brosser, décrotter, vergeter.
BUILD, *va.* bâtir, construire, édifier.
— ON, *m.* compter *sur.*
BUILDING, *s.* édifice, bâtiment, *m.*
BUNCH, *s.* bosse, tumeur, *f.* nœud, *m.* grappe, botte, *f.* faisceau, trousseau, fagot, *m.* touffe, *f.* panache, *m.*
BURIAL, *s.* sépulture, *f.*
BURIAL-PLACE, *s.* lieu de sépulture, *m.*
BURN, *v.* brûler.
BURST, *v.* crever *de*, éclater, débonder, fondre, enfoncer.

BURST OUT A LAUGHING, *v.* éclater de rire.
BURY, *va.* enterrer, ensevelir.
BURYING-PLACE, *s* sépulture, *f.*
BUSINESS, *s.* affaire, *f.*
BUSY, *a.* affairé, occupé, actif, ve.
— *va.* occuper, employer.
BUSYBODY, affairé, entremetteur, intrigant, *m.* tracassier, ère.
BUT, *c.* mais, hormis que, seulement, excepté.
BUTTON, *s.* bouton, *m.*
BUY, *va.* acheter, *à, de.*
BUYER, *s.* acheteur, euse.
BY, *pr.* par, de, à, au, à la, près, proche, à côté de, près de, sur, en.
— *ad.* à quelque distance d'un endroit.
— AND BY, *ad.* tout à l'heure.
BY PLACE, *s.* réduit, lieu écarté, *m.*
BY-STANDER, *s.* spectateur, trice.

C.

CADI, *s.* cadi, juge, *m.*
CALAMITY, *s.* calamité, *f.* malheur, *m.*
CALCULATE, *va.* calculer, compter.
CALCULATION, *s.* calcul, *m.*
CALIPH, CALIF, *s.* calife, *m.*
CALL, *s.* appel, *m.* invitation, *f.*
— *v.* appeler, à, *à*, venir, nommer, convoquer.
— AGAIN, rappeler, faire revenir, repasser.
— ALOUD, pousser un cri, s'écrier.
— ASIDE, tirer de côté.

CALL AT A PLACE, passer par un endroit.
— AT ONE'S HOUSE, passer *chez.*
— AWAY, faire sortir, emmener.
— BACK, rappeler, révoquer.
— DOWN, faire descendre.
— FOR, appeler, demander, venir chercher, aller chercher.
— FORTH, faire sortir *ou* venir.
— IN, retirer, rétracter, mander, de, *à*, faire entrer *dans.*
— OFF, détourner, de, *de*, dissuader, de, *de.*

CALL ON exhorter, à, animer, à, invoquer, passer chez.
— OUT, faire sortir.
— OVER, repasser, se rappeler.
— TOGETHER, assembler, convoquer.
— TO ONE, en appeler à, invoquer.
— UP, faire monter, éveiller, évoquer.
— UPON ONE, aller voir quelqu'un.
CALMLY, ad. tranquillement.
CALMNESS, s. sérénité, tranquillité.
CAMP, s. camp, m.
— vn. camper, se camper, se poster.
CAMPAIGN, s. campagne, f.
CAN, vn. pouvoir.
CANDLE, s. chandelle, f.
CANE, s. canne, f. roseau, bâton, m.
— va. donner des coups de canne à.
CANINE, a. canin, qui tient du chien.
CANNON, s. canon, m.
CANNON-BALL, boulet de canon.
CAP, s. bonnet, m. casquette, f.
CAPABLE, a. capable, de, susceptible, de.
CAPITAL, s. capital, chapiteau, m. capitale, f.
— a. capitale, grand, principal.
CAPRICE, s. caprice, m. fantaisie, f.
CAPTAIN, s. capitaine, m.
CAPTOR, s. capteur, preneur, m.
CARAVAN, s. caravane, f. compagnie de marchands en voyage.
CARD, s. carte, carde, f.

CARE, s. soin, souci, m. inquiétude, f.
— vn. se soucier, de, de, s'inquiéter de, de.
CAREFUL, a. soigneux, de, assidu, à, attentif, à, avisé, chagrin.
CAREFULLY, ad soigneusement.
CAREFULNESS, s. attention, f. soin, m.
CARELESS, a. nonchalant, insouciant, négligent, négligé.
CARELESSLY, ad. nonchalamment.
CARELESSNESS, s. nonchalance, négligence, inattention, f.
CARESS, s. caresse, flatterie, f
— vn. caresser, cajoler.
CARRIAGE, s, voiture, f. port, m.
CARRY, va. porter à, mener à, contenir, porter au compte de.
— ALONG, emporter, mener.
— OFF, remporter, emporter.
CART, s. charrette, f. chariot, m.
— va. transporter (sur un charrette).
CART LOAD, s. charretée, f.
CARTER, s. charretier, voiturier, m.
CASE, s. étui, fourreau, m. case, boite, f.
— s. cas, état, sujet, fait, m. place, f.
CAST, v. jeter à, lancer à, fondre, se dépouiller de, condamner, se déjeter ; ma. abattre.
CAST A STATUE, fondre une statue.
CAT, s. chat, m chatte, f. ma. espèce de vaisseau de charge, capon, m.
CATCH, va. attraper, prendre à, ravir à, atteindre.

CATCH AT, chercher, donner prise à, porter les mains sur.
— UP, a. ravi, enlevé.
CAUSE, s. cause, raison, f. motif, sujet, parti, procès, fait, m.
— va. causer, d, faire, d, exciter, à.
— LOVE, donner de l'amour.
— SLEEP, faire dormir.
— SORROW, causer du chagrin.
CAUTION, s. avis, avertissement, m. prudence, precaution, f.
— va avertir, de.
CAVALCADE, s. cavalcade, f.
CAVALIER, s. cavalier, m.
CAVALRY, s. cavalerie, f.
CEASE, v. cesser, de, discontinuer, de, finir, de.
CEASELESS, a. continuel.
CEILING, s. lambris, plafond, m.
CELEBRATE, va. célébrer, louer, de, de.
CELEBRATED, a. célèbre, par, pour.
CELL, s. cellule, f. donjon, m. prison, f.
CENTURY, s. siècle, m. centurie, f.
CEREMONY, s. cerémonie, formalité, f.
CERTAIN, a. sûr, de, de, certain, de, assuré, de, de.
CERTAINLY, ad. certainement.
CHAIR, s. chaise, f. siège à dos, m.
CHAIR (SEDAN), s. chaise à porteurs, f.
— (ARM, ELBOW-), s. fauteuil, m.
CHAISE, s. phaéton, m. chaise, f. cabriolet, m.
CHALLENGE, s. appel, cartel, m. demande, prétention, récusation, f.

CHALLENGE, va. défier, de, réclamer, de, récuser, sommer, de, accuser, de, de.
CHAMBER, s. chambre, f.
CHAMBERMAID, s. femme de chambre, f.
CHANCE, s. chance, f. hasard, m.
— vn. arriver, à.
CHANCELLOR, s. chancelier, garde des sceaux, m.
CHANGE, s. changement, m. la Bourse, f. échange, change, m. monnaie, f.
— va. changer de, échanger.
— FOR, changer pour.
CHANNEL, s. Manche, f. canal, lit, détroit, m.
CHAPLAIN, s. aumônier, chapelaine, m.
CHARACTER, s. caractère, m. marque, écriture, description, lettre, f.
CHARGE, s. charge, dépense, f. monitoire, soin, dépôt, m.
— va. demander, de, à, recommander, de, à, accuser, de.
CHARGER, s. cheval de bataille, m.
CHARLATANRY, CHARLATANISM, s charlatanerie, f.
CHEAP, a. à bon marché, à bas prix.
CHEAPLY, ad. à bon marché, facilement.
CHEAT, s. fourberie, f. fraude, tromperie, f. fourbe, imposteur, filou, m.
— va. fourber, tromper, filouter.
CHEEK, s. joue, f.
CHEERFUL, a. gai, agréable.
CHEESE, s. fromage, m.
— CAKE, s. talmouse, f. raton, m.

CHEESEMONGER, s. marchand de fromages.
CHEMIST, s. chimiste, m.
CHEMISTRY, s. chimie, f.
CHERISH, va. chérir, aimer, à, nourrir, échauffer, caresser.
CHERRY, s. cerise, f.
CHESS, s. jeu des échecs, m. échecs, pl.
CHESS-BOARD, s. échiquier, m.
CHEST, s. caisse, f. coffre, m. poitrine, f.
— OF DRAWERS, s. commode, f.
CHIEF, s. chef, général, coryphée, m.
— a. principal, premier, ère.
CHILD (CHILDREN, pl.), s. enfant, m. f.
CHILLED, a. glacé, refroidi.
CHIMNEY, s. cheminée, f.
CHIMNEY-CORNER, s. le coin du feu.
CHIMNEY-HOOK, s. croissant, m.
CHIMNEY-PIECE, s. manteau de cheminée, m.
CHIMNEY-SWEEPER, s. ramoneur, m.
CHOICEST, a. meilleur, mieux, choici, délicieux.
CHOKE, v. étouffer, suffoquer.
CHRISTIAN, s. chrétien, ne.
CHURCH, s. église, f.
CHURCHYARD, s. cimitière, m.
CIRCLE, s. cercle, m. société, f.
CIRCULATE, vn. circuler, faire circuler.
CIRCUMSTANCE, s. circonstance, condition, f. événement, m. position, f.
CITIZEN, s. citoyen, ne, citadin, bourgeois.
CITY, s. ville, cité, f.
CIVIL, a. civil, honnête, complaisant pour, envers.

CLAIM, s. prétention, demande, f. reclamation, f.
— va. réclamer de, exiger, de, de, demander, de, de.
CLAMOROUS, a. bruyant, tumultueux.
CLAMOUR, s. bruit, m. plainte, clameur, f.
— vn. crier, s'écrier.
CLASSIC, a. classique, approuvé, e.
— The classics, s. les belles-lettres, f.
CLEAR, va. éclairer, expliquer à, liquider, nettoyer, purger, purifier, acquitter, débarrasser de, démêler, absoudre, de.
— ACCOUNTS, v. régler des comptes.
— THE ROOM, vider la chambre, débarrasser de.
— THE TABLE, desservir.
— UP, s'éclairer, devenir clair, éclaircir.
CLEARED, a. vide, éclairci.
CLENCH, va. attacher à, river à.
CLENCHED, a. fermé, serré.
CLERK, s. clerc, homme d'église, commis, m.
CLEVER, a. habile, spirituel.
CLIMB, v. grimper à, monter à, sur, gravir.
— UP WITH A LADDER, escalader.
CLINCH, va. serrer, fermer, river à.
CLOAK, s. manteau, prétexte, m.
— va. couvrir de, déguiser, pallier.
CLOCK, s. horloge, pendule, f.
CLOSE, ad. tout près.
— TO, adv. tout près de, à deux pas de.
CLOSED, a. fermé.

CLOSET, *s.* cabinet, *m.*
— *va.* enfermer dans un cabinet, parler en secret.
CLOTH, *s.* drap, *m.* toile, nappe, *f.*
CLOTHE, *va.* vêtir *de*, revêtir *de*, habiller *de.*
CLOTHES, *s.* hardes, *f. pl.* habillement, habit, linge, *m.*
CLOUD, *s.* nuage, *m.*
— *v.* obscurcir, couvrir *de.*
CLUTCHES, *s.* griffes, pattes, *f. pl.*
COACH, *s.* carrosse, *m.* voiture, *f.*
COACH-BOX, *s.* siége du cocher, *m.*
COACH-HIRE, *s.* louage de carrosse, *m.*
COACH-HOUSE, *s.* remise, *f.*
COACH-MAKER, *s.* carrossier, *m.*
COACHMAN, *s.* cocher, *m.*
COAST, *s.* côte, *f.* rivage, *m.*
— *v.* côtoyer.
COAT, *s.* habit, justaucorps, *m.*
— GREAT COAT, *s.* pardessus, *m.* capote, *f.* carrick, *m.*
— *va.* couvrir *de*, habiller *de*, revêtir *de.*
COCK, *v.* armer (un pistolet, etc.)
COCKNEY, *s.* badaud, *m.*
COFFIN, *s.* cercueil, *m.*
— *va.* mettre dans un cercueil.
COLD, *a.* froid, réservé.
— *To grow cold*, se refroidir.
— *s.* rhume, *m.* froidure, *f.* froid, *m.*
COLLEAGUE, *s.* collègue, associé, *m.*
COLLECT, *va.* rassembler, recueillir, lever.
COLLEGE, *s.* collége, *m.*
— OF PHYSICIANS, faculté de médecine, *f.*

COLLEGIAN, *s.* membre d'un collége, *m.*
COMBAT, *s.* combat, duel, *m.*
— *v.* combattre, se battre.
COME, *vn.* venir, à, *de* arriver *à*, *de*, à, parvenir, à, *à*, aborder, à, se réduire, à, *à*, revenir, s'adresser, *à*, accoster, aboutir, à, *à*, devenir, réussir, à, se terminer.
COME OUT, *vn.* sortir.
COME DOWN, *v.* descendre.
COME UP, *v.* monter, survenir.
COMFORT, *s.* consolation, *f.* agrément, *m.* comfort, *m.*
— *v.* consoler, soulager.
COMFORTABLE, *a.* bon, consolant, bien, comfortable.
— LIFE, *s.* vie douce, *f.*
COMMAND, *va.* ordonner, *à*, de, commander, *à*, de.
COMMENCE, *v.* commencer, à, de, intenter.
COMMISSION, *s.* commission, *f.* brevet, *m.*
COMMIT, *va.* commettre, à, *à*, mettre *à*, remettre, confier.
— TO PRISON, envoyer en prison.
COMMODITY, *s.* commodité, denrée, *f.* article, *m.*
COMMON, *a.* common, vulgaire, ordinaire.
— *s.* bruyères, landes, terre inculte, plaine.
COMMUNICATE, *va.* communiquer, à, communier.
COMMUNICATION, *s.* communication.
COMPANION, *s.* compagnon, camarade, *m.* compagne, *f.*
COMPANY, *s.* compagnie, société, *f.*
COMPEL, *va.* contraindre, à, de, forcer, à, de.

COMPENSATION, s dédommagement, m. indemnité, f.
COMPLAIN, v. plaindre, de, se plaindre, de.
COMPLAINANT, s. complaignant, plaignant, m.
COMPLAINER, s. celui qui se plaint.
COMPLAINT, s. plainte, maladie, f.
COMPLAISANCE, s. complaisance, civilité, f.
COMPLAISANT, a. complaisant, e. affable.
COMPLETE, a. complet, ète, entier, tière, parfait, finie.
— vn. achever, de, compléter, rendre complet.
COMPLETELY, ad. complétement, parfaitement.
COMPLY, vn. acquiescer, à, condescendre, à, d, se commettre à, d, se conformer à, à.
COMPOSE, va. composer, se composer, disposer, constituer, adoucir.
COMPOSITION, s. composition, f. ouvrage, m.
COMRADE, s. compagnon, camarade, m.
CONCEAL, va. celer, d, cacher, d.
CONCEIVE, v. concevoir, imaginer.
CONCERNING, pr. concernant, touchant.
CONCLUDE, v. conclure, terminer, inférer, fixer, determiner, se résoudre, d.
CONDEMN, va. condamner d, à, blâmer, de, de.
CONDEMNATION, s. condamnation, f.
CONDITION, s. condition, f. état, rang, m.

CONDITION, vn. faire un accord, stipuler.
CONDUCT, va. conduire, d, mener, d.
CONDUCT BACK, reconduire, d.
CONFEDERATED, a. confédéré, alliée, fieffé, v.
— va. se liguer, conspirer, s'allier d.
CONFEDERATES, s. alliés, m. pl.
CONFER, v. conférer, d, revêtir de, s'aboucher avec.
CONFESS, v. confesser, d, avouer, d, reconnaitre.
CONFIDE, vn. se fier, d, se reposer sur, confier à.
CONFIDENCE, s. confiance, hardiesse, f.
CONFIDENT, a. effronté, assuré de.
CONFIDENTLY, ad. hardiment, pour certain, avec confiance, sans crainte.
CONFINE, va. confiner, modérer, retenir, emprisonner, borner.
CONFINE ONE'S SELF, se borner, à, d.
CONFINEMENT, s. emprisonnement, assujettisement, m. contrainte, f.
CONFIRMATION, s. confirmation, preuve, f.
CONFISCATE, vn. confisquer, saisir.
CONFORMABLY, ad. conformément.
CONFOUND, va. confondre, rendre confus, desoler, de, troubler.
CONFUSION, s. confusion, ruine, honte, f. embarras, désordre, m.
CONGRATULATION, s. félicitation, f.
CONQUER, v. vaincre, conquérir.

CONQUEROR, *s.* vainqueur, conquérant, *m.*
CONQUEST, *s.* conquête, victoire, *f.*
CONSCIENCE, *s.* conscience, *f.*
CONSECRATE, *a.* consacré, à, dédié, *à.*
CONSECRATE, *va.* consacrer *à*, dédier *à*, dévouer *à.*
CONSENT, *s.* consentement, aveu, *m.*
— *vn.* consentir, acquiescer.
CONSEQUENCE, *s.* consequence, suite, importance, *f.*
CONSEQUENTLY, *ad.* par conséquent.
CONSIDER, *v.* considérer, examiner, avoir égard *à*, songer *à*, méditer *sur*, se présenter, reconnaître, estimer.
CONSIDERABLE, *a.* considerable.
CONSOLE, *va.* soulager *de*, consoler, de, *de.*
CONSPICUOUS, *a.* remarquable, éminent, visible.
CONSPICUOUSLY, *ad* visiblement, d'une manière remarquable.
CONSPIRACY, *s.* conspiration, *f.* complot, *m.*
CONSPIRATOR, *s.* conspirateur, *m.*
CONSPIRE, *vn.* conspirer, conjurer.
CONSTANT, *a.* constant, durable.
CONSTRUCT, *va.* construire, bâtir.
CONSTRUCTION, *s.* construction, *f.* édifice, sens, *m.*
CONSULT, *v.* consulter, deliberer *sur.*
— *s.* consultation, *f.* avis, *m.*
CONSULTATION, *s.* consultation, *f.* délibération, *f.*

CONTAGION, *s.* contagion, peste, *f.*
CONTAIN, *v.* contenir, tenir, réprimer.
CONTEMPLATE, *va.* contempler, regarder en face.
CONTEMPT, *s.* mépris, *m.*
CONTENT, *s.* contentment, contenu, *m.*
— *a.* content, de, *de,* satisfait, de, *de.*
— *va.* contenter, satisfaire, plaire *à.*
CONTENTS, *s.* contenu, *m.*
CONTINUAL, *a.* continuel, perpetuel.
CONTINUALLY, *ad.* continuellement.
CONTINUE, *v.* continuer, de, à, persister, à, durer, prolonger, perpétuer, conserver, séjourner *à*, demeurer, à, *à*, poursuivre.
CONTRACT, *v.* contracter, convenir, de, *de,* amasser, abréger, resserrer, rétrécir, se retirer.
CONTRARY, *s.* contraire, *m.*
— *a* contraire, opposé.
— *va.* contrarier, contradire.
CONTRIVE, *v.* inventer, de, imaginer, de, pratiquer, ménager, tramer, méditer, de, concerter, de, faire, parvenir, *à.*
CONVERSATION, *s.* conversation, *f.* entretien, commerce familier, *m.*
CONVERSE, *s.* habitude, conversation, familiarité, communication, *f.*
CONVERSE, *va.* converser, s'entretenir *de,* frequenter.
CONVEY, *va.* transporter *à*, envoyer *à.*
— AWAY, emporter.

Convict, s. condamné, m.
Convicted, a. condamné.
Convince, va. convaincre, de, de, persuader d, de, vaincre, subjuguer.
Convulsion, s. convulsion, f. tumulte, accès.
Cook, s. cuisinier, ère.
Cook, va. apprêter, faire cuire.
Cookery, s. l'art du cuisinier, m.
Cook-maid, s. cuisinière, f. servante de cuisine, f.
Cook-shop, s. rôtisserie, f. traiteur, m.
Coquetry, s. coquetterie, f.
Coquette, s. coquette, f.
Cork, s. liége, bouchon, m.
Corn, s. blé, m.
Corn-field, s. champ de blé, m.
Corner, s. coin, angle, m. encoignure, f.
— house, s. maison du coin, f.
Correct, a. correct, exact.
— va. corriger, châtier.
— ad. correctement.
Correction, s. correction, f. châtiment, m.
Cost, s. prix, frais, dépens, m.
Cost, v. coûter, de, à, revenir à.
Cottage, s. chaumière, cabane, f.
Cottager, s. (qui vit dans une cabane ou chaumière) paysan, m.
Counsel, s. conseil, avis, avocat, m.
— va. conseiller, à, de, donner conseil à, de.
Counsellor, s. conseiller, avocat, m.
Count (earl), s. comte, m.
— v. compter, croire, faire fond sur.

Countenance, s. figure, f. contenance, f.
Country, s. patrie, f. pays, champ, m. contrée, campagne, région, f.
— a. rustique, rural, champêtre.
Countryman, woman, s. provincial, campagnard, compatriote.
Country-seat, s. maison de campagne, f.
Courage, s. courage, m. bravoure, f.
Courageous, a. courageux.
Courageously, adv. courageusement.
Courageousness, s. intrépidité, f.
Course, s. cours, courant, m.
Court, s. cour, ruelle, f. parvis, m.
Court, va. faire la cour à, courtiser.
Courtier, s. courtisan, m.
Cover, s. couvert, couvercle, couvre-plat, m. couverture, enveloppe, f.
— (pretence), prétexte, manteau, m.
Cover, va. couvrir de, déguiser, cacher avec, remplir de, combler de, obscurcir.
Cow, s. vache, f.
Coward, s. poltron, ne, lâche.
Cowardice, s. poltronnerie, f.
Cowardly, a. lâche, poltron, ne.
— ad. lâchement, en poltron.
Cradle, s. berceau, m. éclisse, f.
— va. coucher dans un berceau.
Crane, s. grue, f. siphon, m.

CRAWL, *vn.* ramper, se traîner, s'insinuer *dans.*
— OUT, sortir.
— UP, grimper *sur.*
CREDITOR, *s.* créancier, ère.
CREDULITY, *s.* crédulité, facilité de croire, *f.*
CREDULOUS, *a.* crédule.
CREEP, *v.* ramper, se traîner, glisser, s'insinuer *dans*, aller doucement.
— INTO, s'introduire *dans.*
CREW, *s.* equipage, *m.* bande, *f.*
CRIER, *s.* crieur, *m.*
CRIME, *s.* crime, forfait, *m.*
CRIMINAL, *a. s.* criminel, de, coupable, de, *de.*
CRITICISE, *v.* critiquer, censurer.
CROSS, *s.* croix, traverse, affliction, *f.*
— *a.* oblique, en travers, de travers.
— (*abusive*), choquant, dur.
— (*contrary*), contraire.
— (*peevish*), bourru, fantasque.
— (*troublesome*), fâcheux, se.
— (*untoward*), revêche, têtu.
— *v.* traverser, croiser, passer, fâcher, de, contrarier, faire mal *à.*
CROSS-QUESTION, *s.* quiproquo, *m.* méprise, *f.*
CROWD, *s.* foule, multitude, presse, *f.*
CROWD, *v.* presser, serrer, fourmiller.
— IN, se jeter dedans en foule, entrer en foule, enfoncer.
CROWN, *s.* couronne, *f.* diadéme, *m.*
— (*coin*), écu, *m.*
CROWN, *va.* couronner *de.*
CRUEL, *a.* cruel *envers*, rude *envers*, impitoyable *envers.*

CRUELLY, *ad.* cruellement.
CRUELNESS, CRUELTY, *s.* cruauté, *f.*
CRUSH, *v.* écraser.
CRY, *s.* cri, pleurs, *m. pl.* clameur, *f.*
— *vn.* crier *à*, pleurer *de*, appeler, publier.
— ALOUD, élever la voix.
— DOWN, décrier, décréditer.
— OUT, s'écrier, crier, se récrier.
CRYING, *s.* cri, *m.*
CULPABLE, *a.* blâmable, coupable.
CULPRIT, *s.* accusé, criminel, *m.*
CULTIVATE, *va.* cultiver, perfectionner.
CUNNING, *a.* fin, rusé, adroit, subtil, malin, igne.
CUP, *s.* coupe, tasse, *f.*
CURATE, *s.* vicaire, curé, *m.*
CURIOSITY, *s.* curiosité, *f.*
CURIOUS, *a.* curieux, exact, exquis, admirable, délicat, fin.
CURIOUSLY, *ad.* curieusement.
CUSTODY, *s.* garde, prison, *f.*
CUSTOM, *s.* coutume, habitude, *f.*
CUT, *v.* couper *à*, tailler, *à*, trancher *à*, se couper.
— A FIGURE, faire figure.
— A LOAF, entamer un pain.
— ASUNDER, déchirer, couper, briser.
— DOWN, abattre, scier.
— OFF, extirper, élider, séparer, priver, de, *de*, retrancher *à*, tailler, couper.
— OUT, tailler, couper.
— SMALL, hacher, apetisser.
— SHORT, interrompre, abréger.
CUTLER, *s.* coutelier, fourbisseur.

D.

DAILY, a. journalier, ère, quotidien, ne.
DAINTY, a. friand.
DAMAGE, va. endommager, nuire à.
— s. dommage, tort, m. ma. avarie, f.
DAMAGES, s. pl. dommages-intérêts, m. pl.
DANCE, s. danse, f.
— v. danser, faire danser.
DANCING, s. danse, f.
DANCING MASTER, s. maître de danse, m.
DANGER, s. danger, péril, risque, m.
DANGEROUS, a. dangereux.
DANGEROUSLY, ad. dangereusement.
DARE, s. défi, appel, m.
DARE, v. oser, défier, de, braver.
— SAY, v. oser dire, à, croire bien.
DARK, s. ténèbres, f. pl. obscurité, f.
— a obscur, sombre, noir.
— LANTERN, s. lanterne sourde, f.
DART, s. dard, javelot, trait, m.
— v. darder, lancer à, se lancer.
DATE, s. date, f. quantième, m.
DAUGHTER, s. fille, f.
DAUGHTER-IN-LAW, s. belle-fille, bru, f.
DAUNT, v. dompter, effrayer.
DAUPHIN, s. dauphin, m.
DAY, s. jour, m. journée, f.
— BEFORE YESTERDAY, avant-hier.
— (time, life), s. jour, temps, siècle, m. vie, f.

DAY-SCHOLAR, s. externe, m.
DAY (TO-), ad. aujourd'hui, ce jour.
DEAD, s. les morts, m. pl.
— mort, lâche, pesant, lourd, éventé, engourdi.
DEADLY, a. mortel, terrible.
DEAF, DEAFEN, v. assourdir.
DEAF, a. sourd, e. qui n'entend pas.
DEAL (A GREAT), ad. beaucoup, de.
— v. trafiquer, en agir, traiter, distribuer, faire.
DEAN, s. doyen, m.
DEAR, a. cher, ère. de grand prix, chéri.
— ad. cher, beaucoup.
DEARLY, ad. chèrement, tendrement.
DEATH, s. mort, f. trépas, m.
DEATH BED, s. agonie, f. lit de mort, m.
DEATH-HUNTER, s. croque-mort, m.
DEBT, s. dette, f.
DECAPITATE, va. décapiter, décoller.
DECEASE, s. décès, trépas, m. mort, f.
— vn. décéder, mourir de.
DECEASED, a. mort, décédé.
DECEIVE, vn. tromper, abuser, attraper.
DECEPTION, s. tromperie, fraude, f.
DECIDE, va. décider, de, à, terminer, finir, de.
DECISION, s. décision, détermination, f.
DECLARE, v. déclarer à, avouer, notifier à, de.

DECLARER, s. celui qui déclare.
DECLENSION, s. déclinaison, décadence, f. déclin, dépérissement, m.
DEEP, a. profond, grand, haut, chargé, rusé, caché, abstrus.
DEEPLY, ad. profondément, bien avant.
— IN DEBT, chargé de dettes, m.
DEFEAT, s. défaite, déroute, f.
— va. mettre en déroute, battre.
— (a design), frustrer.
— (make void), annuler, casser.
DEFENCE, s. défense, protection, f.
DEFENDANT, s. défendeur, défenderesse (en loi), accusé.
DEFER, v. différer de, remettre de, déférer à.
DEFY, s. défi, appel, m.
— va. défier, de, braver, mépriser.
DEGRADED, a. avili, disgracié.
DEGREE, s. degré, rang, m. condition f.
DEIGN, vn. daigner, permettre, à, de.
DELIBERATE, a. avisé.
— v. délibérer, sur, aviser, à, à, considérer.
DELIBERATELY, ad. mûrement, avec délibération, de propos délibéré.
DELICACY, s. délicatesse, friandise, f.
DELICIOUS, a. délicieux, se, exquis.
DELIGHT, s. délices, f. pl. plaisir, m.
— v. plaire, à, délecter, réjouir, récréer, aimer, à, se plaire, à, se divertir, charmer, ravir.

DELIGHTFUL, a. délectable, charmant.
DELIGHTFULLY, ad. délicieusement.
DELIVER, va. délivrer, de, livrer, à, prononcer, s'énoncer, exprimer, accoucher, de, remettre, à, abandonner, à.
— IN TRUST, confier, à.
— UP, livrer, à, remettre, à, rendre, à.
DEMAND, s. demande, requête, f.
— va. demander, à, à, de, réclamer, de.
DEMOLISH, va. démolir, abattre.
DEMOLITION, s. démolition, f.
DENOUNCE, va. dénoncer, à, déclarer, à.
DENY, va. nier, dénier, refuser, à, de; renier, renoncer, à, à, abjurer.
— ONE'S SELF, se faire celer, se refuser, à.
DEPART, s. départ, m. mort, f.
— v. partir, de, sortir, de, mourir, quitter, diviser, séparer.
DEPARTURE, s. départ, renoncement, désistement, m.
— (death), s. trépas, m. mort, f.
— (deviation), s. égarement, m.
DEPEND, vn. dépendre, de, de.
DEPRIVE, va. priver, de, de, ôter, à, dépouiller, de.
DEPTH, s. profondeur, f.
DEPUTATION, s. députation, délégation, f.
DERVISE, s. dervis ou derviche, m. religieux.
DESCRIBE, va. décrire, représenter.
DESCRIPTION, s. description, f.
DESERVE, v. mériter, de, être digne, de, de.

DESIRABLE, a. desirable, à souhaiter.
DESIRE, s. désir, souhait, m. envie, f.
— (request), s. prière, demande, f.
DESIRE, va. désirer, prier, de, ordonner, à, de.
DESIROUS, a. passionné, qui désire.
DESPAIR, s. désespoir, m.
— vn. désespérer, de, perdre l'espérance, de.
DESPATCH, s. dépêche, expédition, f.
— va. dépêcher, à, expédier, à.
DESPERATE, a. désespéré, au désespoir.
DESPISE, va. mépriser, de, dédaigner, de.
DESTROY, va. détruire, ruiner, défaire.
— (lay waste), saccager, ravager.
— ONE'S SELF, se tuer, se suicider.
DESTRUCTIVE, a. funeste, à, pernicieux, se.
DETAIN, v. détenir, retenir, à, tenir.
DETECT, va. découvrir, à, révéler, à.
DETECTION, s. découverte, f.
DETERMINATION, s. détermination, décision, f.
DETERMINE, v. déterminer, de, à, se resoudre, à, à.
DEVIL, s. diable, m.
DEVOTE, va. dévouer à, vouer à, consacrer, à.
DEVOTEDNESS, s. dévouement, m.
DEVOTION, s. dévotion, disposition, f. dévouement, m.
DEVOUR, va. dévorer, engloutir.

DIABOLICAL, DIABOLIC, a. diabolique.
DIABOLICALLY, ad. diaboliquement.
DIAMOND, s. diamant, m.
— (AT CARDS), s. carreau, m.
DICTATION, s. dictée, f. ordre, m.
DIE (decease), vn. mourir de, périr de.
— (to fade), se flétrir.
DIFFERENCE, s. différence, f. différend, m.
— va. différencier, distinguer.
DIFFERENT, a. différent, de, divers.
DIFFICULTY, s. difficulté, peine, f.
DIG, va. creuser, bêcher, fouir.
— OUT, déterrer, arracher.
— UP, bêcher, enlever (la terre).
DIGNITY, s. dignité, grandeur, f.
DILIGENCE, s. diligence, activité, f.
DINE, v. diner, donner à diner, à.
DINING-ROOM, s. salle à manger, f.
DINNER, s. diner, diné, m.
DIRECT, a. direct, droit, ouvert.
— va. diriger, montrer, à, conduire, à.
DIRECT (a letter), adresser, à.
— (steer), faire voile, faire route, gouverner.
DIRECTION, s. direction, conduite, instruction, f. ordre, m.
DIRECTLY, ad. à l'instant, sur-le-champ, en droite ligne.
DISAPPEARANCE, s. disparition, f.

DISCHARGE, s. congé, m.
— v. décharger, de, acquitter, délivrer, congédier, relâcher, exempter, de, de, expédier, à, se jeter, lancer à, renvoyer.
DISCONCERT, va. déconcerter.
DISCOURAGE, va. décourager, de, rebuter.
DISCOVER, va. découvrir à, apercevoir, s'apercevoir de.
DISCOVERY, s. découverte, f.
DISCUSSION, s. discussion, f. examen, m.
DISDAIN, s. dédain, mépris, m.
— va. mépriser, dédaigner, de.
DISDAINFUL, a. dédaigneux, de, de.
DISDAINFULLY, ad. dédaigneusement.
DISEASE, s. maladie, f. mal, m.
— va. incommoder, rendre malade.
DISENGAGE, v. dégager de, débarrasser de.
DISGRACE, s. disgrâce, honte, f.
— va. disgracier, déshonorer, flétrir.
DISGUISE, s. déguisement, m.
DISGUISE, va. déguiser, feindre, de.
DISHONEST, a. malhonnête, déshonnête.
DISHONESTY, s. malhonnêteté, f. manque de probité, m.
DISHONOUR, s. déshonneur, m.
— va. déshonorer, flétrir.
DISINTERESTED, a. désintéressé.
DISORDER, s. désordre, trouble, embarras, m. confusion, f.
DISORDER (sickness), mal, m. maladie, f.
DISORDERED, a. déréglé, désordonné, confus, dérangé.

DISPERSION, s. dispersion, séparation, f.
DISPLEASE, va. déplaire, fâcher, de.
DISPLEASED, a. fâché, de, de, contre, en colère, de, contre.
DISPLEASURE, s. déplaisir, m. disgrâce, f.
DISPOSE, s. disposition, f. pouvoir, m.
— va. disposer, à, à, donner, à, à, vendre, à, préparer, à, à, ranger, arranger, ordonner, de, à.
— OF ONE, se défaire de quelqu'un.
— OF ONE'S TIME, employer son temps.
DISPOSED, a. disposé, à, à, porté, à, à.
— OF, donné, vendu, loué.
DISPOSITION, s. disposition, inclinaison, f. ordre, penchant, m.
DISPUTE, s. dispute, f. débat, m.
— v. disputer, débattre.
DISSUADE, va. dissuader, de, de, detourner, de, de.
DISTANCE, s. distance, f. intervalle, m.
— at a distance, de loin.
— va. espacer, laisser derrière soi, dépasser.
DISTANT, a. éloigné.
DISTINCTLY, ad. distinctement, à part.
DISTINGUISH, va. distinguer de, juger de.
DISTRACTED, a. troublé, hors de soi.
DISTRESS, s. détresse, f. malheur, m.
DISTURB, va. troubler, interrompre, déranger de, confondre, inquieter.

DIVE, v. plonger *dans*, sonder, approfondir.
DIVER, s. plongeur, m.
DIVIDE, v. diviser, partager *à*.
DIVORCE, va. divorcer, *avec*.
DIVULGE, va. divulguer, publier.
DIVULGER, s. celui qui divulgue.
DO, va. faire *à*, exécuter *à*, finir, de, agir *envers*, réussir *à*, rendre *à*.
DOCTOR, s. docteur, médecin, m.
— OF DIVINITY, docteur en théologie.
— OF LAWS, docteur en droit.
— OF PHYSIC, docteur en médecine.
— va. médeciner, médicamenter, soigner.
DOCTRINE, s. doctrine, f.
DOCUMENT, s. document, titre, m pièce, f.
DOG, s. chien, m.
DOMESTIC, a. domestique, de famille.
— (SERVANT), s. serviteur, m. servante, f.
DONKEY, s. âne, m.
DOOM, va. décréter, de, destiner, à, juger.
— s. sentence, f. arrêt, m.
DOOR, s. porte, f.
DOSE, s. dose, prise, f.
— va donner une dose *à*, régler les doses.
DOUBLE, s. double, repli, pli, doublon, m. copie, f. artifice, tour, m.
— a. double, trompeur, euse.
DOUBLE, v. doubler, *de*, plier, devenir, répéter, *à*, jouer des tours, *à*,
— ad. doublement.

DOUBT, s. doute, scrupule, m.
— v. douter, *de*, soupçonner, de, *de*, hésiter, à.
DOWN, ad. à terre, en bas.
— va. abaisser, à. subjuguer.
— pr. en bas, dans.
— int. bas ! à bas !
DOWNS, s. les Dunes, entre Calais et Douvres
DOWNWARD, DOWNWARDS, ad. en bas.
DRAG, va. traîner ; ma. draguer.
DRAGOON, s. dragon, m.
DRAIN, va. puiser, boire.
DRAMA, s. drame, m.
DRAUGHT, s. trait, tirage, dessin, m.
— (*of drink*), coup, trait, m.
DRAW, v. tirer, *à*, attirer, *à*, traîner, arracher, *de*, *à*, dessiner, approcher, *de*.
— OUT, retirer.
DRAWING-ROOM, s. salon, m. salle, f. réception à la cour, f.
DREADFUL, a. affreux, terrible.
DRESS, s. habillement, habit, ajustement, m. parure, coiffure, f.
DRESS, va. habiller, *de*, parer, *de*, coiffer, garnir, *de*.
— A WOUND, panser une plaie, une blessure.
— ONE'S HEAD, se coiffer.
DRINK, s. boisson, f. boire, m.
— va boire, absorber.
— DOWN, noyer dans le vin.
— OFF or OUT, boire tout.
DRIP, s. ce qui dégoutte.
— v. dégoutter, *de*, laisser dégoutter.
DRIVE, va, forcer, à, de, reduire, *à*, conduire, *à*, mener *à* chasser, enfoncer.

Drive a carriage, mener une voiture.
— a nail, cogner, pousser, enfoncer un clou.
— at, viser, à, d, aboutir, à, d.
— away, chasser, de, bannir, de, renvoyer, de.
— back, repousser.
— in or into, enfoncer.
— off, remettre, d, renvoyer, d, différer.
— on, pousser, partir, avancer, vers.
— out, faire sortir, de, chasser, de.
Drop, s. goutte, f.
— va. lâcher, laisser tomber.
— s. troupeau, m. foule, f.
Drown, v. noyer, inonder, de, submerger, se noyer, obscurcir, effacer.
— one's self, se noyer.
Drub, va. rosser, battre, étriller.
— s. coup, m. tape, f.
Drubbing, s. bastonnade, f.
Drunk, a. ivre, enivrée, ivrogne.
Drunkard, s. ivrogne, m.

Drunken, a. ivre, bachique.
Dry, a. sec, sèche, à sec, aride, tari.
— (thirsty), a. altéré.
— dry, va. sécher.
Ducat, s. ducat, m.
Duchess, s. duchesse, f.
Duel, s. duel, m.
— v. se battre en duel, avec.
Duke, s. duc, m.
Dumb, s. muet, te, silencieux, se.
Dungeon, s. cachot, m.
Dupe, s. dupe, f.
— va. tromper, duper.
During, pr. pendant, durant.
Dust, s. poussière, poudre, f.
— va. couvrir de poussière, épousseter, ôter la poussière de, nettoyer.
Dutiful, a. obéissant, soumis, d.
Dutifully, ad. respectueusement.
Duty, s. devoir, respect, m. fonction, faction, taxe, f. impôt, droit, m.
Dwell, vn. demeurer, d, habiter, d, rester, d.
Dwelling, s. demeure, habitation, f.

E.

Each, pro. chaque, chacun, une.
Each other, pro. l'un l'autre.
Eagerly, ad. ardemment, âprement, précipitamment.
Ear, s. oreille, f.
— of corn, s. épi, m.
Early, a. matinal, avancé, précoce.

Early, ad. de bonne heure, de bon matin.
Earnestly, ad. instamment, ardemment.
Earth, s. terre, f. sol, le globe, m.
Ease, s. aise, assurance, f.
Easily, ad. facilement, aisément.

EASY TO BE SPOKEN TO, affable.
EAT, v. manger.
— UP, dévorer, ronger.
EATER, s. mangeur, euse.
EATING-HOUSE, s. ordinaire, restaurant, m.
ECCLESIASTIC, s. ecclésiastique, m.
ECONOMICAL, ECONOMIC, a. économique.
ECONOMISE, vn. économiser.
ECONOMIST, s. économe.
EDGE, s. bord, tranchant, m.
EEL, s. anguille, f.
EFFECT, s. effet, m. intention, f.
— va. effectuer, exécuter.
EGG, s. œuf, m.
EIGHT, a. s. huit, m.
EIGHTEEN, a. dix-huit.
EIGHTEENTH, a. dix-huitième.
EIGHTFOLD, a. huit fois le nombre.
EIGHTH, a. huitième.
EIGHTHLY, ad. en huitième lieu.
EIGHTIETH, a. quatre-vingtième.
EIGHTY, a. quatre-vingts.
EITHER, pro. l'un ou l'autre, l'un des deux, chaque, un, l'un.
— c. ou, soit, soit que.
EJACULATE, va. s'écrier.
ELECTION, s. élection, f. choix, m.
ELECTOR, s. électeur, m.
ELEMENT, s. élément, rudiment, m.
— va. composer de, constituer.
ELEVATE, va. élever à, hausser.
— (cheer), égayer, réjouir.
ELIXIR, s. élixir, m.
ELSE, pro. autre.

ELSE, ad. autrement, ou.
ELSEWHERE, ad. ailleurs.
EMBARK, v. embarquer, s'embarquer.
EMBARRASS, va. embarrasser, de, de.
EMBRACE, s. embrassement, m.
EMERALD, s. émeraude, f.
EMIGRANT, s. émigrant, émigré, fugitif, ve.
EMINENT, a. éminent, haut.
EMPALE, va. palissader, empaler.
EMPEROR, s. empereur, m.
EMPLOY, s. emploi, m. occupation, f.
— va. employer, à, à, faire usage de.
EMPLOYMENT, s. charge, f.
EMPRESS, s. impératrice, f.
EMPTY, va. vider, transvaser.
— a. vide, vacant, vain, frivole.
ENABLE, va. rendre capable, de, mettre en état, de, donner la force, de.
ENCHANT, va. enchanter, charmer, de.
ENCOURAGE, va. encourager, à, animer, à, à, enhardir, favoriser, protéger.
ENCOURAGEMENT, s. encouragement, m. protection, f.
ENCOURAGER, s. protecteur, trice.
END, s. fin, f. bout, but, m.
— (issue), issue, f. terme, m.
— (make an), achever, cesser.
— v. finir de, achever de, terminer.
ENDEAVOUR, s. effort, m.
— v. tâcher, de, s'efforcer, de.
ENDURE, v. durer, souffrir, supporter.
ENEMY, s. ennemi.

ENGAGE, v. engager, à, d, s'engager.
ENGINE, s. machine, f. instrument, m.
— (device), artifice, stratagème, m.
— fire engine, s. pompe à incendie, f.
ENJOIN, va. recommander d, de, enjoindre d, de.
ENJOY, v. jouir de.
ENLIST, v. enrôler, engager, s'enrôler.
ENORMOUS, a. énorme, atroce.
ENOUGH, ad. assez, suffisamment.
— s. suffisance, f.
— a suffisant, qui suffit.
ENQUIRE, vn. s'informer de.
ENQUIRY, s. recherche, f.
ENRAGE, va. faire enrager, irriter.
ENTER, v. entrer dans, admettre.
— IN THE UNIVERSITY, immatriculer.
— UPON, prendre possession de.
— (write down), enregistrer.
— (list), s'enrôller, s'engager.
— AN ACTION, intenter un procès d.
ENTERTAIN, va. entretenir, recevoir, régaler de, concevoir.
ENTITLE, va. intituler, mettre en droit, de.
ENTRANCE, s. entrée, avenue, f.
passage, commencement, m.
EPITAPH, s. épitaphe, f.
EPITHET, s. épithète, f. titre, m.
EPOCH, EPOCHA, s. époque, ère, f.
EQUAL, a. égal, d, pareil, lo.

EQUAL (just), juste, envers, équitable, envers.
— s. égal, pareil, m.
— va. égaler, d, rendre égal, d.
EQUALITY, s. égalité, uniformité, f.
EQUALLY, ad. également.
ERECT, a. droit, levé.
— v. ériger, élever, bâtir.
ERRAND, s. message, m. commission, f.
ESCAPE, s. évasion, fuite, méprise, f.
— v. échapper, d, éviter, de, s'échapper, de.
ESTABLISH, va. établir.
ESTABLISHMENT, s. établissement, affermissement, état fixe, m.
EVEN, a. plat, au niveau, aplani, uni, droit.
— ad. même, aussi bien.
EVENING, s. soirée, f. soir, m.
EVENT, s. événement, incident, m.
— AT ALL EVENTS, dans tous les cas.
EVER SINCE, ad. depuis.
EVER, ad. jamais, toujours.
EVERY, a. chaque, chacun, tout.
— BODY, tout le monde, chacun.
— DAY, tous les jours, chaque jour.
— THING, tout, chaque chose.
— WHERE, ad. partout.
EVIDENCE, s. témoignage, témoin, acte, m. évidence, f.
EXACT, v exiger, de, de, imposer, d, enjoindre, d, surfaire, extorquer, d, de.
— a. exact, précis, d, ponctuel, le.

EXACTLY, *ad.* exactement, juste.
EXAMINATION, *s.* examen, *m.* perquisition, recherche, *f.*
EXAMINE, *va.* examiner, éplucher, considérer; *na.* reconnaitre, visiter.
EXAMPLE, *s.* exemple, modèle, *m.*
— *va.* démontrer, *d*, donner en exemple, *d.*
EXCELLENT, *a.* excellent, éminent.
EXCESSIVE, *a.* excessif, ve. extrême.
EXCESSIVELY, *ad.* excessivement.
EXCITE, *va.* exciter, à, *d*, animer, à, *d*, réveiller.
EXCLAIM, *vn.* s'écrier, se récrier, déclamer.
EXCULPATION, *s.* excuse, justification, *f.*
— *va.* excuser, de, exempter, de, *de.*
EXECRATION, *s.* exécration, *f.*
EXECUTE, *va.* exécuter, exercer.
EXECUTION, *s.* exécution, saisie, *f.*
EXECUTIONER, *s.* bourreau, *m.*
EXERCISE, *s.* exercice, théme, *m.*
— *v.* exercer, à, *d*, faire l'exercise, former, *d*, à, dresser, *d*, à, s'exercer, à, *d.*
EXERTION, *s.* effort, *m.* production, *f.*
EXHAUST, *va.* épuiser, absorber, tarir.
EXHIBIT, *va.* exhiber, *d*, montrer, *d.*
EXHIBITION, *s.* spectacle, *m.* exposition, *f.*

EXISTENCE, *s.* existence, *f.*
EXPECT, *v.* attendre, espérer, s'attendre, à, *d.*
EXPECTATION, *s.* attente, esperance, *f.*
EXPENSE, *v.* dépense, *f.* frais, *m. pl.* depens, *m. pl.*
EXPERIENCE, *s.* expérience, épreuve, *f.*
EXPERIENCE, *va.* éprouver, expérimenter.
EXPERIMENT, *s.* expérience, épreuve, *f.*
— *va.* expérimenter.
EXPLAIN, *va.* expliquer, *d*, éclaircir.
EXPLANATION, *s.* explication, *f.*
EXPLODE, *va.* éclater, rejeter.
EXPLOSION, *s.* explosion, *f.*
EXPOSE, *va.* exposer, à, *d*, risquer, de.
EXPRESS, *va.* exprimer, *d*, témoigner, *d*, peindre, *d*, representer, *d.*
EXPRESSION, *s.* expression, *f.*
EXPEND, *v.* étendre, élargir s'étendre.
EXTENDED, *a.* étendue.
EXTRAORDINARILY, *ad.* extra ordinairement.
EXTRAORDINARY, *a.* extraordinaire, rare.
EXTREME, *s.* extrémité, *f.* extrême, *m.*
EXTREMELY, *ad.* extrêmement.
EXTREMITY, *s.* extrémité, *f.* bout, *m.*
EYE, *s.* œil, *m.* yeux, *pl.*
— *v.* regarder, épier.

F

FACE, *s.* visage, *m.* face, *f.*
FACETIOUS, *a.* facétieux, farceur, euse.
FACT, *s.* fait, *m.* action, réalité, *f.*
FAIL, *v.* manquer, à, faillir, échouer.
FAILURE, *s.* faillite, faute, *f.* échec, fiasco, *m.*
FAINT, *a.* languissant, débile, faible.
— *vn.* s'évanouir, défaillir, languir.
FAINTED AWAY, *a.* évanoui.
FAIR, *a.* juste, de, franc, che.
FAITH, *s.* foi, croyance, doctrine, *f.*
FAITHFUL, *s.* les fidèles, les élus, *m. pl.*
— *a.* fidèle, à, qui a de la probité.
FAITHFULLY, *ad.* fidèlement.
FALL, *s.* chute, *f.*
— *v.* tomber.
— A CRYING, se mettre à pleurer.
— AGAIN, retomber.
— ALL ALONG, tomber de son long.
— ASLEEP, s'endormir.
— BACK, se reculer, s'acculer.
— (*be cheaper*), baisser de prix.
— DOWN, tomber, se jeter, s'ébouler, descendre, à, baisser.
— IN WITH, rencontrer.
— OFF, tomber.
FALLING, *s.* chute, *f.*
FALSE, *a.* faux, sse. perfide.
— *ad.* faussement, à faux.
FAMILY, *s.* famille, *f.*

FAMOUS, *a.* fameux, célèbre.
FAR, *a.* éloigné, de, de, distant, de.
— *ad.* loin, bien loin, très-avant.
— *a.* de beaucoup.
FARE, *s.* provisions de bouche, *f. pl.* frais de voiture, *m. pl.* chère, *f.*
FARM, *s.* ferme, *f.*
FARMER, *s.* cultivateur, fermier, *m.*
FARRIER, *s.* maréchal-ferrant, *m.*
FAST, *s.* jeûne, *m.* ma. amarre, *f.*
— *a.* ferme, solide, attaché.
— *ad.* ferme, vite, promptement.
— ASLEEP, *a.* bien endormi.
FATAL, *a.* fatal, à, funeste, à.
FATE, *s.* destin, *m.* destinée, *f.*
FATHER, *s.* père, *m.*
— *va.* adopter, imputer, de, à.
FATHER-IN-LAW, *s.* beau-père, *m.*
FATIGUE, *s.* fatigue, peine, *f.*
— *va.* fatiguer, de, de, lasser, de.
FAULT, *s.* faute, *f.* défaut, *m.*
— FIND FAULT, *v.* trouver à redire à.
FAVOUR, *s.* bienfait, *m.* faveur, grâce, *f.*
— (COUNTENANCE), mine, *f.*
— *va.* favoriser de, assister de, flatter.
FAVORITE, *s.* favori, te.
FEAR, *s.* crainte, peur, terreur, *f.*
— *v.* craindre, de, avoir peur, de, de, douter de.

FEAST, s. festin, m. fête, f.
— v. fêter, regaler de, festoyer, être en festin, faire bonne chère.
FEATURE. s. trait, m.
FEED, s. pâture, nourriture, f.
— v. manger, nourrir, de, à, paître, repaître, se nourrir de.
FEEL, s. toucher, m.
— v. sentir, ressentir, tâter, toucher à, sonder, se sentir.
— COLD, avoir froid.
FEIGN, v. feindre, de, faire semblant, de.
FELLOW, s. camarade, égal, m.
— IN OFFICE, collègue, m.
— OF A COLLEGE, boursier, m.
— (PARTNER), associé, m.
— vn. assortir, appareiller.
FELLOW-CREATURE, s. semblable, m. et f.
FELLOW-PRISONER, s. camarade de prison, m.
FELLOW-SERVANT, s. compagnon de service, m.
FELLOW-STUDENT, s. condisciple, m.
FEMININE, a. féminin.
FESTAL, a. joyeux, de fête.
FETCH, va. aller quérir, apporter à, chercher.
FEW, a. peu, un petit nombre, (sing. LITTLE.)
FICTION, s. fiction, fable, imposture, f.
FIDELITY, s. fidélité, constance, f.
FIELD, s. champ, pré, m. prairie, f.
— DAY, s. jour de revue, m.
— OF BATTLE, champ de bataille, m.

FIGHT, v. combattre, se battre avec, resister à; s'opposer à.
— IT OUT, vider un différend, se battre, décider une dispute.
— s. combat, m. bataille, mêlée, f.
FILIAL, a. filial, de fils.
FILL, s. la mesure requise, f.
— v. remplir de, emplir de.
— UP, emplir tout à fait de, combler de.
FIN, s. aileron, m. nageoire, f.
FINALLY, ad. enfin, finalement.
FIND, ad. trouver.
— (perceive), voir, s'apercevoir de.
— AGAIN, retrouver.
— OUT, découvrir, imaginer, de, trouver, à.
— OUT ONE'S WAY, trouver son chemin, se conduire.
FINE, a. fin, beau, bel, m. belle, f.
— (neat), propre, net, te.
— (refined), clair, raffiné.
— AND SOFT, doux au toucher.
— s. amende, fin, f.
— va. mettre à l'amende, épurer de.
— vn. payer l'amende.
FINELY, ad. de la belle manière, richement, fort bien.
FINERY, s. parure, f. ornament, m.
FINGER, s. doigt, m.
— va. manier, toucher à.
FINISH, va. finir, de, achever, de, terminer.
FIRE, s. feu, m. ardeur, chaleur, f.
— va. mettre un feu, incendier.
— (shoot), tirer, à, sur, faire feu sur.

FIRE PLACE, s. foyer de la cheminée.
FIRM, a. ferme, solide, inébranlable.
FIRMNESS, s. fermeté, f.
FIRMLY, ad. fermement, fortement.
FIRST, ad. premier, ière.
— ad. premièrement, d'abord, auparavant, devant.
— OR LAST, tôt ou tard.
FISH, s. poisson, m.
FISH-HOOK, s. hamecon, m.
FISHER, FISHERMAN, s. pêcheur, m.
FISHING, s. pêcherie, pêche, f.
FISHING-TACKLE, s. utensiles de pêche, m. pl. attirail de pêche, m.
FIST, s. poing, m.
— va. battre à coups de poing.
FIT, s. accès, transport, m. attaque de nerfs, f.
— a. propre, à, à, capable, de, de, commode pour, pour, juste, à propos, de, prêt, à, convenable pour, pour.
FIVE, a. cinq.
FLAIL, s. fléau, m.
FLAME, s. flamme, f.
— vn. flamber, s'embraser.
FLAP OF A COAT, s. basque, f. pan, m.
FLAT, a. plat.
— ON THE GROUND, à plate terre.
FLATTER, a. (comp. de FLAT), plus plat.
— va. flatter, louer, de, de, cajoler.
FLATTERER, s. flatteur, euse.
FLATTERY, s. flatterie, cajolerie, f.
FLEE, vn. s'enfuir, de, à, fuir de.
FLESH, s. chair, f.

FLIGHT, s. fuite, f.
— (of birds), volée, bande, f. vol, m.
FLING, v. jeter à, lancer à.
— AWAY, rejeter, jeter loin de soi.
FLOG, va. fouetter, châtier.
FLOGGING, s. punition, action de fouetter, f.
FLOOR, s. plancher, parquet, m.
— (story), s. étage, m.
FLORIN, s florin, m.
FLOUR, s. farine, f.
FLOWER, s. fleur, f.
FLY, va. et n. fuir, de, s'enfuir, de, à, voler, à, se sauver, de.
— s. mouche, f.
— v. voler comme les mouches.
FOB, s. gousset, m. petite poche, f.
FOLD, va. plisser, plier, entourer, enfermer.
— DOUBLE, plier en deux.
— UP, plier, rouler.
FOLLOW, v. suivre, imiter, s'ensuivre.
— AGAIN, resuivre.
— (addict), suivre, s'abandonner, à, à, s'appliquer, à, à.
FOLLOWERS, s. compagnons, m. suite, f.
FOLLOWING, a. suivant, suivante.
FOLLY, s. folie, f. vice, m. sottise, f.
FOND, a. passionné, de.
— (foolish), badin, folâtre.
— (idle), vain, de, fou, folle, de.
— (kind), indulgent, pour, envers, bon, bonne, envers, pour.
FONDLE, va. dorloter, caresser, choyer.
FONDNESS, s. tendresse, f. attachement, m.

FOOL, *s.* sot, te. simple, fou, folle.
— *v.* se moquer, de, badiner, duper.
FOOLHARDY, *a.* téméraire, de.
FOOLISH, *a.* simple, de, sot, te. de, indiscret, ète, de.
FOOLISHLY, *ad.* follement, sottement.
FOOT, *s.* pied, *m.*
— *On foot,* à pied.
FOOTMAN, *s.* laquais, coureur, *m.*
FOR, *pr.* pour, par, de, à, pendant, malgré, nonobstant, que.
— *c.* car.
FORAGE, *s.* fourrage, *m.*
— *v.* fourrager, piller, ravager.
FORBID, *va.* défendre, *d*, de, interdire, *d*, de, faire défense, *d*, de, empecher, de.
FORCE, *s.* force, vigueur, violence, *f.*
— *va.* forcer, à, de, réduire, *d*, à, contraindre, de, à.
— A TRADE, faire valoir son négoce.
FOREIGN, *a.* étranger, ère. éloigné.
FOREIGNER, *s.* étranger, ère. aubain.
FOREMAN OF A SHOP, chef de boutique, contre-maître, maitre garçon, *m.*
FORFEIT, *va.* forfaire, faire confisquer, perdre.
FORGET, *va.* oublier, de.
FORGIVE, *v.* pardonner, *d*, de.
FORK, *s.* fourchette, fourche, *f.*
FORLORN, *a.* triste, abandonné.
FORM, *s.* forme, figure, formalité, *f.*

FORMER, *a.* premier, ère. précédent, celui-là, celle-là.
— *s.* qui forme, qui fait.
FORMERLY, *ad.* autrefois, jadis.
FORTUNATE, *a.* heureux, de, fortuné, de.
FORTUNATELY, *ad.* heureusement.
FORTUNE, *s.* fortune, destinée, *f.*
FORTY, *a.* quarante.
FOUND, *va.* fonder, établir, fondre.
FOUNDATION, *s.* fondation, *f.* fondement, *m.*
FOUNDER, *s.* fondateur, fondatrice.
— OF METAL, fondeur, *m.*
— *va. man.* surmener.
— (*as a ship*), couler bas ou à fond.
FOUR, *a.* quatre.
FOURFOOTED, *a.* quadrupède.
FOURLEGGED, *a.* à quatre pattes.
FOURTEEN, *a.* quatorze.
FOURTEENTH, *a.* quatorzième.
FOURTH, *a.* quatrième.
FOURTHLY, *ad.* quatrièmement.
FRAME, *s.* corps, *m.* forme, *f.*
FRANKLY, *ad.* franchement.
FRENCH, *a.* français.
FRENCH BEANS, *s. pl.* haricots, *m. pl.*
FRENCHIFIED, *a.* francisé, à la française.
FREQUENT, *a.* fréquent.
— *va.* fréquenter, hanter.
FREQUENTLY, *ad.* fréquemment.
FRESH, *a.* frais, fraîche, récent, vif, ve. neuf, ve.
FRIEND, *s.* ami, e.
— *va.* favoriser, protéger.
FRIENDLESS, *a.* sans amis.

FRIENDLINESS, s. amitié, bonté, f.
FRIENDLY, a. serviable, d'ami, favorable, à, propice, à, utile, à, amical.
— ad. en ami, avec amitié.
FRIENDS (relations), s. pl. parents, m. pl.
FRIENDSHIP, s. amitié, f.
FRIGHT, s. épouvantail, m.
FRIGHT, (terror), épouvante, f.
FRIGHT, FRIGHTEN, va. épouvanter, de, effrayer, de.
FRIGHTFUL, a. épouvantable, effroyable.
FRIGHTFULLY, ad. effroyablement.
FROCK, s. frac, fourreau, m. blouse, f.
FROM, pr. de, des, du, à partir de, d'après, de par, de la part de, depuis, dès, par, à, au, à la.
FRONT, s. front, le devant, m.
FRUGAL, a. frugal, sobre, économe.
FRUGALITY, s. frugalité, épargne, f.
FRUGALLY, ad. frugalement.
FRUIT, s. fruit, m.
FRUITLESS, a. vain, stérile.
FRUIT-TREE, s. arbre fruitier, m.

FUGITIVE, a. fugitif, ve. inconstant.
FULFIL, va. remplir.
FULL, a. plein, de, rempli, de, ample.
— ad. plein, à plein, entièrement.
FUMBLE, v. tâtonner.
FUNERAL, s. enterrement, m. funérailles, obsèques, f. pl.
FUNEREAL, a. triste, funèbre.
FURIOUSLY, ad. avec fureur.
FURNISH, va. fournir, à, pourvoir, de.
— (a house), garnir de, meubler, de.
FURNISHER, s. pourvoyeur, fournisseur, m.
FURNISHING, s. l'action de fournir, de meubler, etc.
FURNITURE, s. garniture, f. appareil, m.
— (of a house), meubles, m. pl. mobilier, m. s.
FURTHER, va. avancer, aider à, servir, à, à.
FURTHER, ad. plus loin, de plus, plus avant.
FURY, s. furie, fureur, frénésie, f.
FURY (heat), fougue, f.
FUSEE, s. fusil, m. mèche d'une bombe.

G.

GAILY, ad. gaiement.
GAIN, s. gain, profit, avantage, m.
— v. gagner, acquérir, obtenir, de.
GALLERY, s. galerie, f.

GAME, s. jeu, divertissement, m.
— (hunting), gibier, m. chasse, f.
— va. jouer, à, folâtrer.
GAMEKEEPER, s. garde-chasse, m.

GARDEN, s. jardin, m
— Kitchen garden, potager, m.
GARDEN, vn. jardiner.
GARDENER, s. jardinier, m.
GATE, s. porte, f.
GENERAL, s. général, m, totalité, f.
— a. général.
GENERALLY, ad. en général, ordinairement, d'une manière très-étendue.
GENEROSITY, s. générosité, f.
GENEROUS, a. généreux, se.
GENEROUSLY, ad. généreusement.
GENTEEL, a. galant, noble, poli, (in dress) propre, bien habillé.
GENTEELLY, ad. poliment, galamment, noblement, élégamment.
GENTLEMAN, s. gentilhomme, monsieur, m.
GERMAN, a. germain, allemand.
GERMANY, n. p. Allemagne.
GET, v. gagner, se procurer, obtenir, de, de, remporter, procurer, à.
— OUT, sortir.
— RID, se débarrasser, de.
— TIPSY, se griser.
— UP, lever, se lever, monter, à.
GHOST, s. revenant, esprit, m. âme, f.
GIBBET, s. potence, f. gibet, m.
— va. pendre à une potence, mettre au gibet.
GIN, s. (liqueur), genièvre, eau-de-vie, f.
GIPSY (GIPSIES, pl.) s. Bohémienne, Egyptienne, matoise, f.
GIRL, s. fille, servante, f.
GIVE, v. donner, à, à, rendre, à.

GIVE OUT, donner, à, à, distribuer, à, rapporter, à, annoncer, à, cesser, de, ceder, à.
— THE SLIP, se dérober.
— UP, rendre, à, céder, à, se dessaisir, de, delivrer, à, renoncer, à, à.
— WAY, céder, à, enfoncer, s'abandonner, à, à, se relâcher, se livrer, à.
GLAD, a. content, de, de, charmé, de, de, aise, de, de, joyeux, de, de, réjoui, de, de, heureux, de, de.
GLADDEN, va. réjouir, récréer.
GLADLY, ad. volontiers, avec plaisir.
GLASS, s. verre, m. glace, m. lunette d'approche, f. télescope, m.
GLASS, s. ma. sablier, m.
— a. de verre.
GLAZE, va. vitrer, couvrir de verre.
GLOVE, s. gant, m.
GO, vn. aller, à, s'en aller, à, de, passer, chez, partir, de, pour, marcher.
— ABOUT, faire le tour, se détourner, entreprendre, de.
— ABROAD, sortir, partir, voyager.
— AGAINST, s'opposer, à, être contraire, à.
— ALONG, poursuivre son chemin, accompagner, passer: va-t-en.
— ASHORE, débarquer, aborder.
— ASIDE, se mettre à côté, de.
— ASTRAY, s'égarer, errer.
— ASUNDER, aller séparément.
— AWAY, se retirer, de, sortir, de, s'en aller, de.
— BACK, reculer, s'en retourner, à.

Go BACKWARDS AND FOR-
WARDS, aller et venir, se con-
tredire.
— BEYOND, passer, surpasser.
— BY, passer auprès, *de*, se
régler, *sur*, souffrir, devancer,
duper.
— DOWN, descendre, *à*, aller, *à*,
rétrograder.
— FOR, aller quérir, aller cher-
cher, passer pour.
— FORTH, sortir, se produire.
— FORWARD, avancer, pousser,
profiter, poursuivre.
— FROM, quitter, partir, *de*.
— FROM (*the matter*), s'écarter,
de.
— HALVES, être de moitié.
— IN, entrer, *dans*, rentrer,
dans.
— IN (*wear*), porter.
— NEAR, approcher, *de*, s'ap-
procher, *de*.
— OFF, quitter, partir, *de*, s'en-
fuir, *de*.
— OFF (*sell*), se vendre, se dé-
biter.
— ON, avancer, continuer, de, à.
— OUT, sortir, s'éteindre.
— OVER, passer, *à*, traverser, *à*,
passer, *sur*.
— THROUGH, passer, *par*, pas-
ser au travers, *de*, enfiler,
percer, fendre.
— THROUGH, subir, souffrir.
— UP, *à*, *sur*, monter, s'élever,
sur.
— UP AND DOWN, courir de côté
et d'autre, monter et descen-
dre.
— UPON, entreprendre, se fon-
der.
— WITH, accompagner.
— WITHOUT, se passer, *de*, de.
GOD, *s*. DIEU, *m*.

GOLD, *s*. or, *m*.
GOLDEN, *a*. en or, d'or, doré.
GOOD, *a*. bon, ne. propre, convenable.
— *s*. bien, avantage, profit, *m*.
— *ad*. bien, bon.
— *int*. bien! fort bien.
GOODNESS, *s*. bonté, *f*.
GOOSE, *s*. oie, *f*. imbécile, *m*.
GOSLING, *s*. oison, *m*.
GOSSIP, *s*. commère, causeuse,
f.
— *vn*. jaser, causer, caqueter,
habiller.
GOVERNMENT, *s*. gouvernement,
m.
GOVERNOR, *s*. gouverneur, *m*.
GRACIOUS, *a*. bénin, bénigne,
bon, ne. *pour*, agréable, *pour*,
envers, propice, *à*, bienfaisant,
envers.
GRACIOUSLY, *ad*. gracieusement,
avec grâce.
GRAIN, *s*. graine, *f*. grain, *m*.
GRANARY, *s*. grenier, *m*. grange,
f.
GRANDCHILD, *s*. petit-fils ou
petite-fille.
GRANDFATHER, *s*. grand-père,
m.
GRANDMOTHER, *s*. grand'mère,
f.
GRANT, *s*. octroi, *m*. concession,
f.
— *va*. accorder, *à*, de, céder, *à*,
avouer, *à*.
GRAPE, *s*. raisin, *m*.
— *Bunch of grapes*, grappe de
raisin.
GRASS, *s*. herbe, *f*. gazon, *m*.
GRATIFY, *v*. gratifier, accorder,
à, de, satisfaire, de, faire
plaisir, *à*, contenter, de.
GRATITUDE, *s*. gratitude, reconnaissance, *f*.

GRAVE, s. fosse, f. sépulcre, m.
— a. grave, réservé, retenu.
GREAT, a. grand, gros, se.
— MANY, plusieurs, bien des.
— s. gros, en gros.
GREAT GRANDDAUGHTER, s. arrière-petite-fille, f.
— GRANDFATHER, s. bisaïeul, m.
— GRANDSON, s. arrière-petit-fils, m.
GRECIAN, a. grec, que.
GREEK, s. Grec, m.
GRENADE, GRENADO, s. grenade, f. petite bombe.
GRIEF, s. douleur, f. chagrin, m.
GROAN, s. gémissement, m. plainte, f.
GROAN, vn. gémir, de, de, soupirer, sanglotter.
GROCER, s. épicier, m.
GROCERY, s. épicerie, f.
GROG, s. grog, m. boisson (mélange de rhum et d'eau).
GROSS, a. grossier, ère. gros, se. total.
GROUND, s. terre, f. terrain,

bien-fonds, fondement, sujet, m. raison, f.
GRUFF, a. bourru, rechigné, brusque.
GRUFFLY, ad. d'un air rechigné.
GRUFFNESS, s. mauvais naturel, m.
GUARD, s. garde, défense, f.
— HOUSE, corps de garde, m.
— *King's body-guard*, garde du corps, m.
— va. garder, défendre, contre.
GUESS, s. conjecture, f.
— v. deviner, conjecturer, de.
GUEST, s. convié, e. hôte, hôtesse, convive, m.
GUILT, s. culpabilité, f. crime, m.
GUILTILY, ad. criminellement.
GUILTY, a. coupable.
GUINEA, s. (*coin*), guinée, f.
GUN, s. arme à feu, f. fusil, m.
— *Great gun*, s. canon, m.
GUNPOWDER, s. poudre à canon, f.
— PLOT, s. conspiration des poudres, f.

H.

HABIT, s. habit, habillement, m.
— (*custom*), s. habitude, f.
HAD BETTER, v. ferait mieux.
HAIL, s. grêle, f.
HAIR, s. cheveu, m.
HAIR-DRESSER, s. coiffeur, m.
HALF, s. (pl. HALVES), moitié, f.
— ad. à moitié, imparfaitement.

HALF-PENNY, s. (*coin*), un sou.
HALLOO, v. haler, huer.
— int. le cri par lequel on hale les chiens sur leur proie.
HAND, s. main, f.
— (*at cards*), jeu, m.
— (*measure*), paume, f.
HANDLE, s. anse, poignée, queue, f, manche, bras, m.
— va. manier, toucher à, traiter.

HANDSOME, a. beau, bel, belle.
HANDSOMELY, ad. joliment, avec grâce, généreusement.
HANG, v. pendre à, suspendre à.
— UP, pendre, à, accrocher, à.
— ONE'S SELF, se pendre.
HAPPEN, vn. arriver à, avenir, se passer, à, tomber.
HAPPILY, ad. heureusement.
HAPPINESS, s. bonheur, m.
HAPPY, a. heureux, de, de, fortuné, de, de.
HARD, a. dur.
— AT, a. fortement occupé, de, de.
— ad. fort, fort et ferme, rudement, de près, tout près.
HARDLY, ad. à peine.
HARE, s. lièvre, m.
HARM, s. mal, tort, malheur, m.
— va. nuire, faire du mal.
HARMLESS, a. innocent, sans mal, sans faire de mal.
HARP, s. harpe, f.
HARPER, s. joueur de harpe, m.
HASTE, s. hâte, diligence, vitesse, f.
HASTE, HASTEN, v. se depêcher, de, se hâter, de.
HASTY, a. prompt, à, à, pétulant, violent, emporté, téméraire.
HAT, s. chapeau, m.
HATS OFF! chapeaux bas!
HAT-MAKER, s. chapelier, m.
HAUGHTILY, ad. fièrement.
HAUGHTY, a. altier, ère. fier, ère. arrogant.
HAVE, va. avoir, à, tenir.
— JUST, venir de, ne faire que.
HAY, s. foin, m.
HE, pro. il, celui, lui.
HEAD, s. tête, f. chef, m.
HEALTH, s. santé, f.

HEALTHY, a. sain, salutaire.
HEAR, va. ouïr, entendre, écouter, apprendre, exaucer, donner audience à, prêter l'oreille à.
HEARER, s. auditeur, m.
HEARING, s. ouïe, audience, f.
HEART, s. cœur, milieu, courage, m.
HEARTILY, ad. de bon cœur, avec vigueur.
HEARTY, a. sincère, gai, vigoureux, se. de bon cœur.
HEAVY, a. lourd, pesant.
HEAVILY, ad. pesamment, lentement, fortement.
HEBREW, a. s. Hébraïque, Hébreu, m.
HEEL, s. talon, m.
HEIGHT, s. hauteur, f. comble, m.
HEINOUS, a. odieux, se. à, atroce.
HEIR, s. héritier, m.
HELL, s. enfer, m.
HELP, s. aide, f. support, secours, m.
— v. aider, à, à, secourir, servir, à, à, s'empêcher, de.
HEMORRHAGE, s. hémorrhagie, f.
HENCE, ad. d'ici, de là, loin d'ici.
HENCEFORTH, ad. désormais.
HER, pro. elle, à elle, le sien, la sienne, etc.
HERE, ad. ici, voici, ci, ça, y.
HERE AND THERE, çà et là.
— IS, voici.
HERO, s. héros, m.
HEROICALLY, ad. héroïquement.
HERS, pro. le sien, la sienne, etc., à elle.
HESITATION, s. hésitation, f. doute, m.

HIBERNIAN, s. Irlandais.
HIDE, v. cacher, d, couvrir, se cacher.
HIDING-PLACE, s. cachette, f.
HIGH, a. haut, élevé.
HIGHLY, ad. grandement, infiniment, hautement, fort, sensiblement
HIGHNESS, s. altesse, hautesse, f.
HIGHWAY, s. grand chemin, m.
— MAN, s. voleur de grand chemin, m.
HILT, s. garde, f.
HIM, pro. lui, le.
HIMSELF, pro. lui-même, soi-même, se, soi, seul, tout seul.
HIND, s. biche, f.
HINT, s. idée, f.
HIRE, s. louage, m. gages, m. pl.
— (wages), gages, m. pl. salaire, m.
— va. louer, engager, arrêter.
HIS, pro. son, sa, ses (à lui), le sien, la sienne, les siens, les siennes, à lui.
HISTORICAL, HISTORIC, a. historique.
HISTORICALLY, ad. historiquement.
HISTORY, s. histoire, f.
HOAX, s. plaisanterie, mystification, farce, f.
HOLD, s. prise, f. appui, support.
HOLD, v. tenir, contenir, apprêter.
— UP, lever, soutenir, cesser, appuyer.
HOLE, s. trou, m.
HOLLOW, a. creux, se. vide, enfoncé.
— VOICE, s. voix sourde, sépulcrale, f.

HOLLOW, s. creux, cri, m.
HOLY, a. saint, sacré, pieux, se.
— DAY, s. fête, f. jour de fête, congé, m.
— DAYS, s. vacances, f. pl.
— GHOST, s. le Saint-Esprit, m.
— LAND, s. la Terre-sainte, f.
— ROOD DAY, s. jour de l'exaltation de la sainte croix, m.
— THURSDAY, s. l'Ascension, f.
— WATER, s. de l'eau bénite, f.
— WEEK, s. la semaine sainte, f.
HOME, s. demeure, patrie, f. logis, m.
— a. qui porte coup, bon, bonne.
— ad. au logis, chez soi, hardiment, tout à fait.
HONEST, a. droit, honnête, probe.
— MAN, s. homme de bien, m.
HONESTY, s. droiture, probité, f.
HONOUR, s. honneur, m. honnêteté, gloire, dignité, grandeur, estime, f. amour-propre, m.
HONOURABLE, a. honorable, illustre.
HONOURABLY, ad. honorablement.
HOOK, s. crochet, croc, m.
— va. attraper, accrocher, d.
HOOKED, a. crochu, fourchu, accroché.
HOPE, s. espérance, attente, f. espoir. m.
— v. espérer, de, attendre impatiemment.
HORRID, a. affreux, se. horrible.
HORROR, s. horreur, détestation, f.
HORSE, s. cheval, m. cavalerie. f.

HORSE, *va.* monter un cheval, porter sur le dos.
HORSEBACK (ON), *ad.* à cheval.
HOSPITALITY, *s.* hospitalité, *f.*
HOST, *s.* hôte, *m.* hostie, arméé, *f.*
HOSTAGE, *s.* otage, *m.*
HOUR, *s.* heure, *f.*
HOUSE, *s.* maison, habitation, *f.*
— OF PARLIAMENT, *s.* chambre du parlement, *f.*
HOUSEDOG, *s.* chien de garde, *m.*
HOUSEKEEPER, *s.* femme de charge, personne qui tient maison, *f.*
HOW, *ad.* comment. combien.
— MANY, HOW MUCH, combien, que.
— D'YE DO, *for* HOW DO YOU DO, comment vous portez-vous, comment va la santé?
HOWEVER, *ad.* cependant, quoi qu'il en soit, de quelque manière.
HOWL, *s.* hurlement, cri, *m.*
— *vn.* hurler, faire des hurlements.
HUMAN, *a.* humain.
HUMANE, *a.* bon, ne. bénin, bénigne.
HUMANELY, *ad.* avec humanité.

HUMANITY, *s.* humanité, bonté, *f.*
HUMBLE, *a.* humble, soumis, modeste.
— *va.* humilier, abaisser.
HUMBLY, *ad.* humblement, sans fierté.
HUMILIATING, humiliant.
HUMP, *s.* bosse, *f.*
HUMPBACKED, *a.* bossu.
HUNCHBACKED, *a.* voûté, bossu.
HUNDRED, *a. s.* cent, *m.* centaine, *f.*
HUNGER, *s.* faim, *f.* désir violent, *m.*
— *vn.* avoir faim, sentir la faim, être affamé.
HUNGRY, *a.* affamé, qui a faim.
HURRY, *s.* hâte, presse, précipitation, *f.* fracas, désordre, *m.*
— OFF, *vn.* s'en aller vite.
— *va.* presser, de, hâter, de, précipiter.
HURT, *s.* mal, préjudice, *m.*
— *va.* blesser, faire mal, *à,* nuire, *à,* gâter.
HUSBAND, *s.* mari, époux, *m.*
— *va.* ménager, cultiver.
HUSSEY, *s.* méchante, *f.* coquine, *f.*
HYPOCRISY, *s.* hypocrisie, *f.*

I.

I, *pro.* je, moi.
IDEA, *s.* idée, notion, image, *f.*
IDIOT, *s.* idiot, imbécile, *m.*
IDLE, *a.* fainéant, oisif, ve. paresseux, se. inutile, frivole.
— *v.* faire le paresseux.
IDLEHEADED, *a.* imbécile, fou, folle.
IDLENESS, *s.* fainéantise, paresse, oisiveté, inutilité, frivolité, *f.*
IDLER, *a.* fainéant, paresseux, se.
IDLY, *ad.* en paresseux, sottement, nonchalamment, inutilement.
IF, *c.* si, pourvu que, quand même.

ILL, s. mal, malheur, m. infortune, f.
— a. malade, mauvais, méchant.
ILL-TREAT, va. maltraiter.
ILLNESS, s. indisposition, f.
IMAGINATION, s. imagination, f.
IMAGINE, va. imaginer, de, concevoir, s'imaginer.
IMITATE, va. imiter, copier.
IMMEDIATELY, ad. immédiatement.
IMMORTAL, a. immortel, le.
IMMORTALITY, s. immortalité, f.
IMPART, v. communiquer, à, faire, part, de, à.
IMPATIENT, a. impatient, de, emporté.
— To grow impatient, s'impatienter.
IMPEDIMENT, s. empêchement, obstacle, m.
IMPETUOUS, a. impétueux, se. emporté.
IMPETUOUSLY, ad. impétueusement.
IMPIETY, s impieté, irréligion, f.
IMPLEMENT, s. outil, m.
IMPORTANCE, s. importance, conséquence, f.
IMPORTANT, a. important.
IMPOSE, va. imposer, à.
— UPON, en faire accroire, à, duper.
IMPOSSIBILITY, s. impossibilité, f.
IMPOSTOR, s. imposteur, m.
IMPRISONMENT, s. emprisonnement, m.
IMPROBABLE, a. qui n'est pas probable.
IMPROBABLY, ad. sans vraisemblance.

IMPROVE, va. profiter, fair valoir, tirer parti, de.
IMPROVEMENT, s. perfectionnement, m. amélioration, f.
IMPUDENCE, s. impudence, effronterie, f.
IMPUDENT, a. impudent, effronté.
IMPUTE, va. imputer, à, de, attribuer, à, de.
IN, pr. en, dans, dedans.
— ORDER, pr. afin de, pour.
INCAUTIOUSLY, ad. négligemment, imprudemment.
INCH, s. pouce (mesure), m.
INCREASE, s. augmentation, f. accroissement, produit, m.
INCREDIBLE, a. incroyable.
INCREDULOUS, a. incrédule.
INDECENCY, s. indécence, f.
INDEED, ad. en vérité, vraiment, en effet.
INDEPENDENCE, INDEPENDENCY, s. indépendance, f.
INDIAN, a. indien, ne; des Indes.
— s. Indien, ne.
INDICATE, va. indiquer, à, de, montrer, à.
INDIGNATION, s. indignation, f. courroux, m.
INDIGNITY, s. indignité, f. affront, m.
INDISPOSE, va. rendre incapable, indisposer, déranger.
INEXORABLE, a. inexorable, à.
INFAMOUS, a. infâme.
INFANT, s. enfant, infant, m.
INFEST, va. infester, troubler.
INFIDEL, a. infidèle, à, m. et f.
INFIRM, a. infirme.
INFIRMITY, s. infirmité, infortune, f.
INFLUENCE, s. influence, f.
— va. influer, sur, causer.

INFORM, *v.* instruire, *de,* informer, *de,* animer.
INFORMATION, *s.* information, *f.* avis, *m.*
INGENIOUS, *a.* ingénieux, se.
INGENUITY, *s.* adresse, *f.* talent, *m*
INGRATE, UNGRATEFUL, *a.* ingrat.
INGRATITUDE, *s.* ingratitude, *f.*
INHABITANT, *s.* habitant, *m.*
INJURE, *va.* faire tort, *à,* injurier, faire mal, *à.*
INJURY, *s.* dommage, tort, *m.* injure, *f.*
INJUSTICE, *s.* injustice, iniquité, *f.*
INK, *s.* encre, *f.* noir, *m.*
— *va.* barbouiller d'encre.
INN, *s.* auberge, hôtellerie, *f.*
— *va.* loger, engranger.
INNATE, *a.* inné, naturel, le.
INNKEEPER, *s.* hôtelier, aubergiste, *m.*
INNOCENCE, INNOCENCY, *s.* innocence, *f.*
INNOCENT, *a. s.* innocent.
INNOCENTLY, *ad.* innocemment.
INQUIRE, *v.* demander, *de, à,* examiner, s'enquérir, *de,* s'informer, *de.*
INQUIRER, *s* qui s'enquiert, etc. investigateur.
INSATIABLE, *a.* insatiable.
INSECT, *s.* insecte, *m.*
INSENSIBILITY, *s.* insensibilité, apathie, insouciance, *f.*
INSENSIBLE, *a.* insensible, imperceptible.
INSINUATE, *va.* insinuer, *à,* de.
INSIST, *va.* insister, pour, presser, *de,* persister, *à,* soutenir, *à.*
INSOLENCE, INSOLENCY, *s.* insolence, *f.*

INSOLENT, *a.* insolent, de, effronté, de.
INSOLENTLY, *ad.* insolemment, arrogamment.
INSTANCE, *s.* exemple, *m.*
INSTANT, *s.* instant, moment, *m.*
INSTANTLY, *ad.* à l'instant, instamment, ardemment.
INSTEAD, *ad.* au lieu de.
INSTINCT, *s.* instinct, *m.*
INSTRUCT, *va.* instruire, *de,* enseigner, *à, à.*
INSTRUCTION, *s.* instruction, *f.*
INSTRUMENT, *s.* instrument, *m.*
INSULT, *s.* insulte, injure, *f.* outrage, *m.*
— *va.* insulter, outrager.
INTELLIGENCE, *s.* intelligence, *f.* avis, *m.*
INTELLIGENT, *a.* intelligent.
INTEND, *va.* se proposer, de, avoir dessein, de, avoir égard, *à,* s'appliquer, *à, à.*
INTENSELY, *ad.* fortement.
INTENT, INTENTION, *s.* intention, *f.*
INTENTIONAL, *a.* intentional, le.
INTENTIONALLY, *ad.* par intention, exprès.
INTER, *va.* enterrer, inhumer.
INTERDICTION, *s.* interdiction, *f.*
INTEREST, *va.* intéresser, toucher.
— *s.* intérêt, *m.*
— (*right*), droit, *m.* part, *f.*
INTERESTING, *a.* intéressant.
INTERIOR, *a.* intérieur, interne.
INTERPOSE. *va.* interposer.
INTERROGATE, *va.* interroger, *sur.*
INTERRUPT, *v.* interrompre.
INTO, *pr.* dans, en, entre, sur.
— IT, *pr.* dedans.
INTRINSIC, *a.* intrinsèque.

INTRODUCE, *va.* introduire, présenter, *à.*
INVADER, *s.* agresseur, usurpateur, *m.*
INVENT, *va.* inventer, de, imaginer, de.
INVENTION, *s.* invention, fiction, *f.*
INVITATION, *s.* invitation, prière, *f.*
INVITE, *va.* inviter, *à, de,* à, de, prier, de, convier, à, *à.*
INVITING, *a.* attrayant.
INVOKE, *va.* invoquer, prier, de.
INWARDLY, *ad.* intérieurement.

IRISHMAN, *s.* Irlandais.
IRONICAL, *a.* ironique.
IRONICALLY, *ad.* ironiquement.
IRONY, *s.* ironie, *f.*
IRRITATE, *va.* irriter *de,* provoquer.
ISLAND, *s.* île, *f.*
ISSUE, *v.* provenir *de,* sortir *de,* publier, émaner *de,* faire sortir *de.*
IT, *pro.* ce, il, elle, le, la, en, cela, y.
ITALIAN, *a.* Italien, ne.
ITSELF, *pro.* lui-même, soi-même.

J.

JACK-TAR, *s.* matelot, *m.* loup de mer, Jean goudron, *m.*
JAIL, *s.* prison, *f.*
JAILER, *s.* geôlier, *m.*
JAW, *s.* mâchoire, *f.*
JEW, *s.* JEWESS, juif, ve.
JEWEL, *s.* joyau, bijou, *m.*
JEWELLER, *s.* joaillier, ière.
JOB, *s.* petite affaire, commission, *f.*
JOIN, *v.* joindre *à,* unir *à,* s'unir, *à.*
JOKE, *s.* plaisanterie, *f.* bon mot, *m.*
— *vn.* plaisanter, railler.
JOKER, *s* railleur, euse.
JOLLY-FELLOW, *s.* un bon camarade, un bon vivant, *m.*
JOURNEY, *s.* voyage, *m.*
— *vn.* voyager.
JOY, *s.* joie, *f.* plaisir, *m.*
JOYFULLY, *ad.* joyeusement.
JOYOUSLY, *ad.* joyeusement.

JUDGE, *s.* juge, *m.*
— *v.* juger *de,* penser, à, *à,* décider *de,* de, à.
JUDGMENT, *s.* jugement, avis, sens, goût, arrêt, *m.* décision, *f.*
JUMP, *s.* saut, *m.* saillie, *f.*
— *vn.* sauter, cahoter.
JUNE, *s.* juin, *m.*
JUROR, *s.* juré, *m.*
JURY, *s.* jurés, *pl.* le juré, *m.*
JURYMAN, *s.* juré, *m.*
JUST, *a.* juste, équitable, intègre.
— *ad.* justement, précisément.
JUST AS, tout de même que.
— NOW, tout à l'heure, maintenant.
— SO, tout de même.
JUSTICE, *s.* justice, *f.*
JUSTIFICATON, *s.* excuse, justification, *f.*
JUSTLY, *ad.* à bon droit, justement.

K.

KEEP, v. garder, tenir, conserver, retenir, entretenir, célébrer, demeurer.
KEEPER, s. garde, portier, m.
KEY, s. clef ou clé, f. clavier, quai, m.
KICK, s. coup de pied, m.
— v. donner un coup de pied, à, ruer.
— OUT, chasser à coups de pied.
KILL, va. tuer, faire mourir.
— ONE'S SELF, se tuer, se faire mourir.
KIND, s. espèce, sorte, f.
— a. bon, ne. pour, tendre, envers.
KIND-HEARTED, a. qui a bon cœur.
KINDLY, a. bienfaisant, favorable.
— ad. obligeamment, de bon cœur, en bonne part, avec bonté.
KING, s. roi, m.

KINGDOM, s. royaume, m.
KISSES, s. baisers, embrassements, m. pl.
KNEE, s. genou, m.
KNEE-DEEP, a. jusqu'aux genoux, à la hauteur du genoux.
KNEE, vn. supplier à genoux.
KNEEL, vn. s'agenouiller, devant, se mettre à genoux, devant, fléchir le genou, devant.
KNIFE (pl. KNIVES), s. couteau, m.
KNOCK, v. frapper, heurter.
KNOCK DOWN, terrasser, assassiner.
KNOCKING (noise), s. bruit, m.
KNOW, v. savoir, connaître, être instruit, de.
KNOWLEDGE, s. savoir, m. connaissance science, expérience, f.

L.

LABORIOUS, a. laborieux, se.
LABOUR, s. peine, f. travail, m.
— v. travailler à, à, s'efforcer, de.
LACE, s. dentelle, f.
LAD, s. jeune garçon, jouvenceau, m.
LADDER, s. échelle, f.
LADY, s. dame, demoiselle, f.
LAND, s. terre, f. pays, terroir, m.
— (arable), terre labourable.

LAND (estate), terre, f. biens-fonds, m. pl.
— v. débarquer, faire une descente.
LANDING, s. descente.
LANDING-PLACE, s. palier, atterrage, m.
LANDLADY, s. hôtesse, propriétaire, f.
LANDLORD, s. hôte, propriétaire, m.
LANGUAGE, s. langage, m. langue, f.

LANGUAGE MASTER, s. maître de langue, m.
LANTERN, s. lanterne, f.
LAP, s. genoux, giron, m.
LAPDOG, s. bichon, toutou, m.
LAPSE, s. laps, écoulement, m.
LASH, s. coup de verge ou de fouet, m.
— va. sangler, fouetter.
LAST, s. forme de cordonnier, f.
— a. dernier, ère, passé.
— va. durer, continuer, subsister.
— ad. dernièrement.
— At last, ad. enfin.
LATE, a. dernier, ère, feu, depuis peu, depuis quelques jours, ci-devant.
— ad. tard.
— Of late, ad. dernièrement.
LATELY, ad. récemment, depuis peu.
LATENESS, s. nouveauté, f. retard, m.
LATIN, a. latin.
LATTER, a dernier, ère.
LAUDABLE, a. louable, de.
LAUGH, s. ris, rire, m.
— v. rire, de, de, paraître gai.
— AT, se moquer de, railler, se jouer de.
LAUGHABLE, a. risible, de.
LAUGHTER, s. rire, ris, m.
LAW, s. loi, jurisprudence, f. droit, m.
LAWSUIT, s. procès, m.
LAWYER, s. avocat, homme de robe, m.
LAY, v. mettre, ranger, poser, placer, poster, imposer à, disposer, tendre à, à.
LAZILY, ad. lentement, en paresseux.

LAZINESS, s. fainéantise, paresse, f.
LAZY, a. fainéant, paresseux se.
LAZYBONES, fainéant, paresseux.
LEAD, s. plomb, m.
LEAD, v. mener à, guider, vers, jusque, conduire, à, à, exciter, à, à, pousser, à, à.
LEADING, a. premier, ère, principal.
LEAGUE, s. lieue, f.
LEAP, s. saut, m.
— v. sauter sur, saillir, palpiter.
LEAP-FROG, s. (a boyish game), saute-mouton, m.
LEARN, v. apprendre, à, à, s'instruire, à.
LEARNED, a. savant, docte.
LEARNING, s. étude, littérature, f. belles lettres, f. pl. savoir, m.
LEAST, a. le moindre, le plus petit.
— ad. moins.
— At least, au moins, du moins.
LEAVE, s. permission, f. congé, m.
— v. laisser à, cesser, de, quitter, abandonner à.
— OFF, quitter, cesser, de, finir, de, discontinuer, de.
— OUT, ôter, omettre, de, exclure, de.
LEFT, a. gauche.
LEG, s. jambe, f.
— (of a fowl), cuisse d'un poulet.
— (of mutton), gigot, m.
LEND, va. prêter, à, aider, à, à.
LENGTH, s. longueur, étendue, durée, f.
— At length, ad. enfin, à la fin.

LESS, a. moindre, plus petit.
— ad. moins.
LESSON, s. leçon, f. précepte, m.
— va. instruire, de, enseigner, à, d.
LEST, c. de peur que.
LET, va. louer, laisser.
— BLOOD, saigner.
— DOWN, descendre, abattre, lâcher.
— (hinder), empêcher, de, retarder.
— LOOSE, déchainer, lâcher.
— OFF, or FLY, tirer, décharger.
— OUT, louer, placer, laisser sortir.
— IN, or INTO, faire entrer, dans.
— KNOW, faire savoir, à, faire part, de, à.
LETHARGY, s. léthargie, f. sommeil, m.
LETTER, s. lettre, épitre, f.
— OF ATTORNEY, procuration, f.
— OF MARK, lettre de marque, f.
LETTER, s. celui qui loue, qui permet.
— va. marquer avec des lettres.
LEVANT, s. Levant, Orient, m.
LIBERALITY, s. libéralité, f.
LIBERALLY, ad. libéralement.
LIBERTINE, a. s. libertin.
LIBERTY, s. liberté, f. privilége, m.
LICK, s. petit coup, m.
— va. lécher, laper, rosser.
LICKERISH, a. friand, avide, de.
LIE, s. mensonge, m.
— vn. mentir.
— vn. giter, coucher, reposer.
— DOWN, se coucher, reposer.

LIEUTENANT, s. lieutenant, m.
LIFE, s. vie, vigueur, vivacité, f.
— To depart this life, mourir.
LIGHT, s. lumière, clarté, f. jour, m.
— a. léger, ère. clair, blond.
— v. allumer, éclairer.
LIGHTHOUSE, s. fanal, phare, m.
LIGHTNING, s. éclair, m.
LIKE, v. aimer, à.
— a. semblable, à, comme.
LIMB, s. membre, m. extrémité, f.
LINE, s. ligne, corde, race, f. cordeau, m.
— va. doubler, de, mettre dedans.
LINEN, s toile, f.
LINGUIST, s. savant dans les langues, linguiste, m.
LIP, s. lèvre, f. bord, m.
LIQUID, s. liqueur, boisson, f.
— a. liquide, fluide.
LISTEN, vn. écouter, prêter l'oreille, à.
LISTENER, s. écouteur, euse.
LITERAL, a. littéral.
LITERALLY, ad. à la lettre, littéralement.
LITERARY, a. littéraire.
LITERATURE, littérature, érudition, f.
LITTLE, s. un peu, m.
— a. petit, une petite quantité, de.
— ad. peu, un peu, pas beaucoup.
LIVE, a. vif, ve. en vie, vivant.
— vn. vivre, demeurer, subsister.
— UPON, se nourrir, de.
— UP TO ONE'S ESTATE, dépenser tout son revenu.

LIVELIHOOD, s. vie, nourriture, f.
— (trade), métier, art, m.
LIVING, s. vie, subsistance, f. biens, m. pl.
LOAD, s. charge, f. fardeau, m.
— va. charger, de, embarrasser, de, accabler, de.
— WITH, combler, de.
LAF, s. un pain, m.
LOCK, s. serrure, f.
— v. fermer à clef.
— IN, enfermer, embrasser.
— ONE OUT, fermer la porte à quelqu'un.
— UP, serrer, enfermer.
LODGING, s. logement, logis, m.
LOGICAL, a. qui appartient à la logique.
LOGICALLY, ad. logiquement.
LOGIC, s. logique, f.
LONG, a. long, ue. grand, ennuyant, lent, tardif, ve.
— vn. brûler d'envie, de, avoir envie, de, tarder, de.
— ad. longtemps.
LONGER, a. plus long, ue.
— ad. plus longtemps.
LOOK, s. regard, air, m.
— v. regarder, voir, paraître.
— AT, regarder.
— LIKE, ressembler, à, avoir l'air, de, de, paraître.
LOOKING-GLASS, s. miroir, m. glace, f.
LORD, s. seigneur, m.

LORDSHIP, s. grandeur, seigneurie, domination, f. pouvoir, m.
LOSE, v. perdre, à, d.
LOSER, s. celui qui perd.
LOSS, s. perte, f. dommage, m.
— (in hunting), s. défaut, m.
— To be at a loss, être en défaut.
LOUD, a. haut, fort, grand.
LOUDLY, ad. hautement, à haute voix.
LOVE, s. amour, m.
— v. aimer, à, chérir.
LOVER, s. amant, amateur, m.
LOW, a. bas, se. vil, abattu.
— ad. bas, à bas prix, en bas.
LOYAL, a. loyal, envers, fidèle, d.
LOYALTY, s. loyauté, fidélité, f.
LUCK, s. hasard, bonheur, succès, m.
LUCKILY, ad. par bonheur.
LUCKINESS, s. bonheur, m.
LUCKLESS, a. malheureux, se.
LUCKY, a. heureux, se.
LULL, va. endormir.
LUMP, s. masse, f. bloc, tas, m. motte, f.
LUNCH, LUNCHEON, s. morceau, goûter, m. collation, f. second déjeuner.
LURK, vn. être aux aguets, se tapir, rôder.
LUXURY, s. luxe, m. mollesse, chère délicieuse, surabondance, chose délicate, f.

M.

MAD, v. rendre fou, être fou.
— a. insensé, enragé, fou, folle, de, passionné, folâtre, étourdi.

MADAM, *s.* madame, *f.*
MADMAN, *s.* insensé, furieux, fou.
MAGAZINE, *s.* magasin, recueil, *m.*
MAGISTRATE, *s.* magistrat, *m.*
MAGNANIMITY, *s.* magnanimité, *f.* grandeur d'âme, *f.*
MAGNIFICENCE, *s.* magnificence, *f.*
MAGNIFICENT, *a.* magnifique, superbe.
MAGNIFY, *va.* magnifier, grossir, exagérer.
MAGNIFYING GLASS, *s.* microscope, *m.* lentille, *f.*
MAID, MAIDEN, *s.* servante, vierge, fille, *f.*
MAINTAIN, *v.* maintenir, entretenir, nourrir, *de*, soutenir, *à*, défendre, conserver, prouver, prétendre.
MAKE, *s.* façon, forme, figure, *f.*
— *v.* faire, *à*, exécuter, *à*, créer, former, rendre.
— A FOOL OF, se jouer *de*.
— AGAIN, refaire.
— A MISTAKE, se tromper.
— ANGRY, fâcher, mettre en colère.
— A PEN, tailler une plume.
— AT, suivre, poursuivre.
— AWAY, se sauver, s'en aller, *de*.
— AWAY (*spend*), dépenser, *à*, *à*
— A WONDER, admirer, s'étonner, *de*.
— AWAY WITH, se défaire *de*, détruire.
— CLEAN, nettoyer.
— FOR A PLACE, se diriger *vers*.
— GAIN OF, gagner.

MAKE GOOD, soutenir, prouver, défendre.
— HASTE, se depêcher, *de*, se hâter, *de*.
— HAY, faner l'herbe.
— HOT, chauffer, échauffer.
— LAND, découvrir la terre.
— LEAN, maigrir.
— LESS, apetisser, amoindrir
— LEVEL, aplanir, unir.
— MAD, faire enrager, rendre fou.
— MANY WORDS, chicaner, contester.
— OFF, jouer des talons, s'enfuir.
— ONE OF A COMPANY, être d'une partie.
— ONE'S ESCAPE, se sauver *de*, *à*.
— OUT, prouver, *à*, faire voir, *à*.
— OVER, transférer, *à*, céder, *à*.
— READY, préparer, faire cuire.
— TOWARDS, s'approcher, *de*, aller *vers*.
— UP, achever, réparer, suppléer, *à*, combler, plier, récompenser, *de*, accommoder, compléter.
— UP TO ONE, accoster quelqu'un.
— USE OF, se servir, *de*, faire usage, *de*.
MAKER, *s.* fabricant, *m.*
MALADY, *s.* maladie, *f.* mal, *m.*
MAN, *s.* homme, *m.*
— OF WAR, vaisseau de guerre, *m.*
MANGLE, *va.* déchirer, calandrer, mutiler.
MANHOOD, *s.* virilité, *f.* courage, *m.*
MANKIND, *s.* genre humain, *m.*
MANLY, *ad.* en homme franc.

Manner, *s.* manière, sorte, façon, *f.*
Manœuvre, *v.* manœuvrer.
Manufactory, *s.* manufacture, fabrique, *f.*
— *va.* manufacturer.
Many, *a.* plusieurs, beaucoup, *de,* bien des.
— **a man,** plusieurs hommes.
— **a time,** plusieurs fois.
— **times,** souvent.
March, *v.* marcher, *à, vers,* avancer, *vers,* pousser, *jusque.*
— **on,** marcher, *à, vers,* aller, *à,* être en marche, *pour.*
Marine, *s.* marine, *f.* soldat de marine, *m.*
— *a.* marin, maritime, de mer.
Mariner, *s.* marin, matelot, *m.*
Mark, *s.* marque, trace, preuve, *f.* signe, indice, *m.*
— (*aim*), blanc, but, *m.*
— (*weight and money*), marc, *m.*
— *v.* marquer, *à,* remarquer.
Market, *s.* marché, *m.*
— *v.* marchander, acheter, *à, de,* vendre, *à.*
Market-place, *s.* le marché, *m.*
Market-price, *s.* courant du marché, *m.*
Market-town, *s.* ville à marché, *f.*
Marriage, *s.* mariage, *m.* noce, *f.*
Married, *a.* marié, *à, avec,* conjugal.
Marry, *v.* épouser, se marier, *à, avec,* marier, *à.*
Mask, *s.* masque, prétexte, *m.*
— *v.* masquer, se masquer.
Mass, *s.* messe, masse, *f.* tas, gros, *m.*
— *va.* dire *ou* célébrer la messe.

Master, *s.* maître, monsieur, *m.*
— **of arts,** *s.* maître ès arts, *m.*
— *va.* dompter, surmonter.
Match, *s.* semblable.
— (*fortune*), parti, *m.*
— *v.* assortir, *à,* joindre, *à,* apparier, convenir, marier, *à.*
Matter, *s.* matière, substance, *f.*
— (*thing*), chose, affaire, *f.*
— (*subject*), sujet, *m.* matière, *f.*
May, *auxil. v.* pouvoir.
Mayor, *s.* maire, *m.*
Me, *pro.* me, moi.
Meal, *s.* farine, *f.* repas, *m.*
Mean, *v.* entendre, vouloir dire, être résolu à, *à,* se proposer, *de.*
Meaning, *s.* intention, *f.* sens, *m.* signification.
Means, *s.* moyen, *m.* voie, *f.*
— (*estate*), bien, revenu, *m.*
— **By all means,** *ad.* absolument, par tous les moyens.
— **By no means,** *ad.* nullement.
Measure, *va.* mesurer *à,* estimer.
— (*land*), arpenter.
— *s.* mesure, démarche, *f.* degré, *m.*
Mediterranean, *a. s.* méditerrané.
Meat, *s.* viande, *f.* aliment, *m.*
— (*roast*), rôti, *m.*
— (*boiled*), bouilli, *m.*
Meet, *v.* rencontrer, trouver, éprouver, s'assembler, se joindre, *à,* en venir aux mains, *avec.*
— **with,** rencontrer.
Melancholy, *a.* triste.
— *s.* mélancolie.

MELT, v. fondre, liquéfier, attendrir, fléchir.
MELTER, s. fondeur, m.
MEMBER, s. membre, m.
MEMOIR, s. mémoire, f. souvenir, m.
MEN, pl. de MAN, homme.
MERCHANT, s. marchand, négociant, m.
— SHIP, s. vaisseau marchand, m.
MERCHANTMAN, s. vaisseau marchand, m.
MERCIFUL, a. miséricordieux, se, envers.
MERCIFULLY, ad. avec clémence.
MERCILESS, a. impitoyable envers, cruel, le, envers, pour.
MERCY, s. miséricorde, merci, f.
MERE, a. pur, simple, franc, che.
MERIT, s. mérite, m.
— va. mériter, de.
MESS, s. mets, plat, m. gamelle, portion, compagnie, f.
MESS-ROOM, s. salle à manger (où les officiers mangent ensemble).
MESSAGE, s. message, m. commission, f.
MESSENGER, s. messager, courrier, m.
METAMORPHOSIS, s. métamorphose, f.
METHOD, s. méthode, voie, f. moyen, m.
METROPOLIS, s. métropole, f.
MID-DAY, s. midi, m.
MIDDLE, s. milieu, centre, m.
— a. moyen, ne mitoyen, ne.
MIGHT, prét. de MAY, pouvoir.
— s. puissance, force, f.
MILDLY, ad. doucement, tendrement.

MILE, s. mille, m.
MILESTONE, s. pierre milliaire, f.
MILITARY, s. a. militaire, de guerre.
MILL, s. moulin, m.
MILLER, s. meunier, m.
MIND, s. esprit, m. âme, fantaisie, pensée, envie, résolution, opinion, f. souvenir, dessein, désir, gré, m.
— v. remarquer, songer, à, d, avoir soin, de, de, considérer, faire souvenir, de, de.
MINDFUL, a. attentif, ve. à, d.
MINE, pro. mon, ma, mes, le mien, la mienne, les miens, les miennes, à moi.
MINGLE, v. mêler, d.
MINISTER, s. ministre, agent, m.
— v. servir, à, d, fournir d, administrer, d.
MINUTE, va. minuter.
MIRACLE, s. miracle, m.
MIRACULOUS, a. miraculeux, se.
MISER, s. avare, m.
MISERABLE, a. misérable, malheureux, se. avare, mesquin, vil.
MISERY, s. misère, indigence, f.
MISFORTUNE, s. malheur, m. infortune, f.
MISLAY, va. égarer, déplacer, placer mal.
MISS, s. perte, faute, méprise, f.
— v. manquer, de, de, d, omettre, de.
MISSIONARY, MISSIONER, s. missionnaire, m.
MISTAKE, s. méprise, erreur, faute, f.
— v. se méprendre, se tromper.

Mistress, *s.* maîtresse, *f.*
Mix, *v.* mêler, *à.*
Moan, *s.* gémissement, *m.*
— *v.* gémir, de, *de,* déplorer, de, pleurer, de, *de.*
Mock, *va.* se moquer, *de,* abuser, *de.*
Moderate, *a.* modéré, sage, modique.
— *va.* modérer, adoucir, apaiser.
Modern, *a.* moderne.
Modestly, *ad.* modestement.
Modesty, *s.* modestie, pudeur, *f.*
Moment, *s.* moment, *m.* importance, *f.*
Monarch, *s.* monarque, *m.*
Monarchy, *s.* monarchie, *f.*
Monastery, *s.* monastère, *m.*
Money, *s.* argent, *m.* monnaie, *f.*
Money-bag, *s.* sac à argent, *m.* sacoche, *f.*
Monk, *s.* moine, religieux, *m.*
Monster, *s.* monstre, *m.*
Month, *s.* mois, *m.*
Monument, *s.* monument, *m.*
Moral, *a.* moral.
— *s.* sens moral, *m.* morale, *f.*
More, *ad.* plus, davantage.
Morn, *s.* matin, *m.*
Morning, *s.* matin, *m.* matinée, *f.*
— gown, *s.* robe de chambre, *f.*
Morrow, *s.* demain, le lendemain, *m.*
— *Good morrow,* bonjour.
— *To-morrow,* demain.
Mortal, *a. s.* mortel, le.
Mortification, *s.* mortification, gangrène, *f.*
Mortify, *v.* affliger, se gangrener.

Most, *ad.* le plus, très fort, la plupart.
Mother, *s.* mère, *f.*
Motion, *s.* mouvement, *m.*
Motive, *a.* moteur, trice, qui meut.
— *s.* motif, *m.* raison, *f.*
Mount, *s.* mont, *m.*
— *v.* monter, faire monter.
Mountainous, *a.* montagneux, se.
Mouth, *s.* bouche, *f.*
— of a haven, entrée d'un port, *f.*
— (*of a beast*), gueule, *f.*
— (*of a river*), embouchure, *f.*
— *v.* marmoter, gourmander, manger.
Mouthful, *s.* bouchée, *f.*
Much, *a.* beaucoup, *de.*
Murder, *s.* meurtre, assassinat, *m.*
— *v.* tuer, assassiner.
Murderer, *s.* meutrier, assassin, *m.*
Music, *s.* musique, *f.*
— room, *s.* salle de concert, *f.*
Must, *v.* falloir, devoir, être obligé, de.
Muster, *v.* s'assembler.
Mutual, *a.* mutuel, le. réciproque.
Mutually, *ad.* mutuellement.
Muzzle, *s.* museau, muffle, *m.*
— (*for the mouth*), *s.* muselière, *f.*
— (*of a gun*), *s.* bouche, *f.*
— *va.* emmuseler, museler, dorlotter.
My, *pro.* mon, ma, mes, à moi.
Mysterious, *a.* mystérieux, se.
Mysteriously, *ad.* mystérieusement.
Mystery, *s.* mystère, secret, *m.*

N.

NAME, s. nom, m.
NATION, s. nation, f. peuple, m.
NATIONAL, a. national.
NATIVE, a. natif, ve. natál, indigène.
NATURAL, s. idiot, imbécile.
— a. naturel, le. aisé.
NATURALLY, ad. naturellement.
NATURE, s. nature, f. naturel, m.
NAVIGATE, v. naviguer, sur.
NAVIGATION, s. navigation, f.
N.B. NOTA BENE, remarquez.
NEAR, a. chiche, proche, cher, ère.
— ad. presque.
— pr. proche, près, auprès, de près.
NEARER, a. plus près, de, plus proche, de.
NEAREST, a. le plus près, de.
NEARLY, ad. de près, presque.
— (niggardly), chichement.
NECESSARILY, ad. nécessairement.
NECESSARY, a. nécessaire, à, utile, à, profitable, à.
NECESSITY, s. nécessité, fatalité, f.
NECK, s. cou, m.
— (of a bottle), goulot, m.
NECKLACE, s. collier, m.
NEED, s. besoin, m. indigence, nécessité, exigence.
— va. avoir besoin, de, de, manquer, de.
— vn. être nécessaire, à, falloir.
NEEDFUL, a. nécessaire, à, indispensable, à.
NEEDFULLY, ad. nécessairement.
NEGRO, s. nègre, m.

NEIGHBOUR, s. voisin, prochain, m.
— va. avoisiner, se rapprocher, de.
NEIGHBOURHOOD, s. voisinage, m.
NEIGHBOURING, a. d'alentour, voisin.
NEIGHBOURLY, a. sociable.
— ACT, s. trait de bon voisin, m.
— ad. à l'amiable.
NEITHER, pro. ni l'un ni l'autre.
— c. ni, non plus.
NEVER, ad. jamais, ne pas, point.
— MIND, v. n'importe, c'est égal.
NEVERTHELESS, c. néanmoins, pourtant, malgré cela.
NEW, a. neuf, ve. nouveau, nouvel, le. frais, fraîche, moderne.
— ad. nouvellement, de nouveau.
NEWS, s. nouvelles, f. pl.
NEWSPAPER, s. journal, m. gazette, f.
NEXT, a. prochain, proche, suivant.
— ad. ensuite, puis, immédiatement.
— TO, NEXT AFTER, pr. après.
— DAY, s. lendemain, m.
NIGHT, s. nuit, f. soir, m.
NIGHTCAP, s. bonnet de nuit, m.
NIMBLY, ad. agilement, lestement.
No, ad. non, ne pas, de, point, de.

No, a. nul, le. aucun, pas un ou une.
— MATTER, n'importe.
— MORE, pas davantage.
NOBILITY, s. noblesse, f.
NOBLE (*old coin*) s. noble, m.
— a. noble, illustre, généreux, magnifique, sublime.
NOISE, s. bruit, éclat, fracas, m.
— IN ONE'S EAR, tintement, m.
NONE, a. nul, le. aucun, pas un personne, qui que ce soit.
NONSENSE, s. absurdité, f. galimatias, m. sottise, f. non-sens, m.
NONSENSICALLY, ad. contre le bon sens, contre le sens commun.
NORTH, s. nord, septentrion, m.
— a. du nord, de nord, arctique, septentrional.
NOSE, s. nez, m.
— v. sentir, faire face, à, morguer.
NOSTRIL, s. narine, f.

NOT, ad. ne pas, point, non, non pas.
NOTE, s. note, marque, remarque, f.
— OF HAND, billet, effet, m. traite, f.
NOTE, va. noter, marquer, à, remarquer.
NOTICE, s. note, attention, f.
NOTHING, s. rien, néant, m.
NOTWITHSTANDING, c. nonobstant, malgré, toutefois.
NOW, ad. maintenant, à présent, actuellement, tout à l'heure.
— AND THEN, de temps en temps.
— c. or.
NOWHERE, ad. nulle part.
NUMBER, s. nombre, numéro, m.
— va. nombrer, compter, supputer.
NUMBERLESS, a. innombrable, infini.
NUMEROUS, a. nombreux, nombreuse.

O.

OATS, s. avoine, f.
OBEDIENCE, s. obéissance, f.
OBEY, v. obéir.
OBJECT, s. objet, sujet, m. matière, f.
— va. objecter, à, opposer, à.
OBJECTION, s. objection, f.
OBLIGATORY, a. obligatoire.
OBLIGE, va. obliger, de, faire plaisir, à.
OBSCURE. a. obscur, cache.
— va. obscurcir, rendre obscur.
OBSCURELY, ad. obscurément.

OBSERVATION, s. observation, f.
OBSERVE, va. observer, remarquer.
OBSTINACY, s. obstination, f.
OBSTINATE, a. opiniâtre, obstiné.
OBSTINATELY, ad. obstinément.
OBTAIN, v. obtenir, de, de, remporter, sur, se procurer.
OBTAINING, s. obtention, f.
OCCASION, s. occasion, cause, affaire, f.
— (*want*), s. besoin, m.

OCCULT, *a.* occulte, caché.
OCCUPY, *va.* posséder, jouir, de.
ODOUR, *s.* odeur, senteur, *f.*
OF, *pr.* de, du, des, de l', en, sur, par, à, concernant, parmi, entre.
OFF, *ad.* loin, éloigné.
— *ma.* au large.
OFFEND, *v.* offenser, choquer, pécher.
OFFENDER, *s.* délinquant, *m.*
OFFER, *va.* offrir, à, de, présenter, à, proposer, à, de.
— *vn.* s'offrir, à, se présenter, pour, s'engager, à, à.
— (*expose*), exposer, à, offrir, à.
— ABUSE, maltraiter.
— VIOLENCE, faire violence, à.
— *s.* offre, proposition, *f.*
OFFICER, *s.* officier, *m.*
— (*bailiff*), sergent, *m.*
OFT, OFTEN, OFTENTIMES, OFTTIMES, *ad.* souvent, fréquemment.
OLD, *a.* vieux, vieil, *m.* vieille, *f.*
— (*Of old*), anciennement.
— AGE, vieillesse, *s. f.*
OLDEST, *a.* le plus vieux, *m.* la plus vieille, *f.*
OMNIPRESENT, *a.* présent partout.
ON, *pr.* sur, à, au, de, du, de là, en.
— BOARD, sur le bord.
— THE SPOT, sur-le-champ.
— FOOT, à pied.
— HIGH, en haut.
— HORSEBACK, à cheval.
— IT, dessus.
— PURPOSE, à dessein, exprès.
— THAT DAY, ce jour-là.

ON THE LEFT, à gauche.
— THE RIGHT, à droit.
ONCE, *ad.* une fois, autrefois.
ONE, *s.* quelqu'un, tel, telle.
— *pro.* on, l'on.
— *a.* un, l'un, l'autre, le même.
ONE-EYED, *a.* borgne.
ONE-HANDED, *a.* manchot, te.
ONE'S SELF, *pro.* soi-même.
ONLY, *a.* seul.
— *ad.* seulement, uniquement.
OPEN, *v.* ouvrir, à, entamer.
— (*a bundle*), défaire un paquet.
— (*a letter*), décacheter une lettre.
— (*as flowers do*), s'ouvrir, s'épanouir, éclore.
— (*lay open*), exposer, à, expliquer, à.
— *a.* ouvert, visible, manifeste.
— (*declared*), déclaré.
— (*public*), public, que.
— WEATHER, *s.* temps doux, *m.*
OPERATION, *s.* opération, *f.* effet, *m.*
OPPORTUNITY, *s.* opportunité, occasion, *f.*
OPPOSE, *va.* opposer, à, resister, à.
OPPOSITE, *a.* opposé, à, contraire, à.
OPPOSITION, *s.* opposition, concurrence, *f.*
ORDER, *s.* ordre, décret, *m.*
— (*manner*), manière, méthode, *f.*
— (*rule*), règle, discipline, *f.*
— *va.* ordonner, de, à, régler.
— *In order to*, afin de, pour.
ORGAN, *s.* organe, *m.* orgues, *f. pl.*
ORPHAN, *s.* orphelin, *m. f.*
ORNAMENT, *s.* ornement, *m.*

OSTLER, s. valet d'écurie, m.
OTHER, a. autre.
OTHERS, s. les autres, autrui.
OTHERWISE, ad. autrement, tout autre.
OUGHT, s. quelque chose, f.
OUGHT, v. défect. devoir, falloir.
— *You ought to do it*, vous devriez le faire.
OUR, pro. notre, nos, à nous.
OURS, pro. le nôtre, la nôtre, les nôtres, à nous.
OURSELVES, pro. nous-mêmes.
OUT, va. déposséder, de, dépouiller, de.
— ad. pr. hors, dehors.
— int. qu'on le chasse! foin de lui.
— OF HATRED, par haine.
— OF WHICH, sur lequel.
— OF HAND, tout de suite.
— OF MEASURE, outre mesure.
— OF HOPE, sans espérance.
— OF DESIGN, à dessein, exprès.
— (*expired*), expiré, échu.
— (*extinguished*), éteint.
— OF FAVOUR, disgracié.
— OF PLACE, hors de place.
— OF SIGHT, à perte de vue, hors de vue.
— OF HUMOUR, de mauvaise humeur.
— OF TUNE, désaccordé.
— OF POCKET, déboursé.
OUTSIDE, s. dehors, extérieur, m.

OUTWIT, va. duper, attraper, surpasser en finesse.
OVER, pr. sur, par-dessus, au-dessus.
— ad. d'un bout à l'autre, de, passé, de reste, au delà.
— a, fini, fait.
OVERBOARD, ad. par-dessus bord, hors de vaisseau.
OVERCOME, a. accablé.
OVERHEAR, v. entr'ouïr, entendre.
OVERJOYED, a. charmé, de, de, extasié.
OVERSET, va. renverser, verser détruire, ruiner.
OVERTAKE, va. atteindre, attraper, surprendre, rejoindre.
OVERTAKEN, a. atteint, surpris.
OVERTAKER, s. qui attrape.
OVERTURN, va. verser, renverser.
OWE, va. devoir, à, être obligé, de.
OWING, a. du, qu'on doit, qui est l'effet, de, à cause de, en raison, de.
OWN, a. propre.
— va. avouer, à, confesser, à, convenir.
— (*claim*), réclamer, s'attribuer.
— (*possess*), jouir, de, posséder.
OWNER, s. propriétaire, possesseur, m.

P.

PADDY, s. sobriquet donné aux Irlandais.
PAGE (*at court*), s. page, m.
— (*of a book*), page, f.
— va. marquer les pages, de.

PAIL, s. seau, m.
PAIN, s. douleur, peine, f. mal, m.
— va. faire mal, à, affliger, de.

PAINFUL, *a.* douloureux, se. pénible.
PAINFULLY, *ad.* péniblement.
PALACE, *s.* palais, *m.* maison royale, *f.*
PALTRY, *a.* chétif, ve. pitoyable.
PANG, *va.* tourmenter.
— *s* atteinte, attaque, angoisse, *f.*
PANGS OF DEATH, *s. pl.* l'agonie, *f.*
PAPER, *s.* papier, *m.*
PARCEL, *s.* parcelle, pièce, quantité, *f.*
— (*bundle*), paquet, *m.*
PARDON, *s.* pardon, *m.* grâce, *f.*
— *va.* pardonner, *à,* de, faire grâce, *à.*
PARENT, *s.* père, *m.* mère, *f.*
PART, *s.* partie, part, défense, cause, *f.* parti, quartier, devoir, *m.*
— (*a player's*), rôle, *m.*
— *va.* partager, séparer, se quitter.
PART WITH, se défaire, *de,* céder, se séparer, *de,* abandonner.
PARTAKE, *vn.* participer, *à,* avoir part, *à,* s'intéresser, *dans.*
— OF, partager, prendre part, *à.*
PARTAKER, *s.* participant.
PARTICULAR, *a.* particulier, ère. singulier, ère.
— *s.* détail, point, *m.*
PARTICULARS, *s. pl.* particularités, circonstances, *f. pl.*
— OF AN ESTATE, inventaire, *m.*
— OF A CASE *or* OF A LAWSUIT, *s.* pièces d'un procès, *f. pl.*
PARTRIDGE, *s.* perdrix, *f.*
PARTY, *s.* parti, *m.* partie, *f.*
PASSIONATE, *a.* passionné.

PASS, *v.* passer, traverser, surpasser.
— ALONG, passer, passer le long, *de.*
— AWAY, s'écouler, passer, disparaître.
— BY, passer, omettre, oublier.
— FOR, passer pour, être réputé.
— ONE'S WORD, engager sa parole.
— OVER (*forget*), oublier.
— SENTENCE, prononcer jugement.
PASTRY-COOK, *s.* pâtissier, ère.
PATIENCE, *s.* patience, *f.*
PATIENT, *s.* malade, *m.* et *f.*
— *a.* endurant, patient.
PATTIES, *s.* petits pâtés.
PAVEMENT, *s.* pavé, *m.*
PAVILION, *s.* pavillon, *m.* tente, *f.*
PAW, *s.* patte, griffe, serre, *f.*
PAWN, *s.* pion (au jeu d'échecs), gage, *m.*
— *v.* engager, mettre en gage.
PAY, *va.* payer.
— A VISIT, rendre visite, *à.*
— BACK, rendre, *à,* restituer, *à.*
— DOWN, payer argent comptant.
— OFF, acquitter, battre, punir.
— *ma.* espalmer un bâtiment.
— A SEAM, goudronner une couture.
— OFF A SHIP, désarmer un vaisseau.
— AWAY THE CABLE, filer un câble.
— UP, payer, solder.
PAYMENT, *s.* payement, *m.* récompense, *f.*
PEACE, *s.* paix, tranquillité, *f.*
— OFFERING, *s.* sacrifice propitiatoire, *m.*

PEACE OFFICER, s. officier de police, m.
— int. paix! silence! faites silence.
PEACEABLE, a. paisible, pacifique.
PEACEABLY, ad. paisiblement.
PEASANT, s. paysan, ne.
PEASANTRY, s. corps de paysans, m.
PECK, s. picotin, m.
PEDESTAL, s. piédestal, m.
PEDLAR, PEDLER, s. marchand ambulant, colporteur, petit mercier, m.
PEN, s. plume, f.
PENCE, s. pl. de PENNY.
PENITENT, a. s. pénitent, pénitente.
PENKNIFE, s. canif, m.
PENNY, s. pièce de deux sous, f.
PEOPLE, s. peuple, m. gens, m. et f.
— va. peupler, de, remplir d'habitants.
PEOPLED, a. peuplé, de.
PERCEIVE, v. apercevoir, s'apercevoir, de.
— (beforehand), pressentir.
PEREMPTORY, a. péremptoire, décisif, ve.
PERFECT, a. parfait, achevé.
— va. achever, perfectionner.
PERFECTION, s. perfection, excellence, f.
PERFECTLY, ad. parfaitement, à fond.
PERFORM, v. faire, exécuter, accomplir.
PERFORMANCE, s. ouvrage, m. exécution, f.
PERFORMER, s. artiste, m. exécuteur, trice, musicien, ne. actrice.

PERHAPS, ad. peut-être.
PERISH, vn. périr, mourir, dépérir.
PERJURER, s. parjure, m. et f.
PERMISSION, s. permission, f.
PERMISTION, PERMIXTION, s. l'action de mêler.
PERMIT, permettre, à, de, accorder, à, de.
PERPETUAL, a. perpétuel, le.
PERSEVERANCE, s. persévérance, f.
PERSON, s. personne, figure, f.
PERSUADE, va. persuader, à, de, convaincre, de, de.
PETRIFY, v. pétrifier, se pétrifier.
PHIAL, s. fiole, f.
PHILANTHROPIC, a. philanthropique.
PHILIPPIC, s. philippique, déclamation, f.
PICK UP, v. ramasser, enlever, accrocher.
PICKPOCKET, PICKPURSE, s. filou, m.
PICTURE, s. tableau, m.
PIECE, s. pièce, f. morceau, m.
PIKE (fish), s. brochet, m.
PILL, s. pilule, f.
PINT, s. pinte, f.
PIPE, s. pipe, f. tuyau, conduit, m.
PISTOL, PISTOLET, s. pistolet, m.
PIT, s. fosse, f. creux, trou, m.
— (in a playhouse), s. parterre, m.
PITCHFORK, s. fourche, f.
PITEOUSLY, ad. pitoyablement, à faire pitié.
PLACARD, s. affiche, f.

PLACE, s. place, f. lieu, endroit, m.
— va. placer, mettre, ranger.
— (employment), place, charge, dignité, f. emploi, poste, m.
PLAGUE, s. peste, f. fléau, m.
— va harceler, tourmenter.
PLAINTIFF, s. plaignant, e. demandeur, eresse, accusateur, trice.
PLAY, v. jouer.
— ON (an instrument), jouer, de.
—AT, jouer, à.
PLEAD, vn. plaider, défendre.
— GUILTY, avouer l'accusation.
PLEADER, s. plaideur. m.
PLEASANT, a. agréable, avec, à.
PLEASANTLY, ad. agréablement.
PLEASANTRY, s. plaisanterie, f.
PLEASE, v. plaire, à, agréer, vouloir.
— ONE'S SELF, prendre plaisir, à, à, se plaire, à, à.
PLEASED with, a. content, de, de, satisfait de, de.
— v. plaire, à, contenter.
PLEDGE, s. gage, otage, m.
— va. engager, mettre en gage.
PLENTIFUL, a. abondant.
PLENTIFULLY, ad. abondamment.
PLUM, s. prune, f. raisin sec, m.
PLUMCAKE, s. gâteau aux raisins secs, m.
PLUMPUDDING, s. pouding aux raisins, m.
PLUMS, s. raisins secs, m. pl.

PLUNGE, s. action de plonger, f. embarras, mauvais pas, m.
— v. plonger, enfoncer.
POCKET, s. poche, f.
— v. empocher, mettre en poche.
POCKET-BOOK, s. portefeuille, porte-lettre, m. tablettes, f. pl.
POINT, s. pointe, f. point, degré, état, m. circonstance, f. but, m.
POINT TO, v. montrer du doigt.
— A CANNON, v. pointer un canon.
POISON, s. poison, venin, m.
— va. empoisonner, infecter, de.
POLISH, a. de la Pologne, Polonais.
POLITE, a. poli, civil, honnête.
POLITELY, ad. poliment, civilement.
POLITENESS, s. politesse, f.
POLITICAL, a. politique.
POLLUTE, va. souiller.
POND, s. étang, m.
POOR, a. pauvre, indigent, dénué.
— (lean), décharné, maigre.
— s. les pauvres, m. pl.
POODLE, s. barbet, m.
POPULAR, a. populaire, commun.
PORT, s. port, havre, m.
PORTER, s. forte bière, f.
— s. crocheteur, porte-faix, m.
— OF A HOUSE, s. suisse, portier, m.
PORTION, s. portion, part, dot, f.
— va. doter, partager, deviser.
POSSESS, va. posséder, jouir, de, avoir.

POSSESS ONE'S SELF OF, vr. prendre possession, de, se saisir, de, s'emparer, de.
POSSESSION, s. possession, f.
POSSIBLE, a. possible.
POST, s. poste, f. courrier, m.
— (place), poste, m.
— (piece of timber), poteau, pilier, m.
POSTBOY, s. postillon, m.
POST-CHAISE, s. chaise de poste, f.
POSTILION, s. postillon, m.
POSTMASTER, s. maître de poste, m.
POT, s. pot, vase, m.
POUND (weight), s. livre de poids, f.
— (for cattle), s. enclos, m.
— STERLING, livre sterling, f.
POVERTY, s. pauvreté, misère, f.
POWDER, s. poudre, f.
POWER, s. puissance, autorité, force, f. pouvoir, m.
POWERFUL, a. puissant.
PRAISE, s. louange, f.
— va. louer, de, de, vanter, élever.
PRAY, va. prier, de, supplier, de, implorer.
PRECAUTION, s. précaution, f.
— va. avertir d'avance.
PRECIOUS, a. précieux, se, de prix.
PRECIOUSLY, ad. précieusement.
PREJUDICE, s. préjugé, m. prévention, f.
PREPARATION, s. préparation, f. apprêt, m. préparatifs, m. pl.
PREPARE, v. préparer, à, d, se disposer, à, d.
PRESENCE, s. présence, f.
— OF MIND, sang-froid, m.

PRESENCE (port), mine, f. air, port, m.
PRESENT, a. présent.
— s. présent, don, cadeau, m.
— va. présenter, à, offrir, à, nommer, à.
PRESERVE, va. préserver, conserver, confire.
PRESIDE, va. présider.
PRESS, s. presse, armoire, f.
— GANG, s. presse, f.
PRESS, v. (sailors), forcer à servir.
PRESSGANG, s. matelots qui rôdent pour forcer les gens à servir, m. pl.
PRESUMPTION, s. présomption, f.
PRETENCE, s. prétexte, m.
PRETEND, v. prétendre, à, croire.
PRETTY, a. gentil, le, joli.
PREVALENCE, s. domination, force, prépondérance, f.
PREVENT, va. empêcher, de, détourner, de.
PREVENTER, s. mar. fausse manœuvre, f.
— s. qui empêche, en prévenant, m.
PREY, s. proie, f. butin, m.
— vn. butiner, piller, miner, ronger.
PRICE, s. prix, m. valeur, f.
— Market price, s. cours du marché, m.
PRIDE, s. orgueil, faste, m. fierté, f.
PRIEST, s. prêtre, m.
PRINCE, s. prince, m.
PRINCESS, s. princesse, f.
PRINCIPAL, a. principal, essentiel, le.
— s. chef, principal, m.
PRIOR, s. prieur, m.
— a. antérieure, à.

Prison, *s.* prison, *f.*
— *va.* emprisonner, mettre en prison.
Prisoner, *s.* prisonnier, ère.
Private, *a.* privé, *s.* retiré, *m.* particulier, ère. dérobé, bourgeois, simple soldat.
Private conversation, *s.* un tête-à-tête, *m.*
Privateer, *s.* corsaire, armateur, *m.*
Privately, *ad.* clandestinement, en secret, en particulier.
Privy, *s.* le privé, *m.* les lieux, *m. pl.*
Prize, *s.* prix, *m.* prise, *f.*
Probable, *a.* vraisemblable, probable.
Probably, *ad.* probablement.
Process, *s.* procédé, progrès, *m.*
Procure, *va.* procurer, *à*, produire, occasionner, *à*, se procurer.
Product, *s.* produit, fruit, *m.*
Production, *s.* production, *f.*
Productive, *a.* génératif, ve. fécond, *en.*
Profane, *a.* profane, impie.
— *va.* profaner.
Profess, *v.* professer, exercer.
Profession, *s.* profession, *f.* emploi, *m.*
Professor, *s.* professeur, *m.*
Profit, *s.* profit, gain, avantage, *m.*
— *v.* profiter, *de*, être utile, *à*, avantager.
Profitable, *a.* profitable.
Profound, *a.* profound.
Progress, *s.* progrès, profit, *m.*
— (*journey*), cours, tour, voyage, *m.*

Promote, *va.* avancer, élever, promouvoir.
Promoted, *a.* promu.
Promotion, *s.* avancement, *m.*
Pronounce, *va.* prononcer, décider.
Pronunciation, *s.* prononciation, *f.*
Proof, *s.* preuve, *f.* essai, *m.* épreuve, *f.*
— *a.* à l'épreuve, de.
Property, *s.* naturel, *m.* propriété, *f.*
— (*goods*), biens-fonds, *m. pl.*
Proposal, *s.* proposition, offre, *f.*
Propose, *va.* proposer, *à*, de, offrir, *à*, de.
Proposition, *s.* proposition, *f.*
Proprietor,—tress, *s.* propriétaire.
Proscribe, *va.* proscrire, *de*, bannir, *de.*
Proscript, *s.* proscrit, banni, *m.*
Proscription, *s.* proscription, *f.*
Protect, *va.* protéger, défendre.
Protection, *s.* protection, *f.*
Protective, *a.* défensif, ve. qui protége.
Protector, *s.* protecteur, *m.*
Protest, *s.* protêt, procès-verbal, *m.*
— *v.* protester, jurer, *à.*
Prove, *v.* prouver, *à*, montrer, *à*, *à*, éprouver.
— (*be*), devenir, arriver, *à.*
Provide, *va.* pourvoir, munir, fournir.
— one's self, se pourvoir, *de.*
Provided that, *c.* pourvu que.
Providence, *s.* Providence, *f.*
— (*foresight*), prévoyance, *f.*

PROVIDENCE (*husbandry*), économie, frugalité, *f.*
PROVIDENT, *a.* prévoyant, soigneux, se. de.
PROVIDENTIAL, *a.* de la Providence.
PROVIDENTIALLY, *ad.* heureusement, par un effet de la Providence.
PROVISION, *s.* provision, *f.*
PUBLIC, *s.* public, *m.*
— *a.* public, que. générale.
— HOUSE, *s.* cabaret, *m.* auberge, *f.*
PUBLISH, *va.* publier, faire imprimer.
PUG-DOG, *s.* chien carlin, *m.*
PULL, *s.* l'action de tirer, secousse, *f.*
— BACK, *s.* échec, obstacle, *m.*
PULL, *va.* tirer, *à,* arracher, *à,* cueillir.
— BACK, tirer en arrière, reculer.
— DOWN, faire tomber, démolir.
— DOWN (*humble*), abattre, humilier.
— IN, tirer, dedans.
— OFF, ôter, *de, à,* arracher, *de, à.*
— OUT, arracher, *à,* tirer, *à,* ôter, *à.*
— TO, tirer à soi, serrer.
— UP, tirer en haut, lever, élever.
PUNCTUAL, *a.* ponctuel, le. à, *à,* exact, à, *à.*
PUNCTUALITY, *s.* ponctualité, exactitude, *f.*
PUNCTUALLY, *ad.* ponctuellement.

PUNISH, *va.* punir, de, *de,* châtier, corriger.
PUNISHABLE, *a.* punissable.
PUNISHMENT, *s.* punition, *f.* châtiment, *m.*
PUPIL (*scholar*), *s.* élève, pupille, *m.* et *f.*
PUPPY, *s.* petit chien, *m.*
PURCHASE, *s.* achat, *m.*
— *v.* acheter, *de, à.*
PURE, *a.* pure, simple, bon, ne.
PURPOSE, *s.* dessein, propos, projet, *m.*
— *va.* se proposer, de, avoir dessein, de.
PURSE, *s.* bourse, *f.*
— NET, *s.* bourse, *f.*
— UP, *vn.* embourser
PURSUE, *v.* poursuivre, suivre.
PURSUER, *s.* poursuivant, *m.*
PURSUIT, *s.* poursuite, *f.*
PUSH, *s.* coup, effort, *m.*
PUSH, *v.* pousser, *à,* à.
— ON, pousser, pousser en avant.
PUT, *v.* mettre, *à,* poser, placer.
— AN END TO, mettre fin à.
— A STOP TO, s'opposer, *à,* empêcher, de, arrêter.
— A TRICK UPON, faire un tour, *à.*
— BACK, reculer.
— DOWN, peser à terre.
— FORWARD, pousser, avancer.
— IN FEAR, faire peur, *à.*
— OFF (*delay*), remettre, *à,* renvoyer, *à,* différer, de, traîner, s'excuser.
— BY, mettre de côté, détourner.
— OUT, éteindre.

Q.

QUALITY, *s.* qualité, condition, *f.*
— (*nobility*), la noblesse, *f.*
QUANTITY, *s.* quantité, *f.*
QUARREL, *s.* querelle, dispute, *f.*
— *vn.* se quereller, se disputer.
QUARTER, *s.* quart, quartier, trimestre, *m.*
QUEEN, *s.* reine, *f.*
— (*at cards*), dame, *f.*
QUESTION, *s.* question, demande, *f.* doute, *m.*
— *v.* questionner, interroger, douter.

QUICKLY, *ad.* vitement, vite, bientôt.
QUIET, *s.* repos, *m.* tranquillité, paix, *f.* calme, *m.*
— *a.* tranquille, en repos.
— *va.* apaiser, calmer, assoupir.
QUIETLY, *ad.* paisiblement, tranquillement, sans mouvement.
QUIT, *va.* quitter, se défaire, *de.*
QUITE, *ad.* tout à fait, entièrement.
— CONTRARY, tout au contraire.

R.

RAGE, *s.* fureur, rage, *f.* emportement, *m.*
— *vn.* tempêter, être furieux, se. se courroucer, être courroucé.
RAILLERY, *s.* raillerie, *f.*
RAIN, *s.* pluie, *f.*
— *vn.* pleuvoir, tomber de l'eau.
RAINY, *a.* pluvieux, se. de pluie.
RAISE, *va.* lever, élever, *à,* soulever, *de,* hausser, relever, *de,* rehausser.
RANSOM, *s.* rançon, *f.*
RANK, *s.* rangée, *f.* rang, *m.*
RAPACIOUS, *a.* avide, *de,* rapace.
RAPIDE, *a.* rapide, vif, ve. vite.
RAPIDLY, *ad.* rapidement.
RARELY, *ad.* rarement, exactement.
RATHER, *ad.* plutôt, mieux.

RATTLE, *v.* faire du bruit, remuer avec bruit, secouer.
RAY, *s.* rayon, *m.*
REACH, *s.* portée, *f.*
— (*capacity*), capacité, portée, *f.*
REACH, *v.* atteindre, *à,* tendre, *à,* s'étendre, gagner.
READ, *v.* lire, *à.*
READILY, *ad.* promptement, aisément.
— (*gladly*), avec plaisir, de bon cœur.
READING, *s.* lecture, l'action de lire.
READY, *a.* prêt, *à,* prompt, *à.*
REAL, *a.* réel, le, effectif, ve.
REALITY, *ad.* réellement, en effet.
REALM, *s.* royaume, *m.*
REAPER, *s.* moissonneur, euse.
REASON, *s.* raison, cause, *f.* motif, *m.*

REASON, v. raisonner, de, arguer, discuter.
REASONABLE, a. raisonnable.
REASONER, s. raisonneur, m.
REBUKE, v. reprocher, à, de, blâmer, de, de.
RECALL, v. rappeler, à.
RECEIPT, s. l'action de recevoir, recette, réception, f. reçu, m.
RECEIVE, va. recevoir, de, accueillir.
RECEPTION, s. réception, f. accueil, m.
RECITAL, s. récit, m. narration, f.
RECKON, v. compter.
RECKONING, s. compte, calcul, m.
RECKONING, (at a tavern) écot, m.
— s. ma. estime, f.
RECOGNIZE, va. reconnaître.
RECOLLECT, va. se rappeler, se recueillir, rassembler de nouveau.
RECOLLECTION, s. recollection, f. souvenir, mémoire.
RECOMMENCE, va. recommencer, à.
RECOMMEND, va. recommander, à, de.
RECOMMENDATION, s. recommandation, f.
RECOMPENSE, s. récompense, f. prix, m.
— (amends), dédommagement, m.
— va. récompenser, de, de.
RECONNOITRE, va. reconnaître.
RECOVER, v. recouvrer, de, se ranimer, se rétablir, de, se remettre, de.
RECOVERY, s. recouvrement, m. reprise, rétablissement.

RECOVERY OF HEALTH, convalescence, f.
— (remedy), remède, m. ressource, f.
RED, a. rouge, vermeil, le.
REDEEM, v. racheter, de, retirer, de.
REDUCE, va. réduire, à, à, dompter.
RE-ENTER, va. rentrer, dans.
REFECTORY, s. réfectoire, m.
REFER, va. remettre, renvoyer, à, retirer, rapporter, à, référer, à, s'en référer, à.
— TO ARBITRATION, mettre en arbitrage.
— vn. avoir rapport, à, regarder.
REFLECT, va. réfléchir, rejaillir, sur.
— vn. réfléchir, à, considérer, penser, à.
REFLECTING, s. réfléchissement, m.
REFLECTION, s. réflexion, f. reproche, m.
REFRESHMENT, s. rafraichissement, m. vivres, pl.
REFUGE, s. refuge, asile, m.
— v. réfugier, se réfugier, à.
REFUSAL, s. refus, m.
REFUSE, REFUSING, s. rebut, refus, m.
REFUSE, v. refuser, à, de, rejeter.
REFUSER, s. celui qui refuse.
REGAL, a. royal.
REGALE, s. régale, f. régal, festin, m.
— va. régaler, de, traiter.
REGIMENT, s. régiment, m.
REGIMENTAL, a. de régiment.
REGRET, s. regret, chagrin, m.
— va. regretter, de, être fâché, de.

Reign, *s.* règne, *m.*
— *vn.* régner, dominer.
Reimburse, *va.* rembourser.
Reimbursement, *s.* remboursement, *m.*
Relapse, *s.* rechute, récidive, *f.*
— *vn.* retomber, récidiver.
Relate, *v.* raconter, *à*, rapporter, *à*, conter, *à*, réciter, *à.*
Relation, *s.* relation, *f.* récit, *m.*
— (*affinity*), rapport, *m.*
— (*kinsman*), parent.
Relaxation, *s.* relâche, diversion, *f.*
Release, *s.* décharge, *f.* élargissement, *m.* délivrance, *f.*
— *va.* décharger, *de*, relâcher, élargir, délivrer, *de.*
Relief, *s.* secours, soulagement, *m.* justice, réparation.
Relieve, *v.* secourir, soulager, *de*, faire justice, *à.*
Relish, *s.* saveur, *f.* goût, *m.*
— *va.* donner bon goût, *à*, agréer, *à.*
— *vn.* avoir bon goût, être approuvé, *par*, *de.*
Reload, *v.* recharger, *de.*
Remain, *vn.* rester, *à*, à, demeurer.
Remainder, *s.* restant, reste, *m.*
Remaining, *a.* restant, qui reste.
Remains, *s.* restes, *m. pl.*
Remark, *s.* remarque, *f.*
— *va.* remarquer, observer, faire observer, *à*, faire remarquer, *à.*
Remarkable, *a.* remarquable.
Remember, *va.* se souvenir, *de*, *de*, se rappeler, *de*, rappeler, *à.*

Remove, *v.* ôter, *à*, *de*, déplacer, transporter, *à*, déloger, déménager, enlever.
— *s.* changement, départ, degré, *m.*
Render, *v.* rendre, *à*, remettre, *à.*
Rent, *s.* rente, *f.* revenu, loyer, *m.*
Repast, *s.* repas, *m.*
Repeat, *va.* répéter, *à*, redire, *de*, *à*, réitérer, *de*, *à.*
Repent, *v.* se repentir, *de*, *de.*
Replace, *v.* remettre, remplacer.
Reply, *s.* réplique, repartie, *f.* reponse, *f.*
— *v.* répliquer, *à*, répondre, *à*, repartir.
Report, *s.* bruit, rapport, *m.*
— *va.* rapporter, *à*, dire, *à*, faire du bruit.
Reprimand, *s.* réprimande, *f.* reproche, *m.*
Reproach, *va.* reprocher, *à*, *de*, blâmer, *de*, *de*, faire des reproches, *à.*
Repulse, *v.* repousser.
Reputation, Repute, *s.* réputation, *f.*
Request, *s.* requête, réquisition, demande, *f.*
— *va.* requérir, *de*, prier, *de*, solliciter, *de.*
Rescue, *s.* reprise, délivrance, *f.*
— *va.* délivrer, *de*, reprendre, sauver, *de.*
Resemble, *va.* ressembler, *à.*
Resembling, *a.* semblable, *à.*
Resist, *v.* résister, *à*, s'opposer, à, *à.*
Resolute, *a.* résolu, à, déterminé, à.

RESOLUTION, s. résolution, f.
RESOLVE, s. résolution, f. dessein, m.
— v. résoudre, de, décider, de, se déterminer, à, à, délibérer, se résoudre, à, à, se disposer, à, à.
RESOURCE, s. ressource, f.
RESPECT, s. respect, égard, m.
— (relation), regard, rapport, m.
— va. respecter, honorer, avoir égard, à, avoir du rapport, à.
RESPONSIBLE, a. responsable, solvable.
REST, s. repos, sommeil, m.
— (residue), reste, résidu, m.
— v. se reposer, dormir, faire reposer.
— ON, poser sur, s'appuyer, sur.
RESTORATION, s. rétablissement, m. restauration, f.
RESTORATIVE, s. (med.), restaurant, m.
— a. restauratif, ve.
RESTORE, va. rétablir, restaurer, se rétablir.
— (give back), rendre à, restituer, à.
RESUME, va. résumer, reprendre, continuer, recommencer, à, se remettre, à, à.
— A BUSINESS, renouer une affaire.
RETAKE, va. reprendre, à, rattraper, f.
RETAKING, s. reprise, f.
RETINUE, s. suite, f. cortége, m.
RETIRE, v. retirer, à, de, se retirer, de.
RETURN, s. retour, m. arrivée, f.

RETURN (answer), réponse, f.
— v. retourner, à, revenir, à, de, rendre, à.
REVENGE, s. vengeance, revanche, f.
— vn. venger, se venger, de.
REVERY, s. rêverie, f. songe, délire, m.
REVIEW, s. revue, analyse, f.
REVIVE, va. rétablir, renouveler, ressusciter.
— vn. revivre, reprendre ses forces.
REVOLUTION, s. révolution, f.
REWARD, s. récompense, f.
— va. récompenser, de, de.
RHETORIC, s. rhétorique, f.
RIBAND, s. ruban, m.
RIBBON, s. ruban, m.
RICH, a. riche, opulent, précieux, se.
— WINE, s. vin exquis, m.
RICHES, s. richesses, f. pl.
RIDE, vn. monter, aller à cheval ou en voiture.
RIDICULOUS, a. ridicule.
RIGHT, s. droit, privilége, m. équité, justice, raison, f.
— vn. faire justice.
— a. droit, bien, honnête, sincere, équitable, juste, propre, direct.
— (natural), vrai, bon, ne.
— TRUE, a. vrai, véritable.
— OR WRONG, à tort ou à raison.
RING, v. sonner, tinter, retentir.
RINGLET, s. boucle de cheveux, f.
RIP, vn. découdre, fendre.
RISE, vn. se lever, s'élever, à, hausser, sortir, de, provenir, de.
— AGAIN, se relever, remonter.

RISER, s. qui se lève.
— *Early riser*, matineux, se.
— (*who has got up early*), matinal.
RISING, a. levant, naissant.
RISK, s. risque, danger, péril, m.
— va. risquer, hasarder.
RIVER, a. rivière, f. fleuve, m.
ROAD, s. route, f. grand chemin, m.
— (*for anchoring*), rade, f.
ROAST, va. rôtir, cuire.
— MEAT, s. rôt, m.
ROB, va. voler, piller, priver, *de*.
ROBBERY, s. vol, brigandage, m.
ROCK, s. roche, f. rocher, roc, m.
ROCKY, a. plein de rochers.
ROD, s. verge, bagnette, f.
— (*for measuring*), s. perche, f.
ROGUE, s. coquin, fripon, m.
— (*thief*), voleur, larron, m.
— (*wag*), espiègle, m. et f.
ROGUERY, s. friponnerie, m.
ROLL, v. rouler, tourner, s'écouler.
— UP, plier en rouleau, enrouler.
ROLLING, s. roulement, ma. roulis, m.
— a. roulant, qui roule.
ROOF, s. toit, comble, m.
— (*of a coach*), impériale, f.
— (*of the mouth*), palais, m.
— va. couvrir d'un toit ou d'une voûte.
ROOM, s. place, chambre, f. espace, emplacement, m.
— (*cause*), lieu, sujet, m. occasion, f.
ROOT, s. racine, tige, source, f.
— va. enraciner, fixer en terre.
— UP, déraciner, extirper, *de*.

ROOTED IN, a. enraciné, *dans*.
— OUT, déraciné, extirper.
ROSE, s. rose, f.
ROSY, a. couleur de rose.
ROTTEN, a. pourri.
ROTTEN-WOOD, s. bois pourri.
ROUND, a. rond, circulaire.
— *pr*. autour, *de*, tout autour, *de*.
— *ad*. à la ronde, autour, en rond.
ROVE, vn. rôder, courir.
ROVER, s. rôdeur, corsaire, pirate, m.
ROYAL, a. royal, de roi.
ROYALIST, s. royaliste, m.
RUB, v. frotter.
RUBBISH, s. décombres, débris, m. pl. rebut, m.
— (*dirt*), ordures, saletés, f. pl.
RUDE, a. brutal, envers, grossier, ère, envers.
RUDELY, ad. brutalement.
RUDENESS, s. brutalité, incivilité, f.
RUMBLE, vn. faire un bruit sourd, gronder, résonner.
RUMBLING, s. un bruit sourd.
— (*of a vehicle*), roulement, m.
RUN, vn. courir, *à*, passer.
— AGAINST, heurter, donner contre.
— AGROUND, échouer, engraver.
RUN A RACE, faire une course.
— AWAY, s'enfuir, *de*, s'écouler.
— OVER, passer, *sur*.
— UP, bâtir, faire élever.
RUNAGATE, s. renégat.
RUNAWAY, s. fuyard, fugitif, ve. proscrit, m.
RUSH, s. course précipitée, f.
— vn. se lancer, se jeter, s'élancer.
— FORWARD, se précipiter en avant.

Rush in, entrer de force, *dans.*
— in upon, surprendre.
— out, sortir brusquement, *de.*

Rush through, s'exposer hardiment, *à,* s'élancer, *à travers.*
Rustic, *s.* rustique, rustre.
— *a.* rustre, rustique.

S.

Sack, *s.* sac, *m.*
— *va.* saccager, piller.
— up, mettre dans un sac.
Sacrifice, *s.* sacrifice, *m.*
— *v.* sacrifier, *à,* à, offrir un sacrifice, *à.*
Sadly, *ad.* tristement.
Safe, *a.* sauf, *ve.* sûr, de, heureux, se.
— remedy, *s.* remède sûr, *m.*
Safely, *ad.* sûrement, en sûreté.
Safeness, Safety, *s.* sûreté, *f.*
Sagacious, *a.* pénétrant, subtil.
Sagaciously, *ad.* avec sagacité, pénétration.
Sagaciousness, Sagacity, *s.* sagacité, clairvoyance, *f.*
Sail, *s.* voile, *f.* vaisseau, *m.*
— *vn.* faire voile, mettre à la voile.
— along the coast, ranger la côte.
Sailor, *s.* matelot, marin ; marinier, *m.*
Sake, *s.* amour, égard, *m.* considération, *f.*
— *For his sake,* à sa considération, pour l'amour de lui.
Salary, *s.* salaire, appointements, *m. pl.*
Saloon, *s.* salon, *m.* salle, *f.*
Salutary, *a.* salutaire, sain.
Same, *a.* même.
Sample, *s.* échantillon, *m.*
Sand, *s.* sable, *m.* poussière, poudre, *f.*

Sanguinary, *a.* sanguinaire.
Satan, *s.* Satan, *m.*
Satisfaction, *s.* satisfaction, *f.*
Satisfactorily, *ad.* d'une manière satisfaisante.
Satisfy, *va.* contenter, satisfaire, *de,* de.
— one's passions, assouvir.
— (*with food*), rassasier, *de.*
Satisfying, *a.* satisfaisant, de, satisfactoire.
Saturday, *s.* samedi, *m.*
Saucepan, *s.* marmite, casserole, *f.*
Saucy, *a.* effronté, impudent.
Save, *va.* sauver, *de,* garantir, *de,* préserver.
— (*lay up*), épargner, réserver.
Saving,, *s.* épargne, exception en faveur de, *f.*
Saving, *a.* ménager, ère. salutaire.
— *ad.* à la réserve de, excepté.
Savoury, *a.* savoureux, se. ragoûtant.
Say, *va.* dire, *à,* de, réciter, *à.*
— over again, redire, *à,* répeter, *à.*
Scaffold, *s.* échafaud, échafaudage, *m.*
Scaffoldage, Scaffolding, *s.* échafaudage, *m.*
Scald, *v.* échauder.
Scalding, *s.* l'action d'échauder, *f.*
Scarce, *a.* rare, qui manque.
Scarce, Scarcely, *ad.* à peine.

SCENE, s. scène, coulisse, f.
— OF WAR, théâtre de la guerre, m.
SCHOLAR, s. écolier, ère. homme de lettres, savant, m.
SCHOOL, s. école, f.
— v. censurer, instruire.
— *Boarding school*, s. pension, f.
SCHOOLBOY, s. écolier, m.
SCHOOLFELLOW, s. camarade d'école, m.
SCHOOLMASTER, s. maître d'école, m.
SCIENCE, s. science, f.
SCIENTIFIC, a. scientifique.
SCIENTIFICALLY, ad. scientifiquement.
SCOLD, a. criailleur, euse. grondeur, euse.
— vn. gronder, de, *de*, quereller.
SCOTCH, a. écossais, e.
SCOTSMAN, s. Écossais, m.
SCOUNDREL, s. scélérat, vaurien, m.
SCREAM, s. cri perçant, m.
SCREAM, vn. jeter des cris perçants, s'écrier.
— OUT, s'écrier, jeter des cris perçants.
— UP, s'écrier, jeter des cris perçants.
SCULPTOR, s. sculpteur, m.
SEA, s. mer, f.
SEAMAN, s. matelot, marin, m.
SEA-PORT, s. port de mer, m.
SEA-VOYAGE, s. voyage par mer, m.
SEARCH, s. visite, recherche, f.
— v. chercher, visiter.
— INTO or AFTER, rechercher.
— ONE, fouiller quelqu'un.
— OUT, faire une exacte recherche, de.

SEAT, s. siége, banc, m. chaise, f. château, m. maison de campagne, f.
— va. poser, situer, placer, s'asseoir, établir.
SEATED, a. assis.
SECOND, a. deuxième, second.
— RATE, second ordre, m.
— s. un second appui, témoin, m.
— (*of time*), seconde, f.
— va. appuyer, seconder.
SECOND-HAND, a. de la seconde main, de rencontre, de hasard, d'occasion.
SECONDLY, ad. secondement.
SECRET, a. secret, ète. caché, inconnu.
— s. secret, m.
SECRETARY, s. secrétaire, m.
SECRETLY, ad. en secret, secrètement.
SECURE, a. sûr, en sûreté, qui se croit assuré, intrépide.
— va. mettre en sûreté, assurer. exempter, grantir.
SECURED, a. mis en sûreté, sauvé.
SECURELY, s. ad. sûrement, en sureté, à l'abri, à couvert.
— (*quietly*), ad. tranquillement.
SECURITY, s. sûreté, sécurité, f.
— (*bail*), caution, f.
SEE, v. voir, regarder.
— (*conceive*), voir, comprendre.
— (*inquire*), voir, s'informer, de.
— INTO, pénétrer, voir le fond, de, examiner.
— (*take heed*), prendre garde, à, à.
SEEK, va. chercher, à, rechercher.
SEEK AFTER, rechercher

Seek out, chercher de côté et d'autre.
— out (*as a dog*), quêter.
Seem, *va.* sembler, à, paraître, à.
Seize, *va.* saisir, prendre, se saisir, de.
Seldom, *ad.* rarement, peu souvent.
Select, *a.* choisi, d'élite.
— *va.* choisir, de, recueillir, avec choix.
Self, *pro.* même.
Self-love, *s.* amour-propre, *m.*
Selfish, *a.* intéressé, propre, personnel, égoïste, de.
Sell, *v.* vendre, à, débiter, à, trafiquer, se vendre, avoir du débit.
— off, vendre tout.
— by auction, vendre à l'encan.
Send, *v.* envoyer, à.
— back, renvoyer, à.
— away, renvoyer.
— for, envoyer chercher.
— off, envoyer, faire partir, expédier.
Sense, *s.* sens, *m.* perception, signification, *f.*
— (*feeling*), ressentment, *m.*
— (*wit*), esprit, *m.*
Senseless, *a.* comme mort, sans vie.
— (*foolish*), sot, te. de, absurde, de, ridicule, de.
Senselessly, *ad.* contre le bon sens, sans jugement, sottement.
Sensibility, *s.* sensibilité, *f*
Sensible, *a.* sensible, à, de bon sens, raisonnable, de.
Sentence, *s.* sentence, *f.* jugement, *m.* opinion, maxime.
— *va.* condamner, à, à, pro-

noncer un jugement, contre.
Sentiment, *s.* sentiment, avis, *m.* pensée, *f.*
Sentinel, Sentry, *s.* sentinelle, *f.*
Sergeant, *s.* sergent, *m.*
— at law, avocat, docteur en droit, *m.*
Serious, *a.* sérieux, se. grave.
Seriously, *ad.* sérieusement.
Sermon, *s.* sermon, *m.* prédication, *f.*
— *va.* sermonner, prêcher, à, de.
Servant, *s.* serviteur, domestique, *m.*
Serve, *v.* servir, à, à, assister, de, fournir, à.
— one a trick, jouer un tour à quelqu'un.
— one's turn, suffire.
Service, *s.* service, *m.* servitude, *f.*
Set, *v.* poser, mettre, placer.
— about, se mettre, à, à.
— off, *v.* partir.
— up, établir, fixer, ériger.
Settle, *v.* établir, fixer, régler, se fixer, à.
Seven, *a.* sept.
Seventeen, *a.* dix-sept.
Seventeenth, *a.* dix-septième.
Seventhly, *ad.* en septième lieu.
Seventieth, *a.* soixante et dixième.
Seventy, *a.* soixante et dix.
Several, *a.* plusieurs, divers.
Severe, *a.* sévère, *envers.* dur, *envers,* cruel, *envers,* intense.
Severely, *ad.* sévèrement.
Sew, *v.* coudre.
Shake, *v.* branler, ébranler, trembler, secouer.

SHAME, s. honte, f. opprobre, m.
— v. déshonorer, faire honte.
SHAPE, s. forme, figure, taille, f.
SHAPE, va. former.
SHARE, s. part, portion, f.
— v. partager, à, avoir part, à.
SHARK, s. requin, filou, escroc, m.
— v. escroquer, à, fourber, tromper.
SHATTER, s. éclat, m.
— va. fracasser, endommager.
SHE, pro. elle.
SHEET, s. drap, linceul, m.
— OF PAPER, feuille de papier, f.
SHELTER, s. abri, couvert, m.
— (refuge), asile, refuge, m.
— va. donner le couvert, protéger, contre.
SHILLING, s. schelling (24 sous), m.
SHIP, s. vaisseau, navire, m.
— va. embarquer, sur.
SHIPMAN, s. marin, matelot, m.
SHIPMATE, s. camarade, m.
SHIPWRECK, s. naufrage, m.
SHOCK, s. choc, combat, dégoût, m.
SHOCK, v. choquer, de, de, heurter, offenser, de.
— AT, choquer de, de.
SHOOT, va. tirer un coup de fusil, à, sur, lancer, à, darter, jeter, à.
— AT ONE, tirer sur quelqu'un.
SHOOTING, s. chasse au fusil, l'action de pousser, pousse, f.
— EXCURSION, partie de chasse, f.
SHOP, s. boutique, f.
SHOPKEEPER, s. boutiquier, m.
SHOPMAN, s. garçon de boutique, m.

SHORE, s. bord, rivage, m. terre, f.
SHORT, a. court, succinct.
— ad. court.
SHORTLY, ad. courtement, bientôt.
SHOT, s. coup d'arme à feu, m.
— (reckoning), écot, compte, m.
— Cannon shot, s. boulet de canon, m. portée d'un canon, f.
— Small shot, s. dragée, f. plomb de chasse, m.
SHOT-BAG, s. sac à plomb, m.
SHOULDER, s. épaule, f. épaulement, m.
— va. épauler, appuyer.
SHOW, v. montrer, à, faire voir, à, démontrer, à, avoir l'air, de, de, sembler, faire semblant, de.
— MERCY, faire grâce.
SHOW RESPECT, porter du respect, à.
— TRICKS, faire des tours, à.
SHOWING, s. l'action de montrer, f.
SHRUG, s. haussement d'épaules, m.
— va. hausser les épaules.
— UP, hausser, lever.
SHUN, va. éviter, de, fuir, échapper, à.
SHUT, v. fermer.
— IN, enfermer.
— OUT, exclure, de, refuser l'entrée, à.
— UP, renfermer, fermer.
SICK, a. malade.
SIDE, s. côté, flanc, parti, m.
— OF A HILL, penchant, m. pente, f.
— a. de côté, indirect, latéral.
SIDEBOARD, SIDE-TABLE, s. buffet, m.

SIFT, va. cribler, sasser, tamiser.
SIGHT, s. vue, vision, f.
SIGN, s. signe, indice, m. enseigne, f.
SIGN (footstep), trace, f. vestige, m.
— v. signer, faire signe, à.
SIGNAL, s. signal, m.
— a. éclatant, signalé.
SIGNIFY, s. signifier, de, à, notifier, à, de.
— What does it signify? qu'importe?
SILENCE, s. silence, m.
— v. fermer la bouche, à, interdire, à, faire taire, faire silence.
— THERE, int. paix là!
SILENT, s. silencieux, se. paisible.
SIMILAR, a. similaire, semblable, à, homogène.
SIMPLY, ad. simplement.
SIN, s. péché, crime, m.
SINCE, c. puisque.
— ad. pr. depuis, depuis que.
SINCERE, a. sincère, franc, che.
SINCERELY, ad. sincèrement.
SINGLE, a. seul, unique.
SINGULAR, s singulier, m.
— a. singulier, ère. rare, extraordinaire.
SINK, v. abaisser, enfoncer, foncer.
— (as a ship), couler bas.
SINLESS, a. sans péché.
SINNER, s. pécheur, pécheresse.
SIR, s. monsieur, m.
SIRE, s. père, sire, m.
SISTER, s. sœur, f.
SIT, v. s'asseoir, se tenir, se mettre, à, à, être assis.
— CLOSE, se serrer.
— DOWN, s'asseoir.
— UP, veiller, se lever, visiter.

SITUATION, s. situation, condition, place, f. emploi, m.
SIXTEEN, a. seize.
SIXTEENTH, a. seizième.
SIXTH, a. sixième.
SIXTHLY, ad. sixièmement.
SIXTIETH, s. soixantième.
SIXTY, a. soixante.
SLAVE, s. esclave, m. et f.
— vn. travailler comme un esclave.
SLEEP, vn. dormir.
— WITH, coucher avec.
SLIGHT, a. mince, léger, ère. chétif, ve.
SLIGHTLY, ad. légèrement.
SLILY, ad. secrètement, artificieusement.
SLIP, v. glisser, couler, laisser, échapper.
SLIP AWAY, s'échapper, se sauver.
SLOW, a. lent, tardif, ve.
SLOWLY, ad. lentement.
SMACK, s. bruit, m.
— v. claquer.
SMACKING, s. claquement, m.
SMALL, a. petit, menu, léger, ère.
SMELL, v. sentir, flairer, rendre quelque odeur.
— OUT, découvrir.
— s. odorat, m. odeur, f.
SMELLING, s. l'odorat, m.
SMELLING-BOTTLE, s. flacon d'essence, m.
SMILE, s. sourire, m.
— vn. sourire, à, de, rire, de, favoriser.
SMILING, a. riant, gai, favorable.
SMILINGLY, ad. en souriant, d'un air riant.
SMOCK, s. blouse, f.
SMOCK-FROCK, s. blouse, f.

SMOKE, s. fumée, f.
— v. fumer, jeter de la fumée.
SMOKER, s. fumeur, m.
SMOOTH, a. uni, poli, lisse.
— (soft), doux, ce. affable, flatteur, euse.
SMOOTH, va. unir, polir, lisser.
SNATCH, s. accès, m. happée, f. court intervalle, m.
— v. happer, arracher, de, à, attraper, saisir, ravir, à.
SNEAK, vn. ramper, rôder.
— ALONG, se glisser furtivement, aller la tête baissée.
— AWAY, se cacher.
SNUFF, s. tabac en poudre, m.
— OF A CANDLE, mèche, f.
SNUFF BOX, s. tabatière, f.
SNUG, a. agréable, gentil, le.
SO, ad. ainsi, de même, cela, de cette manière, comme cela, de sorte, si.
— MUCH, tant, si, aussi.
— THAT, tellement que, de sorte que.
— WELL, ou SO ILL, si bien, ou si mal.
SOB, s. sanglot, m.
SOFT, s. mou, m.
— a. mou, mol, le. doux, ce. tendre.
SOFTLY, ad. doucement, la la.
SOLDIER, s. soldat, militaire, m.
SOLEMNLY, ad. solennellement.
SOLICIT, va. solliciter, de, de, demander, à, à.
SOLICITATION, s. sollicitation, instance, f.
SOLITARY, a. solitaire, retiré.
SOME, a. quelque.
— pro. quelqu'un, pl. quelques uns.
— (little), un peu de, du, de la, des.

SOME (some men), les uns, les autres, il y en a qui.
SOMEBODY, s. quelqu'un, e.
— ELSE, quelque autre.
SOMETHING, s. quelque chose, m.
SOMETIME, ad. autrefois, jadis.
SOMETIMES, ad. quelquefois.
SOMEWHERE, ad. quelque part.
SOON. ad. bientôt.
SOUND, s. son, bruit, m.
SOUTH, s. midi, sud, m.
— a. méridional, du sud.
— ad. vers le midi.
SOVEREIGN, a. s. souverain, e.
SPACE, s. espace, m. intervalle, m. etendue, f.
SPAIN, np. Espagne, f.
SPANIARD, s. Espagnol.
SPANISH, a. d'Espagne.
SPARE, v. épargner, à, de, ménager, à, accorder, à, de, se dispenser, de.
— a. maigre, de réserve, de reste.
— DIET, s. maigre chère, f. régime, m.
— HOURS, s. pl. heures perdues, f. pl..
— MONEY, s. argent mignon, m.
— TIME, s. loisir, temps de réserve, m.
SPEAK, v. parler, à, de, dire, à, déclarer, à.
SPEAK FAIR, flatter, parler sincèrement, à.
SPEAKABLE, a. ce dont on peut parler.
SPEAKER, s. orateur, m.
SPECTATOR, s. spectateur, trice.
SPECTRE, s. spectre, fantôme, m.
SPEECH, s. parole, langue, f. discours, m. harangue, conversation, f.

SPEND, v. dépenser, à, consumer, à, se dissiper.
SPENDTHRIFT, s. prodigue, dissipateur, m.
SPIDER, s. araignée, f.
SPIDER'S WEB, s. toile d'araignée, f.
SPIRIT, s. esprit, m.
SPORT, s. divertissement, jeu, plaisir, badinage, m.
— (*hunting, fowling*, etc.), chasse, f. le plaisir de la chasse, de la pêche, m.
— v. jouer, se divertir, folâtrer.
SPOT, s. endroit, m. tache, salissure, marque, f. place, f.
— OF GROUND, s. morceau de terre, m.
— *On the spot*, sur la place.
SPREAD, v. étendre, tendre, répandre, ouvrir, étaler, s'étendre, se répandre.
— a. déployé.
SPUR, s éperon, m.
— va. piquer, pousser, aiguillonner.
— vn. aller vite, se presser, de.
SPY, s. espion, émissaire, m.
— va. découvrir, épier, observer.
SQUARE, a. carré.
SQUARE, s. carré, m. place, case (d'un echiquier), f.
SQUEEZE, va. serrer, à, presser.
— OUT, exprimer, de, extraire, de.
SQUIRE, s. écuyer, seigneur, châtelain, m.
STAB, s. coup de poignard, m.
— va. poignarder.
STABLE, a. stable, ferme, constant.
— s. écurie, f.
STABLEBOY, s. valet d'écurie, m.

STAFF, s. bâton, état-major, appui, soutien, m.
STAGE, s. théâtre, m. scène, f.
STAGE-COACH, s. diligence, voiture publique, f. coche, m.
STAIR, s. marche, f. degré, escalier, m.
STAIRCASE, s. escalier, m.
STAND, v. se tenir debout, être situé, ne pas bouger.
— AGAINST, résister, à, s'exposer, à.
— (*be*), être, se tenir.
— BY, soutenir, appuyer, se ranger *du côté de*, se joindre, à, prendre parti, *pour*, être présent, à.
— (*for an office*), postuler, briguer.
— (*cost*), coûter, revenir, à.
— IN STEAD OF, servir, de, tenir lieu de.
— OFF, reculer, se tenir à l'écart, de.
— ONE'S GROUND, ne pas céder, à.
— OUT, soutenir, à, maintenir.
— SENTRY, être en sentinelle, en faction.
— STILL (*as water*), croupir.
— (*stop*), s'arrêter, à, demeurer, à.
— UP, se lever, être debout.
— UP ON END, se hérisser, se dresser.
— UP FOR, défendre, maintenir.
— WITH, s'accorder, *avec*, compatir, à.
— s. station, halte, f. poste, chantier, guéridon, m.
START, v. partir.
STARVE, v. mourir de faim, de froid.
STATE, s. état, m. condition, f.

State (*pomp*), pompe, grandeur, *f.*
— (*pride*), fierté, hauteur, *f.*
— *vn.* régler, établir, déterminer.
Statue, *s.* statue, figure, *f.*
Stay, *s.* séjour, *m.*
— *v.* attendre, rester, à, *d,* arrêter, retarder.
Stead, *s.* lieu, *m.* place, *f.*
— *vn.* servir, *d,* rendre service, *d.*
Steadfast, *a.* ferme, constant.
Steadfastly, *ad.* constamment, fixement.
Steal, *v.* voler, *d,* dérober, *d.*
— off, *or* away, s'esquiver, se sauver, se dérober, s'envoler, s'enfuir.
Steed, *s.* cheval, coursier, *m.*
Step, pas, *m.* enjambée, démarche, *f.* degré, *m.* marche, *f.*
— *vn.* aller, passer.
— in *or* into, entrer, *dans.*
— from, sortir *de.*
Sterling, *s.* sterling, *m.*
— *a.* pur, vrai, sterling.
Sternly, *ad.* sévèrement.
Stick, *va.* attacher, *d,* ficher, enfoncer, coller, *d, sur.*
Stocking, *s.* bas, *m.*
Stone, *s.* pierre, *f.*
— (*of a mill*), meule, *f.*
Stoop, baisser, s'abaisser, à, *d.*
Stop, *s.* retardement, point, obstacle, *m.* pause.
— *v.* arrêter, de, retarder, de, s'arrêter, à, *d.*
— short, s'arrêter court.
Storm, *s.* orage, *m.* tempête, *f.*
— (*assault*), assaut, *m.*
— tempêter, foudroyer, s'emporter, donner l'assaut, *d.*

Story, *s.* histoire, *f.* conte, *m.*
— (*in building*), étage, *m.*
Strait, *s.* détroit, gorge, *f.*
Strange, étrauge, étonnant.
— (*foreign*), étranger, ère.
— *int.* chose étrange !
Stranger, *s.* étranger, ère.
Straw, *s.* paille, brin de paille, *m.*
— bed, *s.* paillasse, *f*
Stream, *s.* courant, fil de l'eau.
— *vn.* couler, ruisseler, rayonner.
Street, *s.* rue, *f.*
Street-door, *s.* porte de devant, *f.* (sur la rue).
Strength, *s.* force, vigueur, *f.*
Stretch, *s.* étendue, *f.* effort, *m.*
— *s. ma.* bordée en louvoyant, *f.*
— *v.* étendre, prêter, raidir.
— out, tendre.
Strict, *a.* strict, à, rigide, *envers,* exact, *d,* à, précis, formel, le. étroit, serré.
Strictly, *ad.* étroitement, exactement, strictement, formellement.
Strike, *v.* frapper, *de,* battre.
Strong, *a.* fort, puissant, robuste.
Student, *s.* étudiant, proposant, *m.*
Studied, *a.* érudit, affecté.
Studier, *s.* étudiant, qui étudie, *m.*
Studious, *a.* studieux, se. diligent.
Studiously, *ad.* soigneusement, avec application à l'étude.
Study, *s.* étude, *f.* cabinet, *m.*
— *v.* étudier, s'étudier, à.
Stuff, *v,* empailler, garnir.
Stun, *va.* étonner, étourdir, assourdir.

STUPID, a. stupide, hébété.
STUPIDITY s. stupidité, bêtise, f.
STUPIDLY, ad. stupidement.
SUBJECT, s sujet, m.
— a. sujet, te. à, d, exposé, d, à.
— va. assujettir, à, d, dompter.
— one's self, s'exposer, à, d, s'assujettir, à.
SUBMIT, v. se soumettre, à, d, abaisser, à, d.
SUBSCRIPTION, s. souscription, f. seing, m.
SUBSTITUTE, s. remplaçant, m.
SUCCEED, v. réussir, à, succéder, d, suivre.
SUCCESS, s. succès, m. réussite, f.
SUCH, pro. tel, le. de même, si, pareil, le.
— (before an adj.), si, aussi.
SUCCOUR, va. secourir.
SUDDEN, a. soudain, inopiné.
SUDDENLY, ad. subitement, tout à coup.
SUFFER, v. souffrir, de, de, supporter, être puni, de.
SUFFERING, s. souffrance, f.
SUFFICIENT, a. suffisant, habile.
SUFFICIENTLY, ad. suffisamment.
SUFFOCATE, va. suffoquer, étouffer.
SUFFOCATED, a. étouffé, suffoqué.
SUFFOCATION, s. suffocation, f.
SUIT, s. suite, f. assortiment, procès, m.
— (at cards), couleur, f.
— OF CLOTHES, habillement complet, m.
SUIT, va. assortir d, avec, ajuster, d, habiller.

SUIT, vn. convenir, d, s'accorder, avec.
SUM, s. somme, f. précis, sommaire, m.
— va. nombrer, nommer.
SUMMER, s. été, m.
SUMMON, va. sommer, de, citer, devant, assigner, d, interpeller, appeller, devant.
SUMMONS, s. sommation, semonce, interpellation, f.
SUN, s. soleil, m.
SUNDAY, s. dimanche, m.
SUP, v. souper, humer, avaler.
SUPERB, a. superbe, magnifique.
SUPERBLY, ad. avec orgueil.
SUPERINTEND, v. surveiller.
SUPERINTENDENT, s. surintendant, m.
SUPERIOR, a. s. supérieur.
SUPERIORITY, s. supériorité, f.
SUPERNATURAL, a. surnaturel, le.
SUPPER, s. souper, soupé, m.
SUPPLICATE, va. supplier, de, implorer, de.
SUPPLY, s. renfort, secours, subside, m.
— va. fournir, d, suppléer, d, remplir.
SUPPORT, s. soutien, support, appui, m.
— va. soutenir, appuyer, supporter.
— (keep), entretenir.
SUPPORTABLE, a. supportable.
SUPPOSE, va. supposer, penser.
SURE, a. sûr, de, de, assuré, de, de.
— ad. assurément, certainement.
SURFACE, s. surface, superficie, f.
SURGEON, s. chirurgien, m.
SURNAME, s. surnom, m.

Surpass, va surpasser, exceller, surmonter.
Surprise, va. surprendre, de, de, étonner, de, de.
Surprising, a. surprenant, de.
Surround, v. entourer, cerner.
Survey, v. voir, observer, contempler.
Survive, v. survivre, à.
Suspect, va. soupçonner, de, de, se defier, de.
— vn. soupçonner, concevoir, avoir des soupçons, sur.
Suspend, va. suspendre, à, arrêter.
— a. suspensif, ve.
Suspicion, s. soupçon, m.
— (in law), suspicion, f.

Suspicious, a. suspect, soupçonneux, se.
Suspiciously, ad. avec soupçon.
Swallow, va. avaler, gober.
— up, engloutir, absorber.
Swear, v. jurer, à, de, assurer, à.
Sweep, s. ramoneur, balayeur, m.
— v. ramoner, balayer.
Sweet, a. doux, ce.
Swim, vn. nager.
— over, passer à la nage.
Swimmer, s. nageur, m.
Sympathy, s. sympathie, f. sensibilité, f.

T.

Table, s. table, liste, f. tableau, m.
— v. être ou prendre en pension.
Tail, s. queue, f.
Take, va. prendre, à, mener, à, se saisir, de.
— vn. aller, prendre, voguer, réussir.
— after one, ressembler, à.
— again, reprendre, à.
— a leap, faire un saut, sauter.
— asunder, séparer, défaire.
— a turn, se promener.
— away, ôter, emporter, à, desservir, emmener, de.
— care, avoir soin, de, prendre garde, à, prendre soin, de.
— down, descendre, abaisser, défendre, humilier, mortifier.
— from, tirer, ôter, à, retirer, à.
— hold, se saisir, de.
— in, prendre, tromper.

Take in hand, entreprendre, de.
— off, lever, ôter, à, de, enlever, de, détacher, de.
— on, prendre, revêtir.
— out, faire sortir, à, de, tirer, retirer, à, de.
— place, avoir lieu.
— (receive), recevoir.
— up, prendre, emporter, à, déterrer, ramasser.
Taken, a. pris, surpris, saisi.
Tale, s. conte, m. fable, sornette, f.
— s. histoire, f.
Talent, s. talent, m. capacité, f.
Talk, s. entretien, caquet, f.
— vn. causer, à, parler, à.
— over, raconter, à, conter, à.
Tame, v. apprivoiser.
Tap, s. tape, f. coup, m.
— va. taper, frapper, percer.

Tap-room, s. salle de cabaret, f.
Tar, s. goudron, matelot, m.
— va. goudronner, brayer.
Tarnish, v. ternir, flétrir, se ternir.
Taste, s. goût, m. saveur, f.
Taste, v. goûter, avoir quelque goût.
Tasting, s. goût, m.
Tax, s. taxe, f. impôt, m.
— va. taxer, lever des impôts, accuser, de, de.
Teach, v. enseigner, à, à, instruire, de, montrer, à, à, apprendre, à, à.
Team, s. attelage, m. ligne, file, f.
Tear, s. larme, f. pleurs, m. pl. déchirement, m. déchirure, f.
— va. déchirer.
— vn. se chagriner, s'emporter.
Tell, v. dire, à, de, conter, à, compter, nombrer, dicter, à.
Temper, s. caractère, tempérament, esprit, m. humeur, f.
Tempest, s. tempête, f. orage, m.
Temple, s. temple, m. (anat.), tempe, f.
Tempt, va. tenter, de, exciter, essayer, de.
Temptation, s. tentation, f.
Ten, a. dix.
Tender, s. offre, f.
Tender, a. tendre, délicat.
Tent, s. tente, f. abri, m.
Tenth, a. dixième.
Tenthly, ad. dixièmement.
Terrible, a. terrible, épouvantable.
Terror, s. terreur, épouvante, f.
Testimony, s. témoignage, m.

Thames, s. la Tamise, f.
Than, a. que, de.
Thank, va. remercier, de, de, rendre grâce, à, de.
Thankful, a. reconnaissant, de, envers, de, qui a de la gratitude.
Thanks, s. pl. grâces, f. pl.
That, pro. ce, cet, cette, cela, celui-là, celle-là, celui, celle qui, que, lequel, laquelle, quoi.
— c. que, afin que, pour que.
— is, c'est-à-dire.
Thatch, s. chaume, m.
The, art. le, la, les.
Thee, pro. toi, te.
Theft, s. larcin, vol, m.
Their, pro. leur, leurs.
Them, pro. eux, elles, les, leur, en, y.
Themselves, pro. pl. eux-mêmes, elles-mêmes.
Then, ad. alors, pour lors, ensuite.
— c. donc, par conséquent.
There, ad. là, y, en cela.
Therefore, ad. c'est pourquoi, aussi.
These, pro. ceux, ces, celles, ceux-ci, celles-ci.
They, pro. ils, elles, eux.
Thickness, s. épaisseur, f.
Thief, s. larron, voleur, m.
Thief-taker, s. officier de police, m.
Thieve, va. voler, à, dérober, à.
Thin, a. maigre, mince, clair, léger, ère.
— va. éclaircir.
— ad. clair, peu.
— To grow thin, maigrir.
Thing, s. chose, affaire, f.
Think, va. penser, à, à, songer, à, à, croire, s'imaginer, de.

THIRD, *a.* troisième.
THIRDLY, *ad.* troisièmement.
THIRSTY, *a.* altéré, qui a soif.
THIRTEEN, *a.* treize.
THIRTEENTH, *a.* treizième.
THIRTIETH, *a.* trentième.
THIRTY, *a.* trente.
THIS, *pro.* ce, cet, cette, ceci, celui-ci, celle-ci.
THORN, *s.* épine, *f.*
THOSE, *pro.* ces, ceux-là, celles-là, ceux, celles.
THOU, *pro.* tu, toi.
THOUGH, *c.* quoique, encore que, bien que, quand, pourtant, si.
— *s.* pensée, réflexion, opinion, *f.*
THOUSAND, *a.* mille, mil.
— *s.* millier, *m.*
THOUSANDTH, *a.* millième.
THREATEN, *va.* menacer.
THREATENING, *s.* menaces, *f. pl.*
— *a.* menaçant, qui menace.
THREE, *a.* trois.
THRONE, *s.* trône, *m.*
THROUGH, *pr.* à travers, par, dedans.
— *ad.* de part en part, jusqu'au bout.
THROW, *v.* jeter, *d.*
— AWAY, jeter, prodiguer, dépenser, à.
— OFF, quitter, se défaire, *de*, rejeter.
— ONE'S SELF, se jeter.
THUNDER, *s.* tonnerre, *m.*
— *v.* tonner, foudroyer, fulminer.
THUS, *ad.* ainsi, de la sorte, tant.
— FAR, jusqu'ici, jusque-là.
THY, *pro.* ton, ta, tes.
TICKLE, *v.* chatouiller, flatter.
TIDE, marée, *f.*
— *vn.* aller à la faveur de la marée.

TIE, *va.* nouer.
TILL, *pr.* jusqu'à, jusques à.
— *c.* jusqu' à ce que, avant que, que.
TIME, *s.* temps, terme, *m.* fois, *f.* moment, *m.*
TIMID, *a.* timide, craintif, ve
TIN, *s.* fer-blanc, *m.*
TIPSY, *a.* ivre, gris.
— *Get tipsy*, *v* se griser.
TIPTOE, *s.* la pointe du pied, *f.*
TIRE, *s.* parure, *f.* attirail, *m*
— *va.* orner, *de*, parer, *de*, lasser, *de*, fatiguer, *de*
— *vn.* se lasser, de, *de*, se fatiguer, de, *de*, s'ennuyer, de, *de.*
TIRESOME, *a.* ennuyeux, se, fatigant.
To, *pr.* de, à, à la, à des, au, aux, en, vers, jusque, pour.
TOGETHER, *ad.* ensemble, à la fois.
TOKEN, *s.* signe, *m.* marque, *f.* enseignes, *f. pl* renseignement, *m.*
TOMB, *s.* tombeau, monument, *m.*
— *v.* ensevelir, enterrer,
TOMBSTONE, *s.* tombe, *f.*
TONGUE, *s.* langue, *f.* langage, *m.*
— *v.* gronder, quereller, jaser.
TOO, *ad.* aussi, même, trop.
— MUCH, TOO MANY, trop, trop de.
TOOTH, *s.* dent, *f.*
TOP, *s.* cime, surface, *f.* sommet, haut, faîte, comble, *m.*
TOPIC, *s.* topique, sujet, *m.* matière, *f.*
TORMENT, *s.* tourment, supplice, *m.*
— *va.* tourmenter, souffrir.

TORTURE, s. torture, gêne, f.
— va. mettre à la torture.
TOSS, s. secousse, f. jet, m.
— v. jeter.
TOUCH, s. toucher, tact, m.
— v. toucher, à, arriver, à, émouvoir.
TOUCHING, a. touchant, pathétique.
TOWARDS, pr. vers, du côté de, pour, envers.
TOWN, s. ville, f. bourg, m.
TRACE, va. suivre à la piste, à la trace, decouvrir.
TRADE, s. métier, commerce, m.
— va. trafiquer, négocier.
TRAGICAL, TRAGIC, a. tragique.
TRAGICALLY, ad. tragiquement.
TRAITOR, s. traitre, esse.
TRANSACTION, s. fait, m. transaction, f.
TRANSMIT, v. envoyer, à, rémettre, à, faire parvenir, à.
TRANSPORT, s. transport, m. extase, f. accès, m.
— SHIP, s. bâtiment de transport, m.
— vn. transporter, à, exiler, à.
TRANSPORTATION, s. transport, m.
— (of criminals), déportation, f.
TRAVEL, s. voyage, m.
TRAVELLER, s. voyageur, euse.
TRAVELLING, s. l'action de voyager, f.
TREASURE, s. trésor, m.
— UP, thésauriser, amasser.
TREAT, v. traiter, régaler, de, négocier.
— s. régal, repas que l'on donne, m.
TREATMENT, s. traitement, m.

TREE, s. arbre, m.
TREMBLE, vn. trembler, de, de, trembloter.
TREMBLING. s. tremblement, m.
— a. tremblant, de, de.
TRESSES, s. tresses, f. pl.
TRIAL, s. épreuve, preuve, tentative, f.
— AT LAW, jugement, procès, m.
TRICK, s. ruse, manigance, f. tour, m.
— (at cards), s. levée, f.
— v. tromper, duper, escroquer, à.
TRICKERY, s. tromperie, f.
TRIFLE, s. bagatelle, f.
TRIFLING, a. léger, ère. peu de chose.
TROOPS, s. troupes, f. pl.
TROT, s. trot, m. vieille femme, f.
— vn. trotter, aller le trot.
— OFF, s'en aller au trot.
TROUBLE, s. peine, misère, f. embarras, m.
— (disturbance), trouble, désordre, m.
— va. troubler, incommoder, fâcher.
TRUE, a. vrai, véritable, certain.
TRULY, ad. vraiment, véritablement, sincèrement.
TRUSS, s. botte, f.
TRUST, s. confiance, assurance, f. crédit, dépôt, m.
— v. confier, à, croire, faire crédit, à, se fier, à, se confier, à.
TRUTH, s. vérité, f. vrai, m.
TRY, v. essayer, à, de, tâcher, de, faire ses efforts, pour, examiner, considérer, éprouver.
— (at law), juger.

TRY EXPERIMENTS, faire des expériences.
TUB, *s.* cuve, *f.* baquet, *m*
TUG, *s.* effort, *m.* peine, fatigue, *f.* action de tirer.
TUITION, *s.* direction, instruction, conduite, *f.*
TUMBLE, *s.* chute, *f.*
— *v.* tomber, renverser, rouler.
TURBULENT, *a.* turbulent.
TURKEY, *s.* la Turquie.
TURN, *va.* tourner, retourner, *à*, détourner, *de*, changer, métamorphoser, rétorquer, se tourner.
— OUT, chasser, *de*, sortir, *de*, déloger.

TURN TO, tourner, *vers*, se tourner, *vers*.
TURPITUDE, *s.* turpitude, bassesse, *f.*
TWELVE, *a.* douze.
TWELVEMONTH, *s.* an, *m.* année, *f.*
TWENTY, *a.* vingt.
TWICE, *ad.* deux fois.
TWO, *a.* deux.
TYRANNICAL, TYRANNIC, *a.* tyrannique.
TYRANNICALLY, *ad.* en tyran.
TYRANNY, *s.* tyrannie, oppression, *f.*

U.

UNABLE, *a.* incapable, de, impuissant, à, inhabile, à, *à.*
UNACQUAINTED, *a.* qui ignore.
UNCERTAINTY, *s.* incertitude, *f.* délai, *m.*
UNCONSCIOUS, *a.* ne sachant pas, ignorant, *de.*
UNDER, *ad. pr.* sous, dessous, par-dessous, au-dessous de.
— (*less*), moins, à moins, de.
— FAVOUR, *ad.* avec permission.
UNDERSTAND, *va.* entendre, comprendre.
UNDERSTANDING, *s.* entendement, *m.* intelligence, *f.* jugement, *m.*
UNDERTAKE, *v.* entreprendre, de.
UNDERTAKER, *s.* entrepreneur, entrepreneur de pompes funèbres, *m.*
UNEASY, inquiet, ète. *de,* incommode, embarrassé, *de*, de.

UNEXPECTED, *a.* inspiré, inattendu.
UNEXPECTEDLY, *ad.* inopinément.
UNFORTUNATE, *a.* infortuné, malheureux, se. de.
UNFORTUNATELY, *ad.* malheureusement.
UNGOVERNABLE, *a.* indomptable, qui n'obéit pas.
UNGRATEFUL, *a.* ingrat, *envers*, désagréable, *à.*
UNGRATEFULLY, *ad.* avec ingratitude, désagréablement.
UNHAPPY, *a.* malheureux, se. de.
UNITE, *va.* unir, *à*, joindre, *à.*
UNITEDLY, *ad.* de concert, avec union.
UNIVERSITY, *s.* université, *f.*
UNINTENTIONALLY, *ad.* sans intention, sans le vouloir.
UNJUST, *a.* injuste, *envers*, inique.

UNJUSTLY, *ad.* injustement.
UNKINDNESS, *s.* méchanceté, dureté, *f.*
UNKNOWN, *a.* inconnu, *à,* insu.
— TO ME, à mon insu.
UNLESS, *ad.* à moins que, si ce n'est que.
UNLOAD, *va.* décharger, alléger.
UNLUCKY, *a.* malheureux, se. de, infortuné, de.
— (*mischievous*), méchant, malin, gne.
UNMASK, *v.* démasquer.
UNNECESSARY, UNNEEDFUL, *a.* inutile, *d.*
UNOBSERVED, *a.* qui n'est pas observé.
UNPARDONED, *a.* pas pardonné.
UNPUNISHED, *a.* impuni.
UNREASONABLE, *a.* déraisonnable, de.
UNSUCCESSFUL, *a.* qui n'a pas réussi, sans succès, infructueux.
UNSUSPECTING, *a.* qui ne soupçonne rien.
UNTIL, *ad.* jusqu'à, jusques à, jusqu'à ce que, en attendant que.
UNWEARIED, *a.* délaissé, infatigable.
UNWILLING, *a.* pas disposé, à, *à,* ne voulant pas.
UNWORTHY, *a.* indigne, de, *de,* méprisable.
UP, *pr.* au haut de, au, sur.
— *ad.* en haut.
— AND DOWN, çà et là, partout.

UP, *int.* debout ! courage !
— HILL, qui va en montant.
— (*not sitting*), debout, sur pied.
— THERE, là-haut.
— TO, jusqu'à.
UPON, *pr.* sur, dessus, à, en, vers.
— IT, *pr.* dessus.
UPPER, *a.* superieur, haut, dessus.
UPPERMOST, *a.* le plus élevé, le plus haut, qui a le dessus.
URCHIN, *s.* hérisson, *m.*
— (*unruly child*), petite peste, *f.* vaurien, *m.*
URN, *s.* urne, *f.* vase, *m.*
US, *pro.* nous.
USE, *s.* usage, emploi, *m.*
— (*habit*), coutume, habitude, *f.*
— (*interest*), intérêt, *m.*
— *v.* user, employer, à, se servir, *de,* avoir coutume, de.
— A PLACE, fréquenter un endroit.
— ILL, en user mal, maltraiter.
USED, *a.* en usage, usité, consommé.
USEFUL, *a.* utile, *à,* nécessaire, *à.*
USELESS, *a.* inutile, *d.*
USUAL, *a.* ordinaire, accoutumé, usuel, le. usité, commun, *d.*

V.

VAGRANT, *s.* vagabond.
VAINLY, *ad.* vainement.

VALUABLE, *a.* precieux, se.
VALUE, *s.* valeur, estime, *f*

VALUE, *va.* évaluer, *à*, estimer, *à*, apprecier.
VANQUISH, *va.* vaincre, dompter.
VAPOUR, *s.* vapeur, fumée, *f.*
— *v.* faire le fier, s'évaporer.
VEIL, *s.* voile, prétexte, *m.*
— *va.* voiler, couvrir d'un voile.
VEIN, *s.* veine, *f.*
VENERABLE, *a.* vénérable, respectable.
VENGEANCE, *s.* vengeance, *f.*
VENTRILOQUIST, *s.* ventriloque, *m.*
VENTRILOQUY, *s.* action du ventriloque, *f.*
VENTURE, *v.* se hasarder, *à*.
— *s.* risque, hasard, *m.* entreprise hasardeuse, pacotille, *f.*
VERY, *a.* vrai, véritable, réel, le, même, fieffé, franc, che.
— *ad.* fort, bien, très.
VESSEL, *s.* vaisseau, vase, *m.*
VEXATION, *s.* déplaisir, *m.* vexation, *f.*
VICE, *s.* vice, défaut, *m.*
VICTOR, *s.* vainqueur.
VICTORY, *s.* victoire, *f.*
VICTUALS, *s. pl.* vivres, mets, *m. pl.*
VIEW, *s.* vue, *f.* coup d'œil, *m.*
VILE, *a.* vil, abject, méprisable.
VILLAGER, *s.* villageois.
VILLAIN, *s.* scélérat, coquin, *m.*

VINDICATE, *va.* soutenir, maintenir, justifier, de, défendre, venger.
VINDICATION, *s.* justification, défense, *f.* maintien, *m.*
VINEGAR, *s.* vinaigre, *m.*
— CRUET, *s.* vinaigrier, *m.*
VIOLATE, *va.* violer, profaner.
VIOLATION, *s.* violation, *f.* infraction, *f.*
VIOLENT, *a.* violent, impétueux, se.
VIOLENTLY, *ad.* violemment.
VIRTUE, *s.* vertu, *f.*
VIRTUOUS, *a.* vertueux, se.
VISIT, *s.* visite, *f.*
— *va.* visiter, rendre visite, *à*.
VISITER, *s.* visiteur, *m.*
VIVACITY, *s.* vivacité, *f.*
VOCAL, *a.* vocal, de voix.
VOICE, *s.* voix, *f.* suffrage, *m.*
VOLUME, *s.* volume, tome, *m.*
VORACIOUS, *a.* vorace, dévorant.
VORACIOUSLY, *ad.* goulûment.
VOW, *s.* vœu, *m.* promesse solennelle, *f.*
— *v.* vouer, *à*, faire vœu, de.
— (*to swear*), jurer, *à*, de, protester.
VULGAR, *s.* le bas peuple, *m.* populace, *f.*
— *a.* vulgaire, commun, de mauvais goût, de.
VULGARITY, *s.* bassesse, grossièreté, *f.*
VULGARLY, *ad.* vulgairement.

W.

WAG, *s.* drôle, badin, espiègle.
— *va.* remuer, agiter.
WAGER, *s.* gageure, *f.* pari, *m.*
— *va.* gagner, parier.
WAISTCOAT, *s.* gilet, *m.*

WAIT, *s.* guet-apens, piége, *m.*
— *v.* attendre, demeurer, se rendre, *à*.
— ON, servir, accompagner, vi

siter, aller voir, se rendre, chez.
WALK, s. promenade, allée, f.
— (gait), démarche, f.
— v. marcher, à, vers, promener, se promener.
— AWAY, s'en aller, s'éloigner.
— IN, entrer, dans.
— OFF, décamper, de, se sauver.
— OUT, sortir, de.
— THE ROUNDS, faire la ronde.
WALKER, s. marcheur, euse.
WALKING, s. l'action de promener.
WALKING-CANE, s. canne, canne à marcher, f.
WALKING STAFF, s. bâton, m. canne, f.
WALL, s. muraille, f. mur, m.
WANDER, va. rôder, errer, s'écarter, aller ça et là.
— ABOUT, vn. courir ça et là.
WANT, s. besoin, m. faute, f. manque, m.
— (poverty), s. indigence, disette, f.
— In want, dans la nécessité.
— For want of, ad. faute de.
WANT, v. avoir besoin, de, de.
WANTON, a. sans provocation, inutile.
WAR, s. guerre, f.
— vn. faire la guerre, à.
WAR OFFICE, s. ministère de la guerre, bureau du ministère de la guerre, m.
WARM, a. chaud, tiède.
— (zealous), zélé, ardent.
— To be warm, avoir chaud.
— v. chauffer, échauffer, faire chauffer.
— AGAIN, réchauffer.
WARMLY, ad. chaudement, ardemment.
WARNING, s avertissement, m.

WASH, va. laver, à, blanchir, à, nettoyer, à.
— AWAY, OFF or OUT, emporter, effacer.
WATCH, va. observer, épier.
— A SICK PERSON, veiller.
— vn. veiller, faire le quart.
— AND WARD, faire le guet.
— s. montre, f. guet, m. veille, f.
WATCHHOUSE, s. corps de garde, m.
WATCHMAKER, s. horloger. m.
WATCHWORD, s. mot d'ordre, m. consigne, f.
WATER, va. arroser, baigner.
— (a horse), abreuver.
— s. eau, f.
WATERMAN, s. batelier, m.
WAX, s. cire, f.
WAY, s. chemin, m. route, voie, f.
— ma chemin d'un vaisseau, sillage.
— (custom), coutume, habitude, f.
— (manner), manière, sorte, méthode, f.
— (means), moyen, expédient, m.
— (pass), état, m. passe, f.
— (side), côté, sens, m.
— IN, entrée, f.
— OUT, sortie, issue, f.
— THROUGH, passage, m.
WE, pro. nous.
WEAK, a. faible, infirme, débile.
— SIDE, s. côté faible, le faible, m
WEAKNESS, s. faiblesse, f
WEAPON, s. arme, f. instrument d'attaque ou de défense, m.
WEAR, va. porter.
— OUT, épuiser.

WEB (of a spider), toile, *s. f.*
WEEK, *s.* semaine, *f.*
WELCOME, *s.* bon accueil, *m.*
— *a.* bienvenu, agréable.
— *va.* faire accueil, bien accueillir.
— *int.* soyez le bien-venu.
WELFARE, *s.* bien être, *m.* prospérité, *f.*
WELL! *int.* Eh! bien.
WELL, *s.* puits, *m.* source, *f.*
WESTPHALIA, *np.* Westphalie, *f.*
WET, *s.* humidité, *f.*
— *a.* mouillé, humide, moite.
— WEATHER, *s.* temps pluvieux, *m.*
— *va.* mouiller, humecter, arroser.
WHAT, *pro.* quoi, que, qui, quel, le. ce que, ce qui, quelque.
— *int.* quoi !
WHATEVER, WHATSOEVER, *pro.* quel que, quoi que ce soit, tout ce que *ou* qui.
WHEAT, *s.* froment, blé, *m.*
WHEN, *ad. c.* quand, lorsque, au lieu que, pendant que.
WHENCE, *ad.* d'où, pour cette raison.
WHENEVER, WHENSOEVER, *ad.* toutes les fois que, quand.
WHERE, *ad.* où.
WHETHER, *pro.* lequel, laquelle.
— *ad.* si, soit, soit que.
WHICH, *pro.* quel, quelle, lequel, laquelle, qui, que.
WHICHSOEVER, *pro.* quel que soit celui, qui, *ou* ceux qui, quiconque.
WHILE, *s.* temps, espace de temps, *m.*

WHILE, *s. It is not worth while*, cela n'en vaut pas la peine.
— *v.* remettre, différer, de, s'amuser, à.
— *ou* WHILST, *ad.* pendant que, tant que, tandis que.
WHIP, *s.* fouet, *m.*
WHISPER, *s.* chuchotement, *m.* voix basse, *f.*
— *va.* parler bas, *d.*
WHITE, *s.* blanc, *m.*
— OF AN EGG, blanc d'œuf, *m.*
— *a.* blanc, che.
— *va.* blanchir, rendre blanc.
WHO, *pro.* qui.
WHOEVER, *pro.* quiconque, qui que ce soit, toute personne qui.
WHOLE, *a.* entier, ère. tout.
WHOLE, *s.* tout, *m.* totalité, *f.*
WHOM, *pro.* qui, que, lequel, laquelle.
WHOSE, *pro.* dont le, la, les, de qui, à qui.
WHY, *ad.* pourquoi, que, mais.
— TRULY, vraiment.
WICKED, *a.* méchant.
WIDE, *a.* large, grand, étendu.
WIDOW, *s.* veuve, *f.*
— *va.* priver une femme de son mari.
WIDOWER, *s.* veuf, *m.*
WIFE, *s.* femme, *f.*
WILD, *a.* étourdi, sauvage.
WILL, *s.* volonté, disposition, *f.*
— (*testament*), *s.* testament, *m.*
— *v.* vouloir, souhaiter, avoir envie, de.
— (*desire*), prier, de, supplier, de.

WILL (*order*), ordonner, *à*, de.
WILLING, *a.* d'accord, prêt à faire.
WILLINGLY, *ad.* volontiers.
WIN, *v.* gagner, *sur*, obtenir, *de*, conquérir, *sur*, remporter, *sur*.
WILLIAM, *sp.* Guillaume.
WIND, *s.* vent, *m.* haleine, *f.*
WINDOW, *s.* fenêtre, *f.*
— *v.* faire des fenêtres.
WINE, *s.* vin, *m.*
— BOTTLE, *s.* bouteille à vin, *f.*
WINTER, *s.* hiver, *m.*
— *v.* hiverner, passer l'hiver.
WISE, *a.* sage, savant, judicieux, se.
— MAN, *s.* sage, philosophe.
WISELY, *ad.* sagement, discrètement.
WISH, *s.* souhait, vœu, désir, *m.*
— *v.* souhaiter, *à*, de, vouloir, désirer.
WIT, *s.* esprit, bon sens, *m.*
— (*person*), bel esprit, génie, *m.*
WITCHCRAFT, *s.* sortilége, *m.* sorcellerie, *f.*
WITH, *pr.* avec, de, par, à, en, contre, chez, parmi, sur.
WITHDRAW, *v.* se retirer, *de.*
WITHOUT, *pr.* sans, au delà, au dehors.
— *ad.* dehors, en dehors, par dehors.
— *c.* à moins que, si ce n'est que, sans que.
WITNESS, *s.* témoin, témoignage, *m.*
— *v.* témoigner, attester.
WITTY, *a.* spirituel, le. d'esprit.
WOE, *s.* malheur, *m.*
WOE TO, *int.* malheur!

WOMAN, *s.* femme, *f.*
WOMANKIND, *s.* le sexe féminin, *m.*
WONDER, *s.* étonnement, *m.* merveille, surprise, *f.* prodige, *m.*
— *vn.* s'étonner, de, *de*, être surpris, de, *de.*
WOOD, *s.* bois, *m.* forêt, *f.*
WOODEN, *a.* de bois, fait de bois.
WORD, *s.* mot, *m.* parole, *f.*
— *By word of mouth*, de bouche.
— *High words*, *s.* grosses paroles, *f. pl.*
WORK, *v.* travailler, à, *d*, mettre en œuvre, manufacturer, fabriquer.
— *va. ma.* manœuvrer.
WORKMAN, *s.* ouvrier, artisan, *m.*
WORKSHOP, *s.* atelier, *m.*
WORLD, *s.* le monde.
WORLDLY, *a.* mondain.
WORK, *s.* travail, *m.* occupation, *f.*
— (*thing wrought*), ouvrage, *m.* œuvre, *f.*
WORTH, *s.* prix, *m.* valeur, *f.*
— (*personal*), mérite, *m.*
— *a.* qui vaut, valant.
WORTHIES, *s.* les grands hommes, *m. pl.*
WORTHILY, *ad.* dignement, avec raison.
WORTHY, *s.* homme illustre, *m.*
— *a.* digne, de, *de*, estimable, bon, ne.
WOUND, *s.* blessure, plaie, *f.*
— *va.* blesser, *de*, offenser, *de.*
WRAP, *va.* envelopper, *de*, enrouler, *de*, entortiller, *de.*
— UP, envelopper, *de.*

WRECK, s. débris, naufrage, m.
— va. briser un vaisseau, perdre, détruire.
— vn. faire naufrage.
WRECKED, a. naufragé.
WRETCH, s. misérable.
WRETCHED, a. malheureux, se.
WRITE, v. écrire, à, de.
— OUT, transcrire, copier.
WRITE OVER AGAIN, récrire, mettre au net.
WRITHE, va. tortiller, tordre.
— vn. souffrir une rude agonie, se tordre, de.
WRONG, s. tort, m. injustice, f.
— ad. mal, à tort, mal à propos.
— a. faux, sse. de travers, injuste.

Y.

YARD (*inclosed place*), s cour, f.
YEAR, s. an, m. année, f.
YET, ad. encore, outre cela, même.
— c. néanmoins, cependant.
YOU, pro. vous.
YOUNG, a. jeune.
— BEGINNER, s. novice, commençant.
— ONES, les petits, m. pl.
YOUNGEST, a. le ou la plus jeune, cadet, ette.
YOUR, pro. votre, vos.
YOURS, pro le vôtre, les vôtres, à vous.
YOURSELF, pro. vous-même.
YOURSELVES, pro. vous-mêmes.
YOUTH, s. jeunesse, f. bas âge, m. les jeunes gens, m. pl. un jeune homme, un jeune garçon, m.
YOUTHFUL, a. jeune, de jeunesse.

APPENDIX TO THE DICTIONARY.

As stated page 175, headed "Abreviations du Dictionnaire:"
The prepositions printed in *Roman* after the verbs or adjectives, are to be used before the next infinitive; those printed in *Italic* govern the *indirect* regimen of the verb or the complement of the adjective.

Some verbs and adjectives govern sometimes one preposition, sometimes another, according to the meaning.—As limited space commands brevity, also, as confusion might result from profuseness of details, it has been left to the Teacher to direct the student in the use of either of the prepositions when two are introduced, or to supply the lack in exceptional cases.

However, much difficulty would be removed by consulting the following directions:

"The English preposition *to*, used before a verb in the sense of *in order to*, must be translated *pour*.

"All adjectives following the verb *to be*, used impersonally, require *de* before the next infinitive; as: It is noble to die for one's country. Il est noble *de* mourir pour sa patrie.

"Adjectives used after *assez, trop, trop peu* (enough, too, too little), require *pour* before the next infinitive; as: she is *too* kind *to* refuse you. Elle est *trop* bonne *pour* vous refuser.

"Adjectives requiring *à* before their complement, generally express an idea of *inclination, readiness, opposition, habit, fitness*.

"Adjectives requiring *de* generally refer to *content* or *discontent, abundance, scarcity, happiness* or *misfortune, pride, shame, certainty*. They are often followed in English by: *with, of, from, by*.

"Those, requiring *envers*, express *behaviour, kind* or *unkind* feelings towards others."

THE END.